Ellery Queen's
Circumstantial Evidence

Novels by Ellery Queen

The Roman Hat Mystery
The French Powder Mystery
The Dutch Shoe Mystery
The Greek Coffin Mystery
The Egyptian Cross Mystery
The American Gun Mystery
The Siamese Twin Mystery
The Chinese Orange Mystery
The Spanish Cape Mystery
Halfway House
The Door Between
The Devil to Pay
The Four of Hearts
The Dragon's Teeth
Calamity Town
There Was an Old Woman
The Murderer Is a Fox
Ten Days' Wonder

Cat of Many Tails
Double, Double
The Origin of Evil
The King Is Dead
The Scarlet Letters
The Glass Village
Inspector Queen's Own Case
The Finishing Stroke
The Player on the Other Side
And On the Eighth Day
The Fourth Side of the
   Triangle
A Study in Terror
Face to Face
The House of Brass
Cop Out
The Last Woman in His Life
A Fine and Private Place

Books of Short Stories by Ellery Queen

The Adventures of Ellery Queen
The *New* Adventures of Ellery Queen
The Casebook of Ellery Queen
Calendar of Crime

Q.B.I.: Queen's Bureau of Investigation
Queens Full
Q.E.D.: Queen's Experiments in
   Detection

Edited by Ellery Queen

Challenge to the Reader
101 Years' Entertainment
Sporting Blood
The Female of the Species
The Misadventures of Sherlock Holmes
Rogues' Gallery
Best Stories from *EQMM*
To the Queen's Taste
The Queen's Awards, 1946-1953
Murder by Experts
20th Century Detective Stories
Ellery Queen's Awards, 1954-1957
The Literature of Crime
Ellery Queen's Mystery Annuals:
   13th-16th
Ellery Queen's Anthologies: 1960-1980
The Quintessence of Queen
   (edited by Anthony Boucher)
To Be Read Before Midnight
EQ's Mystery Mix

EQ's Double Dozen
EQ's 20th Anniversary Annual
EQ's Crime Carousel
EQ's All-Star Lineup
Poetic Justice
EQ's Mystery Parade
EQ's Murder Menu
EQ's Minimysteries
EQ's Grand Slam
EQ's The Golden 13
EQ's Headliners
EQ's Mystery Bag
EQ's Crookbook
EQ's Murdercade
EQ's Crime Wave
EQ's Searches and
   Seizures
EQ's A Multitude of Sins
EQ's Scenes of the Crime
EQ's Circumstantial Evidence

Ellery Queen's Mystery Magazine (40th Year)

Ellery Queen's International Case Book   The Woman in the Case

Critical Works by Ellery Queen

The Detective Short Story   Queen's Quorum   In the Queens' Parlor

Under the Pseudonym of Barnaby Ross

The Tragedy of X
The Tragedy of Y

The Tragedy of Z
Drury Lane's Last Case

**34th
Mystery
Annual**

ELLERY QUEEN'S

Circumstantial Evidence

22 stories from
Ellery Queen's Mystery Magazine

Edited by

Ellery Queen

THE DIAL PRESS
DAVIS PUBLICATIONS, INC.
380 LEXINGTON AVENUE, NEW YORK, N.Y. 10017

ACKNOWLEDGMENTS

The editor hereby makes grateful acknowledgment to the following authors and authors' representatives for giving permission to reprint the material in this volume:

Barrie & Jenkins, Ltd. for *This Is Death* by Donald E. Westlake, © 1978 by Barrie & Jenkins, Ltd.

Georges Borchardt, Inc. for *Born Victim* by Ruth Rendell, © 1978 by Ruth Rendell.

Curtis Brown, Ltd. for *Reasons Unknown* by Stanley Ellin, © 1978 by Stanley Ellin; and *The Writing on the Wall* by Patricia McGerr, © 1978 by Patricia McGerr.

John Cushman Associates, Inc. for *Dover Goes to School* by Joyce Porter, © 1977 by Joyce Porter.

Brian Garfield for *Charlie's Shell Game,* © 1977 by Brian Garfield.

Kathryn Gottlieb for *Dream House,* © 1977 by Kathryn Gottlieb.

Edward D. Hoch for *The Spy and the Cats of Rome,* © 1978 by Edward D. Hoch.

International Creative Management for *Going Backward* by David Ely, © 1978 by David Ely.

John Lutz for *The Other Runner,* © 1978 by John Lutz.

McIntosh & Otis, Inc. for *When in Rome* by Patricia Highsmith, © 1978 by Patricia Highsmith.

Ann Mackenzie for *I Can't Help Saying Goodbye,* © 1978 by Ann Mackenzie.

Harold Q. Masur for *One Thing Leads to Another,* © 1978 by Harold Q. Masur.

Harold Ober Associates, Inc. for *Milady Bigamy* by Lillian de la Torre, © 1978 by Lillian de la Torre; and *The Forgotten Murder* by E. X. Ferrars, © 1977 by E. X. Ferrars.

Barbara Owens for *The Cloud Beneath the Eaves,* © 1977 by Barbara Owens.

Bill Pronzini for *Caught in the Act,* © 1978 by Bill Pronzini.

Ernest Savage for *Count Me Out,* © 1978 by Ernest Savage.

Larry Sternig Literary Agency for *No Wider Than a Nickel* by Jack Ritchie, © 1978 by Jack Ritchie.

Robert Twohy for *Installment Past Due,* © 1978 by Robert Twohy.

Thomas Walsh for *The Sacrificial Goat,* © 1977 by Thomas Walsh.

Stephen Wasylyk for *The Krowten Corners Crime Wave,* © 1978 by Stephen Wasylyk.

The Dial Press
1 Dag Hammarskjold Plaza
New York, New York 10017

6

CONTENTS

INTRODUCTION

Dear Reader:

Do you believe in and accept circumstantial evidence? How reliable is circumstantial evidence? Let's look at the matter in an oblique way.

In Eudora Welty's essay titled "The Point of the Story," she writes: "It's all right, too, for words and appearances to mean more than one thing—ambiguity is a fact of life."

Ambiguity is a fact of life. Is ambiguity a fact of life in circumstantial evidence?

Is ambiguity also a fact of life in a mystery or detective story? Yes, in most of the story—in the beginning, in the middle, and in the approach to the denouement. Ambiguity adds to mystery, but when the story comes to its end, the reader wants all ambiguities resolved—that is, the reader wants the mystery solved. Indeed, the reader insists on full clarification and the tying-up-of-all-loose-ends.

True, there have been mysteries which authors have deliberately ended ambiguously. Four classic short stories come to mind: Mark Twain's *Awful, Terrible Medieval Romance* (1871), Frank R. Stockton's *The Lady, or the Tiger?* (1884), Cleveland Moffett's *The Mysterious Card* (1896), and W. W. Jacobs' *The Lost Ship* (1898). Note that they are all Nineteenth Century stories—today's readers generally do not care for mystery or detective stories that end without clearcut solutions or that leave readers with impenetrable riddles. Today's readers ask for hard evidence—or at the least, circumstantial evidence—leading to the truth.

So we come back to Eudora Welty's "life's uncertainty"—ambiguity is a fact of life. And in this volume of mystery, crime, and detective stories we offer you just enough ambiguity to tease your wits, to

9

baffle and fascinate and entertain you, to stimulate your imagination. Ambiguity is thought- and theory-provoking, but in our genre it must finally be dispelled or dissolved by hard or circumstantial evidence.

ELLERY QUEEN

P.S. This postscript is not merely an afterthought. Eudora Welty's short essay, "The Point of the Story," is a model of instruction, a marvelously economical lesson in creative writing for all aspiring authors, young and old. You will find it in her book titled THE EYE OF THE STORY (Random House, 1978).

Barbara Owens

The Cloud Beneath the Eaves

This is the 485th "first story" published by Ellery Queen's Mystery Magazine . . . the poignant, moving story of Alice Whitehead, an unsophisticated farm girl who has run off to the big city . . .

The author, Barbara Owens, is in her early forties, "a housewife with a fine arts degree in drama." She is an "avid reader and bridge player, and enjoys the outdoors and travel." She and her husband are originally from Illinois and they have two teenage sons.

Since she started devoting her time to writing—"for 2 years now"—she has "never been happier at work," and she writes every moment she can spare. Which is good news indeed for the future—for all the readers on our staff agreed that Barbara Owens' first story is "something special" . . .

May 10: I begin. At last. Freshborn, dating only from the first of May. New. A satisfying little word, that "new." A proper word to start a journal. It bears repeating: I am new. What passed before never was. That unspeakable accident and the little problem with my nerves are faded leaves, forgotten. I will record them here only once and then discard them. Now—it's done.

I have never kept a journal before and am not sure why I feel compelled to do so now. Perhaps it's because I need the proof of new life in something I can touch and see. I have come far and I am filled with hope.

May 11: This morning I gazed long at myself in the bathroom mirror. My appearance is different, new. I can never credit myself with beauty, but my face is alive and has lost that indoor pallor. I was not afraid to look at myself. That's a good sign.

I've just tidied up my breakfast things and am sitting at my little kitchen table with a steaming cup of coffee. The morning sun streams through my kitchen curtains, creating lacy, flowing patterns on the cloth. Outside it's still quiet. I'm up too early, of course—difficult to break years of rigid farm habits. I miss the sound of birds, but there are several large trees in the yard, so perhaps there are some. Even a city must have some birds.

I must describe my apartment. Another "new"—my own apartment. I was lucky to find it. I didn't know how to find a place, but a waitress in the YWCA coffee shop told me about it, and when I saw it, I knew I had to have it.

It's in a neighborhood of spacious old homes and small unobtrusive apartment houses; quiet, dignified, and comfortably frayed around the edges. This house is quite old and weathered with funny cupolas and old-fashioned bay windows. The front and side yards are small, but the back is large, pleasantly treed and flowered, and boasts a quaint goldfish pond.

My landlady is a widow who has lived here for over 40 years, and she's converted every available space into an apartment. She lives on the first floor with several cats, and another elderly lady lives in the second apartment on that floor. Two young men of foreign extraction live in one apartment on the second floor, and I have yet to see the occupant of the other. I understand there's also a young male student living in part of the basement.

That leaves only the attic—the best for the last. It's perfect; I even have my own outside steps for private entry and exit. Because of the odd construction of the house, my walls and ceilings play tricks on me. My living room and kitchen are one large area and the ceiling, being under the steepest slope of the roof, is high. In the bedroom and bath the roof takes a suicidal plunge; as a result, the bedroom windows on one wall are scant inches off the floor and I must stoop to see out under the eaves, for the ceiling at that point is only four feet high. In the bath it is the same; one must enter and leave the tub in a bent position. Perhaps that's why I like it so much; it's funny and cozy, with a personality all its own.

The furnishings are old but comfortable. Everything in my living-room area is overstuffed, and although the pieces don't match, they get along well together. The entire apartment is clean and freshly painted a soft green throughout. It's going to be a delight to live here.

I spent most of yesterday getting settled. Now I must close this and be off to the neighborhood market to stock my kitchen. I've even been giving some thought to a small television set. I've never had the pleasure of a television set. Maybe I'll use part of my first pay-check for that. Everything is going to be all right.

May 12: Today I had a visitor! The unseen occupant from the apartment below climbed my steps and knocked on my kitchen (and only) door just as I was finishing breakfast. I'm afraid I was awkward and ill-at-ease at first, but I invited her in and the visit ended pleasantly.

Her name is Sarah Cooley. She's a widow, small and stout, with gray hair and kind blue eyes. She'd noticed I don't have a car and offered the use of hers if I ever need it. She also invited me to attend church with her this morning. I handled it well, I think, thanking her politely for both offers, but declining. Of course I can never enter a car again, and she could not begin to understand my feelings toward the church. However, it was a grand experience, entertaining in my own home. I left her coffee cup sitting on the table all day just to remind myself she'd been there and that all had gone well. It's a good omen.

I must say a few words about starting my new job tomorrow. I try to be confident; everything else has worked out well. I'm the first to admit my getting a job at all is a bit of a miracle. I was not well prepared for that when I came here, but one trip to an employment agency convinced me that was pointless.

Something must have guided me to that particular street and that particular store with its little yellow sign in the window. Mr. Mazek was so kind. He was surprised that anyone could reach the age of 32 without ever having been employed, but I told him just enough of my life on the farm to satisfy him. He even explained how to get a Social Security card, the necessity of which I was not aware. He was so nice I regretted telling him I had a high-school diploma, but I'm sure he would never have considered someone with a mere eighth-grade education. Now my many years of surreptitious reading come to my rescue. I actually have a normal job.

May 13: It went well. In fact, I'm so elated I'm unable to sleep.

I managed the bus complications and arrived exactly on time. Mr. Mazek seemed pleased to see me and started right off addressing me as Alice instead of Miss Whitehead. The day was over before I realized it.

The store is small and dark, a little neighborhood drugstore with two cramped aisles and comfortable clutter. Mr. Mazek is old-fashioned and won't have lunch counters or magazine displays to encourage loitering; he wants his customers to come in, conduct their business, and leave. He's been on that same corner for many years, so almost everyone who enters has a familiar face. I'm going to like being a part of that.

Most of the day I just watched Mr. Mazek and Gloria, the other clerk, but I'm convinced I can handle it. Toward the end of the day he let me ring up several sales on the cash register, and I didn't make one mistake. I'm sure I'll never know the names and positions of each item in the store, but Mr. Mazek says I'll have them memorized in no time and Gloria says if she can do it, I can.

I will do it! I feel safer as each day passes.

May 16: Three days have elapsed and I've neglected my journal. Time goes so quickly! How do I describe my feelings? I wake each morning in my own quiet apartment; I go to a pleasant job where I am needed and appreciated; and come home to a peaceful evening of doing exactly as I wish. There are no restrictions and no watchful eyes. It's as I always dreamed it would be.

I'm learning the work quickly and am surprised it comes so easily. Gloria complains of boredom, but I find the days too short to savor.

Let me describe Gloria: she's a divorced woman near my own age, languid, slow-moving, with dyed red hair and thick black eyebrows. She's not fat, but gives the appearance of being so because she looks soft and pliable, like an old rubber doll. She has enormous long red fingernails that she fusses with constantly. She wears an abundance of pale makeup, giving her a somewhat startling appearance, but she's been quite nice to me and has worked for Mr. Mazek for several years, so she must be reliable.

I feel cowlike beside her with my great raw bones and awkward hands and feet. We're certainly not alike, but I'm hoping she becomes my first real friend. Yesterday we took our coffee break together, and during our conversation she stopped fiddling with her nails and said, "Gee, Alice, you know you talk just like a book?" At first I was taken aback, but she was smiling so I smiled too. I must listen more to other people and learn. Casual conversation does not come easily to me.

Mr. Mazek continues to be kind and patient, assuring me I am learning well. In many ways he reminds me of Daddy.

I've already made an impression of sorts. Today something was wrong with the pharmaceutical scales, so I asked to look at them and had them right again in no time. Mr. Mazek was amazed. I hadn't realized it was a unique achievement. Being Daddy's right hand on the farm for so many years, there's nothing about machinery I don't know. But I promised I wouldn't think about Daddy.

May 17: Today I received my first paycheck. Not a very exciting piece of paper, but it means everything to me. I hadn't done my figures before, but it's apparent now I won't be rich. And there'll be no television set for me. I can manage rent, food, and few extras. Fortunately I wear uniforms to work, so I won't need clothes soon.

Immediately after work I went to the bank and opened an account with my check and what remains of the other. I did that too without a mistake. And now it's safe. It looks as though I've really won; they would have come for me by now if she had found me. I'm too far away and too well hidden. Bless her for mistrusting banks; better I should have taken it than some itinerant thief. She's probably praying for my soul. Now, no more looking back.

May 18: I don't work on weekends; Mr. Mazek employs a part-time student. I would rather work since it disturbs me to have much leisure. It's then I think too much.

This morning I allowed myself the luxury of a few extra minutes in bed, and as I watched the sun rise I noticed an odd phenomenon beneath the eaves outside my window. Because of their extension and perhaps some quirk of temperature, the eaves must trap moisture. A definite mist was swirling softly against the top of the window all the while the sun shone brightly through the bottom. It was so interesting I went to the kitchen window to see if it was there, but it wasn't. It continued for several minutes before melting away, and nestled up here in my attic I felt almost as though I were inside a cloud.

This morning I cleaned and shopped. As I was carrying groceries up the steps, Sarah Cooley called me to come sit with her in the backyard. She introduced me to the other widow from the first floor, Mrs. Harmon. Once again Sarah offered her car for marketing, but I said I like the exercise.

It was unusually soft and warm for May, and quite pleasant sitting idly in the sun. A light breeze was sending tiny ripples across the fishpond, and although the fish are not yet back in it I became aware that some trick of light made it appear as though something were down there, a shadowy shape just below the surface. Neither of the ladies seemed to notice it, but I could not make myself look away. It became so obvious to me something was down there under the water that I became ill, having no choice but to excuse myself from pleasant company.

All day I was restless and apprehensive and finally went to bed early, but in the dark it came, my mind playing forbidden scenes. Over and over I heard the creaking pulleys and saw the placid surface of Jordan's pond splintered by the rising roof of Daddy's rusty old car. I heard tortured screams and saw her wild crazy eyes. I must not sit by the fishpond again.

May 19: I was strong again this morning. I lay and watched the little cloud. There is something strangely soothing about its silent drifting; I was almost sorry to see it go.

I ate well and tried to read the paper, but I kept being drawn to the kitchen window and its clear view of the fishpond. At last I gave up and went out for some fresh air. Sarah and Mrs. Harmon were preparing for a drive in the country as I went down my steps and Sarah invited me, but I declined.

Mr. Mazek was surprised to see me in the store on Sunday. They were quite busy and I offered to stay, but he said I should go and enjoy myself while I'm young. Gloria waggled her fingernails at me. I lingered a while, but finally just bought some shampoo and left.

A bus was sitting at the corner, and not even noticing where I was going I got on. Eventually it deposited me downtown and I spent the day wandering and watching people. I find the city has a vigorous pulse. Everyone seems to know exactly where he's going.

I must have left the shampoo somewhere. It doesn't matter. I already have plenty.

May 20: Today I arrived at the story early. Last week I noticed that the insides of the glass display cases were dirty, so I cleaned them. Mr. Mazek was delighted; he said Gloria never sees when things need cleaning.

Gloria suggested I should have my hair cut and styled, instead of letting it just hang straight; she told me where she has hers done. I'm sure she was trying to be friendly and I thanked her, but I have to laugh when I think of me wearing something like her dyed red frizz.

Mr. Mazek talked to me today about joining some sort of group to meet new people. He suggested a church group as a promising place to start. A church group, of all things! Perhaps he thought I came into the store yesterday because I was lonely and had nothing better to do.

Tonight my landlady, Mrs. Wright, inquired if I had made proper arrangements for mail delivery. Since I've received none, she thought there might have been an error. Again I regretted having to lie.

Only the white coats and she would be interested in my whereabouts, and I have worked too hard to evade them.

I am restless and somewhat tense this evening.

May 24: My second week and second paycheck in the bank, and it still goes well.

I've realized with some regret that Gloria and I are not going to be friends. I try, but I'm not fond of her. For one thing, she's lazy; I find myself finishing half of her duties. She makes numerous errors in transactions, and although I've pointed them out to her, she doesn't do any better. I'm undecided whether to bring this to Mr. Mazek's attention. Surely he must be aware of it.

On several occasions this week I've experienced a slight blurring of vision, as though a mist were before my eyes. I'm concerned about the cost involved, but prices and labels have to be read accurately, so it seems essential that I have my eyes tested.

May 26: What an odd thing! The little cloud has moved from under the eaves in my bedroom to the kitchen window. Yesterday when I awoke it wasn't there, and as I was having breakfast, suddenly there it was outside the window, soft and friendly, rolling gently against the pane. Perhaps it's my imagination, but it seems larger. It was there again today, a most welcome sight.

Yesterday was an enjoyable day—just cleaning and shopping.

Today was not so enjoyable. Just as I was finishing lunch, I heard voices under my steps where Sarah parks her car. The ladies were getting ready for another Sunday drive and when I looked out, they were concerned over an ominous sound in the engine. Before I stopped to think, I heard myself offering to look at it. All the way down the steps I told myself it would be all right, but as soon as I raised the hood, the blackness and nausea came. I couldn't see and far away I heard a voice calling, "Allie! Allie, where are you?"

Somehow I managed to find the trouble and get back upstairs. Everything was shadows, threatening. I couldn't catch my breath and my hands wouldn't stop shaking. Suddenly I was at the kitchen window, straining to see down into the fishpond. I'm afraid I don't know what happened next.

But the worst is over. I'm all right now. I have drawn the shade over the kitchen window so I will never see the fishpond again. It's going to be all right.

I wish it were tomorrow and time to be with Mr. Mazek again.

May 30: Gloria takes advantage of him. I have watched her carefully this week and she is useless in that store. Mr. Mazek is so warm and gentle he tends to overlook her inadequacy, but it is wrong of her. I see now she's also a shameless flirt, teasing almost every man who comes in. Today she and a pharmaceutical salesman were in the back stockroom for over an hour, laughing and smoking. I could see that Mr. Mazek didn't like it, but he did nothing to stop it. I've been there along enough to see that he and I could manage that store quite nicely. We really don't need Gloria.

I have an appointment for my eyes. The mist occurs frequently now.

June 2: The cloud *is* getting bigger. Yesterday morning the sun shone brightly in my bedroom, but the kitchen was dim and there was a shadow on the shade. When I raised it a fraction, there were silky fringes resting on the sill. I stepped out on the landing and saw it pressed securely over the pane. It is warm, not damp to the touch—warm, soft, and soothing. I have raised the kitchen shade again—the cloud blots out the fishpond completely.

Yesterday I started down the steps to do my marketing, my eyes lowered to avoid sight of the fishpond, and through the steps I saw the top of Sarah's car. Something stirred across it like currents of water, and suddenly I was so weak and dizzy I had to grip the railing to keep from falling as I crept back up the stairs.

I have stayed in all day.

June 7: I have been in since Wednesday with the flu. I began feeling badly Tuesday, but I worked until Wednesday noon when Mr. Mazek insisted I go home. I'm sorry to leave him with no one but Gloria, but I am certainly not well enough to work.

I came home to bed, but the sun shining through my window made disturbing movements in the room. Everything is so green, and the pulsing shadows across the ceiling made it seem that I was under-water. Suddenly I was trapped, suffocating, my lungs bursting for air.

I've moved my bedding and fashioned a bed for myself on the living-room couch. Here I can see and draw comfort from the cloud. I will sleep now.

June 10: I have been very ill. Sarah has come to my door twice, but I was too tired and weak to call out, so she went away. I am feverish; sometimes I am not sure I'm awake or asleep and dreaming. I just realized today is special—the first month's anniversary of my new life. Somehow it seems longer. I'd hoped

June 11: I've just awakened and am watching the cloud. Little wisps are peeping playfully under my door. I think it wants to come inside.

June 12: I am better today. Mrs. Wright used her passkey to come in and was horrified to find I'd been so sick, and no one knew. She and Sarah wanted to take me to a doctor, but I cannot get inside that car, so I convinced them I'm recovering. She brought hot soup and I managed to get some down.

The cloud pressed close behind her when she came in, but didn't enter. Perhaps it's waiting for an invitation. Poor Mrs. Wright was so concerned with me she didn't notice the cloud.

June 13: Today I felt well enough to go downstairs to Mrs. Wright's and call Mr. Mazek. I couldn't go until after noon—Sarah's car was down there. I became quite anxious, sure that he needed me in the store. He sounded glad to hear my voice and pleased that I am better, but insisted I not come in until Monday when I am stronger.

I am so ashamed. Suddenly wanting to be with him today, I heard myself pleading. Before I could stop, I told him my entire plan for letting Gloria go and having the store just to ourselves. He was silent so long that I came to my senses and realized my mistake, so I laughed and said something about the fever talking. After a moment he laughed too, and I said I would see him on Monday.

I have let the cloud come in. It sifts about me gently and seems to fill the room.

June 21: Didn't go to the bank today. Crowds and lines begin to annoy me. I will manage with the money and food I have on hand.

Mr. Mazek, bless him, is concerned about my health. I see him watching me with a grave expression, so I work harder to show him I am strong and fine.

I've started taking the cloud to work with me. It stays discreetly out of the way, piling gently in the dim corners, but it comforts me to know it's there, and I find myself smiling at it when no one's looking.

Yesterday afternoon I went to the back stockroom for something, and I'd forgotten Gloria and another one of her salesmen were in there. I stopped when I heard their voices, but not before I heard Gloria say my name and something about "stupid hick"; then they laughed together. Tears came to my eyes, but suddenly a mist was all around me and the cloud was there, smoothing, enfolding, shutting everything away.

A note from Mrs. Wright on my door tonight said that the eye doctor had called to remind me of my appointment. No need to keep it now.

June 23: Sarah's car was here all day yesterday, so I did not go out.

I don't even go into the bedroom now. I am still sleeping on the couch. Because it's old and lumpy, perhaps that's what's causing the dreams. Today I awoke suddenly, my heart pounding and my face wet with tears. I thought I was back there again and all the white coats stood leaning over me. "You can go home," they chorused in a nasty singsong. "You can go home at last to live with your mother." I lay there shaking, remembering. They really believed I would stay with *her!*

Marketed, but did not clean. I am so tired.

June 27: You see? I function normally. I reason, so I am all right. It's that lumpy old couch. Last night the dream was about Daddy choking out his life at the bottom of Jordan's pond. I was out of control when I awoke, but the cloud came and took it all away. Today I fixed my blankets on the floor.

June 28: Dear Mr. Mazek continues to be solicitous of my health. Today he suggested I take a week off—get some rest or take a little vacation. He looked so troubled, but of course I couldn't leave him like that.

Sometimes I feel afraid, feel that everything is slipping away. I am trying so hard.

Maybe I should be more tolerant of Gloria.

July 5: After several hours inside my blessed cloud, I believe I am calm enough to think things through. I have been hurt and betrayed. I cannot conceive such betrayal!

Today I discovered that Gloria is—how shall I say it?—"carrying on" with Mr. Mazek and has evidently been doing so for years. Apparently they were supposed to spend the holiday yesterday together, but Gloria went off with someone else. I heard them through the closed door of Mr. Mazek's little office—their voices were very loud—and Gloria was laughing at him! The cloud came to me instantly and I don't remember the rest of the day.

Now I begin to understand. It explains so many things. At first I was terribly angry with Mr. Mazek. Now I realize Gloria tempted him and he was too weak to resist. The evil of that woman. Something must be done. This cannot be allowed to continue.

July 8: I found my opportunity today when we were working together in the stockroom. I began by telling her my finding out was an accident, but that now she must stop it at once. She just played with her fingernails, smiled, and said nothing until I reminded her he was a respected married man with grandchildren and she was ruining all their lives. Then she laughed out loud, said Mr. Mazek was a big boy, and why didn't I mind my own business.

July 11: I'm afraid it's hopeless. For three days I've pursued and pleaded with her to stop her heartless action. This afternoon she suddenly turned on me, screaming harsh cruel things I can't bring myself to repeat. I couldn't listen, so I took refuge in the cloud. Later I saw her speaking forcefully to Mr. Mazek; it looked almost as though she were threatening him. What shall I do now?

I am not sleeping well at all.

July 12: I have been let out of my job. There is no less painful way to say it. This afternoon Mr. Mazek called me into his office and let me go as of today, but he will pay me for an extra week. I could say nothing, I was so stunned. He said something about his part-time student needing more money in the summer, but of course I know that's not the reason. He said he was sorry, and he looked so unhappy that I felt sorry for him. I know it isn't his fault. I know he would rather have me with him than Gloria. Even the cloud has not been able to save me today.

July 16: I have not left here for four days. I know, because I have marked them on the wall the way I did when I was there. Tomorrow I will draw a crossbar over the four little straight sticks.

I think I have eaten. There are empty cans on the floor and bits of food in my blankets.

The cloud sustains me—whispering, shutting out the pain.

July 19: It is all arranged. Gloria was alone when I went in this morning for my last paycheck. She seemed nervous and a bit ashamed. We were both polite and she went back to Mr. Mazek's office for my pay.

I felt a great sadness. I love that little store. And I have memorized it so well in the time I was allowed to be a part of it. It is fortunate that I know precisely where everything is kept.

At first she refused my invitation to have lunch with me today. She said she begins her vacation tomorrow. But I was persistent, pleading how vital it is to me that we part with no hard feelings between us. Finally she agreed, and I am calm inside the cloud, and strong and confident again.

She came here to my apartment and it went well. Lunch was pleasant and Mr. Mazek's name was never mentioned. I even told her all about myself, and she seemed no more upset than could be expected . . .

Tonight I put a note on Mrs. Wright's door saying I'd been called away for a few weeks. I've moved my heavy furniture in front of the door. I must be very still and remember not to turn on lights. There is enough light from the street to write by and the cloud is here to protect and keep me. I have come a long way. This time it is right.

July   : All goes back, goes back. The white coats were wrong. I can't do it.

I saw Daddy again. We stood under the lantern in the big old barn. He showed me all the parts of his old car and how each one of them worked. It felt so safe and good to be with him, and he told me again that I was his good right hand. I wanted

Bad. Oh bad. Everyone said you were crazy. Mean. Your Bible and your praying and church, over and over, your church every night, shouting and praying, never doing anything to help Daddy and me on the farm. Sitting at the kitchen table with your Bible, singing and praying, everything dirty and undone, then into the old car and off to church to shout and pray some more while Daddy and I did all the work.

Never soothed him, never loved him, just prayed at him and counted his sins. Couldn't go to school, made me stay home and work on the farm, no books, books are the devil's tools, had to hide my books in the barn high up under the eaves. Ugly, you're a big ugly child, girl, and you prayed for my soul, prayed for mine and Daddy's souls. Poor sad Daddy's soul.

Took it too hard they said, oh yes, took it too hard, so they sent me away for the white coats to fix and then they made me go back to you, your Bible, and your praying, and everyone said it was an accident, a tragic accident they said, but you knew, you never said but you knew, and you prayed and sang and quoted the Bible and you broke my Daddy's life. In the clouds, girl's always got her head in the clouds, I loved my Daddy and you prayed for souls and went to church every night and every night It is hot in here. It must be summer outside. All the windows are closed up tight and it is very hot here under the eaves. In the clouds

Today: I do not know what day it is. How many days I have been here. Markings on my walls, words and drawings I do not understand. I lie here on the floor and watch my cloud. It sighs and swirls and keeps me safe. I can't see outside it anymore. It is warm and soft and I will stay inside forever. No one can find me now.

Gloria is beginning to smell. Puffy Gloria and her long red claws. Silly foolish Gloria who didn't even complain when the coffee tasted strange. I have set my Daddy free.

I am in the barn. Night. I am supposed to be milking the cow. I am peaceful, serene. I have done it well and now life will be rich and good. The old car coughs and soon I hear it rattling toward the steep hill over Jordan's pond. It starts down. I listen. Content. The sound fades, a voice, the wrong voice, calling my name: "Allie! Allie, where are you?" The light goes out of the world.

Odaddydaddydaddy, where were you going in the car that night? Wasn't supposed to be you   supposed to be her her her

EDITORIAL POSTSCRIPT

The story you have just read was awarded the coveted Edgar by MWA (Mystery Writers of America) as the best new mystery short story published in American magazines and books during 1978.

Thomas Walsh

The Sacrificial Goat

The two lovers had one obstacle to their future happiness—one person who stood in their way. With that person eliminated the lovers would have freedom, money, everything their hearts desired. To accomplish their purpose they needed a patsy, a tool, a fall guy ... Thomas Walsh at his best ...

They met one bright August afternoon in one of the elegant red and gold Hotel Versailles elevators, and since it was a bit crowded at the moment they had to stand close together, though without touching. Yet even on that first occasion, in the way that such people instinctively recognize each other's morality and inclinations, there was something communicated between them. They touched eyes for only a brief instant, yet even so the man knew the woman from then on, and the woman the man.

They were very careful, however. Mistakes were always possible. So it was mid-October before the man rented a small furnished apartment on East 78th Street under the name of Robinson, after which the woman came over there to spend a few hours in the afternoon with him about twice a week. They were both experienced in such matters, the man very experienced, and after he had made sure there was an automatic elevator in the building and no doorman, everything could be managed with the most admirable discretion.

Nobody knew about them. Nobody suspected about them. But something unforeseen happened. Little by little the thing got more serious, or perhaps only more passionate, and by January it had become very serious. That was when they began to think with increasing hatred of the one person who stood in their way. Without that one person they would have more money than they could use. Without him they could have everything they wanted and enjoy a long happy life together.

At first, however, they only considered the thing silently, in their thoughts. But one afternoon the man remarked as if jokingly how fortunate it would be if only some sort of accident occurred, and the woman responded in the same manner. But an accident, the man pointed out, might be very dangerous for them. Details could go wrong; mistakes could be made; everyone concerned, husband or wife, son or daughter, would be thoroughly checked out, even down to the hotel staff—unless, of course, someone else could be found who obviously had the means, the motive, and the opportunity to eliminate that one person.

After that, no longer jokingly, they began to discuss who the someone might be. First, there must be no question as to his identity. And second, the police must be made to realize at once who had done the thing and the reason for it. If that part could be set up, only one very simple question remained. Who would the tool of murder be? Whom would they pick as the sacrificial goat?

Finally the solution presented itself and they both immediately understood it was the perfect solution. Soon a pleasantly conspiratorial excitement carried them ahead faster and faster, and by the last week in January, with every possible difficulty taken care of, they arranged the whole thing from beginning to end.

The Versailles was an old but still extremely elegant New York hotel. It had been designed by a famous architect many years ago, and though by now its quiet but luxurious high-society tone had perhaps faded a little, it still was considered by all the right people as far superior to the newer and more commercial establishments. It had a famous Garden Room, several expensive restaurants much too costly for the common herd, and half a dozen exclusive shops—jewelry, interior decorating, gentlemen's furnishings, and three French couturiers all just off the main lobby.

It was no longer, however, as in its first haughty years, restricted as to all minorities, and although its employees were screened much more carefully than the patrons upstairs, a few blacks and Puerto Ricans were beginning to be accepted. It had twenty-odd floors, and on the north side a magnificent view over Central Park. Every floor had a desk clerk and a page boy, and the page boy on the 17th floor was named Ramon Rodriquez.

One day he was on duty from seven in the morning until twelve noon, and again from six until nine in the evening. On the following day, conversely, he worked from twelve noon until six. He was a slim undersized boy with black hair and cheerfully glistening black eyes, only 15 years old—but the Versailles, needing a page boy, had not bothered to make sure that he was old enough to work full time according to the laws of New York State. Interviewed only by the bell captain, he was paid no more than the minimum wage—one reason perhaps that the Versailles needed a page boy—and out of that, the bell captain said, the Versailles would deduct $5 a month to keep his uniform cleaned and pressed. But in addition, it was also explained to Ramon, there would be a great many tips from all the rich society people who patronized the Versailles and those tips would be entirely Ramon's.

So Ramon expected great things for himself on his first job, although he soon discovered that the tips were more a promise than an actuality. Most of the better suites on the 17th floor were reserved for permanent guests, and all had maids who answered the door. It happened, consequently, that when Ramon delivered a package to one of the suites, or ran an errand for the occupant, the only thanks he got, if that, was a nod from the maid.

There were no more than a few generous exceptions. A rich mining man named Mr. Lahrheim in 1734 gave Ramon a dollar for anything he did, and a Mrs. McLeod in 1748 gave him a crisp five-dollar bill every Saturday morning, although she required less service from him than anyone on the whole floor. But most of the other permanent guests, in sharp distinction, must have thought that what Ramon did for them was well covered by the exorbitant rent they paid the Versailles, and that there was no need of further largess.

And Ramon did a great many things for them which most never even thought about. On early mornings, for instance, he delivered newspapers to their doors, which they could read while having breakfast comfortably in bed; and on Sunday mornings, when the papers were five or six times the daily size, he had to go downstairs on the service elevator three or four times, pile the papers onto a cart, then wheel the cart from Suite 1701 at the northwest corner of the Versailles to Suite 1794 at the southwest corner. He ran all their errands, brought all their packages, since no outside delivery boy was ever admitted into the Versailles corridors, and 20 or 30 times a day, when a guest was out, he took a telephone message from Miss Riley, the floor clerk, and then hung it on the proper doorknob for the guest's return.

In between times he had to sit on a small straight-backed chair by Miss Riley's desk, and when a guest appeared, was required to jump up, ring for the elevator, and then stand as rigidly at attention as a West Point cadet until the guest had been wafted down. On Christmas morning, when he also had to work, he did that for old Mrs. Terwilliger in 1707.

"Oh, yes," old Mrs. Terwilliger beamed, toddling into the floor clerk's office with a nurse supporting her on one side and a uniformed chauffeur on the other—on her way, probably, at that time of the morning, to one of the more exclusive Park Avenue churches.

"Christmas Day. We mustn't forget the boy, must we? Now let me see."

And Ramon had great expectations at that moment. For month after month he had done chore after chore for Mrs. Terwilliger, but never yet had he been given so much as a five-cent piece for any of them. His expectations proved much too optimistic, however. Mrs. Terwilliger rummaged through her purse, then rummaged again.

"Oh, dear," she exclaimed. "It appears that I—would you have change for a dollar, Miss Riley?"

And Miss Riley, who liked Ramon very much, made a great show of examining her desk drawer.

"No," she said. "I'm very sorry, Mrs. Terwilliger. But no, I haven't."

"Oh, dear," Mrs. Terwilliger repeated, hesitating with anxious distress for a moment, then reluctantly extending the dollar bill. "Then I suppose—well, Christmas Day, after all. Here you are, boy."

Then the elevator went down and Miss Riley violently slammed in her desk drawer.

"Mean, miserable old bitch," she said. "Change for a dollar! It's a wonder she didn't want change for a dime, Ramon."

But still Ramon liked his job very much. The long and quiet Versailles halls, finished with subdued elegance in gold and green, were a great change for him from Spanish Harlem, and on his early morning shifts there were always wheeled breakfast trays outside many of the guest suites. Then Arturo the waiter would allow him to help himself to a leftover sausage or some buttered toast, and whatever remained in the silver coffee pots. In that way Ramon could have a fine breakfast for himself, leaving a little more at home for his four smaller brothers and sisters, although he had to be careful that none of the guests came along and caught him. They would probably have been very indignant at such low-class vulgarity in the Versailles and in all likelihood have reported it at the main desk on their way out.

Ramon even liked his gray and blue Versailles uniform. He always kept it immaculately neat—and of course his shoes polished, his hair brushed, and his fingernails cleaned, as the bell captain had impressed on him. But then Ramon had a certain ambition. He hoped, by hard and painstaking attention to duty, to become in time a bellhop down in the main lobby where he had heard that the tips amounted to more than $100 a week. And the sum would make a vast difference at home where Ramon was the only breadwinner. Therefore he was always quickly and cheerfully responsive to a guest's need, tip or no tip, and off like a flash to get them toothpaste or cigars from the drug store downstairs, or *Fortune* magazine or a Paris newspaper from the hotel newsstand.

There was an electric signboard on the wall over Miss Riley's desk, and on that, when a guest pressed the bell in his room, the corresponding number would appear—1714, 1729, 1765. Then Ramon, after pushing up the release disk so that the number dropped back into place, would be up and away on the instant. And every night at home, when he had to crowd into a rickety daybed with his two little brothers, he would first pray fervently for the bellhop's job, so that in his first months at the Versailles there was never any kind of mark against him.

Only a bare year out of San Juan, Ramon was a very good boy, and a very innocent boy, with almost no experience in the world. The man and the woman had chosen him out of sure instinct. Ramon had no money, no influential friends, and no way to get himself even half-competent legal help. And early in February it developed that if Arturo and Miss Riley liked him, there were other members of the Versailles staff who did not like him at all.

That proved itself one night when two security men appeared in the hall and beckoned him out silently from Miss Riley's desk. Each of them took him by an arm, gripping him painfully, and the blond, very good-looking one even twisted his arm painfully. They marched him down to the service stairway and there, with the hall door closed behind them, the blond security man immediately slapped him across the mouth.

"Know what we got here?" he remarked to the other one. "A real smart little operator, Walter. Okay. I guess what we have to do now is to show him pretty damned quick just how smart he is to try and pull something like this."

"Guess we will," Walter said, and smashed Ramon's head into the wall. "Now tell me something, you little punk. You deliver a package to 1727 about six thirty tonight?"

Ramon was frightened and in much pain. He backed against the wall, shaking his head. It was not to deny that he had delivered the package to Mr. Curtis in Suite 1727. It was to show that in his pain and confusion he did not quite understand what they were asking him.

"No?" Walter said, smacking him again. "You mean you didn't? You mean the maid never left you all alone in the living room when she went inside to get the receipt signed, and that you weren't standing right beside old man Curtis' coin case when she came out with it? You better own up, punk, or me and Harry are going to knock the hell out of you. Where did you hide that coin you stole? What did you do with it? Take a look in his pockets, Harry."

But in Ramon's pockets there were only the few tips he had made, a subway token, and his locker key. That Harry handed to Walter.

"Probably stashed it away down there," he said. "Check it out, Walter. I'd bet on the thing."

Then, all alone, Harry twisted Ramon's arm even more viciously and kept on slapping his face. He also said things, but Ramon—15 years old, after all—was in no condition to understand what they were. He did not want to cry, but he had to. He crouched lower against the wall, shielding his face.

Walter came back.

"Nope," he said. "Nothing at all. Only his overcoat ain't there. Nothing but a crummy old sweater."

"Ees all I have to wear," Ramon whispered to them. "Ees all I have."

"That right?" Harry said. Crisply curling, reddish-gold hair; coldly sharp blue eyes with thick lashes; hard, hatingly contemptuous grin. "Then maybe they'll give you one up the river, because that's where you're going straight from here, cutie. You got just one chance before we take you around to the precinct house. What did you do with that coin you took? Where did you hide it?"

"No coin," Ramon whispered. "No, no. I bring the package, yes. I wait for the maid to come back. But—"

They led him out into the hall and down to Suite 1727, where Mr. Curtis and Mr. and Mrs. Purnell, his daughter and son-in-law from 1739, were talking together in front of the door.

"Well, here's your answer," Harry said, brutally slapping Ramon's head forward. "He's the one stole it, Mr. Curtis, sir. We checked it all out for you, Walter and me, and the maid said he's the only one she left into your suite tonight. So it's got to be him. It's the only answer. No one else could have taken it."

Mr. Curtis glanced in helplessly at a glass-topped case, just like a museum case, that stood against one wall of the foyer. Each coin in there was nestled in a circle of red velvet that fitted exactly around it. One circle was empty. Mr. Curtis was a coin collector.

"Well, I know it was there," he said. "And now it isn't. And I paid over $15,000 for it in London last year. I'm sure you're right, men. But why you employ boys of this type—"

Mrs. Curtis came out of Suite 1727. She was a slim platinum-blonde, much younger than her husband, and had the aloof, haughtily disinterested expression of the fashion model she had been before Mr. Curtis married her. There was a coin in her right hand.

"Is this what you're so concerned about?" she asked calmly. "Really, Charles. I said that you only mislaid it somewhere. I found it under some letters on your desk inside. And you yourself put it down there last night after showing it to Ted Bannister and his wife. I saw you do it."

Mr. Curtis' mouth gaped.

"But I put it back in the case," he cried. "I did, Adele. I remember coming out into the living room after the Bannisters left and—"

"Oh, Daddy," Mrs. Purnell said, making an impatient gesture. "You remember so many things lately that you don't do at all. You forgot your dinner appointment with us only last Saturday. And you forgot about that Charity Ball at the Waldorf. I don't know what's getting into you."

"But I only made a mistake in the dates," he insisted feebly. "That's all, Barbara. I just—"

There was a pause. Mrs. Curtis and Mrs. Purnell murmured together. Mr. Purnell shook his head sadly. Harry and Walter glanced slyly at each other, grinning. But nobody looked at Ramon or appeared to notice the tears on his face. It was just as if Ramon were not present.

"Well, I guess it's all right," Mr. Curtis said finally to Harry and Walter. "I'm so sorry, so sorry, men. But I could have sworn—"

After that, rubbing the back of his gray head wearily, he went into 1727, with the other members of his family following him. The door closed, and after it had, Harry uttered a curt, jeering laugh.

" 'I'm so sorry,' " he mimicked. " 'So sorry, men.' But not a damn dime for us, Walter, not even after I told him all the trouble we went to. Only the best people here, hah? But all I hope is that they come up here some night and clean out the whole damn suite on him."

And Ramon was left all alone in the hall, with not one word of regret or apology having been spoken to him. It was at least five minutes before he could go back to the office again and face Miss Riley. His head hurt. His eyes felt hot and dry. But worst of all he felt deeply ashamed. It was as if no one had realized that Ramon was a human being. It was as if he had been, not only to Harry and Walter, just nothing at all.

About a week after that, a few minutes before nine in the evening and just as Ramon was preparing to go off duty, they found Curtis' body sprawled in front of the coin case in Suite 1727. It was Harry, making one of his regular house rounds, who saw the door to 1727 half open and discovered Mr. Curtis with blood all over his white evening shirt, and the one coin again missing from its place in the glass-topped museum case.

After that many things happened. Policemen came up by way of the service elevator, first two in uniform, then several more in ordinary civilian clothes. There was a great deal of feverish but subdued excitement in the 17th floor corridor, and even Mr. Lenormand the manager appeared, wringing his hands and whispering in agitated low tones to Walter and Harry by the side of Miss Riley's desk. But soon Mr. Lenormand, very distinguished-looking in a tail coat and white tie, nodded as if distractedly at Harry, and Ramon was again marched down to Suite 1727 where he had to close his eyes and swallow three times at the way Mr. Curtis looked.

By that time there were a great many other men in the suite. Some measured things; some took pictures; and some spoke to the maid, then to Mrs. Curtis, who looked very pale and shaky, though without tears. But Mrs. Purnell sobbed quietly in one corner, while Mr. Purnell stared out of the window at Central Park.

It was all very frightening to Ramon, the way all the policemen kept whispering to Harry and then looking around at him, and it was only a little better when a tall slim man with hard eyes and a saturnine face had Ramon sit down on the couch with him—the only time Ramon had ever been permitted to sit in Suite 1727.

But the man had a calm quiet voice, almost a friendly voice, and could speak Spanish to Ramon. At first he asked very simple questions—how old Ramon was, whether he went to church, and how long he had been working at the Versailles. But Ramon hardly knew what he answered, having to close his eyes when they lifted Mr. Curtis' body onto a stretcher, covered it with a gray blanket, and carried it off in the direction of the service elevator so that none of the other guests would see it. Then only the slim man was left, and

Harry and Mr. Lenormand, until another man came in from the hall holding something that was wrapped carefully in a white cloth.

Then all the men turned around to look at Ramon again, and the tall slim one, who had been called Lieutenant Da Costa by the others, walked across the room holding the white cloth in his hand.

He put his other hand under Ramon's chin and made him look straight into his eyes. Then he opened the cloth very suddenly, without even the least warning, and Ramon saw all the blood that had been wiped off on it, and under the blood a razor-sharp knife with a wood handle. It was done so suddenly that Ramon started to shake all over, and then he closed his eyes from the knife. But Da Costa forced his head back and turned over the knife.

"R.R.," he said, pointing a forefinger at two initials on the handle. "You see that, Ramon? And you just told me what your name is—Ramon Rodriquez. How about those initials, then? Is this your knife? Did you ever see it before?"

"I do not know it," Ramon whispered. "I swear, senor. I never see it before."

Harry came over to them.

"What the hell are you wasting time for?" he demanded angrily. "Just slap it out of him, Lieutenant. What else do you want? Mr. Curtis mislaid that same coin last week and this little jerk heard how much it was worth—about $15,000. We heard Mr. Curtis say that himself, all of us. So this little punk snuck in here to grab it tonight and Mr. Curtis caught him. And all of these people are the same kind, aren't they? Ain't one of them that doesn't have a knife handy, just in case."

"One of these people myself," Da Costa murmured, still looking down at Ramon. "But I never owned or used a knife in my life. And you know what, Hannegan? A lot of us don't."

"Well, of course," Hannegan said, coloring a bit. "Didn't mean anything like that, Lieutenant. Only trying to say—"

"Yes, I know," Da Costa put in. "How about the coin, O'Brien? Anybody find it yet?"

"Not yet," O'Brien said. "But it's around somewhere, Lieutenant. Got to be. Miss Riley says the kid ain't been off the floor since about 8:15. The last call he answered was at eight o'clock when somebody wanted him in 1735. Right down the hall."

"How long did the call take him?"

"Not long at all, Miss Riley says. He was always quick as a shot, according to her. She's sure he was back again in about two minutes.

All he had to do for 1735 was take some letters and drop them down the mail chute in Miss Riley's office."

"So all in two minutes," Da Costa murmured, "he goes down to 1735, passes 1727 here on the way back, finds the door open or at least unlocked, comes in and opens the coin case, takes the right coin out, stabs Curtis when he's caught doing it, then walks back to the floor office cool as a cucumber, after dropping the knife behind that hall radiator where you found it, and sits down again just like nothing has happened. Not excited at all; not in any kind of crazy panic—and only fifteen years old, he tells me. All he says to Miss Riley is about the money he's saving up for his little sister's birthday next week. How about that, Hannegan? He sure knew how to handle himself, didn't he? *All* in two minutes?"

"Well, like I said," Hannegan said, shrugging insolently. "Them people. Maybe Miss Riley got a degree in child psychology, Lieutenant. You ought to ask her."

"Maybe I ought to start asking a lot of people," Da Costa said. "Starting with you. Were you up on this floor any time tonight before you discovered the body in here?"

"Yeah, flew up," Harry Hannegan said, and laughed jeeringly. "Why, none of the elevator operators saw me. Go ahead. Ask them."

"Stairs," Da Costa murmured. "Service stairs. And deserted, I should imagine, about nine-tenths of the time."

"I was up here a bit earlier," Mr. Lenormand said, wiping his face harriedly with the flowing linen handkerchief that he took out of his breast pocket. "Mr. Curtis wanted to discuss the menu for a dinner he was giving for a few friends tomorrow night in the Garden Room. Then when I came out, I passed Mr. Purnell in the hall. I believe he can verify that, if you think it's necessary."

"We will," Da Costa said. "Although it looks like the boy, all right. He made a very serious mistake talking to me, even if he doesn't realize that he did. All we need to prove on him now is that he stole the coin and we have him dead to rights."

"Lost his nerve," Harry suggested, "and got rid of it. Probably threw it down one of the toilets."

"Or better yet," Da Costa thought, "dropped it down the mail chute with those letters from 1735. What's your first mail pickup in the morning, Hannegan?"

"I think eight o'clock," Hannegan said. "That right, Mr. Lenormand?"

"I believe so," Mr. Lenormand said, still wiping his face. "But a thing like this to happen at the Versailles! My God!"

"Then have somebody here when the mailman comes around," Da Costa ordered. "If we find the coin down there, we got Ramon. Once we face him with that, we'll give him half an hour downtown with Frank Sandstrum and we'll have the whole story."

But still the man and the woman were very careful, even after it became known the next morning that the coin had been found right where Da Costa had suggested it would be. They arranged a meeting only two weeks later at the East 78th Street apartment. The man got there first and the woman had just taken off her coat when the hall door opened. Da Costa and O'Brien walked in.

"Nice little place," Da Costa said, glancing around casually. "Not so high-toned as the Versailles, of course—but fair enough for what you needed. How long you been meeting here?"

The woman sat down as suddenly as if her legs had given way under her, but the man had better control of himself.

"Now just a minute," he blustered. "You have nothing against us. What we're doing here is our own personal business."

Da Costa cuffed him across the mouth with hard knuckles.

"From a kid named Ramon," he said. "Keep your mouth shut. I don't have to ask what you did because I know it already. You got damned cozy at the Versailles first, meeting each other nearly every day there, and then you got even more cozy in this place. You—" he glanced contemptuously at the woman"—had to set up the first scene. I mean how the old man forgot the coin, or apparently forgot it, leaving it on his desk when he hadn't left it there at all. You also made out that he had begun forgetting a lot of things, giving him the wrong dates for appointments and so on till he began to believe it himself. In addition, you made sure that he said right in Ramon's hearing how much the coin was worth, and if he hadn't said it you'd have slipped it in yourself. Following me so far?"

Neither one answered. The man sat silently. The woman, shaking her head time after time, had become pale as death.

"Then we might as well proceed," Da Costa went on. "I had to prepare the ground too, because I know kids like Ramon, and I knew by the way he acted that he didn't even understand what was happening to him. So I told you"—glancing down contemptuously at the man—"how important the coin was and how Ramon made a very serious mistake when he was talking to me. Well, the coin was important, important as all hell, because whoever took it out of the case obviously killed the old man. Where to find it, though? It could have been hidden in any place at all in the Versailles, if Ramon hadn't taken it.

"So I made another suggestion while we were all in the same room. I suggested that maybe Ramon dropped it down the mail chute, and asked what time the first pickup was the next morning. Only before that I had O'Brien get in touch with the post office and they sent a man up here to open the chute right away, take the letters out, and close it up again, empty.

"And what do you know? The letters from 1735 were in there already, just like Ramon said—but the coin wasn't. Next morning, though, with a lot of other letters, there it was. Which meant that whoever dropped it into the chute, it wasn't Ramon. It couldn't have been. He was in our hands already. See what I mean?"

There was still dead silence. The man had put his head in his hands. The woman had begun to weep brokenly.

"Guess you do," Da Costa said, his lips curled. "You figured that coin would be the last thing to damn the kid, only it turned out to be the one thing that nailed you. So if it couldn't be Ramon, it had to be somebody else. Who? That was the poser.

"Well, it was quite a little trouble for us, but from then on everybody involved was given a good careful tail wherever he went.

"So what do you think happens? Our hero here leaves the Versailles at two o'clock this afternoon, and his dear lady fifteen minutes later. Then where do you suppose they both come? Right here. And then where do you suppose we come? Right here too. All we have to do then is talk to the superintendent downstairs, get his passkey—and here we are. We know how long ago you rented the place; we know how long you've been coming here; and so all we have to do is to leave it to a jury as to what the reason might be.

"Slap the cuffs on them, O'Brien. I want them to feel it just the way a little Puerto Rican kid did when I had to do it to him, even if it was only for show that time. Now come on. Up on your feet, both of you. You get one phone call apiece to any lawyer you want, but I'll lay fifty to one that no lawyer can help you. Anybody talking?"

There did not appear to be. Mrs. Curtis, her face stony-hard under the tears, stood up like a sleepwalker. Across from her, his head still in his hands but his eyes open and staring down with savage hopelessness at the brilliantly polished tips of his black shoes, sat the Versailles manager, Mr. Lenormand.

Joyce Porter

Dover Goes to School

Which detective of fiction is rude, mean, nasty, ungracious, and
unpleasant, always grunting, growling, grumbling, snarling,
yelping, screaming, bullying, scowling, and roaring? Only
one—Chief Inspector Wilfred Dover of Scotland Yard, admittedly
not a fair or typical representative of that noble body ... Well,
Dover and his long-suffering Sergeant MacGregor are back at
work, investigating the murder of a County Councillor found
strangled in—where else for Dover?—a bathroom ...

Detective Chief Inspector Dover was a creature of habit. Whenever he entered a room he made a point of selecting the most comfortable-looking seat and heading straight for it. On this occasion, as he waddled across the threshold of the large old-fashioned bathroom at Skelmers Hall College, he was not embarrassed by choice. The rim of the bath was definitely out and he didn't fancy the three-legged stool. That left only one place where 241 pounds of flab could be safely deposited, and the Chief Inspector sank gratefully onto the oval of polished mahogany. That flight of stairs up from the ground floor had taken it out of him.

Two other men entered the bathroom. One was the young and handsome Detective Sergeant MacGregor, Chief Inspector Dover's long-suffering assistant; the other was an older man in uniform, Inspector Howard. He was the representative of the local police force whose unenviable job it was to put these two clever devils from Scotland Yard in the picture.

It was Inspector Howard's first encounter with members of the prestigious Murder Squad and he was understandably somewhat diffident. Still, a man had to do what a man had to do. He cleared his throat. "Er—excuse me, sir."

Dover's mean little eyes opened slowly and balefully. "What?"

"Your—er—feet, sir."

"What about 'em?"

"They're resting on the—er—body, sir."

Dover glanced down and with ill grace shifted his boots back a couple of inches from the corpse that lay sprawled, in pajamas and dressing gown, over the bathroom floor. "Thought you were supposed to be telling us what's happened," he observed nastily.

Inspector Howard swallowed. "Oh, yes, I am, sir."

"Well, get on with it, then! I don't want to sit here all morning gawping at a stiff!" Dover's pasty face twisted in a grimace.

Not surprisingly, Inspector Howard's account of the murder which had taken place in the bathroom at Skelmers Hall College was somewhat incoherent. Shorn of his stammerings and splutterings, and expurgated of Dover's increasingly obscene interjections, the story ran something like this:

Skelmers Hall College was an Adult Education Centre where members of the general public could attend courses on subjects of interest to them. The course which had been planned for that week-end was on icons and half a dozen enthusiasts had assembled just before supper on the previous evening, Friday. After supper they had been treated to an introductory lecture by the visiting expert, Professor Ross, and had then dispersed to their various bedrooms for the night. It was in the early hours of Saturday morning that one of the students, a young woman named Wenda Birkinshaw, had discovered the body.

"What's his name?" asked Dover, giving the corpse a poke with his boot.

"Er—Rupert Andrews, sir. Quite a well-known building contractor, I understand, and a County Councillor too."

"How was he croaked?"

"Ah, now that's rather interesting, sir." Inspector Howard's boyish enthusiasm didn't find much echo in his audience. "He was knocked unconscious, then strangled with the cord of his own dressing gown. This was probably one of the weapons, sir."

"This" proved to be a sausage-shaped object, about two feet long, still lying where it had been found on the floor by the washbasin.

Dover inspected it from a safe distance. "What the hell is it?"

"It's a draft excluder, sir. Mrs. Crocker, the Warden's wife, made it herself. It's just a tube of cloth some three inches in diameter filled with sand. You stretch it out along the window sill to keep the draft out. There are several more of them about the Hall. These old houses generally seem to have badly fitting windows, don't they? This particular draft excluder weighs several pounds, sir, and would make a highly efficient cosh. It belongs here in the bathroom."

Dover had slumped back until his spine rested comfortably against the wall. "You always this bloody long-winded?" he asked unpleasantly. "Or is it just for my benefit? And don't," he added as poor Inspector Howard produced yet another prize exhibit, "bother telling me what that is because I know. It's a bath brush."

"It's another murder weapon, sir," explained Inspector Howard. He glanced for sympathy at Sergeant MacGregor, but that young gentleman was prudently keeping his head well down over his note-book. "The handle of the bath brush, sir, was inserted into the dressing-gown cord and used like a tourniquet to tighten it round the neck of the unconscious victim. The victim was a middle-aged man, sir, but quite strong. In the doctor's opinion quite a frail person could have killed him using this method."

"When I want the bloody doctor's opinion," grunted Dover, who really worked at being ungracious, "I'll ask for it. Anything else?"

"I don't think so, sir," replied Inspector Howard miserably.

"What about bloody suspects?"

"Oh, yes, well, virtually everybody in the house last night is a suspect, sir." Inspector Howard shifted uneasily from one foot to the other. Things weren't going at all as he'd expected. Where was that friendly cooperation between one copper and another? That profes-sional camaraderie— That happy exchange of— He caught Dover's jaundiced eye and hurriedly took up the thread of his story. "The Hall is securely locked up at night, sir, and there's no sign of a break-in. Of course we can't definitely exclude—"

"Let's have a few names," growled Dover.

"Of the suspects, sir?"

Dover rolled his eyes toward the ceiling.

"Well, there's Brigadier and Mrs. Crocker, sir, the resident War-dens of the College, and—"

"Here," said Dover as the thought suddenly struck him, "do you have to pay to come to this dump?"

"Oh, yes, sir. Not very much, though. The students' fees, I un-derstand, only cover part of the cost of running the place. The rest comes from the government."

"Bully for some!" grumbled Dover. "Well, get on with it!"

There were, it turned out, no less than eight possible murderers currently at the Skelmers Hall College for Adult Education—and Chief Inspector Dover's face fell at the news. Apart from the Crock-ers, they were in alphabetical order: Miss Wenda Birkinshaw (who had discovered the body), Miss Betsy Gallop, Mr. and Mrs. Mappin, Professor Ross (the lecturer), and Peter Thorrowgood.

To everyone's surprise, Dover had actually been listening.

"No Mrs. Anfield?" he demanded indignantly.

"Anfield, sir?"

Sergeant MacGregor was more accustomed to the great man's idiosyncracies. "I think you mean Andrews, sir," he said, looking up from his notebook. "The dead man was named Andrews."

"What I said!" snarled Dover before turning again on the shrinking Inspector Howard. "So where's his wife?"

Inspector Howard gave up trying to understand. "I gather he was divorced, sir."

"Pity," said Dover, sinking back into lethargy.

"Sir?"

In an untypical flush of generosity Dover tossed one pearl of his investigatory wisdom to this poor provincial bluebottle. "If Mrs. Ashford had been on the scene, laddie, we could just have arrested her and all gone home." He sensed that Inspector Howard needed something more. "Husbands, laddie," he added, disgruntled at having thus to gild the lily, "are always murdered by their wives. And vice versa."

Inspector Howard, to his eternal credit, took his courage in both hands. "Always, sir?"

"Near as damn it!" grunted Dover, hauling himself to his feet and stepping clumsily over the dead body. "It's a law of nature." He headed for the door. "If anybody wants me I'll be downstairs." As he passed MacGregor he fired off a valedictory behest in a voice that carried just far enough to do the most damage. "And get rid of *him!*"

Whether it was Dover's sensitive ears that had caught the clink of bottles or his delicate nostrils that had picked up the aroma of good malt whiskey at 150 paces, the world will never know. Suffice it to say that he made his way unerringly downstairs and straight into the small parlor that served Skelmers Hall College as a bar just as Brigadier Crocker raised his tumbler to his lips.

Caught red-handed, there was nothing a retired officer-and-gentleman could do but reach for another glass. The Brigadier introduced himself. "You look," he said, erroneously attributing Dover's habitual pallor to shock, "as though you could do with this."

"It wasn't a pretty sight," agreed Dover, reaching out an eager paw.

The Brigadier proposed a toast. "Absent friends!"

Dover emptied his glass and prudently got a refill before putting the boot in. "Pal of yours, was he?"

The Brigadier's indignation nearly sobered him. "Good lord, no!

I never set eyes on the bounder before last night."

"Bounder?" queried Dover, who liked seeing people squirm.

"Well, what would you call a chappie of fifty who attends a week-end study course on icons accompanied by his teenage popsie?"

Dover mulled it over. "You sure?"

"Of course I'm sure. Him and Miss Birkinshaw—well, you only had to see them together to realize precisely what was going on."

Dover slowly examined his surroundings. "Bloody funny setup for a romantic weekend," he commented.

"It's a jolly sight cheaper than a hotel," the Brigadier pointed out, replenishing the drinks with an unsteady hand. "And he'd be less likely to run into any of his business chums. County Councillor, indeed!" He stared sullenly into the depths of his glass. "I should have a good look at Miss Birkinshaw, if I were you, Chief Inspector. She found Andrews, you know, and in my opinion—"

There might have been further revelations if it hadn't been for the arrival of a very tall, very thin man who moved with the preternatural leisureliness of a giraffe.

"Ah, Professor Ross!" Brigadier Crocker accompanied his greeting with legerdemain which had the bottle of whiskey out of sight before you could say "usquebaugh."

"I simply want to know how much longer I'm supposed to keep on," bleated Professor Ross. "I've just finished my lecture on Iconography, Part One, but it's hard going. They're hardly a very receptive audience."

"Business-as-usual was my idea," the Brigadier told Dover proudly. "Takes their minds off the tragedy, keeps 'em out of your hair, and stops 'em asking for their money back." He addressed Professor Ross again. "What are they doing now?"

"Having their coffee break," whined the Professor. "That's what's on the timetable."

The Brigadier emerged reluctantly from behind his bar. "I'd better go and give the lady wife a hand before she starts feeling put upon, what? I'll bring you your coffee back here."

Left alone, Dover and the Professor eyed each other moodily. In the end it was Dover, his tongue no doubt loosened by the strong drink, who cracked first.

"You don't look like a professor to me," he said, just to be rude.

Professor Ross's face turned scarlet. "Well, actually," he admitted hoarsely, "I'm not, really."

Dover leered in evil encouragement.

"No," confessed the unfortunate academic with an agonized grimace. "It's just that people have got into the habit of calling me one."

Dover removed his bowler hat the better to scratch at his head. "And you didn't stop 'em?"

Professor Ross (as we may as well continue to call him) murmured, "Well . . ."

"Here," yelped Dover, almost overwhelmed by the audacity of his imagination, "did Ainsworth know about this?"

"Ainsworth?"

"The dead man!" screamed Dover. "Did he know you were sailing under borrowed plumes?"

"Good heavens, no!" wailed the Professor. "The loud-mouthed bully was unpleasant enough to me without that! Oh, *dear!*" Too late—far, far too late—Professor Ross clamped a restraining hand over his mouth.

The only thing left in life that gave Dover real pleasure was bullying the weak and helpless. Naturally he preferred pushing widows and orphans around but, failing them, Professor Ross would do. It wasn't long before the whole story poured out.

It had happened during Professor Ross's introductory lecture, given on the previous evening immediately after supper. Professor Ross had been guilty of a couple of slips of the tongue and Councillor Andrews had pounced on them with unconcealed relish. Professor Ross realized with dismay that he'd encountered every lecturer's nightmare—an expert in the audience. And there were eight more sessions to get through!

"I *knew*," whimpered Professor Ross, "that I was showing them a Hodegetria Mother of God, and I can't think *why* I called it Glykophilusa. It was just a momentary mental aberration."

Dover grunted. It was all Greek to him.

"And then, when I was talking about the metal covers, he pulled me up again. I was simply trying to keep things simple. I know there's a *technical* difference between a riza and an oklad, but really the terms are—"

Dover's threshold of boredom could be measured in microns, so it was fortunate that the Brigadier chose this moment to return with coffee and biscuits. Mrs. Crocker came bustling in behind him. She was one of those women who are always busy.

"You forgot the sugar, Tom." The empty whiskey glasses on the bar counter caught her eye and her routine wifely exasperation turned to real fury. "Oh, for God's sake, you've not been at the booze already, have you?"

Her husband grinned sheepishly at his male companions. "Just a quick snifter to speed poor old Andrews on his way, m'dear."

If this reference to the dear departed was an attempt to inhibit Mrs. Crocker's wrath, it failed. "Poor old Andrews?" she repeated incredulously. "That's not what you called him last night, my lad. Last night you couldn't find words bad enough for him. I don't know when I've seen you in such a blind temper."

She was so absorbed in rinsing out glasses and wiping the bar top down that she failed to notice her husband's frantic signals, and went blithely on, "I'm surprised you need reminding, Tom, that 'poor old Andrews' is the same bloody interfering swine who was going to get us both turned out into the streets without a penny to our name."

Brigadier Crocker glanced at Dover to see if he was paying any attention to this tirade. Strangely enough, he was. "Nonsense, old girl," said the Brigadier desperately. "Andrews hadn't that much influence. He wasn't God Almighty, y'know."

"He was chairman of that special committee the Council set up for slashing local government expenditures," snapped Mrs. Crocker, draping her towel over the beer pump. "And he's not the only one who thinks Skelmers Hall College is a waste of public funds. He just happens to be the most influential and dangerous one we've come across to date."

The arrival of MacGregor to announce that the body had been removed interrupted this heated exchange of views.

Dover hoisted himself to his feet. "About bloody time!"

"They'll let us have the post-mortem report as soon as possible, sir," said MacGregor as he followed Dover upstairs. "And then I was wondering if you'd like to examine Andrews' room now, sir. He only brought one small suitcase, of course, but—"

Dover marched straight into the bathroom and locked the door firmly behind him.

When he emerged five minutes later, he was not pleased to find Professor Ross waiting for him on the landing. The Professor jerked into life and caught Dover by the sleeve. "Remember the old adage," he advised hoarsely. *"Cherchez la femme!"*

Dover tried to brush him off but the Professor was tenacious.

"It's the fair sex you ought to be looking at, Chief Inspector. That Mappin woman for a start."

Dover progressed, carrying Professor Ross with him as he went. "And who's she when she's at home?"

Having twined himself right round Dover, Professor Ross was now able to whisper confidentially in his ear. "She's a student of the course. With her husband. Not that that's cramping her style. They arrived early last night, like Councillor Andrews. You should have seen the pair of them in the bar—Mrs. Mappin and Andrews. Getting on like a house on fire! Flirting. Making suggestive remarks. Saying things with double meanings."

"What was her husband doing?" asked Dover, trying without success to break Professor Ross's wrist.

"Oh, he was maintaining a very low profile. Most of the time he wasn't even there. No doubt he's used to it, but if it had been my wife carrying on like—"

"I'll bear it in mind," promised Dover. "Jealous husband."

"No, no," moaned Professor Ross frantically. "The *wife,* not the husband."

Dover was trying to use his feet. "Eh?"

"*Mrs.* Mappin!" said the Professor. "Don't you understand? She thought she'd made a conquest. But she hadn't. He was just passing the time until Miss Birkinshaw turned up."

Something stirred in Dover's subconscious. "The girl who found the body?"

"That's right. She arrived just before supper and the minute she arrived on the scene Andrews dropped La Mappin like a hot potato."

"Hmm," said Dover.

Professor Ross was an experienced teacher and he knew that you couldn't repeat a thing too often for some people. "Hell," he announced, "hath no fury like a woman scorned."

MacGregor looked round as Dover burst into the bedroom and slammed the door shut behind him. "Find anything, laddie?"

"Nothing of any significance, I'm afraid, sir."

"No cigarettes?"

"Andrews was a nonsmoker, sir."

"Trust him!" Dover's bottom lip protruded. "You sure you haven't got any, laddie?"

"You smoked all mine on the way down, sir."

Dover crossed over to the bed and flopped down on it sulkily. "You could have brought some more," he pointed out. "And what's that you're holding?"

"It's a tie, sir."

"I can see that!" snarled Dover before sinking back and closing
his eyes.

MacGregor gazed nostalgically at the dazzling blue-and-silver
stripes. "Councillor Andrews must have been a Butcher's Boy, sir."

"Eh?" Unlike his sergeant, Dover had not had the advantage of
a Public School education, and further elucidation was required.

"Oh, that's what we used to call the chaps who went to Bullock's
College, sir," said MacGregor. "Bullock, you see, sir—and the blue-
and-white stripes. Like a butcher's apron."

"So what?"

"Well, so nothing, actually, sir." MacGregor draped the tie back
over the mirror. "Just that we used to play them at cricket and
rugger. Annual events, you know." MacGregor chuckled softly to
himself. "We usually beat 'em too!"

Dover wallowed luxuriously among the pillows. "Are you claiming
you knew this Ambrose, laddie?"

"Andrews, sir." MacGregor made the correction without much
hope. "No, he'd be years before my time."

"Pity," grunted Dover. "I was hoping we'd be able to chuck our
hands in, seeing as how you were personally involved with the
deceased."

MacGregor had given up counting to ten years ago. Nowadays he
found it took 30 or even 40 to get his passions under control.
"Shouldn't we start interviewing the suspects, sir?" he asked eventually.

Dover really fancied a preprandial nap but his superiors at the
Yard had been hounding him a bit recently. "Oh, all right," he
grumbled. "Wheel 'em in."

"We've got the use of a room downstairs, sir."

But Dover had reached the end of his concessions. "Here, laddie,
here."

Miss Wenda Birkinshaw, as befitted her status as finder of the
body, was the first victim and MacGregor fought to keep his eyes
fixed on her face as she undulated, in a miasma of cheap scent, over
to the chair which had been placed ready for her. She even got Dover
sitting bolt upright and taking notice, but this was only because her
first action, after provocatively crossing her legs, was to produce
her cigarettes and ask if anyone minded. MacGregor broke the world
record with his lighter, and Dover was only fractionally behind with
the begging bowl.

"Keep the packet," said Miss Birkinshaw grandly, and thereby insured that, whoever stood before the bar of British Justice to answer for the murder of Rupert Andrews, it wouldn't be she.

She rattled off her story with admirable economy. "I work in the typing pool at County Hall and me and Randy—that's what he told me to call him—have been friends for a couple of months. This awful weekend was his idea. Well, you didn't think I was interested in holy pictures, did you?" Miss Birkinshaw uncrossed her legs.

"Mr. Andrews booked separate rooms for you?" said MacGregor from a tight throat.

"There's elections coming up and he didn't want any filthy talk till they were over. Last night he was supposed to wait till everybody'd got settled down and then nip along to my room. Well, I got cheesed off with waiting, didn't I? Mind you, I was in two minds. The way he'd been chatting with that old Mappin woman, the silly cow! I soon put a stop to that, I can tell you. 'If you're going in for geriatrics nowadays, Randy,' I told him, 'just let me know because I can easily fix myself up elsewhere.' What, dear? Oh, last night? Well, like I said, I went looking for him, didn't I? I saw the bathroom door was half open and the light on, so I popped my head round and—ugh. It was terrible!"

"What did you do then, Miss Birkinshaw?" asked MacGregor.

"Screamed the bleeding place down, dearie, and why don't you call me Wenda?"

"Er—were you and Mr. Andrews intending to get married?"

Miss Birkinshaw blinked her enormous baby-blue eyes. "What for?"

"Do you know anybody who'd want to murder Councillor Andrews?"

"Only just about everybody he ever met, dearie! Let's face it, he could be a right pig. He was on the outs with half the people here before I even arrived on the scene. And the other half after I got here."

Dover lit another of Miss Birkinshaw's cigarettes. "Anybody in particular?"

"Well"—Miss Birkinshaw didn't lose much sleep over the ethics of the situation—"there was that young lad, Peter Thorrowgood, for a start. Wet behind the ears? You wouldn't believe! Randy went over him like a bloomin' steamroller."

"Why?"

"Because of me, dearie! Randy thought he was trying to make

time with me, though anybody could see the kid didn't know how many beans make five. Here"—Miss Birkinshaw changed the subject abruptly—"do I have to keep going to these damn old lectures? It's worse than school. I mean, *icons*—who cares?"

Dover graciously excused Miss Birkinshaw and said she could watch the telly instead. MacGregor barely managed to clear up a couple of minor points before the nubile young woman went on her way rejoicing. No, she'd never been to Skelmers Hall College before. No, she hadn't heard anything suspicious before she went out to look for Councillor Andrews, and finally she thought that Councillor Andrews had booked their places on the course about a month ago.

"What was that all about?" asked Dover after Miss Birkinshaw had departed. His mood had been much improved by the intake of nicotine.

"If the murder was premeditated, sir, the murderer would have had to apply for the course *after* Andrews did."

"Garn," said Dover, his mood not being as rosy as all that, "this murder wasn't premeditated! Stands out a mile—the joker just grabbed whatever was to hand and used it. How could he know in advance there'd be a bath brush and that sausage thing all ready and waiting?"

"He could if he'd attended a course here before, sir. That's why I asked Miss Birkinshaw if this was her first visit."

" 'Strewth," said Dover, gazing fondly at his packet of cigarettes, "you're not suspecting that poor little girl of anything, are you?"

"The doctor did say no great strength would be required, sir. And who better than Miss Birkinshaw to catch him unawares?"

Dover had no intention of wasting his time on theoretical and unpalatable discussions. "Fetch that lad in she mentioned!" he commanded and playfully punched his fist into the palm of his other hand. "Let's see if we can't bash a nice free and voluntary confession out of him!"

Peter Thorrowgood, being immature, weedy, and extremely nervous might have been tailor-made for Dover. He was so eager to cooperate that it wasn't necessary to lay a finger on him. He admitted that he was a frequent student on these weekend courses but insisted that this was his first visit to Skelmers Hall. He wasn't particularly interested in icons—nor in medieval monasticism or pottery for beginners, if it came to that. No, he attended these courses in order to make friends and meet people. Like young ladies of the opposite sex.

Dover sniffed.

Mr. Thorrowgood went pale and launched himself hurriedly into the rest of his *curriculum vitae*. Although currently training to be a shoe-shop manager, he didn't really consider he had as yet found his true vocation. He felt he would prefer a job which brought him more into contact with people. Like young ladies of the opposite sex. Young ladies of the opposite sex were, Mr. Thorrowgood confided, a bit thin at the moment. "Sometimes," he added, "I wonder if it's me."

Had he ever met Councillor Andrews before?

"No, never." Mr. Thorrowgood squared his shoulders. "And if you're going to ask me about that scene at the supper table, I'm quite prepared to admit that I did feel like murdering him—for a moment. He deliberately set out to humiliate me in front of everyone, you know. How was I to know that Miss Birkinshaw was some kind of special friend? In any case, all I did was indulge in some polite conversation. From the way Mr. Andrews went on, you'd have thought I'd tried to— Well, it was all very unpleasant and embarrassing. I'd be a hypocrite if I said I was sorry Mr. Andrews is dead, but that doesn't mean I killed him. Because I didn't."

And from this position, young Mr. Thorrowgood refused to budge. Even Dover couldn't shake him. MacGregor took over the questioning as Dover sank back, sullen and exhausted, on the bed.

Mr. Thorrowgood was willing but unhelpful. He'd neither seen nor heard anything out of the ordinary last night. He'd never met any of his fellow suspects before and his application for the course had been sent in at least six months ago because you never knew if these things would get booked up and, no, he couldn't think of anybody who would have wanted to murder Mr. Andrews except—well—

Young Mr. Thorrowgood paused and licked his lips.

MacGregor exuded encouragement.

Sneaking seemed to be endemic at Skelmers Hall.

"Miss Gallop was getting pretty uptight."

"She's a fellow student?"

Mr. Thorrowgood nodded. "I thought she was going to scratch Councillor Andrews' eyes out at one point."

"Why?"

Mr. Thorrowgood didn't know.

"She sort of railed against him as soon as she realized who he was. Something to do with donkeys. And goats. I couldn't make head

nor tail of it. Anyhow, whatever it was, Miss Gallop claimed it was
all Andrews' fault."

"When did this happen?"

"After the first lecture last night. Andrews had drawn a fair
amount of attention to himself by having quite a heated argument
with Professor Ross." Mr. Thorrowgood took time off to seize another
straw. "That's somebody else you might have a word with—Professor
Ross. He was looking pretty sick by the time Councillor Andrews
had finished with him."

"Let's just stick to Miss Gallop," said MacGregor, who didn't want
Dover getting all muddled up. "What was Mr. Andrews' reaction to
her attack?"

"Oh, he gave back as good as he got." Mr. Thorrowgood was plainly
envious. "Told her he hadn't got where he had in life by letting silly
old maids like her push him around. Miss Gallop looked as though
she was going to have a fit."

Dover and MacGregor were given lunch in a small room by themselves. As Mrs. Crocker explained, even before she'd seen Dover's
table manners, it would be less embarrassing for all concerned.

"I don't suppose," she said as she put the soup on the table, "that
they want to hobnob with you any more than you do with them.
Not," she added as she watched Dover stuffing handfuls of bread
down his gullet, "that one has much to complain about as far as this
course is concerned. They're a fairly civilized lot. We've just had the
one gentleman turning up for supper in an open-necked shirt, but
then we've had nobody going around all day in bedroom slippers or
parking their chewing gum under the chairs in the lecture room."

It was no good looking to Dover for polite conversation at feeding
time, so MacGregor, raising his voice to be audible over the splash-
ing and sloshing, did the honors. "I would imagine you get a pretty
decent type here on the whole," he said politely.

"Yes, we do, really," agreed Mrs. Crocker, finding it hard to tear
her eyes away from the spectacle of Dover eating. "We try to preserve
the old country-house atmosphere, you know, and most people are
very cooperative. Well, we're all starved for gracious living these
days, aren't we? That's what makes it so depressing when somebody
like Mr. Mappin lets the side down. It isn't"—she watched Dover
mop up the last of his soup with the last of his bread—"as though
he hadn't got a tie because he was wearing one when he arrived.
Well, I'll fetch the next course, shall I? It's a beef casserole."

It would be absurd to pretend that Dover's drive, acumen, and general get-up-and-go weren't a little impaired after lunch. Two helpings of everything is hardly the formula for a dynamic afternoon.

The remaining interviews were held in the room in which the two detectives had had their lunch, and there is every reason to believe that Dover slept through the first one. This was no mean feat because Miss Betsy Gallop was a woman of strong character, loud voice, and a distinct aroma of goat.

"Never heard of Gallop Goats?" she said in disbelief. "You do surprise me. Thought everybody'd heard of Gallop Goats. S'why I got so enraged with the late unlamented. I mean, Gallop Goats are practically a national institution. Not," she added in a sour afterthought, "that they would have been much longer if Andrews had had his foul way."

MacGregor's pencil flew over the pages of his notebook as Miss Betsy Gallop let it all come gushing out.

"My small holding is on the edge of Donkey Bridge Wood," she confided. "That rotter, Andrews, bought up a chunk of land about a quarter of a mile away on which he proposed to build a housing tract. Planning permission? A mere formality, dear boy! He was on the Council, wasn't he? That bunch of pusillanimous sycophants would have given him the moon if he'd asked for it. You can see where that left yours truly, can't you? Right up the creek and without a paddle!"

MacGregor raised the shapeliest eyebrows in Scotland Yard, policewomen not excepted.

"Approach roads, dear boy!" explained Miss Gallop. "Scheduled to go right through the middle of my herd of pedigreed beauties! It would have put the kibosh on my whole way of life. Don't just breed goats, you know. See this trouser suit I'm sporting?"

MacGregor nodded. He'd been wondering about that trouser suit.

"Hair from my own goats!" claimed Miss Gallop proudly. "Woven by a chum of mine. That"—her brown eyes filled with tears—"was what Andrews was going to destroy, the philistine. Well, somebody's cooked his goose for him!"

The elegant MacGregor eyebrows rose again.

Miss Gallop's scowl wouldn't have looked out of place on Dover's face. "Certainly not me!"

"What happens to the housing scheme now?"

Miss Gallop turned a grubby thumb downward. "No other

builder's got the pull Andrews had with the Council. I'll be able to
disband my little action committee."

MacGregor turned to other aspects of the case. Was Miss Gallop
interested in icons?

"No jolly fear! Just happens this is the only weekend I could get
a goat-sitter. It's not everybody who can stand it, you know. When
did I book? Oh, a couple of months ago. I generally give myself a
little break at this time of year." She started fishing in her hip
pocket. "Can give you the exact date, if you—"

MacGregor said it didn't matter.

Miss Gallop was equally forthright when it came to the events of
Friday night. "Didn't hear a thing, dear boy! Dead to the world as
soon as my head touches the pillow. Even the screams didn't wake
me," she added. "Had to be wakened specially."

And that was that. The closing of the door must have roused Dover
and there was a great deal of snorting and puffing.

MacGregor tried to put his superior in the picture as tactfully as
possible. "Well, at least Miss Gallop didn't try to pin the murder on
somebody else."

"Gerrumphahugh!" said Dover. He smacked his lips. " 'Strewth,
I could do with a cup of tea."

"Tea's ordered for four o'clock, sir, and we've only got Mr. and
Mrs. Mappin left to see. Just enough time. We've got on quite well,
all things considered."

"People don't realize what a strain it all is," said Dover through
a yawn. He extracted another of Miss Birkinshaw's cigarettes and
waited for MacGregor to give him a light. "Well, fetch 'em in," he
growled. "The sooner we start, the sooner we finish."

"Shall we take the lady first, sir?" asked MacGregor, sensibly
striking while the iron was lukewarm.

He'd reckoned without Dover's cunning. "We'll see 'em both together, laddie! It'll be quicker."

Harold and Cynthia Mappin approached their ordeal with understandable apprehension. MacGregor ran an experienced eye over
them as he invited them to sit down. Mrs. Mappin was well into her
middle forties in spite of fighting every day of the way. From the
way she was dressed MacGregor surmised that a hefty proportion
of the family income finished up on her back. Mr. Mappin was older,
grayer, and shabbier. He was in a sober, badly cut suit which he
had tried to enliven by permitting a tantalizing glimpse of his hairy
chest to peep through the open neck of his shirt.

Dover opened the proceedings. "You can smoke if you want to."
He was out of luck. The Mappins didn't.

Dover washed his hands of the pair of 'em.

MacGregor soon found out that it was Mrs. Mappin who did the talking, answering not only her own questions but her husband's. She had a quick and decisive mind and the preliminaries were soon dispensed with. Her husband was an assistant bank manager, this was their first visit to Skelmers Hall College, and Mrs. Mappin was the one who was passionately "into" icons. Neither of them had ever heard of Councillor Andrews before.

MacGregor cautiously broached the question of the alleged flirtation between Mrs. Mappin and the deceased and was not surprised to be presented with a version which differed considerably from the one supplied by Professor Ross. Mrs. Mappin modestly pictured herself as the innocent target of a lascivious brute's unbridled lust. "I simply couldn't get rid of him," she complained. "Could I, Harold? He just wouldn't leave me alone. And his hands, Sergeant, were *everywhere!*"

MacGregor avoided catching anyone's eye.

"You've no idea what a relief it was when that girl finally turned up," Mrs. Mappin went on, twisting her lips in a sneer. "Such a cheap-looking little thing! Still, she no doubt would provide *exactly* what Councillor Andrews was looking for."

MacGregor tried to draw Mr. Mappin into the conversation but, once again, it was Mrs. Mappin who was much quicker on the draw.

"Jealous?" she echoed with an unpleasant laugh. "Harold? You must be joking, Sergeant! My precious husband wouldn't so much as bat an eyelid if he saw me being attacked on the hearthrug at his feet. Councillor Andrews wasn't the first man to make a pass at me, and I doubt if he'll be the last. I've learned to protect myself and not rely on Harold's strong right arm—if any."

An uncomfortable silence followed, during which Harold Mappin grinned vaguely at nothing in particular.

MacGregor addressed the voluptuous Cynthia again. "Did you hear anything suspicious last night?"

Mrs. Mappin shook her head in a drumroll of oversize earrings. "I was so upset I took a sleeping pill."

"Because of Councillor Andrews' unwelcome attentions?"

"That," said Mrs. Mappin with a spiteful glance at her husband, "and other things."

"How about you, Mr. Mappin?"

Harold Mappin jumped. "Oh, no, nothing! I—er—I sleep very soundly."

"Like a log," agreed his wife.

"Er—twin beds?" asked MacGregor, never very happy when having to deal with such intimate matters.

"What else?" queried Mrs. Mappin.

MacGregor let them go.

"Well, that's that, sir," he said as he resumed his seat. "We've seen all the people who were in the Hall last night."

"Moldy lot," grumbled Dover. "Could have been any single one of 'em."

"I'm afraid it could, sir. Anybody could have guessed that Andrews would be creeping along to Miss Birkinshaw's room as soon as things were quiet. It'd be easy enough to lie in wait for him, strike him down with the draft excluder, drag him into the bathroom, and strangle him. No"—MacGregor tucked his pencil away in his pocket—"we're going to have our work cut out to crack this one. It'll probably take weeks."

Work? Weeks? "I fancy that last joker," Dover said desperately.

"Harold Mappin, sir? To avenge his wife? Oh, I hardly think so. From the looks he kept giving her, I think he'd more likely murder *her.*"

Dover didn't care for being crossed. "He had the opportunity!" he snarled.

"They'd *all* had the opportunity, sir."

Dover scowled. It was rapidly becoming a point of honor to drop a noose round Harold Mappin's scrawny neck. Neck? Dover was reduced to clutching at any straw. "That's why he's not wearing a tie!"

One day, MacGregor promised himself, he really would pick up the nearest blunt instrument and— "Andrews was strangled with the cord of his own dressing gown, sir, not by a necktie."

But Dover was nothing if not a whole-hogger. "Says who? Look, What's-his-name ambushes Who's-your-father and garottes him with his tie. See? But, since he's not a complete idiot, he doesn't leave the corpse lying there with his tie round its neck. No, he removes the tie and substitutes the dead man's own dressing-gown cord. What's wrong with that?"

"Mr. Mappin simply has no motive, sir."

"He's jealous of his wife." Dover looked his sergeant up and down before forestalling his objection. "I mean, you're no flaming expert on married life, are you?" MacGregor's carefree bachelor status never ceased to irritate.

MacGregor retreated to his notebook. "Practically everybody in Skelmers Hall has a better motive than Mappin, sir. The Crockers were in danger of losing their jobs here, and Professor Ross was in much the same boat. Miss Gallop might have been turned out of her goat farm and—"

"What about Wenda Birkinshaw?" demanded Dover, who could remember names perfectly well when he wanted to. "Or that reedy young man?"

"Miss Birkinshaw could have had a hundred reasons for killing Andrews," retorted MacGregor. "As for Mr. Thorrowgood—well, he admitted he could cheerfully have murdered him, given half a chance."

Dover wasn't listening. "Fetch him back!"

"Mappin, sir?"

Dover grinned. "We'll have a confrontation!" Raising his arm he managed to get a couple of wiggles out of the fat over his biceps. "I'll soon clout the whole story out of him. And if you don't like it, laddie," he added contemptuously, "try looking the other bloody way!"

MacGregor knew that he should have put up more of a fight, but there was nothing like a few years of close association with Dover to knock the heroics out of Dover's assistant.

Mr. Mappin returned to the interview room alone, looking even more henpecked without his wife than he did with her.

Dover acknowledged that the burden of this particular examination rested solely on his own shoulders. He opened the proceedings with typical finesse. "Where's your bloody tie?"

Mr. Mappin clutched at his throat. "My—my tie?"

Dover grew bored with all this fencing about. "You killed What's-his-name!" he roared.

To MacGregor's eternal disgust these tactics worked.

"I knew I'd never get away with it," said Mr. Mappin bitterly. "Not with my luck." He looked up and appealed to Dover. "I'm not unintelligent. I work hard. I'm honest. I've got my fair share of imagination. So why am I always a failure? Why me? Why am I the one who's passed over for promotion, left out of the first team? Damn it"—he banged his fist down on the arm of his chair—"I've only got her word for it that the boy's my son!"

It was no good expecting sympathy from Dover. "What did you do it for?"

"I knew Andrews would recognize me sooner or later. Bound to. After all, I knew him right away."

Dover blinked. "You knew Andrews?"

"Of course. We were at school together. He was the school bully and I was the school butt—a poor bespectacled little runt, no good at games, a coward . . . For three years he made my life hell on earth."

" 'Strewth!" said Dover. "And you've been nursing a grudge ever since?"

"Not a grudge exactly," said Harold Mappin wearily. "More of a promise, I suppose. Or the inability to keep a promise."

"And that's as clear as mud!" snapped Dover.

"I'm sorry." Harold Mappin sighed and tried again. "It's just that when I was a kid I always promised myself that one day I'd be a tremendous success at *something*. I didn't know what. I just knew I'd finish up a field marshal or a multimillionaire or . . . something. It was the only thing that kept me going. Without a dream like that to hang on to, I'd have cut my throat. Well"—Harold Mappin shrugged helplessly—"I never made it. I'm an assistant bank manager and that's my limit. I've a wife who flaunts her unfaithfulness and a son who despises me. And I'm up to my ears in debt. I've no money, no friends, and no bloody hopes for the future. Andrews would have had a field day with me. He'd have put the clock back thirty years! Well, I couldn't face it. I kept out of his way as much as I could last night, but I couldn't hope to dodge him for the rest of the weekend."

Dover relaxed with a triumphant smirk at MacGregor. "So you strangled him with your tie."

Mr. Mappin seemed mildly irritated. "No, I used the cord of his dressing gown. Why should I use my tie? I may be unlucky but I'm not stupid."

Dover frowned. Damn it, even murderers started giving you cheek these days. "Look, mate," he snarled, "you arrived here last night wearing a tie. Right? And before supper you took it off and you haven't worn it since. Well, why—if it isn't the bloody murder weapon?"

"But I've explained all that!" protested Mr. Mappin. "I didn't want Andrews to recognize me. Damn it all, that's why I killed him."

Dover leaned across and caught Mr. Mappin by the lapels. "So?"

"So the tie I was wearing was my old school tie, wasn't it? My wife nagged me into putting the damned thing on. She thinks it impresses people. Well, Andrews may not have recognized my face right away, but he would have recognized that tie because it was exactly the same as the one he was wearing!"

MacGregor saw Harold Mappin in a new light. "So you're a Butcher's Boy too!" he cried with evident delight and held out his hand. "I was at St. Spyridon's, myself."

Dover, whose formative years had been spent at the Peony Street Mixed Infants, slumped back in his chair.

Kathryn Gottlieb

Dream House

Kathryn Gottlieb's first two stories in Ellery Queen's Mystery Magazine were published nearly five years apart—too long a hiatus for the work of a fine sensitive writer to be absent from the pages of EQMM. Her third story appeared seven years after her second—again too long a wait. But your Editor will be as patient (or impatient) as EQMM contributors wish or expect him to be. It is never too late to receive a fine sensitive story, never . . .

I'd better begin at the beginning—but when, I ask myself, was that? The day, I suppose, when I agreed to buy the one-acre section of property at the south end of Phil Ritchie's farm. It was one of those days when for want of something better to do, for want of a home to go to, I hung around the station house for an hour after my tour of duty. I am that figure of fun, a small-town cop. Watch some television series and you'll know what I mean. They have small eyes and paunches, and sometimes they spit and beat up on the innocent. It makes my blood boil.

About that no-home-to-go-to business. I was married for over 20 years until my wife died last year, and what I can't understand is why the end of 20 years of an unhappy marriage can leave you feeling lost, at a loss, high and dry in a fog or a desert, take your choice, and without a future. It should be a time for rejoicing, right? Well, the older I get, and I'm 48, the less I know about life. In fact, at my present rate of progress, I should be completely ignorant in another six months, give or take a few.

Well, as I say, on this particular day I ran into Phil Ritchie as I was heading back to my room in Mrs. Plauder's house, having sold my own house on the advice of my friends and enemies when Connie died. Let me give you one piece of advice: never listen to advice. They said the house was too big for me. Well, there are no apartments in this town for rent, and let me tell you that room of mine is big, but it's too small for me. Dismal, is what I was feeling. It's all very well to live in the present when you're a young kid; you can do it because there's that great big bank account of time and the unknown up ahead, but when you're my age and the present is

all you've got, the absence of a desirable future invades the day
you're living through and turns it black around the edges.

Phil Ritchie is the best type of man you find in a town like this,
and I mean that as a compliment. He's a successful farmer; he also
owns the farm-equipment agency down in Skyton, and the only gas
station on this stretch of Route 180. Everything brings in money,
and with it all he is a calm, friendly, honorable guy who does a lot
of good in town, and when he suggested that we stop for a beer and
a bite to eat I was glad to go along and sit with him.

He got onto my mood right away and told me I was a damn fool
for listening to people about selling my house in a hurry. Then he
brightened up and said he had just the solution for me and although
it entailed a bit of profit-taking for him, that wasn't the reason he
was offering the idea, which turned out to be this: he owned a one-
acre piece of land, wooded, lying at the extreme south end of his
farm and between him and the county lands, which as far as he
knew they weren't about to build anything on. It would be an ideal
place for me to build myself a house, he said, and start living like
a human being again.

I asked him why I needed a house for one man.

"Get yourself a wife," he said. He is also blunt.

I felt my face turn red. "Like who?" I asked him.

"There are attractive women in town."

"Name one."

"Mary Ann Shifler."

We went up there just before twilight and looked at the piece of
land. It was beautiful, a little bit hilly, with a gentle slope running
up from the road in a westerly direction, and covered with oak and
dogwood except for a little glade right in the middle of it. I knelt
and scooped up a handful of earth and let it trickle through my
fingers and it smelled of earth and spring and hope and I knew I
would pay any price for that place.

"Name me a reasonable figure and I'll take it off your hands," I
said.

He named a reasonable price, and we shook hands on it.

Ernie and Mary Ann Shifler ran the little grocery store half a
block up from Headquarters next to the Texaco station. It was the
kind of place where they had a little bit of everything on the shelves,
and if you couldn't find exactly what you wanted—well, you could
find something else. It wasn't a restaurant, or even a luncheonette,

but you could get yourself a bit of breakfast there, and there'd be a little crowd in the place before half the town was out of bed.

On the coldest winter morning, you'd see their light go on upstairs over the store along about five o'clock in the morning, and then the light would go on downstairs and you knew they would—she would—be pouring the water into the big coffee urn and it was a friendly feeling it gave you, especially when you'd been on the desk or riding around all night.

When Ernie was still around, they used to serve the coffee from before six in the morning till about eight thirty, along with buttered rolls, or Ernie would cut you a piece of pie. A friendly feeling, as I say, to watch the lights go on, but Ernie was not a friendly man. He was big, broad-shouldered, nice-looking, I guess, but he never smiled. The kind of man who talks too much or not at all, with a surly expression on his face to go with it.

And when he talked, the talk was unkind. Maybe he resented being locked up behind that counter and waiting on people who were not his betters, and maybe he didn't make a good living in the store, but he was unpleasant in my judgment over and above what circumstances called for.

Some people said he beat his wife, and it is true she wouldn't show her face in the store for periods of time, but did he beat her? Joe Patris swears he heard her screaming one night when he was driving by and he went and knocked on the door, and after a while Ernie opened up and Joe asked him if anything was wrong and Ernie said no. Joe said he'd like to talk to Mary Ann and Ernie said she's asleep and then he got a funny look on his face and said, all right, come on up, and they went up to the bedroom and she was sitting up pulling the bedcovers around her. She said, "What's wrong?" and Joe said, "I thought I heard you screaming," and she said, "You did. I was having a terrible nightmare." So what could Joe do but go away?

For a long while after Joe told me that, I pictured Mary Ann Shifler sitting up in her bed pulling those blankets around her. A beautiful woman. How could a man abuse a woman like that? And a nice person, too, just as sweet and cheerful and obliging as she was pretty. Sometimes I'd go in there to pick up cigarettes or odds and ends of groceries, and even while my wife was still alive I'd look at Mary Ann and think, God forgive me, if only I had a wife like that.

And then one night Ernie left her. Just walked out and never came back. You'd think she'd have been glad—everybody else in town who had dealings with him was glad—but it seemed to take her a while to get used to the idea. Probably couldn't believe her luck, I remember Joe saying. Well, I didn't understand it at the time, but now, as I say, I am a living witness to the fact that when a bad marriage ends, things don't necessarily get better right away.

But after a while Mary Ann perked up. She spruced up the store a lot, and she put in a line of ham and eggs along with the breakfast rolls, so I and a lot of the fellows got in the habit of dropping in there fairly regular.

I didn't need Phil Ritchie to tell me she was attractive. But until he mentioned her to me I had just never thought of her in a truly personal way, as maybe somebody who could care for me. The minute I thought of building the house on the acre up by the county farm, then everything changed, and I could see her in that house, my wife, cooking the ham and eggs for yours truly and forget the store. The funny part is, my reaction at first was to stay away from the store for a while. I didn't stop to figure it out, but I think maybe I didn't want to watch her waiting on a bunch of strange men. Not my wife.

And then one day I was walking past the store and there was nobody inside but Mary Ann, so I went in and walked up to her and said, "You and I are alone now. I don't mean there's nobody in the store. We're alone in life now. I want you to come have dinner with me." She said she'd like to do that.

I took her out to the Red Mill up near Slingerstown, not that I was trying to hide anything but I wanted to take her to a nice place where we wouldn't be surrounded by people we knew, so we could be alone together and get to know each other. After that we went up there most of the time, and sometimes out to Poole's place, which isn't as fancy as the Mill but was nice and clean and quiet and usually half deserted. I don't know how the Pooles made a living there, except that wasn't for me to worry about. But being a policeman, you get to thinking after a while that everything's your business; one of the hazards of the trade.

And being a policeman, I am also inclined to be blunt and come out with what's on my mind, so right off I asked her if she had divorced Ernie and she told me it was in the works.

And then, it couldn't have been two weeks later, but I couldn't have been more sure of what I wanted if I'd waited the rest of my life, I asked her to marry me, and she didn't look coy or stall me off. She looked a little startled, and she said yes.

What a moment.

I never said a word to her about the new house I was going to build her, or about the dogwood and the oaks and all I was going to hand her on a platter, because I wanted to be sure it was me she wanted, and not something I could give her above and beyond the ordinary. A feeling of modesty. I wanted to be sure.

I guess you'd like to know what she looked like, although I cannot pretend it doesn't pain me to think of her in that personal way. I am trying to be detached about things. She was a nice height for a woman, just to my shoulder, with a lovely, shapely body, and long shiny hair about the color of a collie dog, one of the reddish brown ones, only sleek and glossy, and a lovely creamy complexion that set off her features so that even if they hadn't been beautiful they would have looked beautiful, and big clear light brown eyes of that shade you only see in natural redheads.

So I asked her, and she said yes, and then the tears rolled down her cheeks.

"Why are you crying?"

"I'm happy."

I put my hand over hers. "I want you always to be happy."

The days started to get longer and I got in the habit of going up to my property in the early evenings when I wasn't with her and I'd just moon around. The buds were swelling on the dogwoods and showing white in the cracks, while the oak trees were still looking like winter was never going to end.

On the first of April I hired a bulldozer from Phil and when I got up there I saw he had delivered it. It had been run in to the edge of the glade, the way I asked, and neatly—count on Phil—with no trees disturbed; some brush lost, that was all, but of course we'd have to put in a driveway out to the road anyway, so that didn't matter. The next day was Mary Ann's birthday, and I planned to spring the big surprise.

I picked her up at the usual time and asked her if she'd like to have dinner at the Red Mill or somewhere else, and she said wherever I'd like, and I said no, I'm asking you; so she said the Red Mill was fine, and then asked me where I was heading, since the Mill was in the opposite direction, and I told her I had something to show her. Something *for* her, and her eyes lit up and she started to smile. "I suppose you're looking for a little bracelet in a red box or something like that," I kidded her.

She shook her head. "I don't know what I'm looking for. I'm not looking for *anything*. I'm happy just the way I am."

"You're going to be happier," I said. "I've got you a house and lot."

"You what!" She turned to me all agape, her eyes shining. "What have you gone and done?"

"I bought us the prettiest piece of land for twenty miles around and you and I are going to build our house on it."

She wrapped her arms around me and landed me a kiss on my ear, don't ask me why.

"Hey!" I said. "Hey, I'm driving!"

She unwrapped her arms and faced front again, but I noticed she kept one hand on my shoulder that was nearer to her, as though she, well, didn't want to stop touching me. After a while she said, "Where is it?"

"You'll see."

"What's it like?"

"Beautiful. Oak trees. Dogwood. A hundred dogwoods getting ready to bloom. It's the one real piece of woods in five miles of town. Beautiful."

She didn't ask me again where it was. I guess she could see the way we were heading, and after a minute she dropped her hand from my shoulder and just sat there staring out the window on her side so I couldn't see her face.

After a while I pulled up to the side of the road under our trees and turned the motor off. "You've got a bulldozer in there," she said. Her voice had a funny tone to it; she was talking in the constrained kind of way that reminded me of when she was Ernie's wife.

I got out of the car, walked around, and opened her door. "What are you going to do?" she asked me.

"Come on," I said. I was impatient. "Let's walk over to where the 'dozer is. That's where we're going to build, right in the little open place. We won't have to touch a tree if you don't want to. It'll be just like a little private castle in the woods." I stretched my arm out, first one way and then the other, to the big open spaces of Phil's farm on the one side and the county lands on the other. "We'll be the lords of it all," I said.

She got out of the car then and stood beside me. Under the shade of the trees her face looked bleached out, and her eyes—I'll never forget her eyes—they looked huge, and hard to read. I took her hand. "Your hands are trembling."

"It's all too much," she said.

"It's beautiful, isn't it?"

She took a deep breath. "I'm grateful to you."

"Come on." I started up the path the bulldozer had crushed through the underbrush and we had got nearly to the clearing when she just sank down beside me. My first thought was that she had tripped over a root, but she hadn't gone down suddenly—she had seemed to drift down. She was kneeling and her head was hanging, and I bent down beside her and put my hand on her forehead. It felt all clammy and cold. She was muttering something and I had to get my head close and ask her what she was saying.

"Just I'm sorry. I'm sorry."

"It's all right."

"I've spoiled my birthday for you."

"It's all right."

"No."

"Are you sick?"

"You'd better take me home."

I was plenty worried about her, but she wouldn't let me come upstairs. She insisted she was going straight to bed and then she'd be as right as rain in the morning. She'd just been feeling queer all day, she said, but trying not to think about it, because of her birthday and all.

I said good night, but I was uneasy. It even crossed my mind that she might be expecting, and what a feeling that was! A father at my age! Well, why not? She said she'd gotten her divorce papers, so we'd just hurry up and get married and ride out the gossip. What did I care? I rejoiced, but I was worried about her just the same.

And the worst of it was the next day it was impossible for me to call her, due to an outbreak of vandalism at the Regional High, the worst mess you ever saw, and the principal spitting with rage and one of the teachers hysterical, and I can't say I blame her. I can understand crime, but there's something about that mindless kind of spite these kids go in for that gets you under the skin so that you feel almost capable of murder yourself and no better than they are.

It was nine o'clock before I got back to her place, and then I saw the lights were out, so I figured I ought not to disturb her. But I was still worried. If she was in bed that early, then didn't it mean she was still not okay? Well, the morning would have to do.

In the morning the store was shut up tight and the lights were out. I banged on the door for a while, then I figured I was drawing too much attention to myself and I went away. The day was endless, and vile. An old lady had been beaten to death and robbed, up on the Slingerstown Road. The road to the Red Mill. It gave me a literal pain across my midsection to drive up that road that day, and I knew I wouldn't be driving up it again, except in the line of duty.

Her letter was waiting for me at the house when I came off duty.

"My heart is broken," she wrote, "and I only hope you will not be too unhappy. I have gone away. I will not be back. It was nothing you did. No one was ever so wonderful to me. But it wouldn't have worked out. I can't say any more.

"Please see that the stuff in the refrigerator goes to the poor before it spoils, milk, eggs, and there is half a ham. You could run it up to the Sisters of Charity in Slingerstown, they will know what to do with it. I hope you don't mind my asking.

"I will ever love you."

It was that last line that got me, because it was poetry, and I believed it was true. My throat got all tight and I couldn't have spoken if I had to, except that I did, I said her name, over and over.

I was awake until dawn, and then I took my car out and ran up to the cursed ground. I climbed onto the bulldozer and began to move back and forth in the open space, as though I was digging a cellar. I made 27 passes—I didn't realize I had been counting—and then I saw it, and I let the load down back in the pit and climbed down and looked close.

A thigh bone was sticking out of the loam; not a horse's, not a dog's, not a part of any of the animals that run wild in the woods.

Ernie's.

I got back on the machine and scraped back all the earth into the pit that I had been piling at the edges, which seemed to take a very long time, and then I smoothed it out and spread out a load of brush and leaves over it. All the time I felt very calm and full of hate and pity. But more hate, for him that drove her to it.

Then I moved the bulldozer back out to the road and up the half mile to the side road into Phil's place, and came back to my car.

I guess the dogwoods bloomed, but I never went back to see them and I guess in God's good time the oaks leafed out. What am I going to do with the place? I can't sell it because someone else will dig there and God knows what they will turn up. My guess is a skull with a bullet hole. And for myself, I never want to see the place again. I told Phil I had changed my mind about building there.

"It's a shame," he said, shaking his head. "That's a beautiful place."

But not a happy one.

Brian Garfield

Charlie's Shell Game

Charlie Dark, the man without nerves, was "overage, overweight,
overeager to stay in the game by the old rules rather than the
new." The game? Espionage and counterespionage—front-page
stuff. But Charlie considered himself "the last of the generation
that puts ingenuity ahead of computer print-outs" . . . The deadly
duel of two professionals in the game—Charlie Dark versus
Gregorius . . .

By the end of the afternoon I had seen three of them check in at
the reception desk and I knew one of them had come to kill me
but I didn't know which one.

Small crowds had arrived in the course of the afternoon and I'd
had plenty of time to study them while they stood in queues to check
in at the reception desk. One lot of 16 had come in together from
an airport bus—middle-aged couples, three children, a few solitary
businessmen; tourists, most of them, and sitting in the lobby with
a magazine for a prop I wrote them off. My man would be
young—late twenties, I knew that much.

I knew his name too but he wouldn't be traveling under it.

Actually the dossier was quite thick; we knew a good deal about
him, including the probability that he would come to Caracas to kill
me. We knew something of his habits and patterns; we'd seen the
corpses that marked his backtrail; we knew his name, age, nation-
ality; we had several physical descriptions—they varied but there
was agreement on certain points: medium height, muscularly slim,
youthful. We knew he spoke at least four languages. But he hadn't
been photographed and we had no fingerprints; he was too clever
for that.

Of the check-ins I'd spied at the Tamanaco desk, three were pos-
sibles—any one of them could be my intended assassin.

My job was to take him before he could take me.

Rice had summoned me back from Helsinki and I had arrived in
Langley at midnight grumpy and rumpled after the long flight but
the cipher had indicated red priority so I'd delivered myself directly

to the office without pause to bathe or sleep, let alone eat. I was famished. Rice had taken a look at my stubble and plunged right in, "You're flying to Caracas in the morning. The eight-o'clock plane."

"You may have to carry me on board."

"Me and how many weightlifters?" He glanced at the clock above the official photograph of the President. "You've got eight hours. The briefings won't take that long. Anyhow you can sleep on the plane."

"Maybe. I never have," I said, "but then I've never been this exhausted. Have you got anything to eat around here?"

"No. This should perk you up, though—it's Gregorius."

"Is it now."

"I knew you'd wag your tail."

"All right, you have my attention." Then I had to fight the urge to look straight up over my head in alarm: Rice's smile always provokes the premonition that a Mosler safe is falling toward one's head.

"You've gained it back. Gone off the diet?" Now that he had me hooked in his claws he was happy to postpone the final pounce—like a cat with a chipmunk. I really hate him.

I said, "Crawfish."

"What?"

"It's what you eat in Finland. You take them fresh out of a lake, just scoop them up off the bottom in a wooden box with a chickenwire bottom. You throw them straight into the pot and watch them turn color. I can eat a hundred at a sitting. Now what's this about Caracas and Gregorius?"

"You're getting disgustingly fat, Charlie."

"I've always been fat. As for disgusting, I could diet it off, given the inclination. You, on the other hand, would need to undergo brain surgery. I'd prescribe a prefrontal lobotomy."

"Then you'd have no one left to spice your life."

"Spice? I thought it was hemlock."

"In this case more likely a few ounces of plastique. That seems to be Gregorius' preference. And you do make a splendid target, Charlie. I can picture two hundred and umpty pounds of blubber in flabby pieces along the ceiling. Gregorius would be most gratified."

He'd mentioned Gregorius now; it meant he was ready to get down to it and I slumped, relieved; I no longer enjoy volleying insults with him—they cut too close and it's been a long while since either of us believed they were jokes. Our mutual hatred is not frivolous. But we need each other. I'm the only one he can trust to do these jobs without a screw-up and he's the only one who'd give me the jobs. The slick militaristic kids who run the organization don't offer their plums to fat old men. In any section but Rice's I'd have been fired years ago—overage, overweight, overeager to stay in the game by the old rules rather than the new. I'm the last of the generation that puts ingenuity ahead of computer print-outs.

They meet once a month on the fifth floor to discuss key personnel reassignments and it's a rare month that goes by without an attempt being made by one of the computer kids to tie a can to my tail; I know for a fact Rice has saved me by threatening to resign: "If he goes, I go." The ultimatum has worked up to now but as we both get older and I get fatter the kids become more strident and I'm dubious how long Rice can continue the holding action. It's not loyalty to me, God knows; it's purely his own self-interest—he knows if he loses me he'll get the sack himself: he hasn't got anybody else in the section who knows how to produce. Nobody worthwhile will work for him. I wouldn't either but I've got no choice. I'm old, fat, stubborn, arrogant, and conceited. I'm also the best.

He said, "Venezuela is an OPEC country of course," and waited to see if I would attend his wisdom—as if the fact were some sort of esoterica. I waited, yawned, looked at my watch. Rice can drive you to idiocy belaboring the obvious. Finally he went on, "The oil-country finance ministers are meeting in Caracas this time. Starting Thursday."

"I haven't been on Mars, you know. They have newspapers even in Helsinki."

"Redundancies are preferable to ignorance, Charlie." It is his litany. I doubt he passes an hour, even in his sleep, when that sentence doesn't run through his mind: he's got it on tape up there.

"Will you come to the point?"

"They'll be discussing the next round of oil-price hikes," he said. "There's some disagreement among them. The Saudis and the Venezuelans want to keep the increase down below five percent. Some of the others want a big boost—perhaps twenty-five or thirty percent."

"I plead. Tell me about Gregorius."

"This is getting us there. Trust me."

"Let's see if I can't speed it up," I said. "Of course it's the Mahdis—"

"Of course."

"They want Israel for themselves, they don't want a Palestinian peace agreement, they want to warn the Arab countries that they won't be ignored. What is it, then? They've arranged to have Gregorius explode a roomful of Arab leaders in Caracas? Sure. After that the Arab countries won't be so quick to negotiate a Middle East settlement without Mahdi participation. Am I warm?"

"Scalding. Now I know you're awake."

"Barely."

The Mahdi gang began as an extremist splinter arm of the Black Septemberists. The gang is small but serious. It operates out of floating headquarters in the Libyan desert. There's a long and tedious record of hijackings, terror bombings, assassinations. Nothing unique about that. What makes the gang unusual is its habit of using mercenaries. The Mahdis—they named themselves after the mystic who wiped out Gordon at Khartoum—are Palestinian but they're Bedouins, not Arabs; they're few in number and they're advanced in age compared with the teenage terrorists of the PLO. The Mahdi staff cadre consists of men who were adults at the time of the 1947 expulsion from Palestine. Some of the sheiks are in their seventies by now.

Rather than recruit impassioned young fools the gang prefers to hire seasoned professional mercenaries; they get better results that way and they don't need to be concerned about generation-gap factionalism. They are financed by cold-blooded groups of various persuasions and motivations, many of them in Iraq.

They had used Gregorius at least twice in the past, to my knowledge; the Hamburg Bahnhof murders and the assassination of an Israeli agent in Cairo. The Hamburg bomb had demolished not only a crowd of Israeli trade officials but also the main staircase of the railroad station. The Cairo setup had been simpler, just one victim, blown up when he stepped onto the third stair of his entrance porch.

Gregorius was a killer for hire and he was well paid; apparently his fees were second only to those of Carlos the Jackal, who had coordinated the Munich athlete murders and the Entebbe hijack; but Gregorius always chose his employment on ideological grounds—he had worked for the PLO, the Baader-Meinhof Group, the Rhodesian rebels, the Cuban secret service, but he'd never taken a job for the West. Evidently he enjoyed fighting his own private war of liberation. Of course he was psychotic but there was no point dwelling on his lunacy because it might encourage one to underestimate him; he was brilliant.

Rice said, "We've got it on authority—fairly good authority—that the Mahdis have hired Gregorius for two targets in Caracas. Ministers. The Saudi and the Venezuelan. And of course whatever bonus prizes he may collect—bombs usually aren't too selective."

"How good is 'fairly good'?"

"Good enough to justify my pulling you off the Helsinki station and posting you to Venezuela."

"All right." If he didn't want to reveal the source he didn't have to; it wasn't really my affair. Need-to-know and all that.

Rice got down to nuts and bolts and that pleased me because he always hurries right through them: they bore him. He has a grand image of himself as the sort of master strategist who leaves tactical detail to junior staff. Unhappily our section's budget doesn't permit any chain of command and Rice has to do his own staff work and that's why we usually have to go into the field with a dearth of hard information; that's one reason why nobody else will work for him—Rice never does much homework.

"It could happen anywhere," he concluded. "The airport, a hotel lobby, a state banquet, any of the official ministerial meetings, a limousine. Anywhere."

"Have you alerted Venezuelan security?"

"I didn't have to. I've established your liaison out of courtesy."

In other words the tip had come from Venezuelan security. And they didn't feel confident of their own ability to contain Gregorius. Very astute of them; most small-nation security chiefs lack the humility to admit it when a job is too big for them.

Rice continued, in the manner of an afterthought, "Since we don't know where he plans to make the strike we've taken it upon ourselves to—"

"Is that a royal 'we'?"

"No. The fifth floor. As I was saying, it's been decided that our best chance at him is to lure him into the open before the ministers begin the conference. Of course he doesn't tempt easily."

Then he smiled. My flesh crawled.

"You're the bait, Charlie. He'll come out for you."

"In other words it's an open secret that I'll be in Caracas and you've spread the word where you know he'll hear it."

I brooded at him, hating him afresh. "Maybe you've neglected something."

"Oh?"

"Gregorius is like me in one respect. He's—"

"Young, fast, up-to-date, and sexy. Yes indeed, Charlie, you could be twins."

I cut across his chuckle. "He's a professional and so am I. Business comes first. He'd love to nail me. All right. But first he'll do the job he's being paid for."

"Not this time. We've leaked the news that you're being sent down there to terminate him regardless of cost. He thinks you're being set up to nail him *after* he exposes himself by blowing up a few oil ministers. He can't risk that—you got closer to nailing him than anybody else ever has. He knows if you're set on him again you won't turn loose until you've done the job. And he knows if he sets off a bomb while you're in earshot of it you'll reach him. He needs more lead-time than that if he means to get away."

And he smiled again. "He's got to put you out of the way before he goes after the ministers. Once the bombs go off he can't hang around afterward to take you on. He's got to do it first."

I said, "I've heard stronger reasoning. He's confident of his skills. Suppose he just ignores me and goes ahead with the job as if I weren't there?"

"He hates you too much. He couldn't walk away, could he? Not after Beirut. Why, I believe he hates you even more than I do."

Two years earlier we'd known Gregorius was in Beirut to blast the Lebanese-coalition prime minister. I'd devised one of the cleverer stunts of my long career. In those days Gregorius worked in tandem with his brother, who was six years older and nearly as bright as Gregorius. Our plan was good and Gregorius walked into it but I'd had to make use of Syrian back-up personnel on the alternate entrances to that verminous maze of alleys and one of the Syrians had been too nervous or too eager for glory. He'd started the shooting too early by about seven-tenths of a second and that was all the time Gregorius needed to get away.

Gregorius left his brother behind in ribbons in the alley; still alive today but a vegetable. Naturally Gregorius made efforts afterward to find out who was responsible for the ambush. Within a few weeks he knew my name. And of course Gregorius—that's his code name, not the one he was born with—was Corsican by birth and personal revenge is a religion with those people. I knew one day he'd have to come for me; I'd lost very little sleep over it—people have been trying to kill me for 35 years.

Just before Rice sent me to the airport he said, "We want him alive, Charlie."

"You're joking."

"Absolutely not. It's imperative. The information in his head can keep the software boys busy for eight months. Alive—it's an order from the fifth floor."

"You've already blindfolded me and sent me into the cage with him and now you want to handcuff me too?"

"Why, Charlie, that's the way you like it best, you old masochist." He knows me too well.

I'd watched them check in at the hotel desk and I'd narrowed the possibilities to three. I'd seen which pigeonholes the room clerk had taken the keys from so I knew which rooms they were in. I didn't need to look at the register because it wouldn't help me to know what names or passports they were using.

It was like the Mexican Shell Game: three shells, one pea. Under which shell is the pea?

He had to strike at me today because Rice's computer said so. And it probably had to be the Tamanaco Hotel because I had studied everything in the Gregorius dossier and I knew he had a preference—so strong it was almost a compulsion—for the biggest and best old hotel in a city. Big because it was easy to be anonymous there; best because Gregorius had been born dirt-poor in Corsica and was rich now; old because he had good taste but also because old walls tend to be soundproof. In Caracas the Tamanaco was it.

It was making it easy for him, sitting in plain sight in the lobby.

Earlier in the day I'd toured the city with Cartlidge. He looks like his name—all gaunt sinews and knobby joints. We'd traced the route in from the airport through the long mountain tunnel and we'd had a look at the hotel where the Saudi minister was booked in; on my advice the Venezuelans made a last-minute switch and when the Saudi arrived tomorrow morning he'd be informed of the move to another hotel. We had a look at the palace where the conference would take place and I inquired about the choice of halls: to forestall Gregorius, the Venezuelans had not announced any selection—there were four suitable conference rooms in the building—and indeed the final choice wouldn't actually be made until about ten minutes before the session began. They were doing a good job. I made a few minor suggestions and left them to it.

After lunch we'd set up a few things and then I'd staked myself in the Tamanaco lobby and four hours later I was still there.

Between five and six I saw each of the three again.

The first one spent the entire hour at the pool outside the glass doors at the rear of the lobby. He was a good swimmer with the build and grace of a field-and-track contender; he had a round Mediterranean face, more Italian than French in appearance. He had fair hair cut very short—crew cut—but the color and cut didn't mean anything; you could buy the former in bottles. For the convenience of my own classification, I dubbed him The Blond.

The second one appeared shortly after five, crossing the lobby in a flared slim white tropical suit. The heels of his beige shoes clicked on the tiles like dice. He stopped at the side counter to make a phone call—he could have been telephoning or he could have been using it as an excuse to study my abundant profile—and then he went along to the bell captain's desk and I heard him ask the captain to summon him a taxi, as there weren't any at the curb in front. His voice was deep: he spoke Spanish with a slight accent that could have been French. He had a very full head of brown hair teased into an Afro and he had a strong actorish face like those of Italians who play Roman gigolos in Technicolor films. He went right outside again, presumably to wait for his taxi. I dubbed him The Afro. If he'd actually looked at me I hadn't detected it—he had the air of a man who only looked at pretty girls or mirrors.

The third one was a bit more thickly muscled and his baldness was striking. He had a squarish face and a high pink dome above it. Brynner and Savalas shave their heads; why not Gregorius? This one walked with an athlete's bounce—he came down about half-past five in khaki Bermudas and a casual Hawaiian tourist shirt; he went into the bar and when I glanced in on my way past to the gents' he was drinking something tall and chatting to a buxom dark-haired woman whose bored pout was beginning to give way to loose fourth-drink smiles. From that angle and in that light the bald man looked very American but I didn't cross him off the list; I'd need more to go on.

I was characterizing each of them by hairstyle but it was useless for anything but shorthand identification. Gregorius, when last seen by witnesses, had been wearing his hair long and black, shoulder-length hippie style. None of these three had hair remotely like that but the sightings had been five weeks ago and he might have changed it ten times in the interval.

The Blond was on a poolside chaise toweling himself dry when I returned from the loo to the lobby. I saw him shake his head back with that gesture used more often by women than by men to get the hair back out of their eyes. He was watching a girl dive off the board; he was smiling.

I had both room keys in my pocket and didn't need to stop at the desk. It was time for the first countermove. I went up in the elevator and walked past the door of my own room and entered the connecting room with the key Cartlidge had obtained for me. It was a bit elaborate but Gregorius had been known to hook a detonator to a doorknob and it would have been easy enough for him to stop a chambermaid in the hall: "My friend, the very fat American, I've forgotten the number of his room."

So I entered my room through the connecting door rather than from the hall. I didn't really expect to find anything amiss but I didn't want to risk giving Rice the satisfaction of hearing how they'd scraped sections of blubber off the ceiling.

Admittedly I am fat but nevertheless you could have knocked me over with a feather at that moment. Because the bomb was wired to the doorknob.

I looked at it from across the room. I didn't go any closer; I returned to the adjoining room, got the *Do Not Disturb* placard, went out into the hall, and hung the placard on the booby-trapped doorknob. One of the many differences between a professional like Gregorius and a professional like Charlie Dark is that Charlie Dark tends to worry about the possibility that an innocent hotel maid might open the door.

Then I made the call from the phone in the adjoining room. Within two minutes Cartlidge was there with his four-man bomb squad. They'd been posted in the basement beside the hotel's wine cellar.

The crew went to work in flak vests and armored masks. Next door I sat with Cartlidge and he looked gloomy. "When it doesn't explode he'll know we defused it." But then he always looks gloomy.

I said, "He didn't expect this one to get me. It's a signal flag, that's all. He wants me to sweat first."

"And are you? Sweating?"

"At this altitude? Heavens no."

"I guess it's true. The shoptalk. Charlie Dark has no nerves."

"No nerves," I agreed, "but plenty of nerve. Cheer up, you may get his fingerprints off the device."

"Gregorius? No chance."

Any of the three could have planted it. We could ask the Venezuelans to interrogate every employee in the hotel to find out who might have expressed an interest in my room but it probably would be fruitless and in any case Gregorius would know as soon as the interrogations started and it would only drive him to ground. No; at least now I knew he was in the hotel.

Scruple can be crippling. If our positions had been reversed—if I'd been Gregorius with one of three men after me—I'd simply kill all three of them. That's how Gregorius would solve the problem.

Sometimes honor is an awful burden. I feel such an anachronism.

The bomb squad lads carried the device out in a heavy armored canister. They wouldn't find clues, not the kind that would help. We already knew the culprit's identity.

Cartlidge said, "What next?"

"Here," I said, and tapped the mound of my belly, "I know which one he is. But I don't know it here yet." Finger to temple. "It needs to rise to the surface."

"You *know?*"

"In the gut. The gut knows. I have a fact somewhere in there. It's there; I just don't know what it is."

I ordered up two steak dinners from room service and when the tray-table arrived I had Cartlidge's men make sure there were no bombs under the domed metal covers. Then Cartlidge sat and watched with a kind of awed disgust while I ate everything. He rolled back his cuff and looked at his watch. "We've only got about fourteen hours."

"I know."

"If you spend the rest of the night in this room he can't get at you. I've got men in the hall and men outside watching the windows. You'll be safe."

"I don't get paid to be safe." I put away the cheesecake—both portions—and felt better.

Of course it might prove to be a bullet, a blade, a drop of poison, a garrote, a bludgeon—it could but it wouldn't. It would be a bomb. He'd challenged me and he'd play it through by his own perverse rules.

Cartlidge complained, "There's just too many places he could hide a satchel bomb. That's the genius of plastique—it's so damn portable."

"And malleable. You can shape it to anything." I looked under the bed, then tried it. Too soft: it sagged near collapse when I lay back. "I'm going to sleep on it."

And so I did until shortly after midnight when someone knocked and I came awake with the reverberating memory of a muffled slam of sound. Cartlidge came into the room carrying a portable radio transceiver—a walkie-talkie. "Bomb went off in one of the elevators."

"Anybody hurt?"

"No. It was empty. Probably it was a grenade—the boys are examining the damage. Here, I meant to give you this thing before. I know you're not much for gizmos and gadgets but it helps us all keep in touch with one another. Even cavemen had smoke signals, right?"

"All right." I thought about the grenade in the elevator and then went back to bed.

In the morning I ordered up two breakfasts; while they were en route I abluted and clothed the physique that Rice detests so vilely. One reason why I don't diet seriously is that I don't wish to cease offending him. For a few minutes then I toyed with Cartlidge's walkie-talkie. It even had my name on it, printed onto a plastic strip.

When Cartlidge arrived under the little dark cloud he always carries above him I was putting on my best tie and a jaunty face.

"What's got you so cheerful?"

"I lost Gregorius once. Today I'm setting it right."

"You're sure? I hope you're right."

I went down the hall. Cartlidge hurried to catch up; he tugged my sleeve as I reached for the elevator button. "Let's use the fire stairs, all right?" Then he pressed the walkie-talkie into my hand; I'd forgotten it. "He blew up one elevator last night."

"With nobody in it," I pointed out. "Doesn't it strike you as strange? Look, he only grenaded the elevator to stampede me into using the stairs. I suggest you send your bomb-squad lads to check out the stairs. Somewhere between here and the ground floor they'll doubtless find a plastique device wired to a pressure-plate under one of the treads, probably set to detonate under a weight of not less than two hundred and fifty pounds."

He gaped at me, then ran back down the hall to phone. I waited for him to return and then we entered the elevator. His eyes had gone opaque. I pressed the lobby-floor button and we rode down; I could hear his breathing. The doors slid open and we stepped out into the lobby and Cartlidge wiped the sweat off his face. He gave me a wry inquiring look. "I take it you found your fact."

"I think so."

"Want to share it?"

"Not just yet. Not until I'm sure. Let's get to the conference building."

We used the side exit. The car was waiting, engine running, driver armed.

I could have told Cartlidge which one was Gregorius but there was a remote chance I was wrong and I don't like making a fool of myself.

Caracas is a curiously Scandinavian city—the downtown architecture is modern and sterile; even the hillside slums are colorful and appear clean. The wealth of Twentieth Century oil has shaped the city and there isn't much about its superficial appearance, other than the Spanish-language neon signs, to suggest it's a Latin town. Traffic is clotted with big expensive cars and the boulevards are self-consciously elegant. Most of the establishments in the central shopping district are branches of American and European companies—banks, appliances, couturiers, Cadillac showrooms. It doesn't look the sort of place where bombs could go off: terrorism doesn't suit it. One pictures Gregorius and his kind in the shabby crumbling wretched rancid passageways of Cairo or Beirut. Caracas? No; too hygienic.

As we parked the car the walkie-talkies crackled with static. It was one of Cartlidge's lads—they'd found the armed device on the hotel's fire stairs. I'd been mistaken about one thing: it was a trip-wire, not a pressure plate. Again I'd forgotten how indiscriminate Gregorius could be, his indifference to the risk to innocents.

We had 20 minutes before the scheduled arrivals of the ministers. I said, "It'll be here somewhere. The bomb."

"Why?"

"It's the only place he can be sure they'll turn up on schedule. Are the three suspects still under surveillance? Check them out."

He hunched over the walkie-talkie while I turned the volume knob of mine down to get rid of the distracting noise and climbed out of the car and had my look around; I bounced the walkie-talkie in my palm absently while I considered the possibilities. The broad steps of the *palacio* where the conference of OPEC ministers would take place were roped off and guarded by dark-faced cops in Sam Brownes. On the wide landing that separated the two massive flights of steps was a circular fountain that sprayed gaily; normally people sat on the tile ring that contained it but today the security people had cleared the place.

There wasn't much of a crowd; it wasn't going to be the kind of spectacle that would draw any public interest. There was no television equipment; a few reporters clustered off to one side with microphones and tape recorders. Routine traffic, both vehicular and pedestrian. That was useful because it meant Gregorius wouldn't be able to get in close; there would be no crowd to screen him.

Still, it wasn't too helpful. All it meant was that he would use a remote-control device to trigger the bomb.

Cartlidge lowered the walkie-talkie from his face. "Did you hear?"

"No." I had difficulty hearing him now as well: the fountain made white noise, the constant gnashing of water, and I moved closer to him while he scowled at my own walkie-talkie. His eyes accused me forlornly. "Would it kill you to use it? All three accounted for. One in his room, one at the hotel pool, one in the dining room having his breakfast."

I looked up past the rooftops. I could see the upper floors of the Hotel Tamanaco—it sits on high ground on the outskirts—and beyond it the tiny swaying shape of a cable car ascending the lofty mountain. Cotton-ball clouds over the peaks. Caracas is cupped in the palm of the mountains; its setting is fabulous. I said to Cartlidge, "He has a thing about stairs, doesn't he."

"What?"

"The Hamburg Bahnhof—the bomb was on the platform stairway. The Cairo job, again stairs. This morning, the hotel fire stairs. That's the thing about stairways—they're funnels." I pointed at the flight of stone steps that led up to the portals of the *palacio*. "The ministers have to climb them to get inside."

"Stone stairs. How could he hide a bomb there? You can't get underneath them. Everything's in plain sight."

I brooded on it. He was right. But it had to be: suddenly I realized it had to be—because I was here and the Saudi's limousine was drawing up at the curb and it meant Gregorius could get both of us with one shot and then I saw the Venezuelan minister walk out of the building and start down the stairs to meet the limousine and it was even more perfect for Gregorius: all three with one explosion. It *had* to be: right here, right now.

Where was the damned thing? Where?

I had the feeling I needed to find the answer within about seven seconds because it was going to take the Venezuelan minister that long to come this far down the steps while the Saudi was getting out of the limousine; already the Venezuelan was nearly down to the fountain and the Saudi was ducking his berobed head and poking a foot out of the car toward the pavement. The entourage of Arab dignitaries had hurried out of the second limousine and they were forming a double column on the steps for the Saudi to walk through; a police captain drew himself to attention, saluting; coming down the stairs the Venezuelan minister had a wide welcoming smile across his austere handsome face.

They'd picked the limousine at random from a motor pool of six. So it couldn't be in the car.

It couldn't be on the steps because the *palacio* had been guarded inside and out for nearly a week and it had been searched half an hour ago by electronic devices, dogs, and human eyes.

It couldn't be in the fountain either. That had been too obvious. We'd exercised special care in searching the fountain; it had only been switched on ten minutes earlier. In any case you can't plant a bomb under water because the water absorbs the force of the explosion and all you get is a big bubble and a waterspout.

In other words there was no way for Gregorius to have planted a bomb here. And yet I knew he had done so. I knew where Gregorius was; I knew he had field glasses to his eyes and his finger on the remote-control button that would trigger the bomb by radio signal. When the Saudi met the Venezuelan and they shook hands on the steps not a dozen feet from me, Gregorius would set it off.

Six seconds now. The Venezuelan came past the fountain.

The walkie-talkie in my hand cracked with static but I didn't turn it up. The mind raced at Grand Prix speed. If he didn't plant the bomb beforehand—and I knew he hadn't—then there had to be a delivery system.

Five seconds. Gregorius: cold, brutal, neat, ingenious. Then I knew—*I* was the bomb.

Four seconds and my arm swung back. It has been a long time since I threw a football and I had to pray the instinct was still in the arm and then I was watching the walkie-talkie soar over the Venezuelan's head and I could only stand and watch while it lofted and descended. It struck the near lip of the fountain and for a moment it looked ready to fall back onto the stairs, but then it tipped over the rim and went into the water.

His reaction time would be slowed by distance and the awkwardness of handling binoculars and the unexpectedness of my move. Instinctively he reached for the trigger button, but by the time he pressed it the walkie-talkie had gone into the water. The explosion wasn't loud. Water blistered at the surface and a crack appeared in the surrounding rim; little spouts began to break through the shattered concrete; a great frothy mushroom of water bubbled up over the surface and cascaded down the steps.

Nobody was hurt.

We went into the hotel fast. I was talking to Cartlidge: "I assume the one who's still upstairs in his room is the blond one with the crew cut."

"How the hell did you know that?"

"He's Gregorius. He had to have a vantage point."

Gregorius was still there in the room because he'd had no reason to believe we'd tumbled to his identity. He was as conceited as I; he was sure he hadn't made any mistake to give himself away. He was wrong of course. He'd made only one but it was enough.

Cartlidge's bomb-squad lads were our flying wedge. They kicked the door in and we walked right in on him and he looked at all the guns and decided to sit still.

His window overlooked the *palacio* and the binoculars were on the sill. I said to Cartlidge, "Have a look for the transmitter. He hasn't had time to hide it too far away."

The Blond said, "What is this about?" All injured innocence.

I said, "It's finished, Gregorius."

He wasn't going to admit a thing but I did see the brief flash of rage in his eyes; it was all the confirmation I needed. I gave him my best Rice smile. "You'll be pleased to talk in time."

They searched him, handcuffed him, gave the room a toss, and didn't find anything; later that day the transmitter turned up in a cleaning-supplies cupboard down the hall.

To this day Cartlidge still isn't sure we got the right man because nobody ever told him what happened after we got Gregorius back to the States. Rice and I know the truth. The computer kids in Debriefing sweated Gregorius for weeks and finally he broke and they're still analyzing the wealth of information he has supplied. I'd lost interest by that time; my part of it was finished and I knew from the start that I'd got the right man. I don't make that kind of mistake; it didn't need confirmation from the shabby hypodermics of Debriefing. As I'd said to Rice, "The binoculars on the windowsill clinched it, of course. When the Venezuelan and the Saudi shook hands he planned to trigger it—it was the best way to hit all three of us.

But I knew it had to be the Blond much earlier. I suppose I might have arrested him first before we went looking for the bomb but I wasn't absolutely certain."

"Don't lie," Rice said. "You wanted him to be watching you in his binoculars—you wanted him to know you were the one who defused him. One of these days your brain's going to slow down a notch or two. Next time maybe it'll blow up before you throw it in the pond. But all right, since you're waiting for me to ask—how did you pick the blond one?"

"We knew until recently he'd worn his hair hippie length."

"So?"

"I saw him at the pool toweling himself dry. I saw him shake his head back the way you do when you want to get the hair back out of your eyes. He had a crew cut. He wouldn't have done that unless he'd cut his hair so recently he still had the old habit."

Rice said, "It took you twelve hours to figure that out? You *are* getting old, Charlie."

"And hungry. Have you got anything to eat around here?"

"No."

E. X. Ferrars

The Forgotten Murder

Peter Hassall was assigned to write a series of articles on unsolved murders. He began with the murder of Dr. Joseph Armiger five years ago in the village of Newton St. Denis. Now, Dr. Armiger had been a man of violent temper, but he also had had patience—and as Everard Crabbe told Hassall in the village pub, "That's a dangerous mixture, you know." Add subtlety and cunning—and you have a deadly brew . . .

When the *Evening Herald* commissioned Peter Hassall to write a series of articles on forgotten murders they did not, of course, expect him to solve the problems which, over the years, had baffled the police. What they wanted from him was simply an account of the after-effects that the murders had had on the communities in which they occurred. Had they truly been forgotten, or did people still talk about them? If they did, what were they saying now? Had they theories of their own about the truth of what had happened five, or ten, or even 20 years ago? Hassall was left to choose his murders for himself and without hesitation he decided that the first one he would investigate was that of Dr. Joseph Armiger, in the village of Newton St. Denis.

His reason for this was that Dr. Armiger was the only victim of a murder whom Hassall had ever met personally. It had been about seven years ago at a small party in Bournemouth, given by friends of Hassall's with whom he had been spending the weekend. Dr. Armiger at that time had been director of a research station near Bournemouth under the Agricultural Research Council, but he had been just about to retire and that evening he had talked a great deal about his retirement. He had talked with a refreshing lack of the fears and regrets that beset so many people at that stage of their lives.

Dr. Armiger had been a short man, thin, very upright, brisk and abrupt in his movements, with a red, sharp-featured face, thick gray hair, and an amiable, animated manner. Hassall's friends told him that the amiability lasted just as long as no one opposed him, but that when someone did, his temper could flare up suddenly and alarmingly. He had already bought a cottage in Newton St. Denis, he told Hassall, where he was going to live with his sister and where he intended to create the most beautiful of gardens.

He had talked on and on about his plans for the garden. Hassall had not paid much attention at the time, for there had been a beautiful young woman in the room with whom he would far sooner have been talking. But when, about two years later, he read of Armiger's murder, he recalled the evening in Bournemouth and wondered how far that wonderful garden had progressed. Had Armiger achieved anything, or were two years too short a time for results to appear? Had the brief time of his retirement been wholly wasted?

His death had seemed a pure waste, a brutal and senseless tragedy. He had been on his way, late one summer evening, to post some letters in a mailbox near his cottage when he had been set upon by some person or persons unknown and battered to death. The police had tried to obtain information about a gang of boys on motorcycles who had been seen that evening driving wildly through the village; but although they had been traced it had been impossible to prove the guilt of any of them. Whatever suspicions of them the police had entertained, in the end they had to abandon the inquiry. No other suspects had been found and the affair dropped out of the newspapers.

Five years after the murder, driving down to Newton St. Denis, Peter Hassall did not give a thought to the possibility that he might discover the murderer. He assumed the boys on the motorcycles were responsible. But he was curious what impact that self-assertive little man had made on the village. Had he still been too much of a newcomer there for the slow village mind to have become fully aware of his existence, or had he already managed to impose himself on the community as he had certainly intended? Did his sister still live in the cottage? What did she believe or know about his murder?

That was something Hassall never discovered, for Miss Armiger had been dead for a year and was buried in the village churchyard. She seemed to be only vaguely remembered, but a neighbor thought she had heard that the old lady had died of a stroke. The cottage had been sold since her death and the people now living in it, a young couple with several young children, knew nothing about the Armigers. The garden that was to have been so beautiful was now laid out to vegetables, struggling up not too successfully through nettles and bindweed.

The vicar and the doctor were both new since the Armigers' time.

The landlord of The Coach and Horses said he remembered Mr. Armiger, that he used to drop in from time to time for a pint, and that his death had been a bad business, the sort of thing to get the neighborhood a bad name, and that the police hadn't cracked down nearly hard enough on them hooligans.

One or two other village people whom Hassall questioned said more or less the same thing, but on the whole it was disappointing. There was no drama for him to write up, nothing personal about the victim to develop into a story. His own memory of Armiger seemed to be rather more vivid than that of the people among whom he had lived for two years. Regretfully Hassall began to think it best to leave Joseph Armiger in the oblivion in which he rested and go on to investigate the next unsolved murder on his list.

Then one morning he met Everard Crabbe.

They met in The Coach and Horses when Hassall had just made up his mind that after a drink and a sandwich he would drive back to London. There was no one else in the bar but the landlord, who came and went, attending to their wants but leaving Hassall and Crabbe mostly to themselves. Crabbe was sitting on a stool at the bar. He was a quiet-looking, shabby man of about 40, with a deeply lined, nervous face, scanty brown hair, and deepset, watchful blue eyes. He watched Hassall for some minutes before he spoke to him.

Then he said, "Good morning. My name's Crabbe—Everard Crabbe."

Very faintly a bell tinkled in Hassall's mind. He had a feeling he had heard the name, but he could not remember when or where.

"Good morning. Mine's Peter Hassall," he replied.

"I hear you've been asking questions about Dr. Armiger," Crabbe said.

It surprised Hassall to hear the dead man referred to as Dr. Armiger. In general the village had denied him the status of doctor, on the grounds that the title belonged only to members of the medical profession.

"Yes, but I haven't got very far with them," he said.

"Not police, are you?" Crabbe said. "Not after all this time."

"No, I'm a writer. I'm doing a series of articles on forgotten murders."

"Ah, that's what I thought. You've got the look. Possibly I could help you a bit. Not much, I'm afraid. I had some theories of my own at the time, but they were not based on anything you could call evidence. But if you'd be interested—" He paused hopefully, a lonely man probably, badly in need of someone to talk to.

Hassall did not think that anything useful would come out of it, but he was in no hurry and Crabbe's glass was empty. Offering him a drink, he found that Crabbe's preference was for a double whiskey.

Picking up his glass, Crabbe continued, "I hadn't been living here very long when it all happened. Only three or four years. That's nothing in a place like this. And I only knew Armiger casually. But talk gets around and everyone knew he'd a pretty good opinion of himself as a gardener. Not that he'd ever done much gardening before he came here, so far as anyone could make out, but he was going to rely on books and science. He'd been Director of some agricultural research station somewhere—you probably know that—and he was going to show the rest of us a thing or two.

"Of course the old people laughed at him. There wasn't anyone who could teach *them* anything. But it didn't worry him and he went to work and he was a very hard worker, they all admitted that, and he soon had things in what had just been a cabbage patch looking very promising. Of course he didn't mind how much money he spent. He ordered expensive varieties of plants and all kinds of fertilizers and so on and he took no notice of any advice he was given. Given half a chance, he'd lecture you for an hour on what you ought to be doing yourself. A very opinionated man."

"So he wasn't popular," Hassall said.

"Well, not exactly, no. Not that he ever did anyone any harm. That's to say, until his carnations were stolen. That's when the trouble began. Seems they were something very special, from some very special grower. I met him the day after it happened and he was choking with fury. Someone had come into his garden during the night and pinched the whole lot he'd just planted. He said he'd have his revenge.

"But there, you see, he was up against a difficulty, because just how do you recognize your own carnation plants when half the people in the neighborhood have them in their gardens? Not quite such remarkable ones, perhaps, but until they come into bloom, how are you going to distinguish one carnation from another? I pointed that out to him and he muttered, 'Just wait and see,' and walked on, muttering to himself. I didn't like the sound of it much, but what could I do? I didn't really believe he'd do anything."

"I've been told he had a violent temper," Hassall said.

"Oh, that's certain," Crabbe agreed. "But he also had patience, and that's a dangerous mixture, you know. It gives you the makings of a vengeful man. Vindictive and vengeful." He drank some of his whiskey. "He was both, as it turned out. We all thought he'd forgotten about it, but in fact he was just waiting for the annual flower show in the village to see who entered carnations. And there he recognized his own straight away. Anyway, they were the only ones in the show of the right variety and color. And they won first prize. Not that that's what he was interested in. He simply wanted the name of the man who'd entered them.

"It was Albert Riddle. He worked at the garage you'll have passed as you came into the village, and he happened to be a near neighbor of Armiger's. And the night after the show Armiger went into Riddle's garden and poured buckets of weed killer over his lettuces and peas and beans. Very special weed killer that a man like Armiger could know all about, that makes the ground you put it on sterile for years."

"But how did anyone know he'd done it, if he did it at night?" Hassall asked.

"He was seen," Crabbe said. "A couple of boys, coming home late from a dance in town, saw it all happen. Not that they understood what old Armiger was doing, watering Riddle's garden for him in the middle of the night, and they never thought of trying to stop him, but when everything in Riddle's garden went black and shriveled up and died, and he got very drunk in here one evening and made a scene, saying someone in the village must have the evil eye, they told him what they'd seen Armiger doing, and like Armiger before him, Riddle swore he'd have his revenge.

"I was very much more worried than I'd been when Armiger said the same thing, because when Riddle got drunk he could be *very* violent. He'd been in the magistrate's court for it more than once, it wasn't just talk. So I thought someone ought to warn Armiger."

"Which you did," Hassall said.

"Yes, and that's when I learned it was true about the weed killer," Crabbe replied. "He told me about it, said he'd worked on producing it himself. He chuckled and said that would teach Riddle. Only Miss Armiger was worried when I told them the kind of man Riddle was and said she wished her brother would learn to forget and forgive occasionally. But he was crowing with triumph and said he'd still a trick or two up his sleeve if he had any more trouble from Riddle.

"And that night he had it. Riddle got into his garden and cut down a very lovely birch tree in it. Armiger had planted some other young trees after moving into the cottage, but the birch was the only mature one he had, and there it was in the morning, sawed off near the bottom and lying flat on the grass."

"Did someone see that happen too, or how did they know Riddle did it?" Hassall asked.

"No, no one saw it," Crabbe said, "but who else would have done a thing like that? It was sheer malice, you see. If the tree had been stolen we might have said it was the gypsies, taking it to saw up into logs and sell them. But there was something defiant about the way it had just been left lying there. Everyone knew it was Riddle."

"And what did Armiger do?"

"Nothing."

Hassall raised his eyebrows. "Was that in character?"

"No, it wasn't, and I personally found something very disturbing about *that*. I've told you Armiger was a patient man and a vindictive one and I couldn't help remembering what he'd said about having another trick or two up his sleeve. I felt he'd something in store for Riddle which he wouldn't find at all nice when it happened, something even worse, perhaps, than having his garden sprayed with weed killer. But nothing happened until the pigs got into it."

"Pigs?" Hassall said. "Armiger let some pigs into Riddle's garden?"

"So it was thought."

"That doesn't sound to me like Armiger's style."

"Exactly. That's what I said immediately. But no one would listen to me. The pigs belonged to a man called Deakin who owned the field behind Riddle's cottage. Deakin lived in a shack of sorts in the middle of the field and grew vegetables for market and kept a few chickens and pigs, and one night the pigs knocked down the fence round Riddle's garden and rooted up most of the things he'd got left in it and trampled down the rest. The place was a ruin. And everyone said it was Armiger who'd broken down the fence and made sure the pigs got in."

"But you didn't believe that."

"No, as you said, it wasn't Armiger's style. He was a fastidious man, subtle, cunning. If all Riddle's roses had suddenly developed blight, or his apples had all suddenly fallen off his trees, or something of that sort, I might have thought Armiger was at the bottom of it. But I've always believed the pigs got into Riddle's garden by themselves. There was an old sow among them and old sows, as you probably know, are very belligerent, very destructive, quite dangerous, really. I thought the whole affair was Riddle's own fault, for not keeping his fence in better order. But he was sure Armiger was responsible, that's the important thing. He wouldn't listen to reason. He breathed fire. He swore again he'd have his revenge. And only a week later Armiger was found dead near the letter-box, with his skull battered in."

At this point the landlord, who had been lingering behind the bar, finding small jobs to do in the way of polishing glasses and rearranging the sandwiches under a bell-jar, as if he wanted to hear what the two men were saying to one another, caught Hassall's eye and gave him a swift wink.

Hassall gave no sign of having observed it.

"So what you're telling me," he said, "is that Riddle was the man who murdered Armiger, that it wasn't the boys on the motorcycles at all."

"No, no, you mustn't jump to conclusions like that," Crabbe replied quickly. "All I'm telling you about is a sequence of events. It's just as possible that Riddle *didn't* kill Armiger, however murderously he was talking, as that Armiger didn't let the pigs into Riddle's garden."

"Logically, I'm sure you're right. But what did everyone believe?"

Crabbe gave a grave shake of his head. "I'm afraid I must admit I don't really know much about it. As it happened, I wasn't very well just about then. I didn't go out much. A virus, the doctor said. There was a lot of it about the village at the time."

"What I don't understand, if what you're telling me is true," Hassall said, "is why the police didn't look into the conflict between the two men. Didn't they even suspect Riddle?"

"Perhaps they did. I don't know. Anyway, they didn't find out anything conclusive."

"So it was a victory of brawn over brains. You know, I find that depressing."

"Ah, as to that, I wouldn't be too sure." Crabbe paused. Gazing into the distance, he fingered his glass, which drew Hassall's attention to the fact that it was empty.

He had it refilled.

"What do you mean?" Hassall asked.

"Well, only a few days after Armiger's death, Riddle died, you see," Crabbe said. "Isn't that a remarkable thing?"

"Well, I don't know. People do die, don't they? What was there remarkable about Riddle's death?"

"Nothing, on the surface. He had this virus I told you was going about the village. As a matter of fact, he'd had it for a few weeks, off and on, before Armiger's death. Couldn't seem to shake it off. Gastric trouble, pains in his joints, and so on. Just the same as I got, only worse.

"Old Dr. Turner, who was still in practice here at the time, said it was a virus. That's what they say about everything they can't diagnose nowadays, isn't it? And they give you pills and if they don't work they give you some more of a different color and in the end you probably have to get well on your own, just as you always have.

"But Riddle *didn't* get well. He got steadily worse. And the worse he felt, the worse his temper got. The pigs getting into his garden was the last straw. He was like a maniac the last few days of his life. He may or he may not have attacked Armiger—I have no evidence on that point whatever—but I know he was in a terrible state and would have been capable of anything."

Hassall gave Crabbe a puzzled look. He was eyeing Hassall with his bright, watchful stare, as if to see how his story was affecting him.

"But are you implying that Armiger was somehow responsible for Riddle's condition?" Hassall asked. "You had this virus yourself. You're not suggesting that Armiger managed to give the whole village some mysterious infection?"

"Of course not, no."

"Then what do you mean?"

Crabbe frowned broodingly into what was left of his whiskey. "As I said before, it's just a sequence of events. There may be nothing more to it than that. But I've given the matter a lot of thought and sometimes I can't help feeling there's a pattern in those events. I'll have to begin by making a confession. I stole a cucumber from Riddle's garden."

"A cucumber?" For the first time Hassall began to wonder how many drinks Crabbe had had before he himself had arrived at The Coach and Horses.

"Yes, a ridged cucumber," Crabbe replied. "The kind you can grow in the open. It was a hot summer that year, you may remember, and he had a particularly fine crop. One of the few things that hadn't been spoiled by Armiger's weed killer or the pigs. But Riddle was dead, you see, and it seemed a pity they should go to waste."

"Just a minute," Hassall said. "When was this? How soon after Riddle died?"

"It was the evening after the funeral. Several of us had been to it and we came in here afterwards to have a drink, and one drink led to another, as it tends to when you're feeling low, as you can't help doing after a funeral, and by the time we left we were all fairly drunk. There were about five of us, I think. I remember we started singing some hymn or other when we started home, feeling in a religious state of mind, and we passed Riddle's cottage, which we knew was empty, because his wife had gone to stay with her sister, and there were those cucumbers, looking fat and fine and tempting, where we could see them from the road, because there was only a low stone wall along the front of the garden. And someone, it may have been me, suggested we should nip in and help ourselves, so that's what we did. I took mine home and my wife and I had some of it in a salad that evening. And next morning we were both of us down with that virus."

"Mr. Crabbe," the landlord interrupted, "I've told you I went down with that virus myself and I didn't eat any cucumber."

"Coincidence." Crabbe's enunciation was not quite as clear as it had been. "Yours could have been a different kind of virus. It could have come from anywhere. People coming and going in here all the time from all over the country, you could have picked it up from any of them. It's a fact though, until my wife and I finished that cucumber we didn't begin to get well."

"What about the other four who were with you, singing hymns after the funeral and who helped themselves to cucumbers?" Hassall said. "Did they get ill?"

Crabbe wagged a finger at him. "They did, they did. That's just what I was going to tell you. Every one of them was smitten the next day by that virus. But none of us thought anything about it at the time. We took Dr. Turner's pills and gradually we got well. And I don't suppose I'd have given the matter another thought if I hadn't gone round one day to help Miss Armiger with her garden. Of course she couldn't cope with it herself and it was turning into a wilderness, so I offered to go and mow her lawn for her.

"The lawnmower was kept in the garden shed. I went in to get it and there on a shelf I saw two things, a sprayer and a can of some insecticide. But even then the penny didn't drop. After all, insecticide is a normal enough thing for any gardener to have around. But later, somehow, I got to brooding about it. I thought of the things they tell you about insecticides. D'you know, there was a time when brewers used to spray it on their hops, until it turned out that if you drank eight hundred gallons of beer it would kill you." He looked gloomily into his nearly empty glass.

"You brood too much, Mr. Crabbe," the landlord said. "Now why don't you go home and have a bit of lunch? Your missus'll be expecting you."

"That's right, she will." Crabbe finished his drink and got to his feet. "Nice to have met you, Mr.—Mr.—?"

"Hassall," Hassall said. "But just a minute. What was it in the end that made you think Armiger had been spraying poison over Riddle's cucumbers?"

"The way you jump to conclusions!" Crabbe exclaimed. "Have I said that's what he did?"

"It's what you implied."

Crabbe shook his head. "What I've been telling you is just a sequence of events. You can make what you like of it, so long as you don't quote me. I can rely on you not to quote me, can't I? I always regard my conversation as strictly confidential."

"Very well," Hassall agreed. "But what was the next event in the sequence?"

"Well, something made me think I'd better take that bottle of insecticide to a chemist friend of mine and get him to tell me what it was, and he said it had some chemical in it called fluorophosphonate, which is lethal to things like aphids and in big enough quantities to humans, though it's quite harmless to plants. So d'you know what I did? I got into Riddle's garden again and cut all the remaining cucumbers and put them in a bonfire—just to be on the safe side, you know, not because I seriously thought there was anything the matter with them. And so that was the end of that."

"Leaving you without any real evidence of any kind."

"Not a shred, my dear chap, not a shred!" Crabbe beamed at Hassall suddenly with a look of great happiness. "Now I really must be going."

"But you did believe Armiger had been gradually poisoning Riddle with one cucumber after another, didn't you?" Hassall said.

"I seldom talk about my beliefs," Crabbe answered with dignity. "They're a private matter."

"All the same, what about Mrs. Riddle? Had Armiger anything against her, or didn't he mind if she died?"

"Mrs. Riddle never ate cucumbers. She said they gave her indigestion. I remember my wife and I had her to tea once and she wouldn't touch our cucumber sandwiches. So she was quite safe—from cucumbers, I mean."

"But why didn't you go to the police with your suspicions?" Hassall asked. "Not a word of this came out at the inquest, or later either, did it?"

"Well, they were both dead, weren't they, Armiger and Riddle?" Crabbe said. "And it wasn't going to make Mrs. Riddle or Miss Armiger any happier to think she'd been living with a murderer. Nice old ladies, both of them. No one would have wanted to upset them. So what was to be gained by saying anything? Good day to you now—Mr. Hassall, is it? I've enjoyed our talk."

Concentrating carefully on how he put one foot before the other, the quiet-looking, shabby man made for the door.

When it had closed behind him Hassall said, "You've heard this story he was telling me before, haven't you?"

"Well, it isn't always exactly the same."

"Is there a word of truth in it?"

The landlord began to polish an invisible spot on his shining counter, looking down intently at what he was doing.

"It's true Mr. Armiger and Mr. Riddle are both dead," he said, "and died within a few days of one another. And it's true the old ladies were very well liked and everyone was sorry for them. Miss Armiger's dead now, of course, but Mrs. Riddle still lives in the village."

"So you all got together and decided to keep your suspicions to yourselves," Hassall said. "All except Everard Crabbe."

The landlord applied himself harder still to his polishing.

"Everard Crabbe," Hassall mused. "I seem to know that name, but I can't remember where I've heard it."

"He's a writer, like yourself," the landlord said. "Writes murder stories. I sometimes read them when I'm not busy. They're not bad, but as I see it, they're full of improbabilities. Bit too much imagination for his own good, if you ask me."

Stephen Wasylyk

The Krowten Corners Crime Wave

Homicide and humor—an irresistible combination when the emulsion is achieved, when the emulsifying process is in the hands of a writer with a true comic touch. This story will lighten your day or brighten your evening, especially if you are a TV addict . . . Now read about a case of multiple murder—"This is the work of a madman!"—with a chuckle on every page . . .

When Denny Klinger, the cashier, reported for work that morning, he noticed that the stack of cartons in the storeroom at the rear of the small supermarket had collapsed. He immediately set to work to right them before Mr. Whiffle arrived.

If Denny had known Mr. Whiffle's dead body was under the tumbled boxes, he probably wouldn't have bothered. He had never liked Mr. Whiffle.

Hugh Tint, the tall thin sheriff, blinked behind his heavy spectacles. "First fatal accident in Krowten Corners that I can remember. This is a very average town with very average people who do very average work with no risk involved."

His deputy, young Latham Raster, left his kneeling position at the side of the body and dusted his pudgy hands. "I don't like to say this, Sheriff, but this is no fatal accident. Someone strangled Mr. Whiffle."

"Impossible," said Tint impatiently. "No one ever gets strangled in Krowten Corners. There are no criminal types here. Wake George up and tell him to stop clowning around."

"He's really dead," said Raster. "I guess someone tried to make it look like an accident by toppling these large cartons of toilet tissue down on the body, but the marks on his throat are very clear."

"Now why would someone strangle poor George Whiffle?" asked Tint.

"Perhaps they found his neck squeezably soft," said Raster. "What shall we do with the body?"

"Send it to kindly old Dr. Wilby. He'll take care of it. You and I will start an investigation."

By the end of the day they determined that practically no one in town had liked Mr. Whiffle and quite a few people couldn't stand him because he had been an obnoxious, pompous little man who ran around the supermarket all day demanding that customers stop handling the merchandise. The only reason people shopped in the supermarket at all was because it was the only place in town where they could buy groceries, aside from Cara's General Store, where the selection was severely limited and the prices prohibitive.

One conclusion the two men did reach was that almost anyone could have done it, since it was common knowledge that Mr. Whiffle arrived at the store early every morning to count the cartons of toilet tissue he had on hand, and always entered through the rear door from the parking lot which at that hour of the morning was usually deserted.

"We have reached an impasse," announced Sheriff Tint. "Let's sign off for the day and resume our investigation tomorrow."

Tomorrow brought with it an excited young woman named Convergence O'Toole, who burst into Sheriff Tint's office with the news that Cara, the woman who owned the general store, was dead.

Tint and Raster found the body of the small old woman sprawled behind the wooden counter. Littering the floor were hundreds of cans of coffee.

"Good heaven," said Tint. "This is the work of a madman!"

"You can bet your Smith and Wesson on that," said Convergence indignantly. "He has mixed the perc grind cans with the drip grind. It will take me hours to straighten them out."

Raster examined the body. "Just like Mr. Whiffle," he said. "She's been strangled. Why should someone strangle poor old Cara?"

"I don't know," said Tint. "Send the body to kindly old Dr. Wilby. We will investigate."

Their investigation showed that while Cara had not been as universally disliked as Mr. Whiffle, she had made absolutely the worst coffee in town and was constantly insisting that people who came into her store not only taste it but buy a can whether they wanted one or not.

"It could have been done by a tea drinker," said Raster.

"That is possible," said Tint. "Whatever happened to that big fellow who was around town for a time suggesting thhaat everyone drink tea? He didn't look much like a tea drinker to me. Looked like he'd prefer something much stronger." Mimicking a man tossing off a quick one, he winked. "Know what I mean?"

"Haven't seen him in a long time," said Raster. "I don't think very many people paid any attention to him, so he left."

"Well," said Tint, "I guess we can forget him. But I have the feeling that the same person who strangled Mr. Whiffle also killed Cara."

"We're looking for a common denominator?"

"Since *I* am the sheriff, *I* am looking for a common denominator. Since *you* are the deputy, *you* are looking for fingerprints. Get the super-lightweight but sturdy portable kit and go over the store inch by inch. I'm going home."

That evening Tint had settled in his easy chair, ready for the latest episode of *Upstairs, Downstairs,* when his phone rang. Annoyed, he picked up the receiver.

"I have good news," announced Raster. "I have found an important clue."

"I can't talk now," said Tint. "The King is coming to dinner and Mrs. Bridges is preparing a marvelous feast. You should see it. Those gluttons won't be able to eat again for a week."

"Upstairs, Downstairs is more important than my clue?"

"Of course," said Tint. "After all, the King doesn't come to dinner every night, and your clue will still be there in the morning. Good night."

When Tint entered the office after having breakfasted at the diner, he found Raster waiting for him.

Raster pointed to the sheriff's shirtfront.

"What happened to you?"

Tint frowned. "Rosie, the waitress at the diner, wanted to demonstrate how thirstily absorbent her paper towels are so she slopped some coffee from my cup onto the counter. Unfortunately, a good deal of it landed on my shirt."

"She has a habit of doing that," said Raster. "It can become very irritating at times. However, Hester Gillicuddy claims she has a powerful new foaming-action detergent that leaves clothes whiter-than-white. I'm sure she'll be happy to wash your shirt for you."

"That won't be necessary," said Tint. "I'll let Mordecai Wallbanger wash it in that new top loader he's promoting at the appliance store, the one that starts out with Brahms's *Lullaby* played by musical jets of water as it is filling and ends with Arthur Fiedler conducting the Boston Pops playing *The Stars and Stripes Forever* during the spin-rinse cycle. Now let me see this clue of yours."

Raster proudly held up a pair of fingerprints he had lifted from a heavy coffee mug he had found in the corner of Cara's store behind some rusty garden spades.

"They are a little unusual," he said. "Obviously they represent a thumb and forefinger but the impressions show a ridge on each that simply has to be a callus. Now what sort of occupation could a man have that develops calluses on his thumb and forefinger?"

"I don't know," said Tint, "but I'm sure we'll find out eventually. If we are persistently dogged . . ." He frowned. "Or is it doggedly persistent? No matter. We must somehow bring this culprit to justice. We cannot tolerate violence in a typical American town like Krowten Corners."

Wilmot Krump, the mayor, pushed open the door of the sheriff's office, his bulk quivering with indignation.

"See here, Tint," he said. "I don't know what's going on in this town but you must put a stop to it. I have already lost two people who always contributed generously to my campaigns, and now, when I stopped in at Godwin's Variety Store, what do you think I found?"

"I couldn't guess," said Tint. "Old Smiley is a card."

"Well, somebody dealt him out," said Krump. "He's on the floor, strangled, as dead as yesterday's voter indignation, and I tell you, Tint, it's a real horror in there. The murderer took every tube of toothpaste in the place and mashed it flat. It looks as though Godwin is floating on a sea of fluoride."

"Old Godwin would have liked that," said Tint. "He was a little flaked on the subject of cavities and checkups. Almost beat up the Billings kid last summer because he had a molar pulled." He sighed and motioned to Raster. "I suppose we might as well go over there."

In the variety store the situation was much as Mayor Krump had described it. Mr. Godwin indeed appeared to be floating on the coating of toothpaste that covered the floor.

"I don't understand why the murderer not only kills these people but insists on making a mess," said Tint.

"Perhaps he's angry at more than the people," said Raster.

Tint frowned at him. "That may well be a very penetrating observation. On the other hand, it may be a very stupid remark." He pointed. "What is that?"

Raster gingerly stepped through the coating of toothpaste and leaned over. "It's a footprint."

"Good," said Tint. "It is the best clue we have discovered so far. We must preserve it."

"How?" asked Raster. "The police manual doesn't cover making a cast of a footprint in toothpaste."

Tint scratched his chin. "Correct. We could cut out a section of the floor and take it with us."

"Of this floor? It's solid marble. Did you forget that this was once a drug store of the type that has almost faded from the American scene, complete with a marble soda fountain and a kindly old pharmacist who compounded prescriptions with cool and unerring skill instead of counting out pills from a large bottle into a small one?"

"Hmmm," said Tint. "You're right, but you're not old enough to remember things like that. What TV program was that on?"

"It was called *A Re-examination of Our Past and a Projection of the Next One Hundred Years of Medical Care in America,* complete with a panel of thirty-four distinguished physicians," said Raster.

"Sounds interesting," said Tint. "Wonder how I missed it."

"You had to be alert," said Raster. "They squeezed it in between the end of *Barnaby Jones* and the eleven o'clock news."

Tint grunted. "Well, let's get on with our investigation. Suppose you just measure it with your deputy's rustproof stainless-steel, self-winding tape you received as a premium for sending in three boxtops from that sugar-coated cereal."

Raster measured. "It is exactly twelve inches long and four inches wide."

"Ah," said Tint. He thumbed through a small book. "My compendium of useful information for law-enforcement officers that Steve McGarrett sent to me from Hawaii says that it is a size 9½-D, which indicates a man of medium height."

"Not necessarily," said Raster thoughtfully. "Perhaps the shoe was worn by a short man with large feet." He frowned. "Or perhaps a large man with small feet. Or even a small man with small feet wearing shoes that are too large. It could even be a large man with large feet wearing shoes that are too small."

Tint glared at him. "Just send the body to kindly old Dr. Wilby. I will return to the office and try to think of someone to suspect. We now know we are looking for an average-sized man who has calluses on his thumb and forefinger."

An hour later Raster burst through the door of the office. "I have a suspect!" he announced excitedly. "The washing-machine repairman who has nothing to do but watch what goes on says that Artemis Kaber had a big argument with Mr. Godwin yesterday. It seems that Artemis wanted to buy a tube of non-fluoride toothpaste because he hates fluoride but Mr. Godwin threw him out of the store. Obviously Artemis has a motive."

"Nonsense," said Tint. "You know Artemis is a small man and he would hardly have calluses on his thumb and forefinger because he's the only manicurist in town and constantly soaking his fingers in that dishwashing liquid." The sheriff sighed as he stared out the window. "I'm afraid we are looking for someone more average than Artemis. I have come to the conclusion that the man we are looking for could be either a writer or an accountant, which would explain the calluses on his thumb and forefinger."

"Fantastic thinking!" exclaimed Raster. "It should be easy to check your theory since we have only two accountants and one writer in town."

"One accountant," said Tint. "Several men in white coats came and took away Hapgood Turbuckle the other day. It seems that Hapgood placed a perfectly good eight-hundred-dollar color television set, console model, superbly crafted of Australian wormwood with supermatrix, with a self-tuning twenty-five-inch picture tube out for the trash collectors. Naturally his wife thought this was a little odd, so she sent for the mind mechanics out at the Home to come and take him away for a tune-up."

"That leaves only Sylvanus Grubb," said Raster, disappointed. "He is quite short and very fat and is on a physical-fitness binge right now. He wears his red warmup suit and striped athletic shoes from morning until night and jogs wherever he goes, so I don't think he's our man."

"We still have the writer, Lochinvar Lovelace," said Tint.

Raster shifted uncomfortably. "I don't see how he can be guilty. Lochinvar is ninety years old, even though you wouldn't know it from those passionate love novels he turns out. I often wonder how he does it."

"Nothing wrong with Lochinvar's memory," said Tint. "But I guess you're right. A man who found it necessary to hire a beautiful young girl just to insert the paper into his typewriter is a little too old to run around strangling people. What we need is another clue."

At seven the next morning Tint was awakened by a pounding on his door. He opened it to find a stout handsome woman in her fifties patting her short blonde hair and smiling at him.

"My name is Euphoria Hackenstack," she said. "I live at the west end of town in what everyone calls a typical American suburb. In my typically American way I was out walking my pedigreed dog this morning when I found something lying on the lawn of one of our typically American homes. I asked myself who might be interested in what I had found and it occurred to me that you, as sheriff, might want to know first."

"What did you find?" asked Tint.

"A body," said Euphoria. "Someone has killed poor Mrs. Nelson."

"Who is Mrs. Nelson?"

"Well," said Euphoria, "I guess you would call Mrs. Nelson a typically American busybody. She was forever coming into people's homes and giving wives advice about coffee. I don't know how many broken marriages she has been responsible for."

"Was her advice that bad?"

"Terrible. She subscribed to the theory that a wife should brew excellent coffee for her husband, which is really ridiculous. The opposite is true. No smart wife gives her husband anything but terrible coffee because it gives him something to complain about. Husbands love to complain, so why should a woman stick her neck out? Let him complain about the coffee. It will take his mind off the money spent at the beauty parlor or something equally important."

"You sound like an expert," said Tint.

"I have thirty years of domestic bliss and tranquillity behind me," said Euphoria proudly. "I think that perhaps you had better come look at this body, Sheriff. While I may not have cared much for Mrs. Nelson, my social consciousness tells me she should not be left lying there indefinitely. Furthermore, since I assume you are interested in catching the person responsible, I am forced to point out you can't do so standing here gossiping with me."

Tint bowed. "I will call my deputy and then you may lead me to the body."

Mrs. Nelson had been an attractive woman of about 40. Surrounded by scattered cans of coffee, she lay on a patch of lawn alongside the back yard of a small corner home, several feet from assorted athletic paraphernalia designed to develop the muscles and motor skills of children and to keep them out of the house on nice days. Raster, kneeling beside the body, looked up as Tint and Euphoria pushed their way through the typically American crowd.

"At least this one wasn't strangled," said Raster. "She has a terrible bruise on her forehead. It's possible she was struck by one of those cans of coffee."

He came close to Tint and whispered. "I think we have discovered our third clue. Look." He opened his palm. "This strand of red hair was clutched in her hand."

Tint pulled a small magnifying glass from his pocket and examined the hair closely. "Ah, yes," he said. "This is obviously a hair from the head of a woman born and raised in the Andante Valley of northern Italy."

"You mean our murderer is a redhaired immigrant?"

"Of course not," said Tint impatiently. "It means our murderer is an average-sized man with calluses on his thumb and forefinger who wears a toupee made of red hair."

Euphoria gasped and clutched her bosom.

"You seem upset," said Tint.

"You have described my beloved husband Alexander," she said.

"Where is he now?" asked Tint.

"Shopping," she said. "He retired a year ago and used to sit around the house watching television day and night but he found very few programs that pleased him. He changed channels so often he developed calluses on his thumb and forefinger. Finally I couldn't stand it any longer. I suggested he take over the shopping. He's been doing it for a week now."

"Quick," said Tint to Raster. "Take the body to kindly old Dr. Wilby and then meet me at the supermarket."

"I can't do that," said Raster. "Kindly old Dr. Wilby said if I bring him one more body he'll punch me in the nose. He says that when he agreed to act as coroner, he thought it was an honorary position. He didn't know he would be dealing with corpses. His specialties are exotic diseases and major personality traumas."

"Cart Mrs. Nelson over there and forget about it," said Tint. "The last time kindly old Dr. Wilby punched anyone in the nose, he was six years old and he's felt guilty about it ever since. Why do you think he became kindly old Dr. Wilby?"

At the supermarket Tint peered through the plate-glass window. Nothing seemed out of the ordinary. Many shoppers, most of them women, were already lined up at the checkout counters while others strolled the aisles pushing carts. Suddenly everyone in the store seemed to turn simultaneously and stare toward the rear.

Tint ran inside and pushed his way through the people toward the center of interest, almost knocking down a tall blonde woman who attempted to shove a buttered cracker into his mouth as he passed.

At the rear of the store he saw a small stout woman dressed in blue. She was screaming and using a roll of paper towels to fend off an elderly redhaired man of average height whose clawed fingers were aimed at her throat.

Tint wrapped a hand in the man's collar.

"That's enough," he said.

The man subsided and the woman lowered the roll of paper towels.

"Now exactly what is going on?" asked Tint.

"He tried to kill me!" yelled the woman.

"Did you?" Tint asked the man.

"You can bet your coffee-stained shirt on that," said the man.

"Why?" asked Tint.

"Listen," said the man. "I came in here to do some shopping for my wife. Paper towels were on the list. I looked over the various brands and made my selection. The next thing I knew, this old biddy grabs me and starts singing in my ear that her brand of paper towels is heavier and that I'm making a big mistake. I told her to get lost, but she grabs my arm and pulls me to a scale, where she weighs her brand of towels and mine and babbles on and on that hers is heavier.

"Give me my towels and get away from me, I said, but she begins screaming at me to stop being so stupid. I told her I didn't want her towels, I didn't care about her towels, and I wouldn't take them as a gift, but she begins screaming louder and beating me on the head with her towels and shouting if I don't buy at least one roll I can't leave the store. So I tried to shut her up."

"Is that true?" Tint asked the woman.

"I was only doing my job," said the woman stiffly. "I'm a consumer-education expert and it's my responsibility to see that this man buys the best paper towel for his money. He is supposed to smile and thank me, but he's too stupid to know what's best for him. If he had bought the towels, I know he would have been grateful to me for the rest of his life, so all I did was apply a little typical American selling persuasion. Now I want him arrested. After all, I simply didn't want to see him waste his money on inferior, second-rate towels even if he did like the smiling camel printed on them in that gruesome magenta ink."

She made a face. "Sort of hokey, don't you agree, Sheriff? Now, mine have a different point of interest from all over the world printed on each oversized, extra-thirsty sheet. Sort of gives you a thrill during the dull workaday existence to realize you are mopping up the dog's muddy footprints with the Eiffel Tower, *n'est-ce pas?* Come,

Sheriff, let me show you."

Tint tore himself from her grasp. "Later," he said. He beckoned to the man. "Come along."

As they walked toward the jail, Tint said, "I guess you're Alexander Hackenstack. Your wife told me where to find you."

"Euphoria is all right," said Hackenstack. "Makes terrible coffee and spends too much at the beauty parlor but a husband learns to live with those things. She also has a tendency to become a little too emotional at times. She cried terribly when the fad for hula hoops died."

"I suppose you strangled all those people," said Tint. "Now why did you do such an unsocial thing?"

"I was defending myself," said Hackenstack, "just as I was in the supermarket just now. Take that Whiffle jerk. I went into the store early that morning, the first customer. I was wandering around when I saw this sign on the toilet tissue that said don't squeeze, so naturally I squeezed. The next thing I knew there was Whiffle carrying on and screaming he would have me arrested. I was so embarrassed I tried to go out the rear door but he wouldn't leave me alone. He said I would have to wait for you and he tried to hold me. In the struggle the boxes of toilet tissue sort of tumbled down on us. To keep from being knocked off my feet, I grabbed the first thing handy. It wasn't my fault it happened to be his neck."

"How about Cara at the general store?"

"Same thing," said Hackenstack. "My wife wanted a super-easy, fast-cutting 1929-type Boy Scout can opener that only Cara stocked, so I stopped in. I never did get the can opener. First thing I knew, she was shoving a cup of coffee under my nose and demanding that I taste it. I told her I didn't want any but she kept pushing it at me and saying I had to buy a can."

Hackenstack shook his head. "Would you believe she actually pushed me to the floor and poured the coffee down my throat so I could see how good it was? In the struggle we knocked over all the coffee shelves and in an effort to protect the poor woman I grabbed her to pull her out of the way. Unfortunately, I grabbed her by the throat."

"That could happen," said Tint. "What about Mr. Godwin?"

Hackenstack sighed. "Would you believe I went in there just to buy a toothbrush? He asked me what kind of toothpaste I used. I told him. That was horrible stuff, he said. The next thing I knew he had me backed against the wall and was squeezing fluoride toothpaste into my mouth, yelling that I had to prevent cavities. I almost choked on the stuff. I tried to push him away but in the struggle we knocked down all the toothpaste and trampled it out of the tubes, which made the floor very slippery. I tried to support myself by hanging onto his neck and accidentally strangled him."

"That sounds reasonable," said Tint. "But there is still Mrs. Nelson."

"I had nothing to do with her death," said Hackenstack. "It's a little embarrassing but I must tell you that the woman had her cap set for me for a long time. Always whispering in my ear about how bad Euphoria's coffee was and if I would go with her she would show me how a *real* woman made coffee. Of course, I tried to avoid her but, busybody that she was, she knew I rose early to do a little jogging before breakfast, so she was waiting for me, carrying that paper bag filled with cans of coffee. Never could understand why the woman always had a paper bag filled with coffee cans with her wherever she went.

"She wanted me to run away with her to her coffee ranch in the mountains of Colombia and pick coffee beans with her cousin Juan Something-or-other. I'm afraid I was rather harsh. I told her to drop dead. She became angry and began throwing coffee cans at me. When I ducked, one hit that crazy bounce-back affair the Baylor kid uses to practise his fielding with the hope that someday he'll be a highly paid big-league shortstop. The can bounced straight back and bonked her on the forehead."

Tint held the cell door open for him. "Well, I guess I'll have to keep you here for a time. You can turn on the TV and relax."

"No, thanks," said Hackenstack. "It seems as though everywhere I look lately, I think I see one of those people in the commercials. Like the woman who collapses with shame because her husband has a ringy-dingy collar and the healthy-looking ones who drink iron. I could swear that just the other day I saw one of those detergent women floating down the street, yelling she had used only one cup in cold water and her clothes had come out squeaky-clean. And as I left a bar yesterday, a guy sprayed deodorant in my face to prove it wasn't an economical way to remain socially acceptable."

Tint patted him gently on the head. "You're just tired. Those people don't really exist, especially in Krowten Corners."

An hour later Tint finished explaining it all to Raster.

"So it really wasn't a crime wave," said Raster.

"More like a series of fatal misadventures brought on by their own actions," said Tint. "I told you there were no bad people in Krowten Corners."

The door of the office opened and an elderly, sweet-faced, motherly woman came in. She smiled at Tint. "I have just heard about your troubles of the past few days. You must be upset."

Tint shook his head. "Not me. I'm an experienced police officer. I don't get upset. However, my deputy is young and not accustomed to these things."

The woman advanced on Raster, smiling. "I'm sure you must have developed indigestion."

"No," said Raster. "I feel fine."

The woman held out a roll of small mints. "Take one," she said. "It will make you feel better."

"I don't need any," said Raster.

"Of course you do," she said soothingly. "A Bummy in your tummy will get rid of all that nasty acid indigestion and make you feel ten feet tall again."

Raster backed away. "I don't have acid indigestion."

The woman became angry. "If Mother Bummy says you have acid indigestion, you have acid indigestion! Now take one of these!" She launched herself at Raster, knocking him to the floor, and astride his chest began to stuff Bummy after Bummy into his mouth.

Tint sighed, picked up the phone, and dialed.

When the man answered, Tint said, "Kindly old Dr. Wilby, I know you don't like to handle the bodies I have been sending over but I want you to know there will be at least one more. A motherly old woman who will be strangled."

He paused and studied the struggling figures.

"On the other hand," he said, "if Raster doesn't get moving, it just might be a young man with an overdose of Bummies."

Harold Q. Masur

One Thing Leads
to Another

*It all began with a summons and complaint in a simple case of
nonpayment of alimony and child support. But you know how
things are in life and law—one thing can lead to another, marriage to divorce, process serving to murder ... Scott Jordan, the
shrewd legal beagle, now has an assistant—Danny Karr, only
months out of law school, an eager beaver working for "probably
the smartest lawyer in New York" ...*

I t was an elegant building, tall and exclusive. The doorman, a
resplendently caparisoned goliath, stood guard at the entrance
like Leonidas defending the pass at Thermopylae. If you live in the
Big Apple and can afford the protection, why not?

I paused alongside the revolving doors and stooped over to tighten
a shoelace just as a taxi pulled up at the curb. Its occupant, apparently a paraplegic, struggled heroically to alight with the aid of
aluminum crutches. As the doorman hastened across the sidewalk
to assist, I ducked into the lobby, sprinted for the elevator, and
jabbed the ninth-floor button.

Just before the door closed, I witnessed a miracle. The passenger
suddenly straightened, tucked the crutches under his arm, saalutedd,
and marched jauntily down the street. The doorman scratched his
head in astonishment and then the elevator was lofting me skyward.

I found Lily Olson's door and rang the bell. It was opened by a
spare, craggy-faced gent. "Mr. George Finney?" I asked.

"Who wants him?"

"This is for you, sir." I handed him a paper. "Summons and complaint. Finney versus Finney. Nonpayment of alimony and child
support. Have a pleasant day."

There was a woman standing behind him, a striking blonde, thin-
lipped now and furious. She ran to the house phone and as I walked
back to the elevator I heard her chewing out the doorman, a ven-
omous tirade in the lexicon of a mule-skinner.

On the way down I could not repress a smile of satisfaction. I had
succeeded where two professional process servers had dismally failed

to breach the building's security. Ordinarily, a lawyer does not serve his own papers. It's undignified. Nor do I generally handle cases of this kind. But Kate Finney had been recommended by an important client. She had a child from a previous marriage, legally adopted by Finney, and she desperately needed financial help.

She gave me the facts on the telephone. George Finney had walked out, left her and the child to shift for themselves, and had moved in with Lily Olson. She did not miss him, not on any emotional level. He drank excessively, worked sporadically, and could squeeze a dime until F.D.R.'s nose came out on the other side.

The elevator door opened on the lobby. The doorman was waiting. He towered over me, shoulders bunched, glowering and belligerent and spoiling for a fight. I handed him one of my cards.

"The name is Scott Jordan," I said. "Counselor and attorney-at-law. So if you decide to use your hands it won't cost me anything to sue the owners for aggravated assault. As a matter of fact, I'm perfectly willing to go a couple of rounds with you, but not at the moment. I'm due at my office for an appointment with the governor."

It gave him pause. The owner's wrath could be more catastrophic than Olson's abuse. While he was considering it, I slipped past him to the street and caught a cab back to the office.

Ten minutes later Danny Karr showed up. Danny, my new assistant, put some bills on my desk. He was grinning from ear to ear. "I returned the crutches, boss. Here's your change. How did you like my performance?"

"A bit gaudy," I said. "But the timing was fine and it worked."

"So how about a raise?"

"You had a raise last week."

"Inflation is killing me."

"You and everyone else. Learn to economize. Your time will come." And I was sure it would. Danny, only eight months out of law school, was young, eager, and bright. I moved some papers around on my desk. "On that environment case, where are those precedents I asked for?"

"We don't have the Minnesota Reports."

"Naturally. There are fifty states. Who has the shelf space? Use the Bar Association library."

"I'm not a member."

"I'm a member and you're my employee. Get over there tomorrow morning. Early, Counselor." He left and I phoned Kate Finney, asking her to stop by for trial preparation.

At four o'clock she arrived accompanied by Sara. The child had enormous eyes and an adult air of gravity. Kate, a slender, somewhat faded woman in her mid-thirties introduced us. "This is Mr. Jordan, Sara. He's my lawyer."

"I don't like lawyers," Sara said.

"Why don't you like lawyers?" I asked.

"George says they're not honest. He says if you don't watch out, they'll steal you blind."

Her mother reprimanded her sharply. "Sara! Apologize at once."

"Okay," she said, not changing her opinion. "I apologize."

Keeping a straight face, I buzzed for Danny Karr. "Danny," I said, "this young lady is Sara Finney. Entertain her in your office while I talk to her mother."

Sara looked him over. "Are you a lawyer too?"

"Yes, ma'am."

She handed her small plastic purse to her mother. "Then you'd better hold this for me."

Danny rolled his eyes, beckoned, and she followed him out. Kate gestured helplessly. "I don't know what to do with that child."

"She'll grow out of it. Is George attached to her?"

"Hah! There is no room in George's emotional equipment for anyone but George. His ego is exceeded only by his selfishness and his penury. The man is incapable of sharing."

"You mentioned that he's a writer."

"Well, he's sold several short stories, but he drinks too much and he can't discipline himself to a full-time schedule."

"You said he has an independent income."

"Yes. From a trust fund administered by an old fossil of a lawyer he inherited from his parents."

"We'll levy an attachment against it."

She smiled. "I'd like to see his face."

"Tell me about Lily Olson."

"He met her through his literary agent, a man named Arnold Procter. She's a writer too, and fairly successful. She writes those romantic Gothic novels. After our last fight George went to live with her. Maybe she's more tolerant than I, or less sensitive." She paused and looked thoughtful. "I—er—have a confession to make." When I said nothing, she continued. "Last week a letter came for George from the editor of a magazine in Chicago. They used to correspond with each other and I guess he didn't know George had moved out. Anyway, I steamed it open. He said he liked the new story Procter had submitted and he would be sending a check to the agent at the end of the month."

"We'll get a court order restraining Procter from turning the money over to George until the determination of your case against him. There's really no way you can lose."

I spent some time preparing her for the court hearing and then I buzzed for Danny Karr. Sara was holding his hand and apparently had changed her mind about lawyers.

He accompanied Kate and Sara to the elevator and then came back, smiling.

I said, "Let's see how good you are, Danny." I told him to get the form book and to prepare a restraining order against Arnold Procter. "Complete the papers and serve them before you go home this evening."

Danny Karr spent the next morning at the Bar Association library. He checked into the office at noon and I saw at once that he was not himself. He seemed dreamy-eyed, dismantled. I had to snap my fingers to get his attention.

"Have you been smoking something, Counselor?" I asked.

He blinked and shook his head.

"You're in a trance, moonstruck. What gives?"

"I—I think I'm in love."

I did a double-take. "With little Sara Finney, for God's sake?"

"No, sir." He smiled foolishly. "With Amy."

"And who, pray, is Amy?"

He sighed. "Amy is a walking poem, a rainbow, a—"

"Whoa, boy! Settle down. Get your head together. Where did you meet this enchantress?"

"In Arnold Procter's office."

"Well, now, George Finney met a female in Procter's office and it changed his whole way of life. Is Amy a writer too?"

He shook his head. "She works for him. She's his secretary."

"Are you telling me you walked in there to serve some legal papers and beheld this vision and bingo, you were hooked, just like that?"

"Almost, Mr. Jordan. You see, Procter was out when I got there. Amy said he'd be back in fifteen minutes. So I waited. And we talked. I liked her. I asked her to have dinner with me last night and she said yes. So we went out and then I took her home and we sat up and talked until three o'clock this morning."

"You kissed her good night?"

"Uh-huh."

"And bells began to ring?"

He nodded, looking rhapsodic.

"I hope you didn't forget to serve that restraining order on her boss."

"I didn't forget. Business before pleasure."

"An excellent maxim, Danny. Never lose sight of it while you're employed in this office. Now go back to the library and finish your research."

My phone rang and Kate Finney was on the line. "Mr. Jordan," she said, sounding tense and subdued, "there's a policeman here. He says George is dead. He wants me to come to the morgue to identify the body."

"Let me talk to him." She put him on and I said, "I'm the lady's lawyer, officer. What happened?"

"Harbor Patrol fished a floater out of the East River early this morning. We got this address from his driver's license. They need the widow downtown for identification."

I spoke to Kate again. I told her to leave Sara with one of the neighbors and to cooperate. I promised to use my contacts at the Police Department for additional information.

My principal contact was Detective Lieutenant John Nola, Homicide, dark, lean, a resourceful and subtly intuitive cop. He sat behind his desk, a thin Dutch cigar smoking itself between his teeth, eyes unblinking, while I explained my connection with the deceased.

"Anything suspicious?" I asked finally.

"All we have now is that he was stoned. There was enough alcohol in his blood to float a rowboat."

"Then it could have been an accident."

"Or someone helped him over the edge. You know anything about his financial status?"

"He had an income from a trust fund."

"Who inherits?"

"The widow, probably."

He lifted an eyebrow. "And he'd strayed from the reservation, was living with another woman? He was tight and behind in his alimony?"

"No, Lieutenant. That's a bad hand. Mrs. Finney is not the type."

The eyebrow moved higher. "There are types of murderers, Counselor? Neatly pegged in categories? Make us a list, please. We can use it." He shook his head. "Tell me about the Olson woman."

I gave him what I had. He stood abruptly. "Let's check her out." The taxpayers provided transport. At Lily Olson's building the same doorman recognized me and blocked our way. "No, you don't," he growled. "Not this time, buster. You're a cute one all right. You almost cost me my job. Now turn around and march, both of you."

But his truculence quickly evaporated at the sight of Nola's shield and was replaced by a lumpy smile of apology. He stepped aside. Nola pointed at the house phone. "Don't use that thing."

"Whatever you say, Lieutenant."

Lily Olson answered the doorbell. Nola identified himself. "And this one?" she demanded, indicating me with a thumb.

"His name is Jordan. He's a lawyer."

"A lawyer!" She snorted. "That explains the trickery. Do you know what he did, Lieutenant? He gained access to this building by subterfuge and served some legal papers on a guest of mine. Isn't there a law against that—criminal trespass or something?"

"I'll look it up," Nola said. "In the meantime I need some information. I understand you had a house guest, a Mr. George Finney."

"I still do."

"Any idea where he is at the moment?"

"No, I don't. He went for a walk the day before yesterday and hasn't returned."

"You're not concerned about his whereabouts?"

She shrugged. "George is a grown man. But he has a problem—drinking. He probably stopped off at a bar and got plastered. He knows how I feel about that, so he probably took a room somewhere to dry out. It wouldn't be the first time. Why are you asking these questions?"

"George Finney is dead."

She gasped. "Oh, no. How—how did it happen?"

"His body was found in the East River early this morning."

"Suicide?"

"We doubt it."

"Had he been drinking?"

"Heavily."

"Then it must have been an accident."

"From the amount of alcohol in Finney's blood we don't see how he could have reached the river under his own power."

"He liked to walk along the river. And he generally carried a flask in his pocket. Surely you don't suspect foul play."

"It's a possibility we have to explore. Admittedly, he could have been the victim of a random mugging, or something more deliberate. Did Finney have any enemies?"

"Everyone liked George."

"Including his wife?"

"There are always exceptions. They fought a great deal."

"And he came to you for comfort?"

"Why not? Life is short."

"It is indeed. We'd like to look at his papers, his correspondence, anything he kept here."

"Do you have a warrant?"

"You invited us in."

"I'm inviting you out."

"It's too late, Miss Olson. Finney is dead. We don't need a warrant to examine his property."

"I think you do. This is my apartment. Ask your lawyer friend here."

He shook his head. "One telephone call and I can have a warrant here within the hour."

She frowned and bit her lip. She debated with herself and finally gestured ungraciously. "Go ahead."

In the bedroom closet Finney's clothes yielded nothing. There was a sunlit workroom at the end of the corridor. It contained a filing cabinet, a shelf of reference books, and a large desk with an electric typewriter. A bridge table in the corner held Finney's portable and an untidy pile of papers. Nola gathered them into a bundle and we started to leave.

"How about his clothes?" Lily Olson called.

"Give them to the Salvation Army," I said and followed Nola out to the elevator and down to the street.

We parted. He went back to the precinct and I returned to my office. My secretary had left for the day. Danny Karr was still at the Bar Association library. I was alone, correcting syntax on an appeals brief when I heard someone moving around in the outer office. I got up and walked to the door for a look.

A young girl smiled at me.

"I'm supposed to meet Mr. Karr here at six," she said. "I'm Amy Barth."

She was neither a rainbow nor a walking poem, but I could easily understand how the sturdy figure and the large eyes and the gamine grin could turn Danny Karr into a marshmallow.

I smiled back. "How do you do, Amy. I'm Danny's boss. He should be back at any moment. You can wait for him in my office, unless you'd prefer to sit out here and read the *Law Journal*."

"Oh, no," she said. She perched herself on the red-leather chair, bouncing restlessly. "Danny says you're probably the smartest lawyer in New York."

"Danny will be sadly disillusioned after he's been around for a while. Is there something wrong with that chair?"

She giggled. "Oh, no," she said, "the chair is fine. It's just that I'm in very high spirits. I work for a literary agency and such exciting things have been happening this week."

"For example?"

"We're handling a new book by Lily Olson. Do you know her work? This one is different than anything she's ever written. It's a political thriller called *The Machiavelli Project*. It's about a millionaire Vice-President who conspires to get rid of the President and take over the White House."

"Sounds interesting," I said.

"It's a real cliffhanger. Readers won't be able to put it down. Mr. Procter got an enormous advance from the hardcover publisher and last Wednesday the paperback rights sold for one million dollars. Three book clubs are taking it and all the major movie companies are bidding for the screen rights. Some of Hollywood's biggest stars have called." She looked awe-struck and said in a hushed voice, "I think I heard Gregory Peck's voice on the phone this morning. I almost fainted."

"Quite a blockbuster," I said.

"Mr. Procter never had one like this before."

Danny arrived. He saw Amy and his expression turned sappy. They smiled at each other. He approached and placed a sheaf of yellow legal cap on my desk. "Here are my notes on the Minnesota Reports."

"No, Danny," I said. "That's not the way to do it. Who can translate your hieroglyphics? Type them out. Neatly."

He looked stricken. "Now?"

"Tomorrow morning will do."

"Yes, sir," he said gratefully and propelled Amy out of the office before I could change my mind.

I sat back and thought about Lily Olson's new novel. Perhaps it was time for me to seek out a few writers as clients. The paperback revolution and the money guarantees made the prospect extremely attractive. I glanced at my watch and dialed Kate Finney's number.

"It was a dreadful ordeal," she told me. "I could hardly recognize George."

"Is there anything I can do?"

"Would you take care of the funeral arrangements?"

"Of course."

"And George's estate too?"

"If you wish."

"Will the court hearing be postponed?"

"I'll call the clerk and explain the situation."

After we broke the connection, I locked the office and headed across town to see Nola. He seldom punched a clock when working on a case. He had been studying Finney's papers. I told him about Lily Olson's successful book.

He whistled. "At least two million in the till so far. I guess I'm in the wrong business."

"Finney's papers tell you anything?"

He shook his head. "Look for yourself."

I pulled up a chair and started reading. There was some correspondence from the lawyer handling Finney's trust fund, signed in a shaky hand; a note from a former army friend now living in Pocatello, Idaho; and a few letters from Kate complaining about support and threatening legal action. Finney's notebooks interested me. And so did a letter from Arnold Procter expressing mild interest in the outline for a prospective novel titled *The Long Night*. The agent had reservations about Finney's ability to complete a full-length work. He doubted that any publisher would commit himself to an advance. As an alternative, he suggested finding a collaborator.

I was distracted by the ringing of Nola's phone. He spoke briefly and I sensed his eyes watching me as I looked up. He cradled the handset.

"The name Daniel Karr mean anything to you, Counselor?"

"Yes. He's my assistant."

"He's in the Emergency Room at Manhattan General."

I sat erect. "What happened?"

"Automobile accident. Hit-and-run. Compound fracture of the right leg, plus assorted contusions and abrasions. He whispered your name several times before they put him under to set the bone."

I was on my feet and moving. Nola came after me. I said, "There was a girl with him."

"Amy Barth. Same accident."

"Hurt badly?"

"She's dead."

Bile leaped into my throat. I took the stairs two at a time. In the street I started to flag a cab, but Nola shouldered me into a police car and snapped instructions at the driver. The siren opened traffic like a carving knife.

We found Danny Karr propped up in bed, his face drawn and white, right leg supported in traction, head in bandages, plaster criss-crossing a cheek. He said in a half-drugged voice, "They won't tell me about Amy, boss. Can you find out how she is?"

"Later, Danny. How did it happen?"

"Amy wanted to go home first and freshen up before dinner. It's a brownstone on West 26th. We came out and started to cross the street. I heard some lunatic gun his engine and I started to turn, but it was too late. He was right on top of us. And then I felt the impact and I guess I passed out. The next thing I knew I was in an ambulance. They brought me here. Did anything happen to Amy?"

I didn't have the heart to tell him. Not yet, anyway. I asked him if there was anything he needed, anything I could do, perhaps notify his parents. They were retired and living in Florida and he didn't want to worry them.

Amy's people, however, would have to be notified. I had no information for Nola except that she worked for Arnold Procter. "Then that's the man we'll have to see," he said. "Let's go."

The telephone directory supplied his home address in the exclusive Beekman Place area. A townhouse, no less. Procter was a man who did not believe in economizing.

Nola banged the knocker and a man opened the door. My jaw fell. Spare and craggy-faced, he stared back. Lazarus rising from the grave. The same man I'd seen in Lily Olson's apartment.

"Finney?" I said on a rising inflection.

"No, sir. The name is Procter—Arnold Procter."

"But you're the man I served with the summons."

"You made an unwarranted assumption, sir. I was visiting Miss Olson on business. You simply handed me that paper and left. What is it now? What do you want?"

"He's with me," Nola said, again presenting his credentials and identifying himself. "His name is Jordan."

"Scott Jordan? The lawyer?" Procter made a face. "I know the name. He dispatched one of his acolytes to my office yesterday with some kind of restraining order. A barrator, Lieutenant, this man is a compulsive barrator."

Nola glanced at me.

"Someone who practices barratry," I explained. "The excessive instigation and promotion of lawsuits."

He turned back to Procter. "You have an employee named Amy Barth?"

"I do."

"I have some sad news. She was struck by an automobile early this evening and killed."

"What?" He stared. "Oh, my God! That lovely child." He shook his head. "It doesn't seem possible. Come in, please." In the living room, his face grim, he shook a stern finger at Nola. "Those damned drunken drivers! Why do you grant them licenses to assassinate pedestrians? Amy Barth. What a dreadful waste!"

"Can you tell us how to reach her family?"

"I know only that she comes from the Midwest. Wichita, I believe. They gravitate here from the provinces, all the bright and eager youngsters, seeking adventure and opportunity." He gestured. "And Jordan? Why is Jordan interested? Because of the accident? Is he chasing ambulances?"

"Jordan's assistant was injured in the same accident."

"The young man should be warned, Lieutenant. He's courting eventual disbarment with his present affiliation."

And Mr. Arnold Procter, I thought, was courting a fat lip.

Nola said, "How long had the girl been working for you?"

"About a month."

"Did she ever discuss her personal affairs?"

"I do not encourage intimacies. We're under constant pressure at the agency. I imagine you could find the necessary information at the girl's apartment." He glanced at his watch. "I really don't have much time, Lieutenant. I'm due at an important meeting."

"Sorry. You'll have to resign yourself to being late."

Procter lifted his chin superciliously. "This city is suffering from a serious fiscal crisis. I understand we've been compelled to reduce the number of law-enforcement officers. Shouldn't you be out catching crooks?"

"That's exactly what he's doing right at this moment," I said.

His head swiveled. "What are you talking about?"

"I'm talking about embezzlement, Procter. I'm talking about murder. Where do you keep your car?"

"What car?"

"The car you parked near Amy's apartment early this evening, waiting for her to come out so you could aim it and step on the gas and put her away. My assistant was with her at the time, so he too was expendable. But it was Amy who caught the full impact."

"Me?" He flattened a palm against his chest. "Are you saying I killed Amy? I don't even own a car."

"Then you rented one. They'll check the rental agencies, Procter. Think about it. Did you return a car with a smashed headlight or a dented fender? Wiped clean of fingerprints?"

"Why in God's name would I want to hurt that girl?"

"Because she knew too much," I said. "She knew about all the money involved in Lily Olson's new book. Almost two million dollars or more. The first time your agency ever hit the jackpot. It might never happen again, either to you or to Lily Olson. Or to George Finney who conceived the idea and developed the plot and was entitled to half of the proceeds."

"Who says so?"

"Finney's notebooks. We have them in his own handwriting, elaborating on the same theme that appears in Olson's book, *The Machiavelli Project*. And a letter you wrote suggesting that he collaborate with some other writer. You put him in touch with Lily Olson. Those papers should have been destroyed, Procter, only the lieutenant showed up unexpectedly and seized them before you had a chance."

"I wrote him a letter, yes. But it referred to a different project."

"It referred to an outline called *The Long Night*. And Olson's book may even have been submitted under that title. Because at that time nobody anticipated this windfall. Shall we call the publishers and ask if they were involved in a change of title?"

It started a vein throbbing in his temple.

I said, "Finney's name had no currency in the publishing world. So he willingly agreed to let Olson appear as the sole author. As a matter of fact, he insisted on it. Because if his wife learned about any new source of income, she had a legal right to demand an increase in alimony. He wanted to avoid that. He hoped to squirrel the money away, so his selfishness played into your hands.

"But then lightning struck. You found yourself in possession of a blockbuster worth millions. Greed obliterated your ethics. You had an idea. You went to Lily Olson and sounded her out. You told her she had written the book, slaved over it for months, bled her talent. Why split with Finney? You made her a proposition. If Finney could be eliminated, with no risk to her, would she split his share with you. And she was receptive. So you worked it out. They celebrated their success and she got him drunk. Then you coaxed him into a car and he kept lapping it up while you drove to an appropriate spot along the river. You got him out, stoned and helpless, and gave him a push."

His mouth was open, breathing harshly, his face moist.

"It never ends," I said. "One thing leads to another. I sent my assistant to your office and he met Amy Barth and they became friends. That posed an instant threat. Because Amy knew about the collaboration. And she could kick over the pail by mentioning it. So she had to be silenced without delay and you took care of it. Who else knew where she lived? Who else had a motive? You, Procter, only you.

"You're finished, mister. They'll put it all together and when they start leaning on Lily Olson she'll come apart, trying to clear her own skirts. You haven't a prayer."

He sank into a chair and covered his face. Nola reached for the telephone and I heard him telling someone to pick up the Olson woman. I looked at Procter. All those snide comments about lawyers. And five will get you twenty, in about two minutes he'd be yelling his head off for one.

Ann Mackenzie

I Can't Help Saying Goodbye

A memorable short-short . . . we doubt if you will ever forget the frisson d'horreur it evokes . . .

My name is Karen Anders I'm nine years old I'm little and dark and near-sighted I live with Max and Libby I have no friends

Max is my brother he's 20 years older than me he has close-together eyes and a worried look we Anders always were a homely lot he has asthma too

Libby used to be pretty but she's put on weight she looks like a wrestler in her new bikini I wish I had a bikini Lib won't buy me one I guess I'd stop being so scared of going in the water if I had a yellow bikini to wear on the beach

Once when I was seven my father and mother went shopping they never came home there was a holdup at the bank like on television Lib said this crazy guy just mowed them down

Before they went out I knew I had to say goodbye I said it slow and clear goodbye Mommy first then goodbye Daddy but no one took any notice of it much seeing they were going shopping anyway but afterwards Max remembered he said to Libby the way that kid said goodbye you'd think she knew

Libby said for gosh sakes how could she know be reasonable honey but I guess this means we're responsible for her now have you thought of that

She didn't sound exactly pleased about it

Well after I came to live with Max and Libby I knew I had to say goodbye to Lib's brother Dick he was playing cards with them in the living room and when Lib yelled Karen get to bed can't you I went to him and stood as straight as I could with my hands clasped loose in front like Miss Jones tells us to when we have choir in school

I said very slow and clear well goodbye Dick and Libby gave me a kind of funny look

Dick didn't look up from his cards he said goodnight kid

Next evening before any of us saw him again he was dead of a disease called peritonitis it explodes in your stomach and busts it full of holes

Lib said Max did you hear how she said goodbye to Dick and Max started wheezing and gasping and carrying on he said I told you there was something didn't I it's weird that's what it is it scares me sick who'll she say goodbye to next I'd like to know and Lib said there honey there baby try to calm yourself

I came out from behind the door where I was listening I said don't worry Max you'll be okay

His face was blotchy and his mouth was blue he said in a scratchy whisper how do you know

What a dumb question as though I'd tell him even if I did know

Libby bent down and pushed her face close to mine I could smell her breath cigarettes and bourbon and garlic salad

She said only it came out like a hiss don't you ever say goodbye to anyone again don't you ever say it

The trouble is I can't help saying goodbye

After that things went okay for a while and I thought maybe they'd forgotten all about it but Libby still wouldn't buy me a new bikini

Then one day in school I knew I had to say goodbye to Kimberley and Charlene and Brett and Susie

Well I clasped my hands in front of me and I said it to each of them slow and careful one by one

Miss Jones said goodness Karen why so solemn dear and I said well you see they're going to die

She said Karen you're a cruel wicked child you shouldn't say things like that it isn't funny see how you made poor little Susie cry and she said come Susie dear get in the car you'll soon be home and then you'll be all right

So Susie dried her tears and ran after Kimberley and Charlene and Brett and climbed in the car right next to Charlene's mom because Charlene's mom was doing the car pool that week

And that was the last we saw of any of them because the car skidded off the road to Mountain Heights and rolled all the way down to the valley before it caught fire

There was no school next day it was the funeral we sang songs and scattered flowers on the graves

Nobody wanted to stand next to me

When it was over Miss Jones came along to see Libby I said good evening and she said it back but her eyes slipped away from me and she breathed kind of fast then Libby sent me out to play

Well when Miss Jones had gone Libby called me back she said didn't I tell you never never never to say goodbye to anyone again

She grabbed hold of me and her eyes were kind of burning she twisted my arm it hurt I screamed don't please don't but she went on twisting and twisting so I said if you don't let go I'll say goodbye to Max

It was the only way I could think of to make her stop

She did stop but she kept hanging on to my arm she said oh god you mean you can make it happen you can make them die

Well of course I can't but I wasn't going to tell her that in case she hurt me again so I said yes I can

She let go of me I fell hard on my back she said are you okay did I hurt you Karen honey I said yes and you better not do it again and she said I was only kidding I didn't mean it

So then I knew that she was scared of me I said I want a bikini to wear on the beach a yellow one because yellow's my favorite color

She said well honey you know we have to be careful and I said do you want me to say goodbye to Max or not

She leaned against the wall and closed her eyes and stood quite still for a while and I said what are you doing and she said thinking

Then all of a sudden she opened her eyes and grinned she said hey I know we'll go to the beach tomorrow we'll take our lunch I said does that mean I get my new bikini and she said yes your bikini and anything else you want

So yesterday afternoon we bought the bikini and early this morning Lib went into the kitchen and fixed up the picnic fried chicken and orange salad and chocolate cake and the special doughnuts she makes for company she said Karen are you sure it's all the way you want it and I said sure everything looks just great and I won't be so scared of the waves now I have my bikini and Libby laughed she put the lunch basket into the car she has strong brown arms she said no I guess you won't

Then I went up to my room and put on my bikini it fitted just right I went to look in the glass I looked and looked then I clasped my hands in front I felt kind of funny I said slow and clear goodbye Karen goodbye Karen goodbye goodbye

Edward D. Hoch

The Spy and the
Cats of Rome

Rand, the former head of the Department of Concealed Communications, the former Double-C man, is retired—or supposed to be. (We never believed for a minute that Rand would really retire, and we hope nothing ever happens to destroy our faith in the perpetuation and continuity of series characters.) In any event, Rand is called back to complete some unfinished business of the past. Would that old matter never end? Was Rand on a fool's errand to Rome and Moscow? And then the old affair became—as it usually did for counterspies—a dangerous, even a deadly mission . . .

Rand felt vaguely uneasy sitting in the familiar chair in Hastings' office at British Intelligence. He'd sat there on a thousand prior occasions over the years, but this time was different. He'd retired from the Department of Concealed Communications the previous autumn, and though he'd been involved in one or two cases since then, this was his first visit back to the old building.

"Good to see you again, Rand," Hastings said. "How's your wife?"

"Leila's fine. Teaching archeology at Reading University."

"You live out that way now, don't you?"

"That's right. We have a house west of London, about halfway to Reading. It's an easy drive for her."

"And yourself?"

Rand shrugged. "Writing a book. What everyone does when they retire from here, I suppose."

"I wanted you to know how much I appreciated your help on that Chessman toy business a few months back."

"You told me so at the time," Rand reminded him. "What is it now?"

"Does it always have to be something?"

"You're too busy a man to invite me down for a mere chat. What is it?"

At that instant Hastings seemed old and bleak. "The sins of our

119

youth catching up with us, Rand. It's Colonel Nelson."

Rand stiffened. That had been—how many years ago?—ten at the very least.

Colonel Nelson had been in charge of certain international operations for British Intelligence. He'd lied to Rand about the nature of a Swiss assignment, and some good people had died. Shortly afterward Colonel Nelson suffered a nervous breakdown and was retired from the service. Even after ten years Rand had never forgotten the man and what he did. He'd thrown it up to Hastings in moments of anger, and had cited the affair to younger members of Double-C as a glaring example of what could go wrong if an overseas agent was not in possession of all the facts.

"What about him?" Rand asked.

"We have reports from Rome that he's stirring things up, recruiting white mercenaries to fight in Africa."

"Not on behalf of British Intelligence, surely!"

"No, no, of course not. And I doubt if he's working for the Americans, either. Frankly, we don't know what his game is. But it's most embarrassing at this time."

"Where do I come in?"

"Could you fly down to Rome for a day or two? Just see what mischief he's up to?"

"Oh, come on now, Hastings! I'm out of the service. I helped you on that toy business because—"

"I know, I know. But I don't want to send anyone officially. You know Colonel Nelson. You'd recognize him, even after ten years."

"And he'd recognize me."

"That might be enough to scare him off what he's doing, or at least make him assume a lower profile. You'd be strictly unofficial, but he'd get the message."

"I don't want to be away—" Rand began, still resisting.

"Two nights at most. Certainly your bride could spare you that long."

Perhaps it was the enforced bleakness of the winter months, or the simple need for activity. Perhaps it was a gnawing sense of unfinished business with Colonel Nelson. Ten years earlier Rand had wanted to kill him. Now, perhaps if he saw the man, he could write a finish to it, finally forget it.

"All right," he said, "I'll go."

Hastings smiled. "I thought you would. I have your plane ticket here. . . "

Rand phoned Leila at the university and explained, as best he could, that he'd been summoned to Rome for two days. "Back at it, aren't you?" she asked accusingly.

"Not really. It's some unfinished business. A fellow I used to work with."

"Be careful, Jeffery."

"Don't worry. I'm through taking chances."

He gathered up some things into an overnight bag and flew to Rome that evening. It was a city he'd visited only briefly in the past, and perhaps his impressions of it were different from most. To him it was not so much a city of churches as a city of fountains and cats.

This night, having settled into a hotel room not far from the Spanish Steps, he took a taxi to a restaurant near the Forum, where the cobblestoned street was cluttered with cats of all sizes waiting to be fed the scraps from the kitchen. Some said the cats had been there since the Fifth Century B.C., when they were imported from cat-worshipping Egypt. They ran wild in many parts of the city, often simply sitting and watching a passerby with a regal indifference that made one believe they might well have inhabited the city for 2500 years.

The restaurant itself was unspectacular. It was called Sabato—Saturday—and perhaps that was the only night it did any business.

Certainly on this Thursday night there were plenty of empty tables. Rand saw a few men at the bar—young Italian toughs of the sort that might make good mercenary material. If Colonel Nelson did his recruiting here, business might be good.

A young woman wearing a tight satin skirt and scoop-necked blouse appeared from somewhere to show him to a table. She asked him something in Italian and he answered in English, "I'm sorry. My Italian is a bit rusty."

"Do you wish a menu?" she asked, speaking English almost as good as his.

"Thank you, no. My name is Rand. I've come in search of a friend. I understood I could find him here."

"What is his name?"

"Colonel Nelson."

"Ah! The man with the cats!"

"Cats?"

"He feeds them. They trail him down the street when he leaves."

"Does he come here every night?"

"Usually, but you have missed him. He's been and gone."

"I see. You wouldn't happen to know where he lives, would you?"

She shrugged. "Ah, no."

Rand glanced at the line of men standing by the bar. "Any of his friends around?"

"Colonel Nelson's friends are the cats."

"But if he comes in here he must drink with somebody."

"Ask them," she answered, indicating the men at the bar.

"Thank you, Miss—"

"Anna."

"Thank you, Anna."

The first man Rand approached spoke only Italian, but his companion had a knowledge of English. He also had a knowledge of Colonel Nelson. "I take you to him if you want. He lives not far from here."

"Fine. Does he work around here?"

"No, no, he's an old man. He feeds the cats, that is all."

Rand figured Colonel Nelson to be in his early sixties, but the effects of the nervous breakdown might have aged him. Still, it seemed odd that a neighborhood character who fed the stray cats of Rome would be seriously recruiting mercenaries to fight in Africa.

"All right, take me to him."

The man gestured with his hands. "I must pay for the drinks I have."

Rand took the hint and put down a couple of Italian bills. The man smiled, pocketed one of them, and left the other for the bartender. Then he led the way outside, heading down a dim alley lit only by the curtained glow from the restaurant windows.

"How far is it?" Rand asked.

"Not far from here," the man said, repeating his earlier words, and Rand wondered if he was being set up for a trap. But presently they reached a seedy stone building that obviously contained small apartments, and the man motioned him inside. "I leave you. Sometimes he does not like visitors."

Rand checked the mailboxes—some standing open with their hinges broken—and found one for *Col. A. X. Nelson.* Ambrose Xavier Nelson. Rand hadn't thought of the full name in a decade. He glanced around to thank the man who'd brought him, but the man had already vanished into the night.

The apartment was on the third floor and Rand went up the dim steps with care. The place smelled of decay. Not all that quiet, either, he decided, hearing the noise of a family quarrel from one of the second-floor apartments as he passed it. There was a man's body sprawled on the third-floor landing, and he thought for an instant it was Colonel Nelson, cut down by enemy agents. But it was only a drunk, wine bottle empty at his side, who opened his mouth and snored when Rand turned him over.

He knocked at the door of Colonel Nelson's apartment and waited. Nothing happened. After a moment he knocked again, harder.

Finally a voice reached him from inside. "Who is it?"

"An old friend, Colonel Nelson. I'm in Rome and thought I'd look you up."

The door did not open. "Who is it?" the question was repeated.

"Jeffery Rand, from London."

"Rand. Rand?"

"That's right. Open the door."

He heard latches being undone and bolts pulled back. The heavy oak door opened a crack and a white kitten squeezed out. Then it opened farther, revealing a wrinkled face and balding head. Tired eyes peered at Rand through thick glasses. "I'm Colonel Nelson," the man said. "Why did you come here?"

"To see you. May I come in?"

"All right. The place is a mess."

Two more cats came into view, running across the floor in Rand's path. He lifted a pile of newspapers from a chair and sat down. The place was indeed a mess. "Do you remember me?" Rand asked.

The man opposite him waved his hand. "The memory comes and goes. The old days are clouded sometimes. But I think I remember you, yes."

"That surprises me," Rand said, almost casually, "because I've never laid eyes on you before. You're not Colonel Nelson."

The old man smiled then, showing a missing tooth. "Didn't think I could fool you, but I had to give it a try, right?"

"Who are you, anyway? Where's Nelson?"

"He's away. Hired me to take care of his cats and things. My name's Sam Shawburn."

"You're English."

"Sure am! There's a great many of us in Rome, you know. I was with the British Embassy in my younger days. That's how I met old Nelson."

"But this place—!"

"Isn't very tidy, is it? He's fallen on bad times, Colonel Nelson has. Gets a small pension, you know, but not enough to live on."

"Yet he can afford to pay you to stay here while he goes off traveling. That doesn't make sense."

"He was called away on business. He expects to make scads of money and then he says he's going to move to a better place. Maybe take me with him, too."

"I see. Are the cats his?"

"Sure are! They're not mine, I can tell you that. He feeds them in alleys and sometimes they follow him home. He's got close to a dozen around here, maybe more."

"I really would like to see him while I'm in Rome. When's he due back?"

"Who knows? He's been gone a week now."

"I understand he has business connections in Africa."

Sam Shawburn's eyes narrowed.

"Where'd you hear that?"

"The word gets around. I heard he was recruiting mercenaries to fight in Africa."

"Old Nelson's a sly one. I wouldn't want to say what he's up to. But I never heard anything about Africa."

"All right," Rand said. "Good talking to you, anyhow. And be sure to tell him I was asking for him."

"Sure will!" the old man said.

Rand left the apartment and went back downstairs. The drunk was gone from the landing now, and he wondered what that meant. Was Colonel Nelson's apartment being watched, and if so by whom? Rand hadn't noticed a telephone in the shabby quarters and once he reached the street he decided to wait a few minutes and see what happened. If anything.

Luck was with him. Within five minutes Sam Shawburn left the building and headed down the street, followed by a couple of cats. He might have been taking them for a walk, but Rand was willing to bet he was headed for a telephone.

The streets in that section of the city were all but deserted at night, and it was difficult for Rand to follow too closely. Once or twice he thought he'd lost the trail, but finally he saw Shawburn enter a little tobacco store and make for a telephone in the rear. The cats waited outside, scanning the street for some unseen prey.

He waited until the old man emerged from the shop and started back down the street. Then Rand crossed quickly to intercept him. "Hello again, Mr. Shawburn."

"What?"

"It's Rand. I wonder if you've been in touch with Colonel Nelson."

The old man took a step backward, as if frightened by the sudden encounter. "No, no, I haven't talked to him."

"Who'd you call just now?"

"When?"

"Just now, in the tobacco store."

"My daughter. I called my daughter."

"Here in Rome?"

"Yes. No—I mean, near here."

"You phoned Colonel Nelson, didn't you?"

The old man's head sagged. "I sent him a telegraph message. I thought he'd want to know."

"Where did you send it?"

"Moscow."

"Colonel Nelson is in Moscow?"

"Yes."

Rand cursed silently. What in hell had he got himself into? The brief favor for Hastings was opening before him like an uncharted swamp. "What's he doing there?"

"I don't know. Business, I guess."

"Where's he staying?"

"I don't know."

"You had to send the telegram somewhere."

Shawburn seemed to sag a bit. "The Ukraine," he replied at last. "He's staying at the Ukraine Hotel in Moscow."

There was never any doubt in Rand's mind that he'd be going to Moscow. He phoned Hastings in London to tell him the news and then made arrangements to catch a flight the following morning. As Hastings had quickly pointed out, the possibility of establishing a link between the Russians and the recruiting of African mercenaries was too good an opportunity to be passed over.

Rand had been in Moscow before, in 1970, and he was surprised to see the fresh coats of paint on buildings that had long been neglected. The city was spruced up; it was more modern and lively than he remembered it, and riding down Kalinin Prospekt in the taxi from the airport he might have been in any large city of western Europe. He could see the Gothic spires of the Ukraine Hotel in the distance, looking like some sort of medieval anachronism, contrasting sharply with the modern offices and apartment buildings that lined the thoroughfare. And he couldn't help wondering if his chances of finding Colonel Nelson were any better in a grand Moscow hotel than in the cat-filled alleys of Rome.

The desk clerk at the Ukraine spoke some English, and he knew of Colonel Nelson. "I think he is in the dining room," he told Rand.

The difference in time between Rome and Moscow had made it the dinner hour without Rand's realizing it. He thanked the room clerk and entered the dining room. It was long and fairly wide, with a raised bandstand at the far end and balconies running the length of either side. A huge chandelier hung from the center of the ceiling, adding a surprisingly ornate touch. Most of the side tables were set for large parties, but at one of the small center tables he found Colonel Nelson dining alone. This time there could be no mistake, even after a decade. "Hello, Colonel."

The old smile greeted him, though the face around it had aged and the eyes above it had taken on a slightly wild look. "Well, Rand—good to see you! I trust your flight from Rome was a pleasant one."

"So Shawburn sent a second telegram."

"Of course! Did you think he wouldn't? The old man is quite faithful."

"Mind if I join you?" Rand asked, already pulling out a chair.

"Not at all!"

"How's the food here?"

"Predictable. And the service is slow, as in all Moscow restaurants. But I can recommend the soup. It's so thick your fork will stand in it unsupported."

"I'll try some." Rand smiled. "What brings you to Moscow, Colonel?"

"Business prospects. Nothing of interest to Concealed Communications, I shouldn't think."

"Oh, I'm retired from there," Rand said casually.

"Are you now? Then why are you tracking me across Europe?"

"I was in Rome and thought I'd look you up, see how you're doing. I'll admit when I heard you were in Moscow my curiosity got the better of me. Not changing sides after all these years, are you?"

Colonel Nelson glanced around nervously, as if fearing they'd be overheard. "I have no side in London any more. Surely you remember how I was booted out of the service."

"I remember how you lied to me about that Swiss assignment and caused the deaths of several people."

"We are in the business of lying, Rand. You know that. Didn't Hastings ever lie to you?"

"Not to my knowledge."

"Ah, the good gray Hastings! A knight in shining armor! But he's the only one of the old crowd left, isn't he? You and I are out of it—and I hear that even some of the Russians like Taz are gone."

"Taz was blown up in a car shortly before I retired. He made the mistake of coming out of retirement."

Colonel Nelson smiled. "I hope you don't make the same mistake."

Rand leaned forward. "What are you doing here, Colonel?"

"A business matter."

"You're playing a dangerous game. Your apartment in Rome is being watched."

"No doubt by British Intelligence."

Rand decided to lay his cards on the table. "They know you're recruiting mercenaries," he said quietly. A small combo was tuning up on the bandstand, and he doubted if even a directional microphone could have picked up his words.

Colonel Nelson merely shrugged. "There is very little for an aging man to do in my line of work. One must make a living."

"Are the Russians paying you?"

Nelson thought about the question for a moment, then said, "Look here, Rand, come with me tomorrow morning and see for yourself. It will save you the trouble of following me all day."

"Tomorrow morning?"

"At ten, in the lobby. We're going to Gorky Park. It's the first warm weekend of spring and there's certain to be a crowd there."

He'd been right in his weather prediction, at least. The temperature had climbed to 22 degrees on the Celsius scale, and the park was crowded with strollers. Gorky Amusement Park was located on the Moscow River, a few miles south of the central city. Rand had never been there before, and somehow the sight of the giant Ferris wheel startled him.

"They come here in the winter to ride the ice slide," Colonel Nelson said, "and in the summer to sun-bathe on the hillside. It is a park for all seasons."

"A good place for a meeting," Rand agreed. "Especially on a mild spring weekend."

"The man I'm to meet is named Gregor. Make a note of it if you wish, for Hastings."

"That won't be necessary."

They strolled deeper into the park, past the amusement area to the bank of the river. There were people resting on its grassy shore, and Colonel Nelson said, "It's too cold for swimming except in mid-summer, but they like to wade."

"You know a great deal about Moscow."

"After so many trips it's like London or Rome to me. But come, there's Gregor now."

Gregor was a heavy-set Russian wearing a dull gray suit that seemed too heavy for the weather. Rand's unexpected presence made him nervous, and after a few words in Russian the two of them moved off out of earshot. "You understand, old chap," Colonel Nelson said.

Rand found a bench and sat down, watching some children at play with a fat yellow cat. He couldn't help thinking that the cats of Moscow seemed better fed than those of the Rome alleys. Presently he saw the two men part and Colonel Nelson joined him on the bench. He bent to pet the cat, then sneezed suddenly and sent the creature scurrying into the bushes. "That was simple," he said. "My business in Moscow is finished."

"You handed him an envelope."

"Down payment. In three weeks' time he will deliver five hundred Russian and East German weapons, mainly automatic rifles."

"You're buying arms here?"

"Of course! What else would bring me to Moscow?"

"For your African mercenaries?"

"Yes," Colonel Nelson answered smugly. "Then if the arms are captured it appears the Russians supplied them."

"Who really supplies them?"

"You know as well as I do, Rand. The British are footing the bill, perhaps with the C.I.A.'s help. I'm still with British Intelligence, you see. I never really left."

"I can't believe—"

"Can't believe what? That Hastings didn't tell you? Good clean Hastings who's always so aboveboard? Hastings knows what I'm doing, all right. He sent you on a fool's errand, going through the motions in the event anyone asked questions later on. I'm working for the British, supplying guns and men to various African factions. You might as well accept it, Rand, because it's true."

Rand was stunned by the words. He didn't want to believe them, didn't want to believe that Hastings had lied to him just as Colonel Nelson had done a decade earlier.

But before he could speak, a man wearing a black raincoat detached himself from the nearby strollers and headed toward them. Rand's first thought was that the man looked vaguely familiar. Then he saw the gun come into view and he thought they were under arrest.

But the gun was a 9mm German Luger, and it was pointed at Nelson's chest.

"Volta, Colonel Nelson!" the man shouted, and fired three quick shots.

Rand saw it all as if in slow motion. He saw Nelson topple backward as the bullets tore into his chest, saw the assassin drop the weapon at Rand's feet and disappear into the bushes.

Then Rand was running—knocking screaming women and frightened men from his path, running after the gunman who'd already melted into the crowd on the next footpath. It was impossible to find him, and to most witnesses Rand must have looked like the killer himself. He saw a policeman coming his way, guided by the pointing fingers of the crowd.

He ducked behind a signboard as the officer approached, and quickly bought a ticket on the Ferris wheel. As soon as he began his ascent, he spotted the policeman still searching the crowd for him. And higher up, with a view of the entire park, he could see the crowd gathered around the spot where Colonel Nelson's body lay. It was hard for him to believe that the tiny figure at the center of that crowd was Nelson, who'd survived a dozen intrigues to die like this in a Moscow amusement park.

He thought about that, and about Hastings back in London.

Had Hastings really lied to him? Was Colonel Nelson working for British Intelligence all this time, financing his African venture with money from England and possibly from America?

And had the killing of Colonel Nelson been part of the ultimate double-cross?

Rand left the Ferris wheel after three more trips around. The view hadn't answered any of the questions for him, but at least he'd seen Colonel Nelson's body being carried off and he knew the police had stopped searching the immediate area. He took a taxi back to his hotel and was just entering the lobby when he noticed the two men in belted black raincoats talking with the room clerk. This time there could be no mistake. These really were Russian police.

He went back out the revolving door without pausing.

They were looking for him and they knew where to find him.

He was being nicely framed for the murder of Colonel Nelson.

As Rand saw it, there were only two courses of action open to him. He could attempt to leave the country by the first available airliner—and no doubt be stopped and arrested at the gate. Or he could go to the British Embassy and try to get help there. The embassy seemed the better bet. Once inside a Russian prison, he knew he'd be a long time getting out.

He was only a few blocks from the embassy building, and he went on foot. The entrance seemed clear as he approached, but almost immediately two Russian detectives emerged from a parked car to intercept him. "Could you state your business, please?" one of them asked in good English.

"My business is with the British Embassy."

"Could we see your passport?"

"I've lost it. That's why I've come to the Embassy."

"You must understand we are looking for a British citizen wanted in connection with a murder. We must ask for identification."

"Are you denying me entrance to my own Embassy?"

The Russian shrugged sadly. "Only until you produce identification. You are still on Russian soil here." He pointed to the ground at his feet, as if daring Rand to step past him.

"All right. I have some identification in my car. I'll go get it." He held his breath as he turned, wondering if the Russians would follow. But their instructions had been to remain at the Embassy entrance, and they only followed him with their eyes. He walked down to the next cross street, where a small Moskvich automobile sat at the curb, its front end hidden from the Russians by a projecting building. Rand bent and pretended to try unlocking the door, then straightened up, shrugged, and made as if to walk around the front of the vehicle to the other side.

As soon as he was out of sight of the Russians he started running, heading down a narrow alley between buildings. He didn't think they'd desert their post to follow him too far, but he wasn't taking any chances.

Finally, panting for breath and fearful of attracting attention, he slowed to a walk as he emerged onto a busy avenue. No one stopped him. For the moment he was safe.

But what should he do now?

Hunted in a strange country for a murder he didn't commit, unable to leave the city or reach the British Embassy, knowing very little of the language, it seemed only a matter of time before he was taken into custody.

He descended into one of the ornate Moscow subways with its gilded chandeliers and sculptured archways and rode to a point not far from the American Embassy. But as he approached he saw a familiar-looking car with two men inside. He kept on walking, wondering how many embassies in Moscow had teams of police watching their doors.

Next he entered a small shop and asked for a public telephone. When he finally made his message clear, the woman behind the counter led him to a telephone—but there was no phone book. He remembered reading somewhere that telephone numbers were hard to come by in Moscow. With some difficulty he might reach the British or American Embassy by phone, but then what? They would hardly risk an international incident by coming into the street to rescue an accused killer. The best they'd offer would be a visit to his prison cell after he was arrested.

And what if he was arrested? Even his friends back in London might half believe the charge against him. He'd hated Colonel Nelson for ten years, and that hate might have boiled over into a murderous attack. And though several strollers must have seen the real killer in Gorky Park, Rand was not deceiving himself into believing that any of them would dare come forward to testify. If the government said he was guilty, he was guilty.

He wondered about the man who had really shot Colonel Nelson. Was he in the pay of the Russian, Gregor, who'd accepted his down payment for the weapons and promptly ordered Nelson killed? Or was it a more complex plot than that?

Someone had told the Russians his name, and only Hastings in London had known he was going on to Moscow. Was it possible that Hastings was in on it after all, as Colonel Nelson had insisted?

No. Rand refused to believe that.

The British hadn't been financing Nelson for all these years. He'd bet his life on it.

In fact, he'd bet his life on Hastings.

He took a trolleybus to the Central Telegraph Building and addressed a message to a cover address Hastings maintained in London: *Negotiating early landing shipment of new diesel engines at desirable seaport. Eastern nations don't pose any serious supply problem or route trouble.* He signed it *L. Gaad* and indicated a reply should be sent to him at the Central Telegraph Building.

Rand was certain Hastings would recognize Mrs. Rand's maiden name signed to the wire. And he was betting Hastings could read the very simple steganographic message hidden in it.

But he knew it would be morning before he could expect a reply.

A hotel would ask to see his passport and might even want to keep it. He couldn't sleep in the subway because they closed for maintenance from one to six in the morning. And he knew from his last visit to Moscow that the streets would be empty by ten o'clock. After that there'd be no crowds in which to hide.

Finally, as night was falling, he took the subway out to the end of the line, beyond Gorky Park, and went to sleep on a park bench.

In the morning, hoping his overnight beard wasn't too noticeable, he returned to the Central Telegraph Building. Yes, the woman clerk informed him, there was a reply for Mister L. Gaad. She handed over the form and Rand read, with rising spirits: *News of our negotiations received. Every dealer should quote under amount received elsewhere.* It was signed with Hastings' code name.

Rand almost shouted. Hastings had come through. The passport was on its way. He would meet the man and—

Unless it was a trap.

Unless Hastings was setting him up for the Russian police, or for the man who had shot Colonel Nelson.

It was a chance he'd have to take.

The message from Hastings had instructed him to be in Red Square at noon, so he assumed the agent bringing him the fake passport would know him by sight. Red Square at noon, with its lines of tourists waiting to visit Lenin's tomb, could be a very busy place.

There would have been time for an overnight flight from London, Rand knew—or the agent meeting him could be someone from the British Embassy. In any event, they would have to find each other in the crowd.

He reached Red Square a little before noon, wandering aimlessly along the fringes of the crowd waiting at Lenin's tomb. Though he kept his head down, his eyes were alert, scanning the faces he passed, looking for someone familiar.

At ten minutes after twelve he was still looking.

Perhaps Hastings had meant noon of the following day. Perhaps—

"Jeffery," a soft voice said at his shoulder.

He spun around, trying not to appear too startled, and looked into the face of his wife, Leila. "What are you—?"

"Hastings sent me. He knew it had to be someone you trusted. I have a passport in the name of Lawrence Gaad for you. And tickets on an evening flight to London."

"My God, he thought of everything!"

She smiled up at him, and at that moment they might have been the only people in the center of Red Square. "He said to tell you he expected something better from the former head of Double-C than a steganograph with the first letters of each word spelling out the message."

"Sometimes the simple things are the easiest to sneak by. And I had to have something that could be read almost at once. But I don't like the idea of his sending you here."

"Jeffery, I once swam the Nile to a boatload of Russian spies! A midnight flight to Moscow is really nothing."

He rubbed the stubble on his face. "Come on. If you don't mind dining with someone who needs a shave, I'll buy you lunch."

They arrived at Sheremetyevo International Airport in the late afternoon to find the usual scene of confusion and delayed flights. Rand asked Leila to check the departure time while he went off to do some checking of his own. He was remembering the words of Colonel Nelson's assassin: "Volta, Colonel Nelson!" It had sounded half Russian then, but he now realized it could have been Italian. *Time, Colonel Nelson!* A time to die.

And if the assassin was Italian—someone who had followed Nelson here from Rome—might not he be returning to Rome?

He confirmed at the information booth that the flight to Rome was six hours late in departing. There was just a chance that—

And then he saw the man.

There was no mistaking him, leaning against the wall smoking a cigarette. He even wore the same black raincoat.

Rand slipped a retractable ballpoint pen from his inner pocket and walked up to the man. Quickly, before he was noticed, he pressed the pen against the skin of the man's neck. "Don't move! Do you understand English? There's a needle in here that could poison you in an instant. You could be dead within a minute. Understand?"

The man was frozen in terror. "Yes. I understand."

"Why did you shoot Colonel Nelson?"

"I—"

Rand pressed harder. "Why?"

"I was paid to."

"By whom? The British?"

Suddenly Rand felt something hard jab him in the ribs, and he realized his mistake. There'd been two of them booked on the flight to Rome. "Let him go, Rand, or you're a dead man," a familiar voice said. "Turn around slowly and drop that pen."

He turned and stared into the deadly eyes of old Sam Shawburn.

It was then Rand remembered where he'd seen the gunman before. "He was the drunk on the landing outside your apartment!"

Sam Shawburn smiled. "Tony here? Yes, that's right. He was just leaving when he heard you climbing the stairs, so he went into his act. We work well together."

"And you had Colonel Nelson killed."

"A matter of necessity. The African business was becoming too complex—and too profitable to share with a partner. One of us had to go, and I simply acted first, before he got the notion of killing me. I thought murdering him in Moscow was a stroke of genius. It presented so many more possible suspects, including yourself, than did Rome."

"I should have known. Someone tipped off the Russian police and I thought of Hastings. But you knew I'd come to Moscow too—you'd even warned Colonel Nelson of my arrival. You followed me here, had Tony shoot Nelson, and gave the Russians my name. It was easy for them to locate my hotel and to place guards at the embassies."

"Very good!"

"And that wasn't Colonel Nelson's apartment. Those weren't his cats," Rand said, remembering the sneezing in Gorky Park. "Colonel Nelson was allergic to cats."

"True."

"You fed the cats and you recruited the mercenaries for Africa, using Nelson's name."

"His business was buying the guns in Moscow, but I found it safer to use his name for the entire operation."

"How will you get the guns now?"

"Gregor will still deliver. He has contacts and he likes money."

Rand had to know one more thing. "The British? Are they financing the operation?"

"The British?" Shawburn laughed. "Not a chance! Did Nelson tell you that? It was his daydream that he still worked for British Intelligence. He couldn't face that he was living a grubby existence in the back streets of Rome. We were in it on our own."

"What now? Will you try shooting me within earshot of five hundred people?"

"Outside," Shawburn decided. "Walk between Tony and me. No tricks now!"

They were almost to the outer doors, walking fast, when Leila was suddenly upon them. There were two burly Russian policemen with her and she was yelling, "Stop those men! They're kidnaping my husband!"

Shawburn tried to pull the pistol from his pocket but he was old and slow. The Russians were on them, and it was over.

Rand and Leila didn't catch the London plane that evening.

It took two days and several telephone calls to London, plus a visit by the British ambassador, to free them from the endless rounds of questioning. By that time the Russians had found Gregor's address in Sam Shawburn's wallet and learned all about the illegal arms deal. They seemed more interested in that aspect of the case than in the murder of Colonel Nelson, but it was enough to insure that Shawburn and Tony would be spending a long time in Russian prisons.

Finally, flying back to London, Rand said, "You saved me twice in one day. I'm beginning to think I should have had you around all my life."

Leila smiled and leaned her head back on the seat. "If you're going to keep on doing little favors for Hastings, you'll need me around."

Ernest Savage

Count Me Out

*San Francisco detective Sam Train was on his annual fishing
vacation and wasn't about to get mixed up in business—no, sir.
He was "in high country and hard country, but they're getting
closer every year—the migrant vandals, the destroyers, the random killers who will burn your house or shoot you or smash your
face on sheer impulse." But trouble was Sam Train's stock in
trade, and there's an old saying: once a cop, always a cop. It's in
the blood . . .*

You get up to Bucky Hagen's place on a footpath that follows the
ridge for a quarter mile and then angles through the trees to
his cabin. You can't drive there, except on a motorcycle. He parks
his Chevy pickup in a little open space alongside the ridge where
the rutted road ends. And then he walks up, unless he brings that
old Harley-Davidson of his, in which case he rides. It's a better walk
than it is a ride, but Bucky, since his wife died and he's gone to hell,
mostly rides. Bucky's 62, quite a bit older than I am, so maybe I
shouldn't criticize.

His Chevy was parked in the open space and I figured he was
there, so I went on up. Walking. It was about 2:30 in the afternoon
of a cool spring day. Tomorrow morning at dawn the fishing season
would open up here in the mountains and for the past ten years
Bucky and I have faced that auspicious moment together. We don't
do anything else together—he lives in Stockton, I in San Francisco—but we do that, and it's a seasoned tradition we both like and
it has the strength of tradition.

Bucky's cabin is situated on a slight rise of otherwise level land
in a grove of giant pines almost park-like in their spacing. Before
his wife Betsy died, she spent patient loving years clearing the
undergrowth from between the trees, and Bucky's place is about as
pretty as you're going to find. Or was, anyway, before she went.
Now it's lapsing back to seed, just as he is. Last year he was drunk
most of the three days we spent together fishing the Upper Eagle,
and you just don't get drunk in places like that.

The Upper Eagle is a series of deep swirling pools strung like jewels between stretches of white water that falls sometimes one foot or two and sometimes 20 feet in a straight drop. It pounds down out of the High Sierra in a gorge of rocks and boulders and shelves of stone worn smooth and bleached white by eons of wind, water, and sun. It's a beautiful river, but it takes all a man's strength and cunning to stay alive on. It has fish in it that have been there forever and will never get caught and will never die. I know some of them and I've given them names which I call out when I fish their special pools. It's the kind of river that will do that sort of thing to a grown man. And it has gold in it too.

Last year on our last afternoon together, Bucky fell in the river and almost drowned and I lost a good rod and reel pulling him out. I told him then I'd never fish with him again when he was drunk and I was coming up now to remind him of that.

The Harley-Davidson was in the woodshed to the left of the cabin. Smoke was coiling lazily out of the stone chimney to the right. I stopped about 40 feet from the place and felt the warmth of anger build behind my eyes. I tried to stop it, to calm myself. I come up here for two weeks every spring to get away from all that—the angering things, human cussedness, sloth, indifference, evil. The thick mat of pine needles on his cabin roof is what turned the heat on behind my eyes—that, and the busted spark arrester on his chimney top.

Normally at this time of year there's still a good snow pack on the ground and rooftops, but this year there wasn't, and that combination of dry pine needles and unscreened chimney stack was dynamite. Fire warnings were posted all over the mountains and Bucky should have known better. I walked up to his door and knocked.

A woman opened it—a girl, about twenty-looking. She surprised me.

"Where's Bucky?" I said.

"Him and Milt went over to the river," she said. She stood hipshot against the doorframe, dark sullen eyes on mine.

"Who's Milt?" I said.

"Who're you?"

I took a deep breath. "My name's Sam Train," I said evenly. "I'm a friend of Bucky's. My cabin's down slope a bit. When's he due back?"

"He di'n't say." She wore a loose red halter and short denim pants over solid hips and thighs. Her feet were bare and dirty and she smelled. She couldn't have gotten into the tackiest beer joint in California, but she could get into Bucky's and I thought, sadly, hell, he's slipped another notch since last year, maybe all the way this time. She was the kind of female I want no part of.

"Well, look," I said civilly, "when he gets back tell him to clean off his roof and fix that spark arrester on his chimney stack." She looked blank, so I said, "Come on out and I'll show you."

"Up yours," she said tonelessly.

I almost reached through the door to grab her and drag her out, but didn't. The heat flared and died behind my eyes. I didn't need this and I didn't need Bucky any more. But this year the fire hazard was too critical to be careless with. "Tell him," I said. "Or the Forestry Service will."

I'd left San Francisco before nine that morning and arrived at my cabin around noon. I turn in off the ridge road a little before Bucky's parking area and can drive the Dart almost to my cabin before the tall trees block me off. The first thing I do each year is check the place for damage and then rake the roof clean, unless it's under snow. So far I've never found damage, but it's a thing you keep your fingers crossed against. This is high country and hard country, but they're getting closer every year—the migrant vandals, the destroyers, the random killers who will burn your home or shoot you or smash your face on sheer impulse.

After I got back from Bucky's I made a list of what I'd need for the two weeks I planned to stay and went down to Mountain City to get it. That chore usually pleases me, but this year it didn't. I kept thinking of Bucky's roof and spark arrester and of Bucky himself. We'd fished and panned for gold through a long stretch of years, nearly a quarter of my life, and it was over now. Bucky hadn't come back from the grievous blow of Betsy's death, and never would.

Last year, after he'd cost me a rod and reel, he'd quit fishing and taken up his perennial hunt for gold—partly if not mostly in the taverns of Mountain City where stories of strikes and lost mines and abandoned claims are as rife as they ever were. Down through the years I've panned about $1500 worth of dust and flakes (at today's prices) from the Upper Eagle and its headwaters, and so has Bucky. And somewhere up there are the veins from which it comes, the mother lode, and men will go on searching for it until it's found or the world ends. But it will not be found by a drunk, I thought, whose secret search is for the soothing grave.

I felt sorry for Bucky, but I did not want him, in the carelessness of his decline, to set fire to my mountain, so on the way back I stopped at the Division of Forestry office. I told the ranger on duty that he should send a man up to Hagen's place and make him shape up, and he said he would first thing in the morning. I could have gone back and talked to Bucky myself—and the ranger's eyes told me that—but it was their job, not mine. I'm on vacation. For 19 years I was a cop on the S.F. Force and for the three years since I've been a P.I.

The next morning I got up at four o'clock and drove down through Mountain City and cross country from there to the north fork of the Feather River. I'd decided Bucky and his friends could have the Upper Eagle for a day or two. Besides, I was fond of the Feather. It's more leisurely and less violent and dangerous than the Eagle and it's a good place to get your legs in shape after the winter's layoff. You fish all Sierra streams from rock to rock and halfway through that first day, sometimes, you wish you were home in bed.

I had good luck there as I usually do. By noon I'd caught my limit and after I ate my sandwich and drank the rest of my coffee I headed home. On the way back I heard over the car radio that a fire was underway north of the Upper Eagle and it gave me the same dark thrill that report always does. I hurried. I went through Mountain City at 3:15 and 20 minutes later was jouncing up the ridge road near the cabin. Just above my turnoff a dark-green Forestry pickup was parked, heading down.

I pulled over, got out, and walked up the road to Bucky's parking area where two more Forestry trucks, a Mountain County Sheriff's car, and a County ambulance were parked. One of the Forestry trucks, a flatbed, had a winch rig on the rear and a cable had been fed down over the lip of the ridge to something out of sight below. A half dozen uniformed men were standing there looking down. Standing by themselves at the point where Bucky's trail leads up slope were the girl I'd talked to yesterday and a big man.

The girl had on a sweater over the same red halter she'd worn yesterday and a pair of dirty sneakers on her feet. She looked at me without apparent recognition from 20 feet away, then whispered something to the man, and he looked at me with quick interest. He was heavily bearded and long-haired and powerful-looking. I returned his stare for a few seconds before walking over to the Deputy Sheriff I recognized and asking him what happened.

"Train!" he said and stuck out his hand. "Hagen's down there," he said, "and a ranger named Miller. They went over the edge in the ranger's truck sometime this morning. The man down below says they're both dead. When'd you get up?"

"Yesterday. I heard there was a fire, Arkins."

"Yeah, there was, but it's out now. North of the Eagle, a small one. One of the helicopters spotted the ranger's truck in the ravine on the way back from there."

"How'd it happen, d'you know? I mean Bucky."

"We got an idea. Miller came out this morning to get Hagen to clean his roof and fix his chimney and evidently they got in a fuss about it. Those people over there"—he gestured toward the girl and the bearded man—"say Miller arrested Hagen and started to take him to town. They said Hagen was drunk. Then, evidently, they had a fight in the truck and Hagen got shot and the truck went over the edge. We'll know more when they get the bodies up, but that could've been the way it went. Miller was a known hothead and you know Hagen, he hasn't been sober for two years."

"Who says Hagen got shot?"

"The man down below there. Miller's the only one at the local station who routinely carries a sidearm. He's quick, like I say, and we've had some trouble with him. Saturday nights he gets drunk too. I see you been fishing, Sam. Any luck?"

"Yeah, my limit. Over on the Feather."

"They tell me Teel Lake is loaded with steelhead."

"I'm not much of a lake man, Arkins. Did you get statements from those two over there?"

"Not yet. We'll take 'em down to town when we get the bodies up."

"Who are they?"

"Friends of Bucky's, they said. They said they met him a couple of weeks ago in Stockton and he invited 'em up for the summer."

"The *whole* summer?"

"That's what they said."

I looked over my shoulder at the girl and our eyes locked instantly, hers sullen and baleful now; maybe she smelled the cop in me. The man was looking at the winch truck, his hands in his hip pockets, flat white belly and hair-matted chest showing through the gap in one of those buttonless wool-lined vests that macho types sometimes wear. It was a bravura touch in the chilly afternoon air.

A radio crackled and the cable, snaking down the steep slope of the ravine, jumped and tightened. You could see the path the truck had smashed through the underbrush, but you couldn't see the truck.

It was below a jutting shelf of rock a hundred feet down and it would be hard to get it back up past that shelf. Maybe they'd just bring up the bodies.

Arkins lit a cigarette and the flare of his match reminded me of a lot of things, chiefly that I had opened the curtain on this lethal show. But I said, "What started the fire, Arkins, do they know yet?"

"Probably one of these things," Arkins said, shaking out the match. "Probably some city dude cooking his breakfast this morning. Roughing it. No offense, Sam." He grinned at me amiably.

Last fall Arkins and I had had a brief encounter in the way of business and he had emerged from it with more egg on his face than I. But he was an easy-going, self-forgiving man, like most mountain men, and I liked him. "Somebody," I said, "has still got to clean off Bucky's roof and fix his chimney."

"Yeah," Arkins said.

"Maybe you can get Grizzly Barlow over there to do it," I said. "He's living there, I guess."

"Yeah, whyn't you ask him, Sam?"

"I asked somebody already," I said. "And besides I'm on vacation." I turned, walked back down to the Dart, and went home.

I usually sleep like a contented child in the cabin and that night was no exception, but when I wakened in the morning I felt for the first time the impact of Bucky's death and the first real lash of guilt.

It was nonsense. Bucky had wanted to die. For three years Bucky had been Death looking for a place to happen, so why should it trouble me? It was nonsense.

I went outside and breathed the cold clean air. Where I go on the Upper Eagle is a long hard uphill hike and you don't take that first step without thinking about it. My legs still hurt from the workout yesterday on the Feather and I knew they would for a couple days yet. They needed more time before tackling the Eagle—more of the Feather maybe, or one of the little tributaries up above where I've found some gold. I was waffling. It had been a bad start for what has always been the most prized two weeks of my year, and there I was just standing there.

I ate breakfast and then got in the Dart and drove the four winding miles down to Mountain City. I'd lost two rooster-tail lures on the Feather yesterday and I wanted to replace them and get a fresh spool of 8-ounce line. Besides, there was a new Daiwa reel I'd heard about and I figured Mickey Johnson would have it in his store down there if anyone did. More waffling—

I was still in Johnson's at ten o'clock and had about 40 bucks worth of stuff lined up to buy when Arkins found me there.

"Saw your car outside, Sam," he said, "and figured you was here."

"So?" I had a particularly fancy new lure in my hand and didn't put it down.

"So how about coming over and identifying Bucky's body?"

"Why me, Arkins? Half the people up here knew him, including you."

"You know *I* can't do it, Sam. Besides, you knew him better than anyone else. Come on."

I didn't want to go. An hour in Johnson's store had reacquainted me with why I was here. "Count me out," I said doggedly. "Get somebody up from Stockton to do it."

"He had no family, Train, you know that."

"Then a neighbor, a friend. How about those hippie guests of his?"

"They're not there this morning. I just got back from there."

"Why didn't you get 'em to do it last night?" I said obstinately.

"We didn't get the bodies up until after dark and they'd gone by then. Come on, Sam, it'll take you ten minutes."

I dropped the lure back in its box and followed him out.

The shot had gone clean through Bucky's heart. Doc Zerbo, who handled autopsies for Mountain County, said death had been instantaneous. Bucky's body was laid out on an embalming table in the back room of Madison's Funeral Parlor on Main Street, down the block from Johnson's. Mountain City is about a mile long and a quarter of a mile wide and 90 percent of the permanent population of the county live there. They can't afford a lot of sophisticated forensic equipment and personnel. Dr. Edward Zerbo does their autopsies in Madison's back room, but he makes his living setting bones during the skiing season and curing snake bite the rest of the year. I'd met him once before and liked him. He said he'd rather be poor here than rich anywhere else, and I understand that.

"Well, it's Bucky," I said, and Arkins duly noted that down.

"The bullet I took out of him looks like a .38," Zerbo said, "and Miller's gun is a .38 and there's probably no doubt he shot him, but we'll have to send them down to Sacramento for a ballistics check."

"Sounds good," I said, and turned to go, but then turned back. Bucky's body was badly battered from the long fall down the slope of the ravine, but there was a motley pattern of marks on his legs that weren't bruises. Little red bumps.

"What're those?" I said to Zerbo, pointing, and he said probably ant bites made while he and Miller were dead in the ravine.

"Does Miller have any?" I said and Zerbo shrugged and pulled the sheet back from Miller's body on the next table. It was as badly battered as Bucky's, but there were no little red marks on his legs.

"What killed him?" I said.

"The fall," Zerbo said. "I haven't done him yet, but it looks like his neck's broken."

"The ants didn't like him, I guess." I'd seen something else on Bucky's body, but didn't mention it. There were marks around his shoulders that looked as if he'd worn a heavy backpack for a long time, and I knew Bucky didn't even own a backpack. It bothered me as it would have bothered me if I were working; but I wasn't working; I was on vacation now and I put it out of my mind.

"Good seeing you again, Doc," I said and left.

I drove up to Teel Lake that afternoon and rented a boat at the marina and caught three good-looking steelhead, but since they were only lip-hooked I threw them back. I don't like lake fishing. Everybody and his Aunt Maude from down below goes lake fishing, especially early in the season, and the surface of the lake that afternoon was as crowded as a supermarket parking lot on dollar day.

The automotive age has produced a law in America as irrevocable as the table of tides: If you can't get to it on wheels, don't go to it. In ten years on the Upper Eagle I've seen no more than a half dozen men, counting Bucky, and that's what I like about it—that and its raw thundering beauty, and its danger. This was no vacation, it was a shopping trip on water. I was back at the cabin by six o'clock.

There's no power cable to the cabin and therefore no radio, TV, or electric lights. There's nothing much in it save a butane-powered cook top and refrigerator, a table, a few chairs, three bunks, and a half dozen books. But there is yourself, there's always yourself and what you've made of yourself in 45 quick years.

Why, I asked myself, did the bugs bite Bucky, but not bite Miller? I put aside the book I'd been trying to read under the cold light of a hissing mantle lantern, and let the question all the way in. It was a cop question, and once a cop, always a cop. Bucky had gotten himself bitten someplace other than down in the ravine. So where, and why?

I got up, went outside, and listened to the world spin for a while. You can hear it up here and it's a good sound; the sound of Time.

The ground underfoot was springy with mulch, the massed and layered detritus of 10,000 years. This noble forest, these tall trees die as we die and are chewed to dust as we are chewed to dust by the million mandibled jaws of the small world. It's their work.

Tie a man to one of these trees, I thought, leave him there for a while and the big black ants will think he's just another job to do. Strap a man by his shoulders somehow— But why?

Dammit! I wanted no part of this. I turned and went back in the cabin and by midnight I finally got to sleep. Bucky was better off where he was anyway, I told myself.

There are two things you have in mind when you fish the Upper Eagle: the first is to stay alive, the second to catch a fish, assuming you've achieved the first. There's a point up there beyond which I've never gone and never will. It's where, for me, the river starts. It pours down between two giant boulders into a boiling pool 20 feet below, breaks there into several streams that gush through and over a ridge of rocks to a larger pool three or four feet lower down. The water is freshly melted snow and viciously cold and the thunder of it is awesome. I drop a line in that lower pool every year, but it's a gesture, a ritual. I don't think any fish could live in it, even if he were fool enough to want to.

Usually in spring the snow is still piled deep along the banks of the Eagle, but this year the pack had been light and there wasn't much there, just grainy patches in the shaded spots, still firm and dry at ten in the morning; but by noon, under the lash of the mountain sun, their substance too would join this cataract, this thundering rush of virgin water, this primitive force. It never seems possible to me that I am just hours away from my apartment on Van Ness in San Francisco, and always that first day I know both joy and fear, but mostly fear.

It is no place to be alone. With every step you're at risk and if you break a leg you stay forever. I wear work shoes up here with thick, cleated, composition soles. Uncleated soles, even of rubber or crepe, are no good. The water bounces and sprays up the sides of the sleek rocks and sometimes wets their tops and they can become like greased slides if you don't have the right kind of shoes on.

I wear heavy cord pants, a heavy wool shirt, and a brimmed hat that otherwise hangs on a peg in the cabin. I carry a canvas creel slung on a strap over my shoulder that lies flat against my side until I put something in it. I carry six lures in a flat plastic box in one button-down shirt pocket, a candy bar in the other, and a single rod and reel. You've got to have one hand free to help you from rock to rock and the fewer things you have dangling from your frame, the fewer chances there are to snag on something.

Moving around up there, I missed Bucky. We always had eye contact with each other and that's almost like having an extra hand.

I worked carefully down to the next lower pool and began some serious fishing. Pierre lived in that pool. Pierre is a trout and, as I said, he always has lived there and always will. I hooked him once two years ago and if I'd had a net I could have landed him. But I never carry a net because it's just one more thing that could get you in trouble; and besides, I didn't want to catch Pierre. He's King here, and I just visit.

I use a green and gold rooster tail as lure, one-eighth ounce in weight if the wind's up, one-sixteenth if the air is still. I drop the lure in the white water in the center of the stream and draw it across his domain, about a foot down and flashing all the way in the clear green pool. He always comes out and sniffs at it—at least once—and two years ago the hook snagged him on the underside of the lower lip and drew him to the edge where he wiggled free and swam away.

It must have embarrassed Pierre, for he didn't show up again all that season. He's about two feet long and there's a pattern of black dots on his mottled brown back that looks like a P. Downstream a way in another pool there's a similar trout with a pattern of dots on his back forming an H and his name is Harry. Up here you talk to the fish if you talk at all, even if a friend's in sight. Your voice carries about a yard through the fractured air and teaches you finally that most of what you say you needn't have.

Back home in San Francisco, sometimes, awake in bed, listening to the rumble and squeal of traffic, the beagle-bawl of ships in the Bay, the screams of muggers' victims, and other not entirely imaginary sounds, I wish I could capture the special thunder of the Eagle, as the roar of the sea is caught in a shell, and lay it on the pillow next to my head. It's a tiring man's whimsy; but I'd sleep better.

Pierre came out that morning and sniffed my lure three times before I bid him goodbye and moved on down to my next station, where Harry lives. I've never hooked Harry, but I usually take one or two of his smaller mates for eating. Their flesh is so hard and firm that it flakes like a cracker when cooked, and there's nothing quite so good. But I didn't take anything that day from Harry's pool, or from anywhere else. Not a fish, anyway.

My legs had been aching all morning and when the sun was straight overhead I sat down in one of my favorite spots and ate my candy bar. I was tired and I missed Bucky. I'd slipped a while back and gotten my right leg wet to the knee and knew suddenly just how alone I was. Bucky would have come a-running, drunk or sober.

A little above and to the right of where I sat on a ledge, 30 feet over the roiling stream below, a nameless creek came tumbling in through the trees and joined its waters with the Eagle. Bucky and I had taken gold higher up on that creek, and a little last year from the curling gravel bar it formed at its junction with the Eagle.

It was a spectacular vantage point, if a little scary. The natural ledge on which I sat tapered away to nothing on my left and was no more than two feet wide at any point as it curved back around the rock on my right to solid ground. Bucky wouldn't come out there and called me a damn fool when I did. But it was always worth it. If I were a bird I'd live on that ledge.

After I finished my candy bar and talked to my legs for a few moments, I stood up carefully and stretched—and saw them from the corner of my eye, Bucky's friends. Somehow I'd half expected to all morning.

And they saw me.

They were 40 feet below me on the south bank of the river, 150 feet away in a straight line. We looked at each other for a long time and then the girl said something to the man and the man reached into a canvas sack at his feet, pulled out a pistol and very deliberately, holding it in both hands, fired at me.

I didn't hear the shot in the roar of the river, but I saw the muzzle flash. He moved a little uphill and fired again, just as I flattened myself on the rock at my back. I heard the zip-hiss of that shot only inches away.

I looked again and he was running up the slope behind me. He had me trapped. If he knew where the ledge I was standing on started, he could walk out on it and shoot me at his pleasure. But he didn't know that. I took another quick peek and saw him clambering up a big domed rock to the right of mine. From its top he'd be 25 feet away and from there he could cover the point at which I'd have to emerge if I retreated around the ledge. But he didn't know that either.

I took another quick look and saw him now nearly on top of the domed rock, but unsure of his feet yet and he wasted a shot that I didn't even hear. I had seconds to do something before he reached the top of the dome and only one thing to do it with—my rod and reel. It was leaning against the rock behind me and it was still armed with the eighth-ounce rooster tail I'd been using in Harry's pool. It was going to have to be a very good cast—

I took another peek to estimate distance. The domed rock was steeper near the top than it looked and the man had on the wrong kind of shoes. His left leg was extended down the side of the rock, his right bent under him holding his weight. He aimed at me one-handed, but didn't fire. He was about 25 feet from me now on a slight uphill line. I wanted him standing.

I took the rod in my right hand and twisted on the ledge, 15 inches wide where I was, so that my face was now pressed against the stone. I took another quick look and saw another muzzle flash and heard the sharp slap of the bullet striking the rock just above my head.

I was ready to go. I could hit him easily with the rooster tail, but that isn't what I wanted. I wanted to drop it over his shoulder or his head and have it go past him by no more than a foot, because a foot was about all I could pull it back without losing my footing on the ledge. I wanted *him* to fall into that murderous water below, not me.

I had to invite one more shot because I wanted him slightly off-balance from the recoil. I held the rod down, ready to whip it up and cast, then I stuck my head far enough around for him to see, raised the rod, and cast in one fluid move. I don't know where his shot went, but the rooster tail snagged in the long hair at the back of his head and when I pulled it back as far as I could before letting it go, he came part way with it. He whirled, his arms flying, his left shoe slipping again, and arced over backward. He tried to twist in mid-air, but didn't have the room and caught a rock full in the chest before bouncing in the water 30 feet below and out of sight.

I shut my eyes for a moment and pressed my cheek against the stone, warm in the afternoon sun. My knees felt as though they could bend either way and I didn't want to try them yet. When I opened my eyes again, the girl was jumping from the shore to a rock about a yard out in the water. There was a cluster of rocks there that in low water could take a sure-footed man halfway across the stream, but not now. The water there was all white and angry; but she didn't seem to see that, she saw her man slipping past, slipping away, his hairy face rolling up for an instant, then an arm, a leg; a broken man out there, dead or dying and lost forever.

She balanced for a moment on the first rock and then jumped for the next and I heard myself mouthing the words, "Go back, go back!"

She slipped, seemed to sit in the air for a moment, then half stood again, turning and falling.

I could see nothing at first but her long black hair, then I could see her face, her mouth wide, her teeth flashing, her eyes on mine. She was clinging to a rock, both arms wrapped around it, her body trailing behind in the fierce grip of the boiling stream. Her dark eyes were riveted on mine and her mouth now was forming the words over and over, "Help me, help me!"

I sidled shakily around the ledge to solid ground and then down to where she'd started her short fruitless trip. She was 15 feet away, but her pleading eyes seemed closer than that.

I was unmoved. Somehow she and her man had harnessed Bucky to something outdoors, a tree probably, and left him there long enough for the ants to chew him up pretty good before, again somehow, killing him. And if that were so, it was a good bet they'd also killed the ranger.

"Please—oh, God, help me, please!" I could almost hear her words in the thundering air.

I wanted to walk away right now and be done with it. She couldn't last another ten minutes in the grip of that frigid powerful stream. They'd killed Bucky and the ranger and then they'd tried to kill me because they thought I knew that; or—it occurred to me just then—because I saw them here, just here. Not somewhere else, but here.

I could walk away from her right now and sleep well tonight. And tomorrow night, and the next. But there is a difference in some of us, and some night—

The flickering spark we call soul is a sacred thing. If hers isn't, then mine is. She could walk away from me laughing; I knew that. But I'm not her. Not yet.

I didn't try to jump out on the rocks as she had. I stepped into the water just upstream of them and felt the breath snap shut in my throat. I moved toward her, belly deep, handing myself from rock to rock, my feet searching out the high spots on the stony bed of the stream. Her eyes were on me all the way until I caught her hands, and then they closed.

I pulled her over the rock she'd been clinging to, got her arms over my shoulders, and hauled her to shore and up the bank a few yards to where the sun burned warm. We were both exhausted and lay there for minutes before I got up and took off my shirt and spread it out to dry. I didn't touch her. She had on a shirt and sweater and those same denim shorts she'd worn before. The skin of her legs was still bluish-white from cold and they were both badly scratched from the rocks.

Her right leg was broken at mid-shin. It didn't go straight down, but bent there in a way that could make you sick if you let it. It didn't bother me at all.

A little later, when the cold wore off, it would begin to hurt again. It had probably hurt sharply when it happened, but then the cold had taken over. It meant that my option was still open; she would die here, too, if I left her, and the temptation was still strong. She opened her eyes and pulled hair away from her face the way women do, lightly, with the tips of the fingers. In any other woman it would have been a charming gesture.

I crouched down by her head on the springy brown earth. "You're gonna tell me how and why you killed Bucky," I said, "or I'm gonna leave you here for the ants. Do you understand me?"

She frowned groggily. "Bucky—?" It took her a while to pick up the thread—Bucky had been several fatal events back. "We have this rig," she said finally. "We hooked it on him and tied him to a tree."

"What rig?"

"This rig we've got. It's like a strait jacket, sort of."

"You've used it before?"

"Well, yes—once or twice."

"Why on Bucky?"

"He had this gold— He wouldn't tell us where it was at first."

My God! I thought; Bucky and his gold, his big strike somewhere. "Gold—where?" I said.

"Right here." She raised her head a little. "Around here somewhere."

"If he told you that—why did you kill him?"

"He fought with Milt. He tried to kill Milt. Milt knocked him out. And just then—"

"What?" The pain in her leg was building now.

"This guy in the monkey suit showed up and—Milt hit him on the head."

Her eyes winced and closed and I picked it up from there. "So Milt took the ranger's gun and put it in the ranger's hand and shot Bucky with it, didn't he? Then the two of you carried them down to the ranger's truck, set them up in it, and ran it over the edge. Right?"

"We had to," she said.

She opened her eyes wide and tried to sell it to me. "We couldn't do anything else, don't you see?"

I saw.

I stood up and gazed down at her with something too close to hate to live with for long. How many times had I heard that plea: "The guy wouldn't give me his money, so I had to kill him. Right?" And we're buying it, a little more each day.

I couldn't think about that.

"Where'd you meet Bucky?" I said.

"In this bar in Stockton. He had this little glass thing full of gold— He was bragging about it, Mr. Train."

Well, he probably was, I thought; there was so little left for him to brag about. I sighed for him just one time. I doubted that he'd fought with Milt. I think that Milt just beat him up for the joy of it, cheered on by this girl. And then the ranger came—the one I'd sent.

"If I take you back, will you tell them all that—the cops?"

"Oh, yes, yes! Just don't leave me here!"

"Promise?"

"I promise, Mr. Train."

I didn't quite grin. She was a pretty girl, good bones in the face and a big bounteous body. Fixed up she'd catch a man's eye quick and dull his good sense. And she would lie; she was born to lie. She'd deny that she and Milt had anything to do with Bucky and the ranger, and that lie might stick. She'd say that I lusted for her and killed Milt to get her—and that would make sense to half of them down there. Otherwise, why would I bring her back? Why not just leave her?

It would be trouble, a tangled, tricky kind of trouble, and in the end some would still believe her. Maybe all of them would. It would take work to clear myself, lots of it, and I didn't come here to work. I came here to get away to fish the Upper Eagle—and not for the like of this.

I looked down at her and said, "I'm gonna leave you here. I can't afford to take the risk."

She knew what I was talking about; her eyes were a mix of pain and guile. She closed them. "I will tell the truth," she said softly. "I'll tell it the way it happened."

"Sure you will," I said. But the decision had been made and there was no going back on it. I went over and put on my half-dry shirt and then I picked her up and draped her over my shoulder. It was about three o'clock, I figured, and it would take me three hours, at least, to get her to town.

I turned her over to the Sheriff at the Mountain City Hospital at 6:30 that evening, and then the trouble started. Just as I knew it would. She told them I'd killed Milt and tried to rape her and she'd broken her leg running away.

It was a week before I cleared myself enough to get back to San Francisco, and the first thing I did was sit down wearily and plan a vacation. Hawaii, maybe.

Next time, count me out.

But they're everywhere you go.

Lillian de la Torre

Milady   Bigamy

(as told by James Boswell, Spring, 1778)

In which James (Bozzy) Boswell plays the double role of an Eighteenth Century Dr. Watson and Perry Mason—with a crucial assist from that moral philosopher, that defender of right and justice, that detector of crime and chicane, the great Cham himself, Dr. Sam: Johnson ... This story is based on a real-life person and event, but for the purposes of fiction the author has reduced the age and size of the Duchess of Kingston, and changed her name, costume, and fate. The Duchess of Kingston was actually tried for bigamy by her Peers in April 1776; all the rest is fascinating reconstruction and creative—as well as poetic—license ...

66 I have often thought," remarked Dr. Sam: Johnson, one Spring morning in the year 1778, "that if I kept a seraglio—"

He had often thought!—Dr. Sam: Johnson, moral philosopher, defender of right and justice, *detector* of crime and chicane, had often thought of keeping a seraglio! I looked at his square bulk, clad in his old-fashioned full-skirted coat of plain mulberry broadcloth, his strong rugged countenance with his little brown scratch-wig clapped on askew above it, and suppressed a smile.

"I say, sir, if I kept a seraglio, the houris should be clad in cotton and linen, and not at all in wool and silk, for the animal fibres are nasty, but the vegetable fibres are cleanly."

"Why, sir," I replied seriously, "I too have long meditated on keeping a seraglio, and wondered whether it may not be lawful to a man to have plurality of wives, say one for comfort and another for shew."

"What, sir, you talk like a heathen Turk!" growled the great Cham, rounding on me. "If this cozy arrangement be permitted a man, what is to hinder the ladies from a like indulgence?—one husband, say, for support, and 'tother for sport? 'Twill be a wise father then that knows his own heir. You are a lawyer, sir, you know the problems of filiation. Would you multiply them? No, sir: bigamy is a crime, and there's an end on't!"

At this I hastily turned the topick, and of bigamy we spoke no more. Little did we then guess that a question of bigamy was soon to engage my friend's attention, in the affair of the Duchess of Kingsford—if Duchess in truth she was.

I had first beheld this lady some seven years before, when she was Miss Bellona Chamleigh, the notorious Maid of Honour. At Mrs. Cornelys's Venetian ridotto she flashed upon my sight, and took my breath away.

Rumour had not exaggerated her flawless beauty. She had a complection like strawberries and cream, a swelling rosy lip, a nose and firmset chin sculptured in marble. Even the small-pox had spared her, for the one mark it had left her touched the edge of her pouting mouth like a tiny dimple. In stature she was low, a pocket Venus, with a bosom of snow tipped with fire. A single beauty-spot shaped like a new moon adorned her perfect navel—

I go too far. Suffice it to say that for costume she wore a girdle of silken fig-leaves, and personated Eve—Eve after the fall, from the glances she was giving her gallants. One at either rosy elbow, they pressed her close, and she smiled upon them impartially. I recognised them both.

The tall, thin, swarthy, cadaverous apparition in a dark domino was Philip Piercy, Duke of Kingsford, once the handsomest Peer in the Kingdom, but now honed to an edge by a long life of dissipation. If he was no longer the handsomest, he was still the richest. Rumour had it that he was quite far gone in infatuation, and would lay those riches, with his hand and heart, at Miss Bellona's feet.

Would she accept of them? Only one obstacle intervened. That obstacle stood at her other elbow: Captain Aurelius Hart, of H.M.S. *Dangerous*, a third-rate of fifty guns, which now lay fitting at Portsmouth, leaving the gallant Captain free to press his suit.

In person, the Captain was the lady's match, not tall, but broad of shoulder, and justly proportioned in every limb. He had far-seeing light blue eyes in a sun-burned face, and his expression was cool, with a look of incipient mirth. The patches of Harlequin set off his muscular masculinity.

With his name too Dame Rumour had been busy. He had won the lady's heart, it was averred; but he was not likely to win her hand, being an impecunious younger son, tho' of an Earl.

So she passed on in her nakedness, giving no sign of which

lover—if either—should possess her.

A black-avised young fellow garbed like the Devil watched them go. He scowled upon them with a look so lowering I looked again, and recognised him for Mr. Eadwin Maynton, Kingsford's nephew, heir-presumptive to his pelf (tho' not his Dukedom), being the son of the Duke's sister. If Bellona married his Uncle, it would cost Mr. Eadwin dear.

The audacity of the Maid of Honour at the masquerade had been too blatant. She was forthwith banished from the Court. Unrepentant, she had rusticated herself. Accompanied only by her confidential woman, one Ann Crannock, she slipped off to her Aunt Hammer's country house at Linton, near Portsmouth.

Near Portsmouth! Where lay the Captain's ship! No more was needed to inflate the tale.

"The Captain calls daily to press his suit."

"The Captain has taken her into keeping."

"There you are out, the Captain has wedded her secretly."

"You are all misled. The *Dangerous* has gone to sea—the Captain has deserted her."

"And serve her right, the hussy!"

The hussy Maid of Honour was not one to be rusticated for long. Soon she was under their noses again, on the arm of the still infatuated Duke of Kingsford. Mr. Eadwin Maynton moved Heaven and earth to forestall a marriage, but only succeeded in mortally offending his wealthy Uncle. Within a year of that scandalous masquerade, Miss Bellona Chamleigh was Duchess of Kingsford.

Appearing at Court on the occasion, she flaunted herself in white sattin encrusted with Brussels point and embroidered with a Duke's ransom in pearls. She would give the world something to talk about!

They talked with a will. They talked of Captain Hart, jilted on the Jamaica station. They talked of Mr. Eadwin Maynton, sulking at home. They were still talking several years later when the old Duke suddenly died—of his Duchess's obstreperous behaviour, said some with a frown, of her amorous charms, said others with a snigger.

It was at this juncture that one morning in the year '78 a crested coach drew rein in Bolt Court and a lady descended. From an upper window I looked down on her modish tall powdered head and her furbelowed polonaise of royal purple brocade.

I turned from the window with a smile. "What, sir, you have an assignation with a fine lady? Am I *de trop*?"

"You are never *de trop*, Bozzy. Pray remain, and let us see what this visitation portends."

The Duchess of Kingsford swept in without ceremony.

"Pray forgive me, Dr. Johnson, my errand is to Mr. Boswell. I was directed hither to find him—I *must* have Mr. Boswell!"

"And you *shall* have Mr. Boswell," I cried warmly, "tho' it were for wager of battle!"

"You have hit it, sir! For my honour, perhaps my life, is at stake! You shall defend me, sir, in my need—and Dr. Johnson," she added with a sudden flashing smile, "shall be our counsellor."

"If I am to counsel you, Madam, you must tell me clearly what is the matter."

"Know then, gentlemen, that in the winter last past, my dear husband the Duke of Kingsford died, and left me inconsolable—inconsolable, yet not bare, for in token of our undying devotion, he left me all that was his. In so doing, he cut off his nephew Eadwin with a few guineas, and therein lies the difficulty. For Mr. Eadwin is no friend to me. He has never spared to vilify me for a scheaming adventuress. And now he has hit upon a plan—he thinks—in one motion to disgrace me and deprive me of my inheritance. He goes about to nullify my marriage to the Duke."

"How can this be done, your Grace?"

"He has resurrected the old gossip about Captain Hart, that we were secretly married at Linton long ago. The whole town buzzes with the tale, and the comedians lampoon me on the stage as Milady Bigamy."

"What the comedians play," observed Dr. Johnson drily, "is not evidence. Gossip cannot harm you, your Grace—unless it is true."

"It is false. There was no such marriage. There might have been, it is true (looking pensive) had he not abandoned me, as Aeneas abandoned Dido, and put to sea in the *Dangerous*—leaving me," she added frankly, "to make a better match."

"Then where is the difficulty?"

"False testimony is the difficulty. Aunt Hammer is dead, and the clergyman is dead. But his widow is alive, and Eadwin has bought her. Worst of all, he has suborned Ann Crannock, my confidential woman that was and she will swear to the wedding."

"Are there marriage lines?"

"Of course not. No marriage, no marriage lines."

"And the Captain? Where is he?"

"At sea. He now commands a first-rate, the *Challenger*, and wins great fame, and much prize money, against the French. I am well assured I am safe in that quarter."

"Then," said I, "this accusation of bigamy is soon answered. But I am not accustomed to appear at the Old Bailey."

"The Old Bailey!" cried she with scorn. "Who speaks of the Old Bailey? Shall a Duchess be tried like a greasy bawd at the Old Bailey? I am the Duchess of Kingsford! I shall be tried by my Peers!"

"If you are Mrs. Aurelius Hart?"

"I am not Mrs. Aurelius Hart! But if I were—Aurelius's brothers are dead in the American war, his father the Earl is no more, and Aurelius is Earl of Westerfell. As Duchess or as Countess, I shall be tried by my Peers!"

Flushed and with flashing eyes, the ci-devant Maid of Honour looked every inch a Peeress as she uttered these words.

" 'Tis for this I must have Mr. Boswell. From the gallery in the House of Lords I recently heard him plead the cause of the heir of Douglas: in such terms of melting eloquence did he defend the good name of Lady Jane Douglas, I will have no other to defend mine!"

My new role as the Duchess's champion entailed many duties that I had hardly expected. There were of course long consults with herself and her solicitor, a dry, prosy old solicitor named Pettigree. But I had not counted on attending her strolls in the park, or carrying her bandboxes from the milliner's.

"And to-morrow, Mr. Boswell, you shall squire me to the ridotto."

"The masquerade! Your Grace jests!"

"Far from it, sir. Eadwin Maynton seeks to drive me under ground, but he shall not succeed. No, sir; my heart is set on it, and to the ridotto I will go!"

To the ridotto we went. The Duchess was regal in a domino of Roman purple over a gown of lavender lutestring, and wore a half-mask with a valance of provocative black lace to the chin. I personated a wizard, with my black gown strewn with cabbalistick symbols, and a conical hat to make me tall.

It was a ridotto *al fresco*, in the groves of Vauxhall. In the soft May evening, we listened to the band of musick in the pavilion; we took a syllabub; we walked in the allées to hear the nightingale sing.

It was pleasant strolling beneath the young green of the trees by the light of a thousand lamps, watching the masquers pass: a Boadicea in armour, a Hamlet all in black, an Indian Sultana, a muscular Harlequin with a long-nosed Venetian mask, a cowled monk—

"So, Milady Bigamy!" The voice was loud and harsh. "You hide your face, as is fit; but we know you for what you are!"

Passing masquers paused to listen. Pulling the mask from her face, the Duchess whirled on the speaker. A thin swarthy countenance glowered at her under the monk's cowl.

"Eadwin Maynton!" she said quietly. "Why do you pursue me? How have I harmed you? 'Twas your own folly that alienated your kind Uncle."

" 'Twas your machinations!" He was perhaps inebriated, and intent on making a scene. More listeners arrived to enjoy it.

"I have irrefutable evidences of your double dealing," he bawled, "and when it comes to the proof, I'll un-duchess you, Milady Bigamy!"

"This fellow is drunk. Come, Mr. Boswell."

The Duchess turned away contemptuously. Mr. Eadwin seized her arm and swung her back. The next minute he was flat on the ground, and a menacing figure in Harlequin's patches stood over him.

"What is your pleasure, Madam?" asked the Harlequin calmly. "Shall he beg pardon?"

"Let him lie," said the Duchess. "He's a liar, let him lie."

"Then be off!"

Maynton made off, muttering.

"And you, ladies and gentlemen, the comedy is over."

Behind the beak-nosed mask, light eyes of ice-blue raked the gapers, and they began to melt away.

"I thank you, my friend. And now, as you say, the comedy is over," smiled the Duchess.

"There is yet a farce to play," said the Harlequin. "*The Fatal Marriage.*" He lifted his mask by its snout, and smiled at her. "Who, unless a husband, shall protect his lady wife?"

The Duchess's face stiffened.

"I do not know you."

"What, forgot so soon?" His glance laughed at her. "Such is the fate of the sailor!"

"Do not mock me, Aurelius. You know we are nothing to one another."

"Speak for yourself, Bellona."

"I will speak one word, then: Good-bye."

She reached me her hand, and I led her away. Captain Hart

watched us go, his light eyes intent, and a small half-smile upon his lips.

That was the end of Milady Duchess's ridotto. What would come of it?

Nothing good, I feared. My fears were soon doubled. Returning from the river one day in the Duchess's carriage, we found ourselves passing by Mr. Eadwin Maynton's lodging. As we approached, a man issued from the door, an erect figure in nautical blue, whose ruddy countenance wore a satisfied smile. He turned away without a glance in our direction.

"Aurelius calling upon Eadwin!" cried the Duchess, staring after him. "What are they plotting against me?"

To this I had no answer.

Time was running out. The trial was looming close. In Westminster Hall, carpenters were knocking together scaffolding to prepare for the shew. At Kingston House, Dr. Johnson was quoting Livy, I was polishing my oration, and old Pettigree was digging up learned instances.

"Keep up your heart, your Grace," said the solicitor earnestly in his rusty voice, "for should the worst befall, I have instances to shew that the penalty is no longer death at the stake—"

"At the stake!" gasped the Duchess.

"No, your Grace, certainly not, not death by burning. I shall prove it, but meerly branding on the hand—"

"Branding!" shrieked the Duchess. Her white fingers clutched mine.

"No *alibi*," fretted old Pettigree, "no testimony from Linton on your behalf, Captain Hart in the adverse camp—no, no, your Grace must put your hope in me!"

At such Job's comfort Dr. Johnson could scarce repress a smile.

"Hope rather," he suggested, "in Mr. Boswell, for if these women lie, it must be made manifest in cross-examination. I shall be on hand to note what they say, as I once noted the Parliamentary debates from the gallery; and it will go hard but we shall catch them out in their lies."

Bellona Chamleigh lifted her head in a characteristick wilful gesture. "I trust in Mr. Boswell, and I am not afraid."

Rising early on the morning of the fateful day, I donned my voluminous black advocate's gown, and a lawyer's powdered wig that I had rented from Tibbs the perruquier for a guinea. I thought that the latter well set off my dark countenance, with its long nose and attentive look. Thus attired, I posted myself betimes outside Westminster Hall to see the procession pass.

At ten o'clock it began. First came the factotums and the functionaries, the yeoman-usher robed, heralds in tabards, serjeants-at-arms with maces in their hands. Then the Peers paced into view, walking two and two, splendid in their crimson velvet mantles and snowy capes of ermine powdered with black tail-tips. Last came the Lord High Steward, his long crimson train borne up behind him, and so they passed into Westminster Hall.

When I entered at last, in my turn as a lowly lawyer, the sight struck me with something like awe. The noble hall, with its soaring roof, was packed to the vault with persons of quality seated upon tier after tier of scaffolding. Silks rustled, laces fluttered, brocades glowed, high powdered foretops rose over all. Around three sides of the level floor gathered the Peers in their splendid robes.

All stood uncovered as the King's Commission was read aloud and the white staff of office was ceremoniously handed up to the Lord High Steward where he sat under a crimson canopy. With a sibilant rustle, the packed hall sat, and the trial began.

"Oyez, oyez, oyez! Bellona, duchess-dowager of Kingsford, come into court!"

She came in a little procession of her own, her ladies of honour, her chaplain, her physician and her apothecary attending; but every staring eye saw her only. Old Pettigree had argued in vain that deep mourning was the only wear; she would have none of it. She walked in proudly in white sattin embroidered with pearls, that very court-dress she had flaunted as old Kingsford's bride: "In token of my innocence," she told old Pettigree.

With a deep triple reverence she took her place on the elevated platform that served for a dock, and stood with lifted head to listen to the indictment.

"Bellona, duchess-dowager of Kingsford, you stand indicted by the name of Bellona, wife of Aurelius Hart, now Earl of Westerfell, for that you, in the eleventh year of our sovereign lord King George the Third, being then married and the wife of the said Aurelius Hart, did marry and take to husband Philip Piercy, Duke of Kingsford, feloniously and with force and arms—"

Though it was the usual legal verbiage to recite that every felony was committed "with force and arms," the picture conjured up of little Bellona, like a highwayman, clapping a pistol to the old Duke's head and marching him to the altar, was too much for the Lords. Laughter swept the benches, and the lady at the bar frankly joined in.

"How say you? Are you guilty of the felony whereof you stand indicted, or not guilty?"

Silence fell. Bellona sobered, lifted her head, and pronounced in her rich voice: "Not guilty!"

"Culprit, how will you be tried?"

"By God and my Peers."

"Oyez, oyez, oyez! All manner of persons that will give evidence on behalf of our sovereign lord the King, against Bellona, duchess-dowager of Kingsford, let them come forth, and they shall be heard, for now she stands at the bar upon her deliverance."

Thereupon Edward Thurlow, Attorney General, came forth, formidable with his bristling hairy eyebrows and his growling voice like distant thunder.

He began with an eloquent denunciation of the crime of bigamy, its malignant complection, its pernitious example, *et caetera, et caetera*. That duty performed, he drily recited the story of the alleged marriage at Linton as, he said, his witnesses would prove it.

"And now, my Lords, we will proceed to call our witnesses. Call Margery Amys."

Mrs. Amys, the clergyman's widow, was a tall stick of a woman well on in years, wearing rusty bombazine and an old-fashioned lawn cap tied under her nutcracker chin. She put a gnarled hand on the Bible the clerk held out to her.

"Hearken to your oath. The evidence you shall give on behalf of our sovereign lord the King's majesty, against Bellona duchess-dowager of Kingsford, shall be the truth, the whole truth, and nothing but the truth, so help you God."

The old dame mumbled something, and kissed the book. But when the questions began, she spoke up in a rusty screech, and graphically portrayed a clandestine marriage at Linton church in the year '71.

"They came by night, nigh upon midnight, to the church at Linton, and desired of the late Mr. Amys that he should join them two in matrimony."

Q. Which two?

A. Them two, Captain Hart and Miss Bellona Chamleigh.

Q. And did he so unite them?

A. He did so, and I stood by and saw it done.

Q. Who was the bride?

A. Miss Bellona Chamleigh.

Q. Say if you see her now present?

A. (pointing) That's her, her in white.

The Duchess stared her down contemptuously.

As I rose to cross-examine, I sent a glance to the upper tier, where sat Dr. Johnson. He was writing, and frowning as he wrote; but no guidance came my way. Making up with a portentous scowl for what I lacked in matter, I began:

Q. It was dark at midnight?

A. Yes, sir, mirk dark.

Q. Then, Mrs. Amys, how did you see the bride to know her again?

A. Captain Hart lighted a wax taper, and put it in his hat, and by that light they were married, and so I know her again.

Q. (probing) You know a great deal, Madam. What has Mr. Eadwin Maynton given you to appear on his behalf?

A. Nothing, sir.

Q. What has he promised you?

A. Nothing neither.

Q. Then why are you here?

A. (piously) I come for the sake of truth and justice, sir.

And on that sanctimonious note, I had to let her go.

"Call Ann Crannock!"

Ann Crannock approached in a flurry of curtseys, scattering smiles like sweetmeats. The erstwhile confidential woman was a plump, round, rosy little thing, of a certain age, but still pleasing, carefully got up like a stage milkmaid in snowy kerchief and pinner. She mounted the platform with a bounce, and favoured the Attorney General with a beaming smile. The Duchess hissed something between her teeth. It sounded like "Judas!"

The clerk with his Bible hastily stepped between. Ann Crannock took the oath, smiling broadly, and Thurlow commenced his interrogation:

Q. You were the prisoner's woman?

A. Yes, sir, and I loved her like my own child.

Q. You saw her married to Captain Hart?

A. Yes, sir, the pretty dears, they could not wait for very lovesickness.

Q. That was at Linton in July of the year 1771?

A. Yes, sir, the third of July, for the Captain sailed with the Jamaica squadron on the fourth. Ah, the sweet poppets, they were loath to part!

Q. Who married them?

A. Mr. Amys, sir, the vicar of Linton. We walked to the church together, the lady's Aunt Mrs. Hammer, and I myself, and the sweet lovebirds. The clock was going towards midnight, that the servants might not know.

Q. Why must not the servants know?

A. Sir, nobody was to know, lest the Captain's father the Earl cut him off for marrying a lady without any fortune.

Q. Well, and they were married by Mr. Amys. Did he give a certificate of the marriage?

A. Yes, sir, he did, he wrote it out with his own hand, and I signed for a witness. I was happy for my lady from my heart.

Q. You say the vicar gave a certificate. (Thurlow sharply raised his voice as he whipped out a paper.) Is this it?

A. (clasping her hands and beaming with pleasure) O sir, that is it. See, there is my handwriting. Well I mind how the Captain kissed it and put it in his bosom to keep!

" 'Tis false!"

The Duchess was on her feet in a rage. For a breath she stood so in her white sattin and pearls; then she sank down in a swoon. Her attendants instantly raised her and bore her out among them. I saw the little apothecary hopping like a grasshopper on the fringes, flourishing his hartshorn bottle.

The Peers were glad enough of an excuse for a recess, and so was I. I pushed my way to the lobby in search of Dr. Johnson. I was furious.

"The jade has lied to us!" I cried as I beheld him. "I'll throw up my brief!"

"You will do well to do so," murmured the Attorney General at my elbow. He still held the fatal marriage lines.

"Pray, Mr. Thurlow, give me a sight of that paper," requested Dr. Johnson.

"Dr. Johnson's wish is my command," said Thurlow with a bow: he had a particular regard for the burly philosopher.

Dr. Johnson held the paper to the light, peering so close with his near-sighted eyes that his lashes almost brushed the surface.

"Aye, sir, look close," smiled Thurlow. " 'Tis authentick, I assure you. I have particular reason to know."

"Then there's no more to be said."

Thurlow took the paper, bowed, and withdrew.

All along I had been conscious of another legal figure hovering

near. Now I looked at him directly. He was hunched into a voluminous advocate's gown, and topped by one of Mr. Tibbs's largest
wigs; but there was no missing those ice-blue eyes.

"Captain Hart! You here?"

"I had a mind to see the last of my widow," he said sardonically.
"I see she is in good hands."

"But to come here! Will you not be recognised, and detained, and
put on the stand?"

"What Peers detain a Peer? No, sir. While the House sits, I cannot
be summoned: and when it rises, all is over. Bellona may be easy;
I shan't peach. Adieu."

"Stay, sir—" But he was gone.

After an hour, the Duchess of Kingsford returned to the hall with
her head held high, and inquiry resumed. There was not much more
harm Mistress Crannock could do. She was led once more to repeat:
she saw them wedded, the sweet dears, and she signed the marriage
lines, and that was the very paper now in Mr. Thurlow's hand.

"You say this is the paper? That is conclusive, I think. (smiling)
You may cross-examine, Mr. Boswell."

Ann Crannock smiled at me, and I smiled back, as I began:

Q. You say, Mistress Crannock, that you witnessed this marriage?

A. Yes, sir.

Q. And then and there you signed the marriage lines?

A. Yes, sir.

Q. On July 3, 1771?

A. Yes, sir.

Q. Think well, did you not set your hand to it at some subsequent
date?

A. No, sir.

Q. Perhaps to oblige Mr. Eadwin Maynton?

A. No, sir, certainly not. I saw them wedded, and signed forthwith.

Q. Then I put it to you: *How did you on July 3, 1771, set your
hand to a piece of paper that was not made at the manufactory until
the year 1774?*

Ann Crannock turned red, then pale, opened her mouth, but no
sound came. "Can you make that good, Mr. Boswell?" demanded
Thurlow.

"Yes, sir, if I may call a witness, tho' out of order."

"Aye, call him—let's hear him—" the answer swept the Peers' benches. Their Lordships cared nothing for order.

"I call Dr. Samuel Johnson."

Dr. Johnson advanced and executed one of his stately obeisances.

"You must know, my Lords and gentlemen," he began, "that I have dealt with paper for half a century, and I have friends among the paper-makers. Paper, my Lords, is made by grinding up rag, and wetting it, and laying it to dry upon a grid of wires. Now he who has a mind to sign his work, twists his mark in wire and lays it in, for every wire leaves its impression, which is called a watermark. With such a mark, in the shape of an S, did my friend Sully the paper-maker sign the papers he made before the year '74.

"But in that year, my Lords, he took his son into partnership, and from thenceforth marked his paper with a double S. I took occasion this afternoon to confirm the date, 1774, from his own mouth. Now, my Lords, if you take this supposed document of 1771 (taking it in his hand) and hold it thus to the light, you may see in it the double S watermark: which, my Lords, proves this so-called conclusive evidence to be a forgery, and Ann Crannock a liar!"

The paper passed from hand to hand, and the Lords began to seethe.

"The Question! The Question!" was the cry. The clamour persisted, and did not cease until perforce the Lord High Steward arose, bared his head, and put the question:

"Is the prisoner guilty of the felony whereof she stands indicted, or not guilty?"

In a breathless hush, the first of the barons rose in his ermine. Bellona lifted her chin. The young nobleman put his right hand upon his heart and pronounced clearly:

"Not guilty, upon my honour!"

So said each and every Peer:

"Not guilty, upon my honour!"

My client was acquitted!

At her Grace's desire, I had provided means whereby, at the trial's end, come good fortune or ill, the Duchess might escape the press of the populace. A plain coach waited at a postern door, and thither, her white satin and pearls muffled in a capuchin, my friend and I hurried her.

Quickly she mounted the step and slipped inside. Suddenly she screamed. Inside the coach a man awaited us. Captain Aurelius

Hart in his blue coat lounged there at his ease.

"Nay, sweet wife, my wife no more," he murmured softly, "do not shun me, for now that you are decreed to be another man's widow, I mean to woo you anew. I have prepared a small victory feast at my lodgings, and I hope your friends will do us the honour of partaking of it with us."

"Victory!" breathed Bellona as the coach moved us off. "How could you be so sure of victory?"

"Because," said Dr. Johnson, "he brought it about. Am I not right, sir?"

"Why, sir, as to that—"

"As to that, sir, there is no need to prevaricate. I learned this afternoon from Sully the paper-maker that a seafaring man resembling Captain Hart had been at him last week to learn about papers, and had carried away a sheet of the double S kind. It is clear that it was you, sir, who foisted upon Eadwin Maynton the forgery that, being exposed, defeated him."

All this while the coach was carrying us onward. In the shadowy interior, Captain Hart frankly grinned.

" 'Twas easy, sir. Mr. Eadwin was eager, and quite without scruple, and why should he doubt a paper that came from the hands of the wronged husband? How could he guess that I had carefully contrived it to ruin his cause?"

"It was a bad cause," said Dr. Johnson, "and he is well paid for his lack of scruple."

"But, Captain Hart," I put in, "how could you be sure that we would detect the forgery and proclaim it?"

"To make sure, I muffled up and ventured into the lobby. I was prepared to slip a billet into Mr. Boswell's pocket; but when I saw Dr. Johnson studying the watermark, I knew that I need not interfere further."

We were at the door. Captain Hart lifted down the lady, and with his arm around her guided her up the stair. She yielded mutely, as in a daze.

In the withdrawing room a pleasing cold regale awaited us, but Dr. Johnson was in no hurry to go to table. There was still something on his mind.

"Then, sir, before we break bread, satisfy me of one more thing. How came Ann Crannock to say the handwriting was hers?"

"Because, sir," said Captain Hart with a self-satisfied look, "it was so like her own. I find I have a pretty turn for forgery."

"That I can believe, sir. But where did you find an exemplar to fashion your forgery after?"

"Why, sir, I—" The Captain darted a glance from face to face. "You are keen, sir. There could only be one document to forge after—and here it is (producing a folded paper from his pocket). Behold the true charter of my happiness!"

I regarded it thunderstruck. A little faded as to ink, a little frayed at the edges, there lay before us a marriage certificate in due form, between Miss Bellona Chamleigh, spinster, and Captain Aurelius Hart, bachelor, drawn up in the Reverend Mr. Amys's wavering hand, and attested by Sophie Hammer and Ann Crannock, July 3, 1771!

"So, Madam," growled Dr. Johnson, "you were guilty after all!"

"Oh, no, sir! 'Twas no marriage, for the Captain was recalled to his ship, and sailed for the Jamaica station, without—without—"

"Without making you in deed and in truth my own," smiled Captain Hart.

At this specimen of legal reasoning, Dr. Johnson shook his head in bafflement, the bigamous Duchess looked as innocent as possible, and Captain Hart laughed aloud.

" 'Twas an unfortunate omission," he said, "whence flow all our uneasinesses, and I shall rectify it this night, my Countess consenting. What do you say, my dear?"

For the first time the Duchess looked directly at him. In spite of herself she blushed, and the tiny pox mark beside her lip deepened in a smile.

"Why, Aurelius, since you have saved me from branding or worse, what can I say but yes?"

"Then at last," cried the Captain, embracing her, "you shall be well and truly bedded, and so farewell to the Duchess of Kingsford!"

It seemed the moment to withdraw. As we descended, we heard them laughing together.

"Never look so put about, Bozzy," murmured Dr. Johnson on the stair. "You have won your case; justice, tho' irregularly, is done; the malignancy of Eadwin Maynton has been defeated; and as to the two above—they deserve each other."

Patricia McGerr

The   Writing   on   the   Wall

*According to available data there have been 24 short stories, 4
novelets, and one novel about Selena Mead whom "The Wall
Street Journal" once called (quite inaccurately) "the female
James Bond." Here is the 25th short story about Selena—a clever
code story. Can you solve the code? The solution is both surprising
and satisfying—always a happy combination . . .*

66 **Y**ou're good at puzzles." Hugh joined Selena at a corner table
in the teashop and placed a slip of paper down in front of her.
"Maybe you can solve this one."

On the paper, which appeared to have been torn from a notebook,
was a series of numbers separated by slanted lines:

81/61/10/26 50/62/13/63 25/137 183/3/5/200
6/17/7 141/8/30 74/65/20/78

"We're on holiday." She glanced at the paper, then looked across
at her husband, her tone reproachful. "You told me this trip to
England was purely for pleasure, that it had no connection with any
intelligence operations."

"It doesn't. Darling, you shouldn't jump to conclusions."

"It's a very short jump from a coded message—that's what this is,
isn't it?" she tapped the paper "—to a job for Section Q. If you're not
working, where did you get it?"

"You left me on my own while you went shopping," he explained.
"So I dropped in on our local representative. Purely a social call, you
understand. I didn't even ask him about current cases."

"But he told you anyway. Ah, Hugh, I was so looking forward to
two weeks when we could just enjoy being together."

"That's what we'll have," he assured her. "The message has nothing to do with us, or with Section Q either. It's evidence in a routine
homicide, probably a gang killing, and Scotland Yard is in charge.
The numbers are circulating through the intelligence network because we're supposed to be experts on hard-to-crack codes. And I
jotted them down to show you. Thought it would be more of a challenge than the *Times* crosswords. It's already stumped everyone
else, including the computers."

"Where's the person who wrote it?"

"Dead. This morning the police were called to a third-rate hotel near the river. The maid had gone into one of the rooms and found a man strangled with his own necktie. He was registered as John Smith and he hasn't yet been identified. But the hotel employees said he sounded American, so his prints were flashed to the F.B.I."

"And these numbers?"

"They were written in ink on the wall behind his bed. That's the only bizarre element in a pretty sordid case. The clerk told the police that Smith, or whatever his real name was, had been in the hotel for five days. The last time he was seen alive was late yesterday afternoon. The man at the desk said he was in a great hurry and looked scared. He ran up the stairs to his room on the second floor and was followed a couple of minutes later by two men described as big and rough-looking. They banged on the door but got no answer. After a short while they gave up and left. That's all the hotel people know—or are willing to tell—until the finding of the body."

"Presumably the men came back during the night."

"Right," Hugh agreed. "Or sent an executioner. The police theory is that he was a small-time crook from the States who got involved with some local villains and then quarreled with them. Once he was locked in his room, he knew how slim his chances were of getting out alive. So he used the time to compose a message and write it on the wall. It may give the names or a description of his murderers, but it's of no use unless it can be translated."

"It's not a simple substitution code, that's clear." Selena studied the paper. "The lowest number is 3 and the highest is 200. Not a single number is repeated."

"That's what makes it so difficult."

"Unless he belonged to an organization that had its own cipher, the chances are he used whatever materials were at hand. The easiest way to devise an extemporaneous code is to open a book, number the letters from the top, then use the numbers to replace the corresponding letters in the message."

"We're almost certain that's what Smith did. Unfortunately, there's no way to read his message without his book."

"I suppose the killers took that away."

"They took everything. It's clear they didn't want us to know who he was or anything about him. The room was stripped of all his belongings. You can be sure that when the police found the writing on the wall, they made a thorough search for even the smallest piece of printed matter."

"But they found nothing?"

"Not a book, not a magazine, not a newspaper. Even the waste-basket was empty."

"In that case," Selena said, "it's impossible."

"That's why I brought it to you, love." He grinned at her. "In times past I've seen you do the impossible. There's no need to work a miracle on this one, though." He folded the paper and put it in his wallet. "In due course Scotland Yard will solve the murder by its usual methods. Meantime, it's no concern of ours."

The next day, however, Hugh's detachment was abruptly ended. Selena was in the bedroom of their suite changing for a luncheon engagement when he switched on a news program for the weather report. Coming into the parlor, she saw on his face a look of consternation that must have been caused by the news.

"What is it, Hugh? Has something happened?"

"Not yet. But they've identified the murder victim. He was Clarence McKettrick of Newark, New Jersey."

"You recognize the name?"

"Yes, I've heard it a few times in connection with subversive groups and terrorist activities. He hadn't been convicted, but unofficially he's credited with making the bombs that killed two people in a California bus station and blinded a teller in a Michigan bank."

"Then we don't have to be sorry he's dead," Selena said.

In the background the announcer was continuing to give the news. ". . . the United States vice president, who arrived in London last night, told a news conference that Anglo-American relations have never—" Hugh turned a knob, cutting him off.

"An American terrorist in London," Selena said slowly. "You think his murder is related to the vice president's visit?"

"It's a strong possibility. There are several groups who'd be glad to strike at the United States and embarrass the British with one blow. If they hired McKettrick, then broke with him, and he decided to betray them—"

"Then his message will tell us what they were going to do."

"Yes—My God, Selena, we've got to break his code and do it fast." He pulled the paper from his wallet and stared at it fiercely. When he raised his eyes to hers, they held an expression of defeat. "It's no use. This is meaningless without McKettrick's book. And that's probably at the bottom of the Thames."

"He was a professional, Hugh. And he had several hours to think while he waited for them to come to him. So he must have foreseen that they'd clear the room of all his books and papers. That's why he wrote the numbers on the wall. He wanted to make sure the authorities got his message. And there was no point in doing that unless he believed someone would be able to read it. You said they took everything belonging to him, but what about the items that came with the room? He might have used a phone book. Or a menu. Even a laundry list."

"It's a very seedy establishment," he told her. "No phones. No other services."

"Were there any notices posted on the wall? Things like turning out the lights or what to do in case of fire?"

"Not a thing. I hate to shoot down all your ideas, Selena, but there was not a single written or printed word in the entire place. Not even a sign he could see from his window."

"The man was in deep trouble." Selena frowned, thinking aloud. "He expected to die and he decided to leave a message. A warning probably. He intended it to be found by the police and he wanted them to figure out its meaning. So there has to be a key and it must be available."

"Good logic," Hugh conceded, "but it doesn't change the numbers into letters. This isn't a parlor game any more. With every hour that passes, the danger increases."

"Perhaps it's something he knew by heart. A favorite poem or quotation. Can they trace his close friends, find one who can tell them if there was anything he used to sing or recite? Like 'Mary had a little lamb' or 'To be or not to be'."

"It's a cinch it won't be the 'Star-Spangled Banner.' " He started toward the phone. "It's a long shot, but it's worth checking. Trouble is, it will take time, something we probably haven't got."

"Then it's not the answer. He wouldn't let his warning hang by so weak a thread. The key must be in our hands now. That's how he planned it. Wait, Hugh!"

The note of excitement in her voice stopped him with his hand on the instrument. "You've thought of something?" he asked.

"What you said—about the 'Star-Spangled Banner'—"

"I only meant that McKettrick's record doesn't give him a high score for patriotism."

"I think I have it." She took the paper from his hand and started toward the bedroom. "I'll check it out and be right back."

It was less than three minutes before she returned and gave the paper to Hugh. A letter was printed above each number:

P L A N   B L O W   U P   V E E P
81/61/10/26 50/62/13/63 25/137 183/3/5/200
C A R   W E D   N O O N
6/17/7 141/8/30 74/65/20/78

"Wednesday noon!" Hugh exclaimed. "That's—" He checked his watch. "That's eighteen minutes away. Are you sure? But of course you are."

He lifted the phone and gave the operator a number, adding, "Hurry, please, it's an emergency." In a few seconds he was connected. "QA," he identified himself. "Where's the vice president?" He listened, nodded his satisfaction. "Good. Don't let him leave the embassy until there's an all clear. McKettrick's message says, PLAN BLOW UP VEEP CAR WEDNESDAY NOON. Get the chauffeur out, block the street, and notify the bomb squad. Understood?"

He put down the phone and took a long slow breath.

"It will be all right," he answered Selena's unspoken question. "The limousine is waiting at the door and the vice president is scheduled to leave at 11:55 for lunch at Ten Downing. He'll be a little late, that's all. Come on, let's go see what's happening."

They could not discuss what was uppermost in both their minds in the taxi and they were too tense to talk trivia. So they rode the short distance in silence. The driver came to a stop near Grosvenor Square.

"This is as far as I can take you, sir." He gestured toward a policeman who was diverting traffic to a side street. "There must be some kind of demonstration at your embassy."

"This is fine." Hugh paid him and they got out. Suddenly there was a loud explosion followed by the crash and clang of falling metal. They hurried forward and got close enough to see the demolished embassy car before being stopped by another policeman.

"Sorry, sir, this street is temporarily closed. The orders are not to let anyone through except on official business." He spoke to them and, over their heads, to a crowd converging from several directions. "Move along, please. Everybody please keep moving."

"Was anyone hurt?" Selena asked him.

"No, the vehicle was unoccupied." He answered politely, then raised his voice again. "Ladies and gentlemen, will you please go about your ordinary business. There is nothing to see but a damaged motor car. No casualties. Please don't block the passage."

Obediently the onlookers turned away. For Londoners a bomb was no longer a novelty.

"Let's go." Hugh tucked Selena's hand inside his arm. "We curious tourists shouldn't interfere with the police in the performance of their duties."

They walked across the Square and stopped near the statue of F.D.R. "And now," Hugh said, "you can tell me how you found the key to McKettrick's code."

"It suddenly struck me when you mentioned the national anthem," she answered. "As an American in a foreign country, there was one document he had to have. And even if it was burned to ashes, he counted on our guessing he had had it."

"And that was—"

"A passport, of course." She took her own from her bag and handed it to him. Opening the dark blue cover, he saw that she had lightly penciled, in sequence from 1 to 209, a number above each letter of the statement on page one:

The Secretary of State
of The
United States of America
hereby requests all whom it
may concern to permit the
citizen(s)/national(s) of
the United States named
herein to pass without delay
or hindrance and in case of
need to give all lawful aid
and protection.

Ruth Rendell

Born Victim

Every once in a while a story's opening sentence is so provocative, so attention-getting, so startling that you will drop everything and plunge into reading the story. One classic example is Francis Iles's first sentence in BEFORE THE FACT *(1932): "Some women give birth to murderers, some go to bed with them, and some marry them." Now read the opening two sentences in Ruth Rendell's short story—and plunge.*

Ruth Rendell was the winner of the Crime Writers Association's Gold Dagger Award for the Best Novel of 1976—for her book titled A JUDGMENT IN STONE. *In the "Sunday Times" (London) Edmund Crispin wrote: "Ruth Rendell can now be judged the best woman crime writer we have since Sayers, Christie, Allingham and Marsh."*

I murdered Brenda Goring for what I suppose is the most unusual of motives. She came between me and my wife. By that I don't mean to say there was anything abnormal in their relationship. They were merely close friends, though "merely" is hardly the word to use in connection with a relationship which alienates and excludes a once-loved husband. I murdered her to get my wife to myself once more, but instead I have parted us perhaps forever, and I await with dread, with impotent panic, with the most awful helplessness I have ever known, the coming trial.

By setting down the facts—and the irony, the awful irony that runs through them like a sharp glittering thread—I may come to see things more clearly. I may find some way to convince those inexorable powers that be of how it really was; to make Defending Counsel believe me and not raise his eyebrows and shake his head; to insure, at any rate, that if Laura and I must be separated, she will know as she sees me in the court that the truth is known.

Alone here with nothing else to do, with nothing to wait for but that trial, I could write reams about the character, the appearance, the neuroses, of Brenda Goring. I could write the great hate novel of all time. In this context, though, much of it would be irrelevant, so I shall be as brief as I can.

Some character in Shakespeare says of a woman, "Would I had never seen her!" And the reply is: "Then you would have left unseen a very wonderful piece of work." Well, would indeed I had never seen Brenda. As for her being a wonderful piece of work, I suppose I would agree with that too. She once had had a husband. To be rid of her forever, no doubt he paid her enormous alimony and had settled on her a lump sum with which she bought the cottage up the lane from our house.

She made the impact on our village that one would expect of such a newcomer. Wonderful she was, an amazing refreshment to all those retired couples and cautious weekenders, with her bright-colored clothes, her long blonde hair, her sports car, her talents, and her jet-set past. For a while, that is. Until she got too much for them to take.

From the first she fastened onto Laura. Understandable in a way, since my wife was the only woman in the locality who was of comparable age, who lived there all the time and had no job. But surely—or so I thought at first—she would never have singled out Laura if she had had a wider choice. To me my wife is lovely, all I could ever want, the only woman I have ever really cared for, but I know that to others she appears shy, colorless, a simple and quiet little housewife. What, then, had she to offer to that extrovert, that bejeweled butterfly? Laura gave me the beginning of the answer herself.

"Haven't you noticed the way people are starting to shun her, darling? The Goldsmiths didn't ask her to their party last week and Mary Williamson refuses to have her on the fête committee."

"I can't say I'm surprised," I said. "The way she talks and the things she talks about."

"You mean her love affairs and all that sort of thing? But, darling, she's lived in the sort of society where that's quite normal. It's natural for her to talk like that, it's just that she's open and honest."

"She's not living in that sort of society now," I said, "and she'll have to adapt if she wants to be accepted. Did you notice Isabel Goldsmith's face when Brenda told that story about going off for a weekend with some chap she'd picked up in a bar? I tried to stop her going on about all the men her husband named in his divorce action, but I couldn't. And then she's always saying, 'When I was living with so-and-so,' and 'That was the time of my affair with what's-his-name.' Elderly people find that a bit upsetting, you know."

"Well, we're not elderly," said Laura, "and I hope we can be a bit more broad-minded. You do like her, don't you?"

I was always very gentle with my wife. The daughter of clever domineering parents who had belittled her, she grew up with an ineradicable sense of her own inferiority. She is a born victim, an inviter of bullying, and therefore I have tried never to bully her, never even to cross her. So all I said was that Brenda was all right and that I was glad, since I was out all day, that she had found a friend and companion of her own age.

And if Brenda had befriended and companioned her only during the day, I daresay I shouldn't have objected. I should have got used to the knowledge that Laura was listening, day in and day out, to stories of a world she had never known, to hearing illicit sex and duplicity glorified, and I should have been safe in the conviction that my wife was incorruptible.

But I had to put up with Brenda myself in the evenings when I got home from my long commuting. There she would be, lounging on our sofa, in her silk trousers or long skirt and high boots, chain-smoking. Or she would arrive with a bottle of wine just as we had sat down to dinner and involve us in one of those favorite debates of hers on the lines of: "Is marriage a dying institution?" or "Are parents necessary?" And to illustrate some specious point of hers she would come out with some personal experience of the kind that had so upset our elderly friends.

Of course I was not obliged to stay with them. Ours is quite a big house, and I could go off into the dining room or the room Laura called my study. But all I wanted was what I had once had—to be alone in the evenings with my wife. And it was even worse when we were summoned to coffee or drinks with Brenda, there in her lavishly furnished, over-ornate cottage to be shown the latest thing she had made—she was always embroidering and weaving and potting and messing about with water colors—and shown too the gifts she had received at some time or another from Mark and Larry and Paul and all the dozens of other men there had been in her life.

When I refused to go, Laura would become nervous and depressed, then pathetically elated if, after a couple of blissful Brenda-less evenings, I suggested for the sake of pleasing her that I supposed we might as well drop in on good old Brenda.

What sustained me was the certainty that sooner or later any woman so apparently popular with the opposite sex would find herself a boy friend and have less or no time for my wife. I couldn't understand why this hadn't happened already and I said so to Laura. "She does see her men friends when she goes up to London," said my wife.

"She never has any of them down here," I said, and that evening when Brenda was treating us to a highly colored account of some painter she knew called Laszlo who was terribly attractive and who adored her, I said I'd like to meet him and why didn't she invite him down for the weekend?

Brenda flashed her long green-painted fingernails about and gave Laura a conspiratorial woman-to-woman look. "And what would all the old fuddy-duddies have to say about *that*, I wonder?"

"Surely you can rise above that sort of thing, Brenda," I said.

"Of course I can. Give them something to talk about. I'm quite well aware it's only sour grapes. I'd have Laszlo here like a shot, only he wouldn't come. He hates the country, he'd be bored stiff."

Apparently Richard and Jonathan and Stephen also hated the country or would be bored or couldn't spare the time. It was much better for Brenda to go up and see them in town, and I noticed that after my probing about Laszlo, Brenda seemed to go to London more often and that the tales of her escapades after these visits became more and more sensational. I think I am quite a perceptive man and soon there began to form in my mind an idea so fantastic that for a while I refused to admit it even to myself. But I put it to the test.

Instead of just listening to Brenda and throwing in the occasional rejoinder, I started asking her questions. I took her up on names and dates. "I thought you said you met Mark in America?" I would say, or "But surely you didn't have that holiday with Richard until after your divorce?" I tied her up in knots without her realizing it, and the idea began to seem not so fantastic after all. The final test came at Christmas.

I had noticed that Brenda was a very different woman when she was alone with me than when Laura was with us. If, for example, Laura was out in the kitchen making coffee or, as sometimes happened on weekends, Brenda dropped in when Laura was out, she was rather cool and shy with me. Gone then were the flamboyant gestures and the provocative remarks, and Brenda would chat about village matters as mundanely as Isabel Goldsmith. Not quite the behavior one would expect from a self-styled Messalina alone with a young and reasonably personable man.

It struck me then that in the days when Brenda had been invited to village parties, and now when she still met neighbors at our parties, she had never once attempted a flirtation. Were all the men too old for her to bother with? Was a slim, still handsome man of going-on-fifty too ancient to be considered fair game for a woman who would never see 30 again? Of course they were all married, but so were her Paul and her Stephen, and, if she were to be believed, she had had no compunction about taking them away from their wives.

If she were to be believed. That was the crux of it. Not one of them wanted to spend Christmas with her. No London lover invited her to a party or offered to take her away. She would be with us, of course, for Christmas lunch, for the whole of the day, and at our Boxing Day gathering of friends and relatives. I had hung a bunch of mistletoe in our hall, and on Christmas morning I let her into the house, Laura being busy in the kitchen.

"Merry Christmas," I said. "Give us a kiss, Brenda," and I took her in my arms under the mistletoe and kissed her on the mouth. She stiffened. I swear a shudder ran through her. She was as awkward, and apprehensive, as repelled as a sheltered twelve-year-old. And then I knew. Married she may have been—and it was not hard now to guess the cause of her divorce—but she had never had a lover or enjoyed an embrace or even been alone with a man longer than she could help. She was frigid. A good-looking, vivacious, healthy girl, she nevertheless had that particular disability. She was as cold as an ice cube. But because she couldn't bear the humiliation of admitting it, she had created for herself a fantasy life, a fantasy past, in which she reigned as a fantasy nymphomaniac.

At first I thought it a huge joke and I couldn't wait to tell Laura. But I wasn't alone with Laura till two in the morning and then she was alseep when I came to bed. I didn't sleep much. My elation dwindled as I realized I hadn't any real proof and that if I told Laura what I'd been up to, probing and questioning and testing, she would only be bitterly hurt and resentful.

How could I tell her I'd kissed her best friend and got a freezing response? That, in her absence, I'd tried flirting with her best friend and been repulsed? And then, as I thought about it, I understood what I really had discovered—that Brenda hated men, that no man would ever come and take her away or marry her and live here with her and absorb all her time. Forever she would stay here alone, living a stone's throw from us, in and out of our house daily, she and Laura growing old together.

I could have moved, of course. I could have taken Laura away.

From her friends? From the house and the countryside she loved? And what guarantee would I have that Brenda wouldn't have also moved, to be near us still? For I knew now what Brenda saw in my wife—a gullible innocent, a trusting everlasting credulous audience whose own inexperience kept her from seeing the holes and discrepancies in those farragos of nonsense and whose pathetic determination to be worldly prevented her from showing distaste.

As the dawn came and I looked with love and sorrow at Laura sleeping beside me, I knew what I must do, the only thing I could do. At the season of peace and good will I decided to kill Brenda Goring for my own and Laura's good and peace.

Easier decided than done. I was buoyed up and strengthened by knowing that in everyone's eyes I would have no motive. Our neighbors thought us wonderfully charitable and tolerant to put up with Brenda at all. I resolved to be positively nice to her instead of just negatively easy-going, and as the New Year came in I took to dropping in on Brenda on my way back from the post office or one of the village shops, and if I got home from work to find Laura alone I asked where Brenda was and suggested we should phone her at once and ask her to dinner or for a drink. This pleased Laura enormously.

"I always felt you didn't really like Brenda, darling," she said, "and it made me feel rather guilty. It's marvelous that you're beginning to see how nice she really is."

What I was actually beginning to see was how I could kill her and get away with it, for something happened which seemed to deliver her into my hands. On the outskirts of the village, in an isolated cottage, lived an elderly unmarried woman named Peggy Daley, and during the last week of January the cottage was broken into and Peggy was stabbed to death with her own kitchen knife. The work of some psychopath, the police seemed to believe, for nothing had been stolen or damaged.

When it appeared likely that they weren't going to find the killer, I began thinking of how I could kill Brenda in the same way so that the killing would look like the work of the same perpetrator. Just as I was working this out Laura came down with a flu bug she had caught from Mary Williamson.

Brenda, of course, came in to nurse Laura, cooked my dinner for me, and cleaned the house. Because everyone believed that Peggy Daley's murderer was still stalking the village, I walked Brenda home at night, even though her cottage was only a few yards up the lane that skirted the end of our garden. It was pitch-dark there as we had all strenuously opposed the installation of street lighting, and it brought me an ironical amusement to notice how Brenda flinched and recoiled when on these occasions I insisted she take my arm.

I always made a point of going into the house with her and putting all the lights on. When Laura began to get better and all she needed in the evenings was to sleep, I sometimes went earlier to Brenda's, had a nightcap with her, and once, on leaving, I gave her a comradely kiss on the doorstep to show any observing neighbor what friends we were and how much I appreciated all Brenda's kindness to my sick wife.

Then I got the flu myself. At first this seemed to upset my plans, for I couldn't afford to delay too long. Already people were beginning to be less apprehensive about our marauding murderer and were getting back to their old habits of leaving their back doors unlocked. But then I saw how I could turn my illness to my advantage.

On Monday, when I had been confined to bed for three days and that ministering angel Brenda was fussing about me nearly as much as my own wife was, Laura remarked that she wouldn't go across to the Goldsmiths' that evening as she had promised because it seemed wrong to leave me. Instead, if I was better by then, she would go on Wednesday, her purpose being to help Isabel cut out a dress.

Brenda, of course, might have offered to stay with me instead, and I think Laura was a little surprised that she didn't. But I knew the reason and had a little quiet laugh to myself about it. It was one thing for Brenda to flaunt about, regaling us with stories of all the men she had nursed in the past, quite another to find herself alone with a not very sick man in that man's bedroom.

So I had to be sick enough to provide myself with an alibi but not sick enough to keep Laura at home. On Wednesday morning I was feeling a good deal better. Dr. Lawson looked in on his way back from his rounds in the afternoon and announced, after a thorough examination, that I still had phlegm in my chest. While he was in the bathroom washing his hands, I held the thermometer he had stuck in my mouth against the radiator at the back of the bed. This worked better than I had hoped—worked, in fact, almost too well. The mercury went up to 103, and I played up to it by saying in a feeble voice that I felt dizzy and kept alternating between the sweats and the shivers.

"Keep him in bed," Dr. Lawson said, "and give him plenty of warm drinks. I doubt if he could get up if he tried."

I said rather shamefacedly that I had tried and I couldn't and that my legs felt like jelly. Immediately Laura said she wouldn't go out that night, and I blessed Lawson when he told her not to be silly. All I needed was rest and to be allowed to sleep. After a good deal of fussing and self-reproach and promises not to be gone more than two hours at the most, Laura finally went off at seven.

As soon as the car had departed, I got up. Brenda's house could be seen from my bedroom window, and I saw that she had lights on but no porch light. The night was dark, moonless and starless. I put trousers and a sweater on over my pajamas and made my way downstairs.

By the time I was halfway down I knew that I needn't have pretended to be ill or bothered with that thermometer ploy. I *was* ill. I was shivering and swaying, great waves of dizziness kept coming over me, and I had to hang on to the banisters for support.

That wasn't the only thing that had gone wrong. I had intended, when the deed was done and I was back home again, to cut up my coat and gloves with Laura's electric scissors and burn the pieces in our living-room fire. But I couldn't find the scissors and I realized Laura must have taken them with her to her dressmaking session.

Worse than that, there was no fire alight. Our central heating was very efficient and we only had an open fire for the pleasure and cosiness of it, but Laura hadn't troubled to light one while I was upstairs ill. At that moment I nearly gave up. But it was then or never. I would never again have such circumstances and such an alibi. Either kill her now, I thought, or live in an odious *ménage à trois* for the rest of my life.

We kept the raincoats and gloves we used for gardening in a closet in the kitchen by the back door. Laura had left only the hall light on, and I didn't think it would be wise to switch on any more. In the semidarkness I fumbled about in the closet for my raincoat, found it, and put it on. It seemed tight on me, my body was so stiff and sweaty, but I managed to button it up, and then I put on the gloves. I took with me one of our own kitchen knives and let myself out by the back door. It wasn't a frosty night, but it was raw and cold and damp.

I went down the garden, up the lane, and into the garden of Brenda's cottage. I had to feel my way round the side of the house, for there was no light there at all. But the kitchen light was on and the back door unlocked. I tapped and let myself in without waiting to be asked.

Brenda, in full evening rig, glittery sweater, gilt necklace, and long skirt, was cooking her solitary supper. And then, for the first time ever, when it didn't matter any more, when it was too late, I felt pity for her.

There she was, a handsome, rich, gifted woman with the reputation of a seductress, but in reality as destitute of people who really cared for her as poor old Peggy Daley had been; there she was, dressed for a party, heating up tinned spaghetti in a cottage kitchen at the back of beyond.

She turned round, looking apprehensive, but only, I think, because she was always afraid when we were alone that I would try to make love to her.

"What are you doing out of bed?" she said, and then, "Why are you wearing those clothes?"

I didn't answer her. I stabbed her in the chest again and again. She made no sound but a little choking moan and she crumpled up on the floor. Although I had known how it would be, had hoped for it, the shock was so great and I had already been feeling so swimmy and strange that all I wanted was to throw myself down too and close my eyes and sleep. But that was impossible.

I turned off the cooker. I checked that there was no blood on my trousers and my shoes, though of course there was plenty on the raincoat, and then I staggered out, switching off the light behind me.

I don't know how I found my way back, it was so dark and by then I was light-headed and my heart was drumming. I just had the presence of mind to strip off the raincoat and the gloves and push them into our garden incinerator. In the morning I would have to get up enough strength to burn them before Brenda's body was found. The knife I washed and put back in the drawer.

Laura came back about five minutes after I had got myself to bed. She had been gone less than half an hour. I turned over and managed to raise myself to ask her why she was back so soon. It seemed to me that she had a strange distraught look about her.

"What's the matter?" I mumbled. "Were you worried about me?"

"No," she said, "no," but she didn't come up close to me or put her hand on my forehead. "It was—Isabel Goldsmith told me something—I was upset—I . . . It's no use talking about it now, you're

too ill." She said in a sharper tone than I had ever heard her use,
"Can I get you anything?"

"I just want to sleep," I said.

"I shall sleep in the spare room. Good night."

That was reasonable enough, but we had never slept apart before
during the whole of our marriage, and she could hardly have been
afraid of catching the flu, having only just got over it herself. But
I was in no state to worry about that, and I fell into the troubled
nightmare-ridden sleep of fever. I remember one of those dreams.
It was of Laura finding Brenda's body herself, a not unlikely even-
tuality.

As it turned out, she didn't find it. Brenda's cleaner did. I knew
what must have happened because I saw the police car arrive from
my window. An hour or so later Laura came in to tell me the news
which she had got from Jack Williamson.

"It must have been the same man who killed Peggy," she said.

I felt better already. Things were going well. "My poor darling,"
I said, "you must feel terrible, you were such close friends."

She said nothing. She straightened my bedclothes and left the
room. I knew I should have to get up and burn the contents of the
incinerator, but I couldn't get up. I put my feet out and reached for
the floor, but it was as if the floor came up to meet me and threw
me back again. I wasn't too worried. The police would think what
Laura thought, what everyone must think.

That afternoon they came, a Chief Inspector and a Sergeant.
Laura brought them up to our bedroom and they talked to us together. The Chief Inspector said he understood we were close friends
of the dead woman, wanted to know when we had last seen her, and
what we had been doing on the previous evening. Then he asked if
we had any idea at all as to who had killed her.

"That maniac who murdered the other woman, of course," said
Laura.

"I can see you don't read the papers," the Chief Inspector said.

Usually we did. It was my habit to read a morning paper on the
way to the office and to bring an evening paper home with me. But
I had been at home ill. It seemed that a man had been arrested on
the previous morning for the murder of Peggy Daley.

The shock made me flinch and I'm sure I turned pale. But the
policemen didn't seem to notice. They thanked us for our cooperation, apologized for disturbing a sick man, and left. When they had

gone I asked Laura what Isabel had said to upset her the night before. She came up to me and put her arms round me.

"It doesn't matter now," she said. "Poor Brenda's dead and it was a horrible way to die, but—well, I must be very wicked—but I'm not sorry. Don't look at me like that, darling. I love you and I know you love me, and we must forget her and be as we used to be. You know what I mean."

I didn't, but I was glad whatever it was had blown over. I had enough on my plate without a coldness between me and my wife. Even though Laura was beside me that night, I hardly slept for worrying about the stuff in that incinerator.

In the morning I put up the best show I could of being much better. I dressed and announced, in spite of Laura's protests, that I was going into the garden. The police were there already, searching all our gardens, actually digging up Brenda's.

They left me alone that day and the next, but they came in once and interviewed Laura on her own. I asked her what they had said, but she passed it off quite lightly. I supposed she didn't think I was well enough to be told they had been inquiring about my movements and my attitude toward Brenda.

"Just a lot of routine questions, darling," she said, but I was sure she was afraid for me, and a barrier of her fear for me and mine for myself came up between us. It seems incredible but that Sunday we hardly spoke to each other and when we did, Brenda's name wasn't mentioned.

In the evening we sat in silence, my arm round Laura, her head on my shoulder, waiting, waiting.

The morning brought the police with a search warrant. They asked Laura to go into the living room and me to wait in the study. I knew then that it was only a matter of time. They would find the knife, and of course they would find Brenda's blood on it. I had been feeling so ill when I cleaned it that now I could no longer remember whether I had scrubbed it or simply rinsed it under the tap.

After a long while the Chief Inspector came in alone.

"You told us you were a close friend of Miss Goring's."

"I was friendly with her," I said, trying to keep my voice steady. "She was my wife's friend."

He took no notice of this. "You didn't tell us you were on intimate terms with her, that you were, in point of fact, having a sexual relationship with her."

Nothing he could have said would have astounded me more.
"That's absolute rubbish!"

"Is it? We have it on sound authority."

"What authority?" I said. "Or is that the sort of thing you're not allowed to say?"

"I see no harm in telling you," he said easily. "Miss Goring herself informed two women friends of hers in London of the fact. She told one of your neighbors she met at a party in your house. You were seen to spend evenings alone with Miss Goring while your wife was ill, and a witness saw you kiss her good night."

Now I knew what it was that Isabel Goldsmith had told Laura which had so distressed her. The irony of it, the irony . . . Why hadn't I, knowing Brenda's reputation and knowing Brenda's fantasies, suspected what construction would be put on my assumed friendship for her? Here was motive, the lack of which I had relied on as my best defense. Men do kill their mistresses, from jealousy, from frustration, from fear of discovery.

But surely I could turn Brenda's fantasies to my own use?

"She had dozens of men friends, lovers, whatever you like to call them. Any of them could have killed her."

"On the contrary," said the Chief Inspector, "apart from her ex-husband who is in Australia, we have been able to discover no man in her life but yourself."

I cried out desperately, "I didn't kill her! I swear I didn't!"

He looked surprised. "Oh, we know that." For the first time he called me sir. "We know that, sir. No one is accusing you of anything. We have Dr. Lawson's word for it that you were physically incapable of leaving your bed that night, and the raincoat and gloves we found in your incinerator are not your property."

Fumbling in the dark, swaying, the sleeves of the raincoat short, the shoulders too tight . . . "Why are you wearing those clothes?" she had asked before I stabbed her.

"I want you to try and keep calm, sir," he said very gently. But I have never been calm since. I have confessed again and again, I have written statements, I have raged, raved, gone over with them every detail of what I did that night. I have wept. Then I said nothing. I could only stare at him. "I came in here to you, sir," he said, "simply to ask if you would care to accompany your wife to the police station where she will be charged with the murder of Miss Brenda Goring."

Robert Twohy

Installment Past Due

Robert Twohy's "Routine Investigation" appeared in the April 1964 issue of EQMM and was selected by Anthony Boucher for his BEST DETECTIVE STORIES OF THE YEAR *(20th Annual Collection), published in 1965. The story, to quote Anthony Boucher, "may have created a new genre"—we had called it "a mystery of the absurd."*

Now, from one point of view it's a mad, mad, mad, mad, mad world, and from another it's a world of the absurd, and from still another it's a world of bizarre behavior. It's all in the eye of the beholder, so take your pick—or choose your own word to describe "what life is all about" . . .

The phone rang. Moorman was lying on his back, on the couch. He was a large man, pushing 40, tousled and unshaved this morning in October. He wore a T-shirt, old slacks, no shoes. A glass of white wine was balanced on his stomach; a bottle of it stood on the floor. It was about eleven o'clock.

Moorman set the glass carefully on the floor, reached back over his head, and groped until his hand connected with the phone on the end table. He put it to his head and said in deep gentle tones, "I'm terribly sorry, but your application is rejected."

A moment of silence. Then, "What?"

"You heard me, Kleistershtroven."

"Klei . . . what is this?"

"You *are* Kleistershtroven, aren't you?"

"No."

"I didn't say you were. Who'd want a name like that? Is it a Welsh name?"

"Listen, is this Mr. Moorman?"

"That doesn't matter. The fact is that no more entries for the quadrennial bobsled steeplechase are being accepted. That's on orders from my psychoanalyst. Would you care for his address?"

"This is Mr. Dooney." The voice was suddenly sepulchral.

Moorman said eagerly, "Dooney? Mr. Dooney? *The* Mr. Dooney? Calling *me*? At this hour?"

"Is this Mr. Moorman?"

"It certainly is. Are you really Mr. Dooney? Well, how in the world are you? How's the wife and all the brood? How's Miss LaTorche?"

"Miss LaTorche?"

Moorman emitted rich laughter. "Come on, Dooley, you old lecher, who do you think you're talking to? Everybody knows about you and Fifi LaTorche!"

"Who is this? Is this Jack Moorman?"

"Wait a minute, I'll find out."

Moorman put his hand lightly over the mouthpiece, and made loud braying noises. Then he said into the phone, "Yeah, Dr. Kleistershtroven says there's no question about it—I've been Moorman for years. Days, even."

"This is Mr. Dooney of Affiliated Finance. I talked to Mrs. Moorman on Friday—is she there?"

"Is she where?"

"Is she home?"

"Hold on." He took the mouthpiece from his mouth, turned his head, and called, "Lisa, some character named Dooley wonders if you're home . . . Where? I don't know where. I'll ask him."

He said into the phone, "She wants to know where you want to go, and if she should wear anything."

There was deep breathing. Moorman said admiringly, "You're a terrific deep breather!"

The voice was low and deadly: "I don't know what you're trying to pull here, Mr. Moorman. You've made a loan through us, and I talked to Mrs. Moorman on Friday and she said the payment would be in the mail. And this is Monday, and—"

"Don't tell me—let me guess. There's nothing in the mail, right?"

"I want to know why not."

"I can explain that. I put the check in one of those new self-destructing envelopes and must have miscalculated the time it would take to reach you. It must have blown up in the mailbox."

"That's very funny," said Mr. Dooney, after a long silence. "Your wife promised Friday that the payment would be in the mail."

"Well, that's Lisa—always the cheerful word. You can't blame her for that. A recent Harris survey indicates that too much bad news is given over the telephone."

"You're very funny, Mr. Moorman. But this isn't funny—this is serious. You have an account with us for $784.47. Your September payment of $71.88 was due two weeks ago, and we haven't received it. We have a chattel mortgage on your furniture . . . I'm on the verge of going to the sheriff. But on the way I'm willing to stop by your place."

"Well, Lisa's not here. And things are kind of a mess."

"I'm leaving my office right now. When I get there I expect a check."

"When you get here I expect a disappointed man. But come anyway. I have some white wine and salami."

"I'm bringing Mr. Hector with me."

"That's okay. I have plenty of salami . . . Hector, eh? Do I know him?"

"No, you don't. I bring Mr. Hector when I want to convince someone that paying legitimate bills isn't a matter for joking. Do you understand?"

"Not really. But he sounds like an interesting guy . . . Does he like salami and white wine?"

"We'll be there in twenty minutes."

"Good. Be nice to see you both."

He hung up, and sipped wine, then lay back, placing the glass on his stomach. There was a pleasant smile on his face.

Inside 20 minutes the door chime sounded. Moorman set the glass on the floor, bounced from the couch, ran to the door, and threw it open, calling, "So good of you to come! How are you? It's Colonel Kleistershtroven, isn't it, formerly with the S.S.? How I remember those wonderful seminars of yours! . . . Ah, you brought a friend with you . . . don't I know him from somewhere?"

He had grasped the nearer man's hand, pumped it, and still held it as he peered in a benevolent manner at the other man. The man whose hand he held wore a neat tan suit, and had a pallid, tense young face with harried eyes. The other man was small, narrow-shouldered, balding, dressed in a dark suit; he had tight lips and cold eyes enlarged by thick-lensed glasses.

The first man, grimacing angrily, pulled his hand free. "I'm Mr. Dooney. This is Mr. Hector."

"Don't I know you, Mr. Hector?"

Mr. Hector's lips went tighter, and he shook his head.

"Sure I do! I've seen you plenty, out at the track."

Mr. Hector's enlarged eyes became more so. He shook his head harder.

"Sure, you're the guy." Moorman laughed in a friendly fashion.

"You're pretty well-known out there. Everybody calls you 'The Stooper.'"

Mr. Hector said, in a strained voice, "What are you talking about?"

"He's being funny," said Mr. Dooney. "He thinks he's a comedian. He thinks this is all a joke."

"It isn't a joke," said Mr. Hector, and hefted his briefcase.

"Sure, the old Stooper—goes around picking up discarded mutuel tickets, looking for a winner somebody missed. You get many of those, Stoop? Is it a living?" He made to pat Mr. Hector in a comradely way on the shoulder; Mr. Hector twisted his narrow shoulder away from Moorman.

Dooney said, "The joke's just about over, Moorman."

"Oh. Well, why don't you come in?" His broad frame filled the doorway. "Why are you standing around in the hot sun? Come in, come in . . . How're the wife and all the brood? How's Miss La-Torche?"

He stepped back. Dooney proceeded in, his face stony. Mr. Hector followed.

"Sit down," said Moorman. "Sit down anywhere. Take that chair there, Stoop. Just throw the clothes on the floor. They're fresh ironed, but what's that to you? Like you say—*you* don't have to wear 'em. Just pitch 'em in the corner . . . right?"

Mr. Hector stared at him, then walked away across the room. There was a folding chair near the dining table. He sat down on it, with his briefcase on his knees, and looked at Moorman, his narrow face lowered and his lips drawn in.

Moorman dropped on the couch, crossing his legs. "Where are *you* going to sit, Dooley?"

"Dooney."

"Right, Dooney. Where are *you* going to sit?"

"I'll sit in this chair here."

"There's an applecore on it."

"I can see the applecore. I'll remove it."

"Good thinking." Moorman nodded approvingly as Dooney picked up the applecore by the stem and dropped it in the near fireplace. "That's a good place for it. You must have been raised in the country. Nothing like a frosty night with the wind howling, and the sweet smell of roasting applecores . . . remember those nights, Dooley?" He blinked, and nodded, smiling reminiscently.

Dooney sat down. He said, his voice flat, "This has been very amusing, Moorman. You're a very funny fellow. Now it's time to face some realities that are going to be a little bit harsher. Do you know what failure to meet the terms of a contract means?"

"Not really, no. Do *you* know, Stoop?"

"Stop calling him Stoop!"

"He doesn't mind, he's used to it. Everybody at the track calls him that." He smiled genially at Mr. Hector, whose thin lips became thinner. "Well, Dooley, what's on your mind? What can I do for you?"

"You can write me a check for $71.88. That's what you can do."

"Sure, I can do that easy enough. Is that all you want?" He slapped various pockets. "I don't seem to have my checkbook. Maybe Lisa's got it. Sorry. Well, I'll get it in the mail tonight—okay? As you know, my word is my bond." He smiled widely.

Dooney said, "You think you're such a comedian. Well, here are some facts." His forefinger picked out various articles in the room. "That color TV there, that dining table, those bookcases, the rug, the drapes—they're all going out of here. All of them. Today, this afternoon. And the beds in the bedroom, and the washing machine in the kitchen. When we leave here, we're going directly to the sheriff. We're going to get an order, Mr. Moorman—Mr. Hector is our company lawyer. He has the contract there in his briefcase—the contract you and Mrs. Moorman signed in our office. You're delinquent. You think it's all a big joke don't you? Tell him, Mr. Hector."

Mr. Hector nodded, fished in his briefcase, and pulled out a document. "This is the contract. It's all here, all signed and witnessed. There's no legal way to block appropriation. The furniture and appliances are all covered by the chattel mortgage—and as of now, it all belongs to Affiliated Finance."

"Oh." Moorman rubbed his jaw and looked solemn. "Well, all right. But I should tell you that the TV doesn't work too good. You got to keep kicking it to hold the picture. When you want to watch it, get some guy to stand by it and boot it every ten seconds. Otherwise, you have to keep throwing things at it."

Mr. Hector looked at him with huge glazed eyes. Moorman said, "Before you escalate your terror tactics . . . you claim to be a lawyer?"

"I am a lawyer."

"Anybody can say that. Do you have a badge?"

"A badge?"

"I didn't think so. Also, a real lawyer always carries a diploma."

"I have a diploma in my office."

"And I have a Thompson submachine gun in *my* office. That makes me the neighborhood hit man."

Dooney said, "This is one of his jokes, Morris—don't pay any attention."

"You say it's a joke?" Moorman sat forward, large hands clasped, face intent, brows drawn down. "Is that what I am to you? Is that what all of us are, all us little people who grub in the grime for our washing machines and color TVs, who sweat and strain to make our monthly payments so you and your flunky here can spend the day joy-riding around in your swanky Mercedes-Benz—"

"I have a Pontiac—'72 Pontiac."

"Whatever. Is that what we are to you—just a contemptible joke?"

He whipped his anguished face to Mr. Hector and jabbed a finger at him, his face gone suddenly hard and grim. "I want the simple truth, fellow—that's all I'm asking. You're The Stooper, and I know it and you know it. Your boss here doesn't know it, but—"

"He's not my boss."

"Well, whatever he is to you . . . that's none of my affair, I'm not going to open *that* can of worms. But the point is, you claim to know something about the law—"

"I'm a lawyer!"

"Yeah. You bragged about your famous diploma. Where'd you get it, some correspondence course advertised on a book of matches? Even from there you should have learned one thing—that if you can't prove the signatures on a contract are valid, that contract isn't worth the paper it's printed on."

Mr. Hector said, "Are you saying that these are not valid signatures?"

"Of course they're valid. Who says they're not? Are you implying that there's been a detent to infraud?"

"This is ridiculous," said Dooney. "Stop it, Moorman—we're busy men."

"Yeah. It's almost noon. You're probably hungry . . . Want some salami?"

"No."

"Bet Stoop does. He looks like he could use a good meal."

He went into the kitchen. They heard him whistling.

Mr. Hector muttered, "I've got a headache. This guy is crazy."

Dooney nodded glumly.

Moorman called, "How do you want your salami?"

"We don't. We're going, but we'll be back. With the sheriff."

Moorman came in. He bore in his right hand a four-foot salami. "Stick around, there's plenty. Stoop really looks hungry. Look at his eyes bug out at the sight of this!" He beamed at Mr. Hector. "Really go for salami, eh, Stoop? You want to wait for a knife, or you just want to start chewing?"

Mr. Hector was tucking the contract in his briefcase. Moorman tossed the salami gently so that it landed across Mr. Hector's knees. The lawyer stared at it in wonderment.

"You want one, Rooney? I got a couple more . . . If you don't want to eat it now, Stoop, shove it in your briefcase."

Dooney was on his feet. Mr. Hector stood up too, the salami rolling off his lap to the rug.

Dooney said, "Enjoy your joke. It'll be a lot of fun when Mrs. Moorman comes home and you tell her that all the furniture and the color TV and the beds and the washing machine are gone."

Moorman was quiet. His face looked suddenly strange and still. He murmured, "I wish I could."

He had turned and was gazing out the wide sliding window at the back lawn.

At the far end, near the redwood fence, was a patch of raw earth, recently spaded.

Dooney said, "What did you say?"

Moorman gazed out the window. The two men stared at him.

Dooney said sharply, "Are you all right, Moorman?"

"What?" Moorman turned quickly. "Of course, of course! Why shouldn't I be?" He shook his head and laughed, a low forced note. "Thinking of something, that's all . . . just thinking of something."

Mr. Hector and Dooney looked at each other. Dooney said, "What's going on, Moorman?"

"Nothing." Moorman's smile looked set; he rapidly blinked his eyes. "Look, uh . . . all right, I did make some jokes. It was because I—well, all right, I wanted to take my mind off . . . listen, we all got problems, is that right? They're not all money problems. There's other things, too. I—I'm sorry if anything I said sounded insulting. It wasn't meant to be, it was just for fun—you seemed like good guys. There's nothing, nothing." He shook his head quickly and his stiff smile widened. "It was all just fooling around. Look, how much was that? Seventy-what?"

Dooney said, "$71.88."

"Okay. I got it right here, in my pocket. "$71.88, eh? I was going to give it to you . . ." He pulled out bills, and counted them off:

"Twenty, forty, fifty, sixty, sixty-five, seventy, seventy-one . . . I got no change. Call it $72.00."

Dooney took the money. He said, "Do you have twelve cents, Morris?"

"I've got nine cents. That's all I have." The lawyer was going through his pockets.

Moorman said, "That's okay. That's fine." He pocketed the coins Mr. Hector held out. "That takes care of it, huh?"

"I'll write you a receipt for $71.91." Dooney had sat down again and taken a receipt book and pen from his pocket.

Mr. Hector was watching Moorman. He said quietly, "I suppose your wife will be pleased when you tell her the bill is paid."

"Yeah. She will." His quick responding smile was only a stretching of his lips. It did not touch his shadowed eyes.

"Is she away on a little trip?"

"What? Yeah. Right. She's visiting some relatives." He glanced out the window, across the lawn, then his glance shot back. "Yeah, she'll be pleased. Look, I'm sorry if I said some silly things, but that's the way the mind works sometimes." He walked them to the door. "Everything okay now?"

Dooney said, "All right, Mr. Moorman. Another payment is due in a couple of weeks."

"I know. It'll be there. You can count on it."

They walked down the drive. He watched them.

Mr. Hector looked back, as he got in the car. He saw Moorman watching, his face set, his eyes still.

He said, as Dooney started the car, "Drive to the police station."

"What?"

"He's crazy. That was plain from the beginning . . . That patch of earth was almost raw."

Dooney stared ahead, as he drove through the tract.

"You saw what happened right after he first glanced out there. How he changed."

Dooney nodded.

"And right after that, so anxious to get things straightened out with us. To know that everything was all right—and that we weren't going to the sheriff."

Dooney said, "We got the payment."

"Yes, but . . . the way he changed, what he said, his craziness, his wife not being there . . . and the look of that spaded earth. This was no joke, Ron. Not that look in his eyes. There was a look of . . . I don't know—something horrible, something recent."

His thin lips tightened into a hint of a smile, and his large eyes glittered behind the thick glasses.

He said softly, "The next joke for Mr. Moorman may be a long time coming."

Moorman cut off a chunk of salami, which he ate as he finished the bottle of wine. Then he lay down on the couch.

The phone rang.

He picked it up, gave a deep vocal yawn, and sighed wearily, "Cannonball Express."

"Honey, how are you doing?"

"Good. Fine."

"How's the day off?"

"Terrific. How's your Aunt Letitia?"

"You mean Aunt Charlotte. She's fine, I'll stay a couple more days, I think."

"Okay."

"Good weather here . . . Love you, honey. Say, did you get hold of Affiliated Finance?"

"They got hold of me. Mr. Dooney called."

"You told him I just plain forgot to send the check, what with hurrying to catch the plane and all?"

"Well, not quite. But he got his money. He came out here with a lawyer. They were going to hijack the furniture."

"Good Lord! Is everything okay?"

"Oh, it's great. They think I've murdered you and buried you in the back yard."

"What! What did you tell them?"

"Nothing. I just looked out at the place I'd dug up Saturday to put in some tomato plants. And they got this weird notion."

"I wonder why."

"Well, you know . . . I have a few days off, and don't want to hang around the bars. I'm drinking a little white wine and missing you, and just hatching up a few things to pass the time . . . I expect the cops here shortly."

"Oh, Jack!" He could picture her shaking her head, and her eyes warm and loving and bewildered and at the same time not unhappy, and accepting the fact that he wasn't quite the standard suburban husband. "So you've been playing your games! When are you going to grow up?"

"Never, I hope. Sounds like no fun at all."

"You're almost forty!"

"That's a *canard*. I'm just sexually precocious. I'm really fourteen."

"Six, more likely."

"You could be right. Six is a good age for games."

"What are the cops going to do?"

"Belabor me with cacklebladders and boil me in midnight oil. Then they'll dig up the tomato plot again."

"You could be in trouble."

"Yeah, if you should get clumsy up there and fall into some bottomless pit. So don't disappear. Come home radiant and rambunctious, and we'll have a lot of fun."

"We always do . . . what'll come of it all?"

"What, game playing? Well, in the end you stop breathing, however you've lived—so why not have some fun while you still see the colors and hear the music?"

"Why not indeed?" she said softly. Then, briskly, "All right, Scarlet Pimpernel—what's the scenario, when I get back?"

"You go to the D.A. and do your damnedest to convince him that you're not dead and buried somewhere, and spring me. Then we sue Affiliated Finance for four hundred and eighty million dollars, for false arrest, slander, and general terpsichore . . . Oh, sweetheart, you know something? You won't believe it!"

"I know I won't. Tell me anyway."

"You know that little creep we've seen at the track a couple of times—long-nosed, ghoulish-eyed, sneaky-looking? Picks up the used tickets and looks them over?"

"The Stooper?"

"Yeah. Well, he's Affiliated Finance's lawyer."

"No!"

"You're right—not really. But I think I've got Mr. Dooney thinking he might be."

"That's terrible."

"I know. But I didn't play favorites. I tried to plant the idea in the lawyer's head that Mr. Dooney has a kept woman on the side—Fifi LaTorche."

"You ought to be ashamed of yourself!"

"I know. Why aren't I?"

"Goodbye, Jack. I love you."

"I love you too. Stay out of drafts and don't let Aunt Mehitabel push you off a cliff."

"I'll be home Wednesday."

"I'll be looking forward. Pick me up at the jailhouse."

He hung up, then snapped his fingers. A new thought had come to him.

He'd better hurry—the cops should be here in a few minutes. He went to her bedroom, grabbed a bra and a pair of stockings from the bureau; slid the rear glass door open, ran in the back door of the garage; got his shovel, ran to the patch of earth, dug quickly, shoved the bra and stockings into the hole, and covered them up. He ran back to the garage with the shovel. Then he sauntered into the kitchen, washed his hands, and hummed in a satisfied way.

They would dig up the items, and their interment wouldn't make any sense, but that was all right; the men wouldn't want to have wasted their time in fruitless digging, so they would attach some kind of sinister significance to what they had uncovered. Bras and stockings always convey a message, and are nice to come upon unexpectedly. So everybody would have a good time. And wasn't that what life was all about?

The door chime rang. He ran to open the door. Standing outside were Dooney, Mr. Hector, and two other men; one of the two was a uniformed policeman, the other looked like a plainclothesman.

Dooney looked firm but a little apprehensive. Mr. Hector looked righteous and retributive. The other two looked like men on a job.

Moorman cried heartily, "Hey! You came back!" He swung a jovial hand, to hammer Mr. Hector's shoulder affectionately; Mr. Hector twisted away. "Hey, all right! How are you, Chief?" He was beaming at the policeman. "Y'all come in, heah? I got plenty of salami—no wine left, though. Stoop, do us a favor, will you?" He thrust bills at Mr. Hector, who drew back. "Run down to the store and pick us up a couple jugs of wine . . . No? Okay, we'll have to do without. Come in, guys . . . Lisa," he called, "some guys have stopped by . . . No, I forgot. She's asleep."

Mr. Hector glanced at the plainclothesman. He and the policeman were gazing fixedly at Moorman.

Mr. Hector said, "You told us she was visiting some relatives."

"What? Yeah, sure. Of course I did. I forgot for a moment. Yeah, that's where she is. She's away. Visiting some relatives."

His face seemed suddenly ashen. They were all looking at him.

His eyes slid away from them and looked out the window.

Their gaze followed his. They all stared out the window, at the patch of fresh-spaded earth at the end of the lawn.

Jack Ritchie

No Wider Than a Nickel

Another Henry-and-Ralph murder investigation in the indefinable and inimitable Jack Ritchie manner. Who said the art of deduction (or should we call it the art of inference?) is dead in detective stories? Not while Henry Turnbuckle and his partner Ralph are on the scene of the crime. They pull deductions out of their heads the way magicians pull rabbits out of their hats and cards out of thin air . . .

I surveyed the stricken apartment. "The murderer was looking for something which was approximately the diameter of a nickel."

Ralph looked at me. "Now how do you know that, Henry? Everything's been torn apart. The sofa, the easy chair, the TV, the stereo, everything. Why did the murderer have to be looking for something the size of a nickel?"

We were in the victim's efficiency apartment, which consisted of one room, its Murphy bed, a cramped kitchenette, and a windowless bathroom.

The victim was, or had been, Everett Sharkey. Ralph—having once worked out of Burglary—recognized the body immediately.

Sharkey, who had expired at the age of approximately 45, had spent most of his adult life in prison, mainly for breaking and entering.

The cause of death, according to an informal on-the-spot diagnosis by our medical officer, had been a blow to the jaw sufficiently heavy so as to cause internal brain damage and fatal hemorrhaging.

Sharkey appeared to have been dead two or three hours. His body had been found by a paperboy who had come this Saturday morning to collect for his papers. The boy had pressed the buzzer, and when he received no answer, had—as most of us automatically do in like situations—tried the doorknob. The door had opened, he had seen the body, and run downstairs to the building superintendent.

I led Ralph back to the bathroom and picked up some of the remains of a broken aspirin bottle in the washbasin. "You will observe, Ralph, that this aspirin bottle has been deliberately broken. If the object for which the murderer was searching was larger than

196

what would pass through the neck of this bottle, then why did he bother to break the container to delve behind its opaque exterior?"

Ralph agreed. "What do you think he was looking for, Henry? Microfilm containing the complete details of our nation's response in case of sneak atomic attack?"

"Ralph," I said, "did you know that the entire Old Testament has been put on a single piece of microfilm one-inch square? It is just a matter of a few more years before one will be able to buy the entire Congressional Library, including periodicals, all of it in a package the size of a matchbox. One simply slips the container into a projector, aims it at a wall or a ceiling, and has access to the printed wisdom and folly of the nation."

I examined the neck of the broken bottle. "You will notice that the cap of this bottle has been unscrewed and removed. This further indicates that whatever the murderer was looking for could possibly have been poured out of the bottle simply by removing its cover. However, our searcher *also* thought it pertinent to break the bottle, obviously to make certain that there was nothing still stuck in the dark depths of the container.

"This would indicate that while the object in question might have been inserted easily, it might not have been so easily withdrawn. From which I deduce that while the object had the diameter of a nickel, or less, it could have been a bit longer. And extremely valuable, of course, or why the devastating search and the murder? I rather suspect that it was a piece of jewelry. A precious stone."

"Why couldn't it have been microfilm?" Ralph asked.

"Well, whatever it was, it wasn't in that bottle."

"Why not?"

We stepped out of the bathroom. Sharkey's body was now being removed. Our fingerprint men had departed earlier with what we fairly assumed might be the fingerprints of the murderer. They had been on almost every object, or shred of object, in the room.

"Ralph," I said, "you agree that our searcher went over this apartment and its contents thoroughly. Inch by inch?"

He agreed. "He took everything apart."

"Not quite everything, Ralph. You will notice that in the completeness of his search he smashed all the light bulbs in the apartment. With one exception. One of the *two* bulbs in the fixture over the kitchenette sink is still intact."

Ralph didn't see the point. "So?"

"He didn't break the remaining bulb because it was no longer necessary. He had just found the thing he was looking for inside the bulb beside it."

Ralph considered that. "*Inside* the bulb?"

"Yes, Ralph. The criminal mind has developed a method of detaching the bulb from its stem without causing the glass to shatter. An object may be hidden inside the frosted bulb and the parts are then glued back together. No traces of the operation are apparent to the naked eye—its only fault, of course, being that the bulb will never burn again."

Ralph and I went downstairs two flights of stairs to apartment 1, which was that occupied by the building superintendent. Like all 30 units in the three-story structure it too was an efficiency apartment.

The super, an elderly man, had been expecting to be questioned, and from the aura about him I suspected that he had spent the time fortifying himself with a few drinks.

"Now, sir," I said. "What can you tell us about your tenant, the late Everett Sharkey?"

He crunched and swallowed the last bits of a breath deodorizer. "Well, nothing much. I mean he was just another tenant. As long as they pay their rent on time, I leave them alone." He felt obliged to explain his duties. "I just keep the boilers going, vacuum the hall runners, and collect the rent for the corporation. It pays my rent and a little extra. It's not much of a job, but I get along fine."

"Did you ever speak to Sharkey?" Ralph asked.

"Just to say hello if we passed in the hall or I happened to be sitting outside on the steps on a warm night and he came or went."

"Then you don't know what his job was? Or if he had a job, for that matter?"

"I think he must have had some kind of night work. I'd see him in the daytime when he'd come downstairs to check his mailbox, but then he'd go back up again. I noticed he left the building nights a lot though."

"Have you ever seen him with anyone else? Man? Woman?"

"Not that I remember. He seemed to be pretty much of a loner."

"Did anybody ever visit him in his apartment?"

"I wouldn't know. Once anybody walks in the front door he's got thirty places to go to and I don't know which one it is unless I follow him and I don't."

When we finished questioning him, Ralph and I walked to our car.

When we got to headquarters, we went to Sergeant Brannigan in the fingerprint department.

He had been waiting for us. "We didn't have any trouble tracking down the fingerprints. They're on file locally and they belong to a man named Alfred Brown Carpenter. He got out of stir just about the same time as Sharkey." Brannigan consulted the folder on his desk. "His specialty is also burglary. He's used three aliases so far. David Email Frazier, George Henna Ingerson, and the last time he was caught, John Khaki Larson."

Ralph cocked his head. "Khaki?"

I chuckled. "Don't you see, Ralph, criminals like to play little indirect games with the police. It bolsters their egos. Our suspect's real name is Albert *Brown* Carpenter. And, as you can see, in each of his aliases, he used a color as his middle name."

They stared at the folder and Brannigan said, "Henna and Khaki, I'll accept. But Email?"

"A sickly greenish blue of low saturation and medium brilliance."

Ralph rubbed his jaw. "I see something else too. His real name is Alfred Brown Carpenter. ABC. His first alias was David Email Frazier. DEF. His second, George Henna Ingerson, GHI. And the third, John Khaki Larson. JKL. In other words, he's going through the alphabet."

I acknowledged Ralph's acuity. "So this time Carpenter is probably using an alias with the monogram MNO?" I fetched the white-pages volume of our telephone book and found Sharkey's name, address, and telephone number listed. "Sharkey has occupied his apartment long enough to get his name in this book. I think it is fairly safe to assume that Carpenter also has a telephone. And given the hope that he too has remained in one spot long enough to be listed in the phone book, I think we may assume that his new alias is herein concealed behind the initials MNO."

Brannigan concurred. "But there must be thousands of MNO's."

I began paging. "There are thirty-four pages in this book containing last names beginning with the letter O. And on each page there are four columns containing approximately one hundred names each. Therefore we have approximately 13,600 people in our metropolitan area whose last names begin with the letter O."

I went to work with pen and paper. "And since the letter M is one-twenty-sixth of the alphabet, we would not be too far off to assume that approximately one-twenty-sixth of the first names of these people would begin with the letter M—which would give us, rounding off—about 500 people whose given names begin with the letter M and surnames with the letter O.

"Further utilizing the principle of one-twenty-sixth, we will find that only *twenty* of these 500 will also possess the middle initial N. And if we eliminate women and take into consideration the fact that half of the people in the phone book do not bother to list their middle initials—though I'm quite certain that Carpenter would, since he is so proud of his aliases—then I would not be at all surprised if we come up with no more than five people whose trio of initials are MNO."

I smiled. "Running a careful and patient finger down these thirty-four pages, I would estimate that it would take one person about three hours to check out the O's. Or two people, one and one-half hours. Or three, one hour. Or four—"

"I get the picture," Brannigan said. "I'll see how many bodies I can get working on it."

"Henry," Ralph said, "that was brilliant, but do you really expect Carpenter to be sitting in his apartment waiting for us to find and arrest him? He's probably halfway across the country by now."

"Very possibly, Ralph. However, you will recall that the cause of Sharkey's death was a single blow to the jaw and subsequent *slow* internal cranial bleeding. Now if a man truly intended to kill another, wouldn't he choose a more efficient means? A gun, a knife, a heavy glass ashtray? A single blow to the jaw is very seldom lethal. Therefore, there exists a strong possibility that while Carpenter struck his partner, he does not know he killed him. When Carpenter left, Sharkey could very well have been still alive and breathing, although unconscious."

We left Brannigan and his men to begin their search of the phone book and continued on to the Robbery Division on the third floor.

I spoke to Sergeant Whitman. "Do you happen to have a jewel robbery in which at least one of the items stolen was a stone approximately the diameter of a nickel and perhaps a bit longer? And quite valuable?"

Whitman went to a filing cabinet and brought back a folder. "Here you are, Henry. Three weeks ago a diamond pendant was stolen from a Miss Vivian Patterson."

"Ah, yes," I said. "And the size of this stone?"

"It says here that it was a blue-white diamond, forty carats, and worth about eighty thousand dollars."

I nodded thoughtfully. "It might be just the thing I'm looking for.

However, do you have anything else?"

"Not right now, Henry. High-class jewel robberies aren't all that common any more. This Patterson caper is the only thing we've got open. Only the diamond pendant was stolen. Nothing else as far as we know. It happened while this Vivian Patterson was on a crowded dance floor in her own home."

I grasped the picture immediately. "Someone surreptitiously snatched the pendant from her neck while she was preoccupied with dance and small talk and she didn't notice the loss until later?"

"That's the way it looks, Henry. She lives with her parents in one of those big places on Lake Drive."

I wrote down the address, sent word to Sergeant Brannigan where he could find us, and then Ralph and I drove to the lake shore. We took the sweeping drive past the estates fronting the water until we found the Patterson entrance. Once past the gateposts, we followed the wood-bordered driveway and finally came to a stop in the oval before a mansion of heroic proportions.

A maid answered the door and led us to a waiting room and then disappeared.

Five minutes later an auburn-haired, dark-eyed girl in her early twenties entered the room. "Sorry to keep you waiting. You are the police? Have you found my pendant yet?"

"No," I said. "However, we are hot on the trail. We would like to go over everything which occurred on the night it was stolen."

"Again? Haven't you people gone over that all pretty thoroughly?"

"We are not from Robbery," I said. "We are Homicide. And we would like to hear for ourselves just what happened."

She was rather impressed. "How did Homicide get into this?"

I smiled grimly. "We suspect a falling out among thieves. One of them is now dead."

"Oh? More than one person was involved in stealing my pendant?"

"It appears so. However, I am certain that we will have the surviving culprit in our custody within two hours, depending on how fast the men at headquarters can go through the O's in the phone book."

She studied me. "Two hours?"

"At the maximum. Now, please start at the beginning."

She nodded. "Okay. Well, it's called the Stele of Zevgolatio."

"What is?"

"The pendant. Or rather the stone itself. The diamond is flattish and rectangular, like a miniature tombstone. That accounts for the

Stele. The Zevgolatio I've never been able to figure out."

"Ah, and this gem, possibly minus the chain, would just slip into an aspirin bottle?"

"I guess so. But why an aspirin bottle?" I amended. "Actually it was not slipped into an aspirin bottle, though it could have been. Instead it was secreted inside an electric light bulb."

She looked at Ralph. "Are you positive he works for the police department?"

Ralph looked out of a window. "Not only that, he outranks me."

She turned back to me. "Do you know who has my pendant now?"

"It is in the possession of a notorious breaking-and-entering man whose present initials are MNO. I haven't his exact address as yet." I rubbed my hands. "Now, I understand that this pendant was stolen some three weeks ago?"

"Yes. We were having a party. No special occasion. My parents just like to give parties and I was dancing with Marvin Dotson, when suddenly he stared at my cleavage and said, 'Vivian, weren't you wearing your pendant a little while ago?' And I looked and I wasn't any more."

I nodded understandingly. "So while you were dancing and conversing gaily someone removed the necklace from your person. Did you know all of your guests?"

"Probably about eighty percent. It wasn't that formal a party that you needed an invitation. We just phoned around and people promised to come and asked if they couldn't bring somebody."

"Did you dance with anyone who was a total stranger to you?"

"Probably a half dozen."

I smiled. "There it is. Either MNO snatched the Stele of Zevgolatio while you were actually dancing with him, or possibly while he was dancing with somebody else he managed to jostle you and took that golden moment to steal the pendant. How many people were at this party?"

"About a hundred and fifty or so. I know there was always some waiting to get into the bathrooms. We spilled all over the place. The terrace, the swimming pool. Matt and Nellie Estes even played tennis, but then they always drink too much."

"After you discovered that your pendant was missing, you called the police?"

"Not right away. I thought that somehow the chain had broken and it had dropped to the floor. So we started looking for it."

"You and Marvin?"

"That's the way it started, but in a little while everybody was helping us to look, but we couldn't find a trace of the Stele of Zevgolatio. Finally more and more of us came to the conclusion that it had been stolen. So Dad finally got on a chair and asked if anybody would mind dreadfully if we called the police. Nobody objected, so we did. I think everybody was really thrilled. Being questioned by the police, you know. Better than party games—well, at least most party games. Some of the guests were genuinely disappointed because the police wouldn't fingerprint them. They just took down names, asked a few questions, and that seemed to be that."

"Do you know if any of your guests slipped off before the police arrived?"

"I suppose some of them could have. But it seemed to me that all of them stayed for the fun."

A maid came into the room. "There's a telephone call for a Sergeant Henry Turnbuckle."

Vivian indicated an extension phone on a side table and I picked it up.

It was Sergeant Brannigan. "Well, Henry, would you believe it, there are only four MNO's in the phone book, and three of them are women."

I laughed modestly. "As I predicted. And who is the man?"

"Merriweather Nile Olson."

"Nile? Ah, yes. As in green."

Brannigan gave me Olson's address and I put down the phone. "The noose is drawing ever tighter. Miss Patterson, you shall have your pendant shortly."

"You mentioned two hours?"

"And I shall be true to my word."

Ralph and I left her and drove to an east-side apartment building where we consulted the mailboxes in the foyer. We found a Merriweather Nile Olson listed for an apartment on the fourth floor.

We took the elevator up and pressed the buzzer beside door 417.

Our man, Alfred Brown Carpenter, currently Merriweather Nile Olson, opened the door. He was quite a hulking man in shirt sleeves, and a patch of surgical tape and gauze covered what appeared to be some damage to the side of his head.

A lifetime of experience seemed to make him instinctively suspect that we were the police and we quickly confirmed his suspicion.

He reluctantly allowed us into his apartment.

I came directly to the point. "Your partner Sharkey is dead."

His mouth dropped. "Sharkey dead?"

It was clear that Sharkey's death was a surprise to him. I pressed the attack. "There is no use denying it, Olson. You are responsible for his demise. That sneak blow to the jaw did it."

He blinked. "I didn't mean to kill him. Not on purpose. I just slugged him in self-defense."

I glanced about the room. Where would Olson hide the pendant? "Where is the Stele of Zevgolatio?"

He looked at me. "Huh?"

"It is called the Stele of Zevgolatio," I said. I spelled stele for him, but did not attempt Zevgolatio.

He looked at Ralph and shrugged.

"Very well," I said. "Since you are not ready to cooperate, then I am forced to find it myself and I have a fairly good idea of where you hid it."

I switched on the floor lamp. One of the bulbs appeared to be burned out. "Ah," I said, "what is sauce for the goose is sauce for the gander, eh?"

I turned to Ralph. "You will notice that this bulb appears to be burned out, and there is a very good reason for that." I unscrewed the bulb, grasped the stem in one hand and the glass in the other, and exerted force in opposite directions.

The bulb exploded in my hands.

There was a silence while I examined my fingers. A few small shards of glass, yes, but not deeply imbedded. I was able to brush them out without drawing more than a drop or two of blood. I cleared my throat. "He is more clever than I thought, Ralph. The pendant was not in that bulb." I glowered at Olson. "All right now, we've had enough of your nonsense. Where is it?"

Olson's mind still seemed befogged by the news of Sharkey's death. He reached absently into his shirt pocket and brought forth a small object. He handed it to Ralph.

I leaned forward. "What is that?"

"Microfilm," Ralph said.

The room seemed a bit warm. I stared aggressively at the small roll. "Actually, Ralph, that is *not* microfilm. Definitely *not* microfilm. Offhand, I would say that it is just an ordinary, general, run-of-the-mill strip of negative from a small camera."

Ralph took the rubber band off the roll and held the film up to the light.

"Well, I'll be damned," he said. "In the event of a threatened atomic attack the entire population of Milwaukee will be evacuated to Sheboygan."

I frowned. Sheboygan?

Ralph replaced the rubber band on the negatives and rubbed at his mouth for a few seconds. "Actually, Henry, I really couldn't make out a damn thing. What is supposed to be on this film, Olson?"

Olson shrugged. "I couldn't see anything either. All I know is that the film is worth five thousand bucks to somebody." He handed us a folded newspaper.

I read aloud the item in the Lost and Found section which had been encircled by ink.

> Would like to contact the gentleman or gentlemen who accidently removed the statuette of the six-armed East Indian goddess from my residence on the night of the 22nd. Would like its return. Keep the other things. Four-figure reward. No questions asked. 563-2740.

Olson began his story. "Two nights ago Sharkey and me pulled this little job in the suburbs. You know how it is, you take what you can turn over for a fast buck. You don't waste time with junk. But at the same time every once in a while, you see something that draws your interest, so you take it along just for the hell of it. And that's what Sharkey done with this statuette which has six arms and a ashtray built into its lap.

"We dropped off all of the stuff we accumulated at this garage we rent for just such purposes, and then I drove Sharkey to his apartment, him still holding on to the statuette.

"Well, in this morning's newspaper I saw that item. And I know it's referring to us, because how many East Indian goddesses with six arms disappear in a week?

"So this loser doesn't care about the TV set, the stereo, and the typewriters we took from his place, he just wants the statuette back and he's willing to pay four figures for it. But why? It's just a chalk thing and I never heard of no valuable antique with a ashtray in its lap.

"First I think, is this some kind of a trap? While I'm making the phone call, are the cops tracing the number? But on the other hand, this 'four figures' was tempting, so I went down to the railroad station where they got this bank of ten phones, and I called the number and also kept an eye out in case I suddenly saw cops.

"I made the connection and the man who answers tells me I can keep the TV and other stuff, all he's interested in is the statuette. And he'll give me one thousand bucks for it.

"Since I wasn't born yesterday, I know that there's got to be more to it—including money—than shows on the surface. So I tell him I want more money. We haggle and finally he won't go no higher than five thousand.

"So I take a chance and say 'Suppose I give you the statuette, but keep what I found *inside* it.'

"There's quiet on the line for a few seconds and then he says, 'You found the film?'

"Naturally I pick it up fast and say, 'That's right, I found the film. And I think it's worth more than five thousand dollars.'

"And he says, 'Maybe. But not to you. You wouldn't know where to peddle it. Five thousand is my limit. If I really have to, I can take the pictures again.'

"So I settle for the five thousand dollars and I'm supposed to meet him at four o'clock in the lobby of the main library downtown. I'll recognize him because he'll have a Smile button in his lapel.

"Well, I drive over to Sharkey's place, tell him about the newspaper item, and ask where's the statuette.

"He looks at me innocent and says, 'I tossed it down the incinerator. I thought it was just a bunch of junk.'

"But I seen that blue-eyed expression on him before and I know he's lying—especially when I look down at the wastepaper basket and there is one of those arms peeking out from under a crumpled newspaper.

"So I picked up the goddess and on the bottom I noticed this hole. It's empty now, but the film must have been in there and sealed over with plaster which was a slightly different color from the rest of the base."

Ralph interrupted. "Sharkey also saw the ad and wondered why the statuette would be worth four figures? He examined it and dug out the hole and found the film? Did he also call the phone number in the ad?"

"I don't think so—at least, not before I did or my contact would have mentioned it for sure. No, I think Sharkey wanted to find out how valuable the film really was before he did any dickering. He was probably going to get prints made, but in the meantime he decided to hide the film, just in case I got wise."

Olson sighed. "I could see that arguing with Sharkey wasn't going to get me anywhere, so I began taking the place apart, doing it slow and not making so much noise that the neighbors might call the police. Sharkey didn't like it, but he wasn't going to call the police to stop me either. I was just about ready to give up, when I thought about the light bulbs. And I was on the right track too because when I start breaking them, Sharkey comes at me with the statuette and breaks it over my head. In self-defense I had to slug him. But I thought he was just knocked out. When I found the film and left, he was still laying there and breathing."

Ralph and I took Olson to headquarters for booking. We turned the negatives over to the photograph department for processing and then drove downtown to the library, arriving there at 3:40.

We began our wait for Olson's contact by inconspicuously studying a butterfly collection under glass in the vaulted lobby.

At five minutes to four Ralph dragged my attention from a Long-tailed Skipper (*Eudamus proteus*). "There's our man, just coming in the door."

He proved to be a thin worried-looking man wearing the Smile button in his left lapel.

Ralph and I approached him. "We are police officers," I said. "Are you 563-2740?"

He paled and seemed about to collapse.

I pressed on. "We have put together the whole sordid tale of the mysterious East Indian goddess, the concealed film, and Murder Two."

He swallowed. "Murder? I wouldn't have anything at all to do with anything that involves murder. I'm just an ordinary average spy."

A vision of Sheboygan flashed before my eyes, but then I pulled myself together. "We know all there is to know about this transaction—except for an insignificant interstice here and there. You might as well unburden yourself and tell us the whole truth and nothing but the truth. It will go much easier for you if you do."

He was thoroughly rattled and ready to talk. "My name is Leander Morgan and my boss is Mr. Erickson, of Erickson Snowmobile. I infiltrated Hollister Snowmobile last March."

"Just one second," Ralph said. "Just what kind of a spy are you?"

Morgan blinked. "An industrial spy. What else did you think?"

Ralph rubbed his neck. "Keep talking."

Morgan did. "As you know, snowmobiling has grown fantastically in the last few years. It is changing the face of the nation, especially in winter. Along with it, the competition between manufacturers for the market is becoming keener and keener and it certainly helps a company to know what its competitors are up to. That's why Mr. Erickson had me infiltrate Hollister Snowmobile, our bitterest rival in this area. I got a job as a draftsman, though I'm really an engineer and know what to look for."

"And the film?" Ralph asked.

"It contains the full plans for the new Hollister Sting Hornet coming out next year. It features a new torque reaction slide suspension, a revolutionary fuel injection system, and a pull-out kidney belt. With that information Mr. Erickson will be ready to match Hollister's Sting Hornet when it begins coming off the assembly line."

We took Morgan down to headquarters, leaving it to the District Attorney's office to figure out whether there really was any law against industrial spying and if there was, did we have anything besides Morgan's confession—which he would probably repudiate as soon as Erickson Snowmobile got him a lawyer.

Ralph and I went upstairs to our desk, preparatory to checking out for the day.

The phone rang and I picked it up.

It was Vivian Patterson. "The two hours are up. Where is my Stele of Zevgolatio?"

I cleared my throat. "Unfortunately, through a set of fortuitous circumstances, I have not yet been able to recover it."

"But you took a sacred oath on your badge."

"I don't quite remember it that way."

"It was implied. Now the very least you can do to salvage the honor and word of the police department is to come over here and ask me more questions."

"But I am Homicide. Not Robbery. And the crime of murder has been disengaged from the disappearance of your pendant."

"I'll expect to see you in half an hour," she said, and hung up.

Ralph had, as is usual, been listening on the extension. "Henry, she's right. You can't just cruelly abandon the Stele of Zevgolatio."

"But I'm off-duty."

"Henry, a good policeman is not a clock watcher."

Ralph went home to his wife, children, and supper, while I drove to the Patterson mansion.

Vivian Patterson met me at the door, smiling.

I got immediately to business. "Now we know that you first noticed that the Stele of Zevgolatio was missing while you were on the dance floor. However, that might not be the spot at which it was stolen. When was the last time you remember still having it on?"

She gave it thought. "I was sitting in one of those chairs beside the swimming pool when Mavis Hutchinson oohed and aahed over it a little."

Vivian led me through the house and to the poolside tables, chairs, and umbrellas. "I was sitting right there."

I nodded. "Between the time when you are positive you had the pendant and the time when you first noticed it was missing, was there any incident, any diversion, which might have captured your attention and that of those about you so that the thief could snatch the necklace from your throat?"

"Well, Freddic Kaltenberg fell into the swimming pool. He can't swim, but it was no tragedy, because I could just reach over and pull him out."

"Ah," I said. "Mr. Kaltenberg fell into this pool and you bent over, offered him a hand, and pulled him up and out?"

"I know just what you're thinking. While I was pulling him out he snatched the Stele of Zevgolatio? But that's nonsense. Freddie's parents are Kaltenberg Breweries and he gets a fabulous allowance."

I stared down at the ten feet or more of water, but could make out nothing, refraction being what it is. "Do you have a pair of swimming trunks I could borrow?"

When I was properly attired for the water, I returned to the pool and jumped into it feet first at the point where Freddie Kaltenberg had fallen into the water.

I plunged to the bottom and almost immediately stepped on a stone and an exceedingly fine chain. I stooped, picked them up, and burst triumphantly to the surface with the Stele of Zevgolatio.

"Just as I suspected," I said. "While you were lending this Kaltenberg a life-saving hand, he, in his thrashing panic, somehow pulled the pendant from your throat and it dropped to the bottom of the pool unbeknown either to you or him." I handed her the pendant. "Madam, the case is closed."

She studied the stone and then me—equally it seemed. Then she moved to the edge of the pool and dropped the Stele of Zevgolatio back into the water at the point where I had recovered it.

I frowned. "Now, why did you do that?"

She smiled. "Actually this case is not closed. It is just beginning and Freddie is the thief."

I rubbed my jaw. "But with all that money, why would he want—"

"I've always suspected that Freddie is a closet kleptomaniac. His eyebrows join. Don't you see how fiendishly clever he's been?"

"No."

"First of all he created the diversion by deliberately falling into the pool practically at my side."

"But if he can't swim, didn't he risk drowning?"

"Bah. He couldn't possibly have drowned with all those people about and he craftily knew it. And while I was lending him a hand and sympathizing with his gasping for air, he chose that moment to snatch the pendant from my neck and let it drop to the bottom of the pool."

"Why would he do that?"

"Because to keep it on his person was too dangerous. If the police searched him, they would surely find it. No, the ideal place to hide the Stele of Zevgolatio was at the bottom of ten feet of wavy blue water where it was invisible. And so now Freddie is biding his time, and one day he will return to the scene of the crime, dive into the pool, and retrieve his loot."

"But if he can't swim, how could he dive into—"

"At this moment I just *know* that he's secretly learning how to swim. I'm psychic about things like that. What we've got to do is remain alert. On our toes. We've got to watch Freddie and this swimming pool whenever they are contiguous. We've got to catch this master jewel thief with the goods on his person."

So far Vivian's invited me to her home to watch Freddie twice and three times when he failed to show up.

I wonder if he suspects a trap?

Patricia Highsmith

When in Rome

How would you like it if every time you took a shower a Peeping Tom grinned through your bathroom window? And nearly every time you went out to the street a "feeler," a pincher, sidled close to you? Well, strange things can happen in Rome these days, in this instance to the wife of a rising young government official ...

Isabella had soaped her face, her neck, and was beginning to relax in the spray of deliciously warm water on her body when suddenly—there he was again! An ugly grinning face peered at her not a meter from her own face, with one big fist gripping an iron bar, so he could raise himself to her level.

"Swine!" Isabella said between her teeth, ducking at the same time.

"Slut!" came his retort. "Ha, ha!"

This must have been the third intrusion by the same creep! Isabella, still stooped, got out of the shower and reached for the plastic bottle of yellow shampoo, shot some into a bowl which held a cake of soap (she removed the soap), let some hot shower water run into the bowl and agitated the water until the suds rose, thick and sweet-smelling. She set the bowl within easy reach on the rim of the tub, and climbed back under the shower, breathing harder with her fury.

Just let him try it again! Defiantly erect, she soaped her facecloth, washed her thighs. The square recessed window was just to the left of her head, and there was a square emptiness, stone-lined, between the blue-and-white tiled bathroom walls and the great iron bars, each as thick as her wrist, on the street side.

"Signora?" came the mocking voice again.

Isabella reached for the bowl. Now he had both hands on the bars, and his face was between them, unshaven, his black eyes intense, his loose mouth smiling. Isabella flung the suds, holding the bowl with fingers spread wide on its underside.

"Oof!" The head disappeared.

A direct hit! The suds had caught him between the eyes, and she thought she heard some of the suds hit the pavement. Isabella smiled and finished her shower.

She was not looking forward to the evening—dinner at home with the First Secretary of the Danish Embassy with his girl friend; but she had had worse evenings in the past, and there were worse to come in Vienna in the last week of this month, May, when her husband Filippo had to attend some kind of human-rights-and-pollution conference that was going to last five days. Isabella didn't care for the Viennese—she considered the women bores with nothing on their minds but clothes, who was wearing what, and how much did it cost.

"I think I prefer the green silk tonight," Isabella said to her maid Elisabetta, when she went into her bedroom, big bathtowel around her, and saw the new black dress laid out on her bed. "I changed my mind," Isabella added, because she remembered that she had chosen the black that afternoon. Hadn't she? Isabella felt a little vague.

"And which shoes, signora?"

Isabella told her.

A quarter to eight now. The guests—two men, Filippo had said, besides the Danish secretary who was called Osterberg or Ottenberg, were not due until eight, which meant eight thirty or later. Isabella wanted to go out on the street, to drink an espresso standing up at the bar, like any other ordinary Roman citizen, and she also wanted to see if the Peeping Tom was still hanging around. In fact, there were two of them, the second a weedy type of about 30 who wore a limp raincoat and dark glasses. He was a "feeler," the kind who pushed his hand against a woman's bottom. He had done it to Isabella once or twice while she was waiting for the porter to open the door. Isabella had to wait for the porter unless she chose to carry around a key as long as a man's foot for the big outside doors. The feeler looked a bit cleaner than her bathroom snoop, but he also seemed creepier and he never smiled.

"Going out for a caffè," Isabella said to Elisabetta.

"You prefer to go out?" Elisabetta said, meaning that she could make a caffè, if the signora wanted. Elisabetta was forty-odd, her hair in a neat bun. Her husband had died a year ago, and she was still in a state of semi-mourning.

Isabella flung a cape over her shoulders, barely nodded, and left. She crossed the cobbled court whose stones slanted gently toward a center drain, and was met at the door by one of the three porters who kept a round-the-clock guard on the palazzo which was occupied by six affluent tenants. This porter was Franco. He lifted the heavy crossbar and opened the big doors enough for her to pass through.

Isabella was out on the street. Freedom! She stood tall and breathed. An adolescent boy cycled past, whistling. An old woman in black waddled by slowly, burdened with a shopping bag that showed onions and spaghetti on top, carelessly wrapped in newspaper. Someone's radio blared jazz through an open window. The air promised a hot summer.

Isabella looked around, but didn't see either of her nuisances, and was aware of feeling slightly disappointed. However, there was the bar caffé across the street and a bit to the right. Isabella entered, conscious that her fine clothes and well-groomed hair set her apart from the usual patrons here. She put on a warm smile for the young barman who knew her by now.

"Signora! Buon' giorno! A fine day, no? What is your wish?"

"Un espress', per piacere."

Isabella realized that she was known in the neighborhood as the wife of a government official who was reasonably important for his age which was still under 40, aware that she was considered rather rich, and pretty too. The latter, people could see. And what else, Isabella wondered as she sipped her espresso. She and Filippo had a fourteen-year-old daughter in school in Switzerland now. Susanna.

Isabella wrote to her faithfully once a week, as Susanna did to her. How was Susanna going to shape up? Would she even *like* her daughter by the time she was 18 or 22? Was Susanna going to lose her passion for horses and horseback riding (Isabella hoped so) and go for something more intellectual such as geology and anthropology, which she had shown an interest in last year? Or was she going to go the usual way—get married at 20 before she'd finished university, trade on her good looks and marry "the right kind of man" before she had found out what life was all about? What *was* life all about?

Isabella looked around her, as if to find out. Isabella had had two years of university in Milan, had come from a rather intellectual family, and didn't consider herself just another dumb wife. Filippo was good-looking and had a promising career ahead of him. But then Filippo's *father* was important in a government ministry, and had money. The only trouble was that the wife of a man in diplomatic service had to be a clothes-horse, had to keep her mouth shut when she would like to open it, had to be polite and gracious to people whom she detested or was bored by. There were times when Isabella wanted to kick it all, to go slumming, simply to laugh.

She tossed off the last of her coffee, left a five-hundred-lire piece, and turned around, not yet leaving the security of the bar's counter. She surveyed the scene. Two tables were occupied by couples who might be lovers. A blind beggar with a white cane was on his way in.

And here came her dark-eyed Peeping Tom! Isabella was aware that her eyes lit up as if she beheld her lover walking in.

He grinned. He sauntered, swaggered slightly as he headed for the bar to a place at a little distance from her. He looked her up and down, like a man sizing up a pick-up before deciding yes or no.

Isabella lifted her head and walked out of the bar-caffé.

He followed. "You are beautiful, signora," he said. "I should know, don't you think so?"

"You can keep your filthy ideas to yourself!" Isabella replied as she crossed the street.

"My beautiful lady-love—the wife of my dreams!"

Isabella noticed that his eyes looked pink. Good! She pressed the bell for the porter. An approaching figure on her left caught her eye. The bottom-pincher, the gooser, the real oddball! Raincoat again, no glasses today, a faint smile. Isabella turned to face him, with her back to the big doors.

"Oh, how I would like to . . ." the feeler murmured as he passed her, so close she imagined she could feel the warmth of his breath against her cheek, and at the same time he slapped her hip with his left hand. He had a pockmark or two, and big cheekbones that stuck out gauntly. Disgusting type! And a disgusting phrase he had used!

From across the street, Peeping Tom was watching, Isabella saw; he was chuckling silently, rocking back on his heels.

Franco opened the doors. What if she told Filippo about those two? But of course she had, Isabella remembered, a month or so ago, yes. "How would *you* like it if a psychopath stared at you nearly every time you took a shower?" Isabella had said to Filippo, and he had broken out in one of his rare laughs. "If it were a *woman* maybe, yes, I might like it!" he said, then he had said that she shouldn't take it so seriously, that he would speak to the porters, or something like that.

Isabella had the feeling that she didn't really wake up until after the dinner party, when the coffee was served in the living room. The taste of the coffee reminded her of the bar that afternoon, of the dark-haired Peeping Tom with the pink eyes walking into the bar and having the nerve to speak to her *again*!

"We shall be in Vienna too, at the end of the month," said the girl friend of the Danish First Secretary.

Isabella rather liked her. Her name was Gudrun. She looked healthy, honest, unsnobbish. But Isabella had nothing to say except, "Good. We shall be looking forward," one of the phrases that came out of her automatically after 15 years of being the wife-of-a-government-employee. There were moments, hours, when she felt bored to the point of going insane. Like now. She felt on the brink of doing something shocking, such as standing up and screaming, or announcing that she wanted to go out for a walk (yes, and have another espresso in the same crummy bar), of shouting that she was bored with them *all*, even Filippo, slumped with legs crossed in an armchair now, wearing his neat, new dinner suit with a ruffled shirt, deep in conversation with the three other men. Filippo was long and lean like a fashion model, his black hair beginning to gray at the temples in a distinguished way. Women liked his looks, Isabella knew. His good looks, however, didn't make him a ball of fire as a lover. Did the women know that, Isabella wondered.

Before going to bed that night, Isabella had to check the shopping list with Luigi the cook for tomorrow's dinner party, because Luigi would be up early to buy fresh fish. Hadn't the signora suggested fish? And Luigi recommended young lamb instead of tournedos for the main course, if he dared say so.

Filippo paid her a compliment as he was undressing. "Osterberg thought you were charming."

They both slept in the same big bed, but it was so wide that Filippo could switch his reading light on and read his papers and briefings till all hours, as he often did, without disturbing Isabella.

A couple of evenings later Isabella was showering just before seven P.M. when the same dark-haired creep sprang up at her bathroom window, leering a "Hello, beautiful! Getting ready for me?"

Isabella was not in a mood for repartée. She got out of the shower.

"Ah, signora, such beauty should not be hidden! Don't try—"

"I've told the *police* about you!" Isabella yelled back at him, and switched off the bathroom light.

Isabella spoke to Filippo that evening as soon as he came in. "Something's got to be done—opaque glass put in the window—"

"You said that would make the bathroom too humid."

"I don't care! It's revolting! I've told the porters—Giorgio, anyway. He doesn't do a damned thing, that's plain! Filippo?"

"Yes, my dear. Come on, can't we talk about this later? I've got to change my shirt, at least, because we're due—already." He looked at his watch.

Isabella was dressed. "I want your tear-gas gun. You remember you showed it to me. Where is it?"

Filippo sighed. "Top drawer, left side of my desk."

Isabella went to the desk in Filippo's study. The gun looked like a fountain pen, only a bit thicker. Isabella smiled as she placed her thumb on the firing end of it and imagined her counterattack.

"Be careful how you use that tear-gas," Filippo said as they were leaving the house. "I don't want you to get into trouble with the police just because of a—"

"*Me* in trouble with the police! Whose side are you on?" Isabella laughed, and felt much better now that she was armed.

The next afternoon around five, Isabella went out, paid a visit to the pharmacy where she bought tissues and a bottle of a new eau de Cologne which the chemist suggested, and whose packaging amused her. Then she strolled toward the bar-caffé, keeping an eye out for her snoops as she went. She was bareheaded, had a bit of rouge on her lips, and she wore a new summer frock. She looked pretty and was aware of it. And across the street, walking past her very door now, went the raincoated creep in dark glasses again—and he didn't notice her. Isabella felt slightly disappointed. She went into the bar and ordered an espresso, lit a rare cigarette.

The barman chatted. "Wasn't it a nice day? And the signora is looking especially well today."

Isabella barely heard him, but she replied politely. When she opened her handbag to pay for her espresso, she touched the tear-gas gun, picked it up, dropped it, before reaching for her purse.

"Grazie, signora!" She had tipped generously as usual.

Just as she turned to the door, the bathroom peeper—her special persecutor—entered, and had the audacity to smile broadly and nod, as if they were dear friends. Isabella lifted her head higher as if with disdain, and at the same time gave him an appraising glance, which just might have been mistaken for an invitation, Isabella knew. She had meant it that way. The creep hadn't quite the boldness to say anything to her inside the caffé, but he did follow her out the door. Isabella avoided looking directly at him. Even his shoes were unshined. What could he do for a living, she wondered.

Isabella pretended, at her door, to be groping for her key. She picked up the tear-gas gun, pushed off its safety, and held it with her thumb against its top.

Then he said, with such mirth in his voice that he could hardly get the words out, "Bellissima signora, when are you going to let me—"

Isabella lifted the big fountain pen and pushed its firing button, maneuvering it so that its spray caught both his eyes at short range.

"Ow!—Ooh-h!" He coughed, then groaned, down on one knee now, with a hand across his eyes.

Even Isabella could smell the stuff, and blinked, her eyes watering. A man on the pavement had noticed the Peeping Tom struggling to get up, but was not running to help him, merely walking toward him. And now a porter opened the big wooden doors, and Isabella ducked into her own courtyard. "Thank you, Giorgio."

The next morning she and Filippo set out for Vienna. This excursion was one Isabella dreaded. Vienna would be dead after eleven thirty at night—not even an interesting coffee house would be open. Awful! But the fact that she had fired a shot in self-defense—in attack—buoyed Isabella's morale.

And to crown her satisfaction she had the pleasure of seeing Peeping Tom in dark glasses as she and Filippo were getting into the chauffeured government car to be driven to the airport. He had stopped on the pavement some ten meters away to gaze at the luggage being put into the limousine by the liveried driver.

Isabella hoped his eyes were killing him. She had noted there was a box of four cartridges for the tear-gas gun in the same drawer. She intended to keep her gadget well charged. Surely the fellow wasn't going to come back for more! She might try it also on the feeler in the dirty raincoat. Yes, there was one who didn't mind approaching damned close!

"Why're you dawdling, Isabella? Forget something?" Filippo asked, holding the car door for her.

Isabella hadn't realized that she had been standing on the pavement, relishing the fact that the creep could see her about to get into the protective armor of the shiny car, about to go hundreds of kilometers away from him. "I'm ready," she said, and got in. She was not going to say to Filippo, "There's my Peeping Tom." She liked the idea of her secret war with him. Maybe his eyes were permanently damaged. She hoped so.

This minor coup made Vienna seem better. Isabella missed Elisabetta—some women whose husbands were in government service traveled with their maids, but Filippo was against this, just now. "Wait a couple of years till I get a promotion," Filippo had said. Years. Isabella didn't care for the word year or years. Could she stand it? At the stuffy dinner parties where the Austrians spoke bad French or worse Italian, Isabella carried her tear-gas gun in her handbag, even in her small evening bag at the big gala at the Staatsoper. *The Flying Dutchman.* Isabella sat with legs crossed, feet crossed also with tension, and dreamed of resuming her attack when she got back to Rome.

Then on the last evening Filippo had an "all-night meeting" with four men of the human-rights committee, or whatever they called it. Isabella expected him back at the hotel about three in the morning at the latest, but he did not get back till seven thirty, looking exhausted and even a bit drunk. His arrival had awakened her, though he had tried to come in quietly with his own key.

"Nothing at all," he said unnecessarily and a little vaguely. "Got to take a shower—then a little sleep. No appointment till—eleven this morning and it won't matter if I'm late." He ran the shower.

Then Isabella remembered the girl he had been talking to that evening, as he smoked a fine cigar—at least, Isabella had heard Filippo call it "a fine cigar"—a smiling, blonde Austrian girl, smiling in the special way women had when they wanted to say, "Anything you do is all right with me. I'm yours, you understand? At least for tonight."

Isabella sighed, turned over in bed, tried to sleep again, but she felt tense with rage, and knew she would not sleep before it was time for breakfast, time to get up. Damn it! She knew Filippo had been at the girl's apartment or in her hotel room, knew that if she took the trouble to sniff his shirt, even the shoulders of his dinner jacket, she would smell the girl's perfume—and the idea of doing that revolted her. Well, she herself had had two, no three lovers during her married life with Filippo, but they had been so brief, those affairs! And so discreet! Not one servant had known.

Isabella also suspected Filippo of having a girl friend in Rome, Sibilla, a rather gypsy-like brunette, and if Filippo was "discreet," it was because he was only lukewarm about her. This blonde tonight was more Filippo's type, Isabella knew. She heard Filippo hit the twin bed that was pushed close to her bed. He would sleep like a log, then get up in three hours looking amazingly fresh.

When Isabella and Filippo got back to Rome, Signor Sore-Eyes was on hand the very first evening, when Isabella stood under the shower about seven thirty in the evening. Now that was fidelity for you! Isabella ducked, giggling. Her giggle was audible.

And Sore-Eyes' response came instantly: "Ah, the lady of my heart is pleased! She laughs!" He had dropped to his feet, out of sight, but his voice came clearly through the stone recess. "Come, let me see more. *More!*" Hands grasped the bars; the grinning face appeared, black eyes shining and looking not at all damaged.

"Get lost!" she shouted, and stepped out of the shower and began to dry herself, standing near the wall, out of his view.

But the other nut, the looler, seemed to have left the neighborhood. At least Isabella did not see him during three or four days after her return from Vienna. Nearly every day she had an espresso at the bar-caffé across the street, and sometimes twice a day she took taxis to the Via Veneto area where a few of her friends lived, or to the Via Condotti for shopping. Shiny-Eyes remained faithful, however, not always in view when she came out of her big doors, but more often than not.

Isabella fancied—she liked to fancy—that he was in love with her, even though his silly remarks were intended either to make her laugh or, she had to admit it, to insult and shock her. It was this line of thinking, however, which caused Isabella to see the Peeping Tom as a rival, and which gave her an idea. What Filippo needed was a good jolt!

"Would you like to come for after-dinner coffee tonight?" Isabella murmured to Shiny-Eyes one day, interrupting his own stream of vulgarity, as she stood not yet pushing the bell of her house.

The man's mouth fell open, revealing more of his stained teeth.

"Ghiardini," she said, giving her last name. "Ten thirty." She had pushed the bell by now and the doors were opening. "Wear some better clothes," she whispered.

That evening Isabella dressed with a little more interest in her appearance. She and Filippo had to go out first to a "buffet cocktail" at the Hotel Eliseo. Isabella was not even interested in what country was host to the affair. Then she and Filippo departed at ten fifteen in their own government car, to be followed by two other groups of Americans, Italians, and a couple of Germans. Isabella and Filippo were earlier than the rest, and of course Luigi and Elisabetta already had the long bar-table well equipped with bottles, glasses, and ice,

and platters of little sausages stuck with toothpicks. Why hadn't
she told Shiny-Eyes eleven o'clock?

But Shiny-Eyes did the right thing, and arrived just after eleven.
Isabella's heart gave a dip as he entered through the living-room
door, which had been opened by Luigi. The room was already
crowded with guests, most of them standing up with drinks, chattering away, quite occupied, and giving Shiny-Eyes not a glance.
Luigi was seeing to his drink. At least he was wearing a dark suit,
a limp but white shirt, and a tie.

Isabella chatted with a large American and his wife. Isabella
hated speaking English, but she could hold her own in it. Filippo,
Isabella saw, had left his quartet of diplomats and was now concentrating on two pretty women; he was standing before them while
they sat on the sofa, as if mesmerizing them by his tall elegant
presence, his stream of bilge. The women were German, secretaries
or girl friends. Isabella almost sneered.

Shiny-Eyes was nursing his Scotch against the wall by the bar-
table, and Isabella drifted over on the pretense of replenishing her
champagne. She glanced at him, and he came closer. To Isabella he
seemed the only vital person in the room. She had no intention of
speaking to him, even of looking directly at him, and concentrated
on pouring champagne from a small bottle.

"Good evening, signora," he said in English.

"Good evening. And what is your name?" she asked in Italian.

"Ugo."

Isabella turned gracefully on her heel and walked away. For the
next minutes she was a dutiful hostess, circulating, chatting, making sure that everyone had what he or she wanted. People were
relaxing, laughing more loudly. Even as she spoke to someone, Isabella looked in Ugo's direction and saw him in the act of pocketing
a small Etruscan statue. She drifted back across the room toward
him. "You put that back!" she said between her teeth, and left him.

Ugo put it back, flustered, but not seriously.

Filippo had caught the end of this, Isabella speaking to Ugo.
Filippo rose to find a new drink, got it, and approached Isabella.
"Who's the dark type over there? Do you know him?"

Isabella shrugged. "Someone's bodyguard, perhaps?"

The evening ended quietly, Ugo slipping out unnoticed even by
Isabella. When Isabella turned back to the living room expecting
to see Filippo, she found the room empty. "Filippo?" she called,
thinking he might be in the bedroom.

Filippo had evidently gone out with some of the guests, and Isabella was sure he was going to see one of the blondes tonight. Isabella helped herself to a last champagne, something she rarely did. She was not satisfied with the evening after all.

When she awakened the next morning, at the knock of Elisabetta with the breakfast tray, Filippo was not beside her in bed. Elisabetta, of course, made no comment. While Isabella was still drinking caffè latte, Filippo arrived. All-night talk with the Americans, he explained, and now he had to change his clothes.

"Is the blonde in the blue dress American? I thought she and the other blonde were Germans," Isabella said.

Now the row was on. So what, was Filippo's attitude.

"What kind of life is it for *me*?" Isabella screamed. "Am I nothing but an *object*? Just some female figure in the house—always here, to say *buona sera*—and smile!"

"Where would I be without you? Every man in government service needs a wife," replied Filippo, using up the last of his patience. "And you're a very good hostess, Isabella, really!"

Isabella roared like a lioness. "Hostess! I detest the word! And your girl friends—*in this house*—"

"Never!" Filippo replied proudly.

"Two of them! How many have you now?"

"Am I the only man in Rome with a mistress or two?" He had recovered his cool and intended to stand up for his rights. After all, he was supporting Isabella and in fine style, and their daughter Susanna too. "If you don't like it—" But Filippo stopped.

More than ever, that day, Isabella wanted to see Ugo. She went out around noon, and stopped for an americano at the little bar-caffè. This time she sat at a table. Ugo came in when she had nearly finished her drink. Faithful, he was. Or psychic. Maybe both. Without looking at him, she knew that he had seen her.

She left some money on the table and walked out. Ugo followed. She walked in an opposite direction from the palazzo across the street, knowing that he knew she expected him to follow her.

When they were safely around another corner, Isabella turned. "You did quite well last night, except for the attempted—"

"Ah, sorry, signora!" he interrupted, grinning.

"What are you by profession—if I dare to ask?"

"Journalist, sometimes. Photographer. You know, a free-lance."

"Would you like to make some money?"

He wriggled, and grinned wider. "To spend on you, signora, yes."

"Never mind the rubbish." He really was an untidy specimen, back in his old shoes again, dirty sweater under his jacket, and when had he last had a bath? Isabella looked around to see if anyone might be observing them. "Would you be interested in kidnaping a rich man?"

Ugo hesitated only two seconds. "Why not?" His black eyebrows had gone up. "Tell me. Who?"

"My husband. You will need a friend with a gun and a car."

Ugo indulged in another grin, but his attitude was attentive.

Isabella had thought out her plans that morning. She told Ugo that she and Filippo wanted to buy a house outside of Rome, and she had the names of a few real-estate agents. She could make an appointment with one for Friday morning, for instance, at nine o'clock. Isabella said she would make herself "indisposed" that morning, so Filippo would have to go alone. But Ugo must be at the palazzo with a car a little before nine.

"I must make the hour the same, otherwise Filippo will suspect me," Isabella explained. "These agents are always a little late. You should be ten minutes early. I'll see that Filippo is ready."

Isabella continued, walking slowly, since she felt it made them less conspicuous than if they stood still. If Ugo and his friend could camp out somewhere overnight with Filippo, until she had time to get a message from them and get the money from the government? If Ugo could communicate by telephone or entrust someone to deliver a written message?

Either way was easy, Ugo said. He might have to hit Filippo on the head, Isabella said, but Ugo was not to hurt him seriously. Ugo understood.

A few moments later, when they parted, everything was worked out for the kidnaping on Friday morning. Tomorrow was Thursday, and if Ugo had spoken to his friend and all was well, he was to give Isabella a nod, merely, tomorrow afternoon about five when she would go out for an espresso.

Isabella was so exhilarated she went that afternoon to see her friend Margherita who lived off the Via Veneto. Margherita asked her if she had found a new lover. Isabella laughed.

"No, but I think Filippo has," Isabella replied.

Filippo also noticed, by Thursday afternoon, that she was in a merry mood. Filippo was home Thursday evening after their dinner out at a restaurant where they had been two at a table of 20. Isabella took off her shoes and waltzed in the living room. Filippo was aware of his early date with the real-estate agents, and cursed it. It was already after midnight.

The next morning Elisabetta awakened them with the breakfast tray at eight thirty, and Isabella complained of a headache.

"No use in my going if you're not going," Filippo said.

"You can at least tell if the house is possible—or houses," she replied sleepily. "Don't let them down or they won't make a date with us again."

Filippo got dressed.

Isabella heard the faint ring of the street-door bell. Filippo went out. By this time he was in the living room or the kitchen in quest of more coffee. It was two minutes to nine. Isabella at once got up, flung on a blouse, slacks and sandals, ready to meet the real-estate agents who she supposed would be twenty minutes late, at least.

They were. Elisabetta announced them. Two gentlemen. The porter had let them into the court. All seemed to be going well, which was to say Filippo was not in view.

"But I thought my husband had already left with you!" She explained that her husband had left the house half an hour ago. "I'm afraid I must ask you to excuse me. I have a migraine today."

The agency men expressed disappointment, but left in good humor finally, because the Ghiardinis were potentially good clients, and Isabella promised to telephone them in the near future.

Isabella went out for a pre-lunch cinzano, and felt reassured by the absence of Ugo. She was about to answer a letter from Susanna which had come that morning when the telephone rang. It was Filippo's colleague, Vicente, and where was Filippo? Filippo was supposed to have arrived at noon at Vicente's office for a talk before they went out to lunch with a man who Vicente said was "important."

"This morning was a little strange," Isabella said casually, with a smile in her voice, "because Filippo went off with some estate agents at nine, I thought, then—"

"Then?"

"Well, I don't know. I haven't heard from him since," Isabella replied, thinking she had said quite enough. "I don't know anything about his appointments today."

Isabella went out to mail her letter to Susanna around four. Susanna had fallen from her horse taking a low jump, in which the horse had fallen too. A miracle Susanna hadn't broken a bone! Susanna needed not only new riding breeches but a book of photographs of German cathedrals which the class was going to visit this summer, so Isabella had sent her a check on their Swiss bank. As soon as Isabella had got back home and closed her door, the telephone rang.

"Signora Ghiardini—" It sounded like Ugo speaking through a handkerchief. "We have your husband. Do not try to find out where he is. One hundred million lire we want. Do you understand?"

"*Where* is he?" Isabella demanded, putting on an act as if Elisabetta or someone else were listening; but no one was, unless Luigi had picked up the living-room extension phone. It was Elisabetta's afternoon off.

"Get the money by tomorrow noon. Do not inform the police. This evening at seven a messenger will tell you where to deliver the money." Ugo hung up.

That sounded all right! Just what Isabella had expected. Now she had to get busy, especially with Caccia-Lunghi, Filippo's boss, higher than Vicente in the Bureau of Public Welfare and Environment. But first she went into her bathroom, where she was sure Ugo would not be peering in, washed her face and made herself up again to give herself confidence. She would soon be putting a lot of money into Ugo's pocket and the pocket of his friend—whoever was helping him.

Isabella now envisaged Ugo her slave for a long time to come. She would have the power of betraying him if he got out of hand, and if Ugo chose to betray *her*, she would simply deny it, and between the two of them she had no doubt which one the police would choose to believe: her.

"Vicente!" Isabella said in a hectic voice into the telephone (she had decided after all to ring Vicente first). "Filippo has been kidnaped! That's why he didn't turn up this morning! I've just had a message from the kidnapers. They're asking for a hundred million lire by tomorrow noon!"

She and Filippo, of course, had not that much money in the bank, she went on, and wasn't it the responsibility of the government, since Filippo was a government employee, an official?"

Vicente sighed audibly. "The government has had enough of such things. You'd better try Filippo's father, Isabella."

"But he's so stubborn!—The kidnaper said something about throwing Filippo in a *river*!"

"They all say that. Try the father, my dear."

So Isabella did. It was nearly six p.m. before she could reach him, because he had been "in conference." Isabella first asked, "Has Filippo spoken to you today?" He had not. Then she explained that Filippo had been kidnaped, and that his captors wanted 100,000,000 lire by tomorrow noon.

"What? Kidnaped—and they want it from me? Why *me*?" the old man spluttered. "The government—Filippo's in the government!"

"I've asked Vicente Carda." Isabella told him about her rejection in a tearful voice, prolonging her story so that Filippo's predicament would have time to sink in.

"Va bene, va bene." Pietro Ghiardini sounded defeated. "I can contribute seventy-five million, not more. What a business! You'd think Italy . . ." He went on, though he sounded on the brink of a heart attack.

Isabella expressed gratitude, but she was disappointed. She would have to come up with the rest out of their bank account—unless of course she could make a deal with Ugo. Old Pietro promised that the money would be delivered by ten thirty the following morning.

If she and Filippo were due to go anywhere tonight, Isabella didn't give a damn, and she told Luigi to turn away people who might arrive at the door with the excuse that there was a crisis tonight—and they could interpret that as they wished, Isabella thought. Luigi was understanding, and most concerned, as was Elisabetta.

Ugo was prompt with another telephone call at seven, and though Isabella was alone in her bedroom, she played her part as though someone were listening, though no one could have been unless Luigi had picked up the living-room telephone. Isabella's voice betrayed anxiety, anger, and fear of what might happen to her husband. Ugo spoke briefly. She was to meet him in a tiny square which Isabella had never heard of—she scribbled the name down—at noon tomorrow, with 100,000,000 lire in old bills in 20,000 and 50,000 denominations in a shopping bag or basket, and then Filippo would be released at once on the edge of Rome. Ugo did not say where.

"Come *alone*. Filippo is well," Ugo said. "Goodbye, signora."

Vicente telephoned just afterward. Isabella told Vicente what she had to do, said that Filippo's father had come up with 75,000,000 and could the government provide the rest? Vicente said no, and wished Isabella and Filippo the best of luck.

And that was that. So early the next morning Isabella went to their bank and withdrew 25,000,000 lire from their savings, which left so little that she had to sign a check on their Swiss bank for a transfer when she got home. At half-past ten a chauffeur in uniform and puttees, with a bulge under his tunic that must have been a gun, arrived with a briefcase under each arm. Isabella took him into the bedroom for a transfer of money from the briefcases into the shopping bag—a black plastic bag belonging to Elisabetta. Isabella didn't feel like counting through all the soiled banknotes.

"You're sure it's exact?" she asked.

The calm and polite chauffeur said it was. He loaded the shopping bag for her, then took his leave with the briefcases.

Isabella ordered a taxi for eleven fifteen, because she had no idea how long it might take her to get to the little square, especially if they ran into a traffic jam somewhere. Elisabetta was worried, and asked for the tenth time, "Can't I come with you—just sit in the taxi, signora?"

"They will think you are a man in disguise with a gun," Isabella replied, though she intended to get out of the taxi a couple of streets away from the square, and dismiss the taxi.

The taxi arrived. Isabella said she should be back before one o'clock. She had looked up the square on her map of Rome, and had the map with her in case the taxi driver was vague.

"What a place!" said the driver. "I don't know it at all. Evidently you don't either."

"The mother of an old servant of mine lives here. I'm taking her some clothing," Isabella said by way of explaining the bulging but not very heavy shopping bag.

The driver let her out. Isabella had said she was uncertain of the house number, but could find out by asking neighbors. Now she was on her own, with a fortune in her right hand.

There was the little square, and there was Ugo, five minutes early, like herself, reading a newspaper on a bench. Isabella entered the little square slowly. It had a few ill-tended trees, a ground of square stones laid like a pavement. One old woman sat knitting on the only sunlit bench. It was a working-class neighborhood, or one mainly of old people, it seemed. Ugo got up and walked toward her.

"Giorno, signora," he said casually, with a polite nod, as if greeting an old acquaintance, and by his own walking led her toward the street pavement. "You're all right?"

"Yes. And—"

"He's quite all right. —Thank you for this." He glanced at her shopping bag. "Soon as we see everything's in order, we'll let Filippo—loose." His smile was reassuring.

"Where are we—"

"Just here," Ugo interrupted, pushing her to the left, toward the street, and a parked car's door suddenly swung open beside her. The push had not been a hard one, only rude and sudden enough to fluster Isabella for a moment. The man in the driver's seat had turned half around and had a pistol pointed at her, held low on the back of the front seat.

"Just be quiet, Signora Isabella, and there will be no trouble at all—nobody hurt at all," the man with the gun said.

Ugo got in beside her in back and slammed the door shut. The car started off.

It had not even occurred to Isabella to scream, she realized. She had a glimpse of a man with a briefcase under his arm, walking only two meters away on the pavement, his eyes straight ahead. They were soon out in the country. There were a few houses, but mostly it was fields and trees. The man driving the car wore a hat.

"Isn't it necessary that I *join* Filippo, Ugo?" she asked.

Ugo laughed, then asked the man driving to pull in at a roadside bar-restaurant. Here Ugo got out, saying he would be just a minute. He had looked into the shopping bag long enough to see that it contained money and was not partly stuffed with newspaper. The man driving turned around in his seat.

"The signora will please be quiet," he said. "Everything is all right." He had the horrible accent of a Milan tough, attempting to be soothing to an unpredictable woman who might go off in a scream louder than a police siren. In his nervousness he was chewing gum.

"Where are you taking me?"

Ugo was coming back.

Isabella soon found out. They pulled in at a farmhouse whose occupants had evidently recently left—there were clothes on the line, dishes in the sink—but the only people now in the house seemed to be Isabella, Ugo, and his driver chum whom Ugo called Eddy. Isabella looked at an ashtray, recognizing Filippo's Turkish cigarette stubs, noticed also the pack empty and uncrumpled on the floor.

"Filippo has been released, signora," Ugo said. "He has money for a taxi and soon you should be able to phone him at home. Sit down. Would you like a coffee?"

"Take me back to Rome!" Isabella shouted. But she knew. They had kidnaped *her*. "If you think there is any *more* money coming, you are quite mistaken, Ugo—*and you!*" she added to the smiling driver, an old slob now helping himself to whiskey.

"There is always more money," Ugo said calmly . . .

"Swine!" Isabella said. "I should have known from the time you first stared into my bathroom! That's your real occupation, you creep!" A fear of assault crossed her mind, but only swiftly. Her rage was stronger just now. "After I tried to—to give you a break, turn a little money your way! *Look* at all that money!"

Eddy was now sitting on the floor counting it, like a child with an absorbing new toy or game, except that a big cigar stuck out of his mouth.

"Sit down, signora. All will be well when we telephone your husband."

Isabella sat down on a sagging sofa. There was mud on the heels of her shoes from the filthy courtyard she had just walked across. Ugo brought some warmed-over coffee. Isabella learned that still another chum of Ugo's had driven Filippo in another car and dropped him somewhere to make his own way home.

"He is quite all right, signora," Ugo assured her, bringing a plate of awful-looking sliced lamb and hunks of cheese. The other man was on his feet, and brought a basket of bread and a bottle of inferior wine. The men were hungry. Isabella took nothing, refusing even whiskey and wine. When the men had finished eating, Ugo sent Eddy off in the car to telephone Filippo from somewhere. The farmhouse had no telephone. How Isabella wished she had brought her tear-gas gun! But she had thought she would be among friends today.

Ugo sipped coffee, smoked a cigarette, and tried to assuage Isabella's anger. "By tonight, by tomorrow morning you will be back home, signora. No harm done! A room to yourself here! Even though the bed may not be as comfortable as the one you're used to."

Isabella refused to answer him, and bit her lip, thinking that she had got herself into an awful mess, had cost herself and Filippo 25,000,000 lire, and might cost them another 50,000,000 (or whatever she was worth) because Filippo's father might decide not to come up with the money to ransom her.

Eddy came back with an air of disappointment and reported in his disgusting slang that Signor Ghiardini had told him to go stuff himself.

"What?" Ugo jumped up from his chair. "We'll try again. We'll threaten—didn't you threaten—"

Eddy nodded. "He said . . ." Again the revolting phrase.

"We'll see how it goes tonight—around seven or so," said Ugo.

"How much are you asking?" Isabella was unable to repress the question any longer. Her voice had gone shrill.

"Fifty million, signora," replied Ugo.

"We simply haven't got it—not after *this!*" Isabella gestured toward the shopping bag, now in a corner of the room.

"Ha, ha," Ugo laughed softly. "The Ghiardinis haven't got another fifty million? Or the government? Or Papa Ghiardini?"

The other man announced that he was going to take a nap in the other room. Ugo turned on the radio to some pop music. Isabella remained seated on the uncomfortable sofa. She had declined to remove her coat. Ugo paced about, thinking, talking a little to himself, half drunk with the realization of all the money in the corner of tho room. Tho gun lay on the center table near the radio. She looked at it with an idea of grabbing it and turning it on Ugo, but she knew she could not keep both men at bay if Eddy woke up.

When Eddy did wake up and returned to the room, Ugo announced that he was going to try to telephone Filippo, while Eddy kept watch on Isabella. "No funny business," said Ugo like an army officer, before going out.

It was just after six.

Eddy tried to engage her in conversation about revolutionary tactics, about Ugo's having been a journalist once, a photographer also (Isabella could imagine what kind of photographer). Isabella was angry and bored, and hated herself for replying even slightly to Eddy's moronic ramblings. He was talking about making a down payment on a house with the money he had gained from Filippo's abduction. Ugo would also start leading a more decent life, which was what he deserved, said Eddy.

"He deserves to be behind bars for the protection of the *public!*" Isabella shot back.

The car had returned. Ugo entered with his slack mouth even slacker, a look of puzzlement on his brow. "Gotta let her go, he may have traced the call," Ugo said to Eddy, and snapped his fingers for action.

Eddy at once went for the shopping bag and carried it out to the car.

"Your husband says you can go to hell," said Ugo. "He will not pay one lire."

It suddenly sank into Isabella. She stood up, feeling scared, feeling naked somehow, even though she still wore her coat over her dress. "He is joking. He'll—" But somehow she knew Filippo wouldn't. "Where're you taking me now?"

Ugo laughed. He laughed heartily, rocking back as he always did, laughing at Isabella and also at himself. "So I have lost fifty million! A pity, eh? Big pity. But the joke is on *you*! Hah! Ha, ha, ha! Come on, Signora Isabella, what've you got in your purse? Let's see." He took her purse rudely from her hands.

Isabella knew she had about twenty thousand in her billfold. This Ugo laid with a large gesture on the center table, then turned off the radio.

"Let's go," he said, indicating the door, smiling. Eddy had started the car. Ugo's happy mood seemed to be contagious. Eddy began laughing too at Ugo's comments. *The lady was worth nothing!* That was the idea. *La donna niente*, they sang.

"You won't get away with this for long, you piece of filth!" Isabella said to Ugo.

More laughter.

"Here! Fine!" yelled Ugo who was with Isabella in the back seat again, and Eddy pulled the car over to the edge of the road.

Where were they? Isabella had thought they were heading for Rome, but wasn't sure. Yes. She saw some high-rise apartment buildings. A truck went by, close, as she got out with Ugo, half pulled by him.

"Shoes, signora! Ha, ha!" He pushed her against the car and bent to take off her pumps. She kicked him, but he only laughed. She swung her handbag, catching him on the head with it, and nearly fell herself as he snatched off her second shoe. Ugo jumped, with the shoes in his hand, back into the car which roared off.

To be shoeless in silk stockings was a nasty shock. Isabella began walking—toward Rome. She could see lights coming on here and there in the twilight dimness. She'd hitch a ride to the next roadside bar and telephone for a taxi, she thought, pay the taxi when she got home. A large truck passed her by as if blind to her frantic waving. So did a car with a single man in it. Isabella was ready to hitch a lift with anyone!

She walked on, realizing that her stockings were now torn and open at the bottom, and when she stopped to pick something out of one foot, she saw blood. It was more than 15 minutes later when Isabella made her painful way to a restaurant on the opposite of the road where she begged the use of the telephone.

Isabella did not at all like the smile of the young waiter who looked her up and down and was plainly surmising what must have happened to her: a boy friend had chucked her out of his car. Isabella telephoned a taxi company's number which the waiter provided. There would be at least ten minutes to wait, she was told, so she stood by the coat rack at the front of the place, feeling miserable and ashamed with her dirty feet and torn stockings. Passing waiters glanced at her. She had to explain to the proprietor—a stuffy type—that she was waiting for a taxi.

The taxi arrived, Isabella gave her address, and the driver looked dubious, so Isabella had to explain that her husband would pay the fare at the other end. She was almost in tears.

Isabella fell against the porter's bell, as if it were home itself. Giorgio opened the doors. Filippo came across the court, scowling.

"The taxi—" Isabella said.

Filippo was reaching into a pocket. "As if I had anything left!"

Isabella took the last excruciating steps across the courtyard to the door out of which Elisabetta was now running to help her.

Elisabetta made tea for her. Isabella sat in the tub, soaking her feet, washing off the filth of Ugo and his ugly chum. She applied surgical spirits to the soles of her feet, then put on clean white woolen booties and a dressing gown. She cast one furious glance at the bathroom window, sure Ugo would never come back.

As soon as she came out of her bathroom, Filippo said, "I suppose you remember—tonight we have the Greek consul coming to dinner with his wife. And two other men. Six in all. I was going to receive them alone—make some excuse." His tone was icy.

Isabella did remember, but had somehow thought all that would be canceled. Nothing was canceled. She could see it now: life would go on as usual, not a single date would be canceled. They were poorer. That was all. Isabella rested in her bed, with some news-papers and magazines, then got up and began to dress. Filippo came in, not even knocking first.

"Wear the peach-colored dress tonight—not that one," he said. "The Greeks need cheering up."

Isabella began removing the dark blue dress she had put on.

"I know you arranged all this," Filippo continued. "They were ready to kill me, those hoodlums—or at least they acted like it. My father is furious! What stupid arrangements! I can also make some arrangements. Wait and see!"

Isabella said nothing. And *her* future arrangements? Well, she might make some too. She gave Filippo a look. Then she gritted her teeth as she squeezed her swollen feet into "the right shoes" for the evening. When she got up, she had to walk with a limp.

John Lutz

The Other Runner

*" 'The wicked flee when no man pursueth,' the Bible says. D'ye
understand that? God help ye if ye do!" said the vicar of Blake-
field, preceding his death from acute alcoholism in Dublin, June
1823 ... This is the epigraph that John Lutz himself chose for
his story, "The Other Runner," a story you will remember with
a shiver for a long time ...*

I jog. Like people all over this mechanized world who have discovered the benefits of jogging, of what really is old-fashioned running.

I'm tired now, in my third mile this evening. I feel that I can't
make it the mile and a half back to my cabin, but a part of me deep
down knows that I will.

What I'm running on is an old bridle path. It once was cinder, but
the mountain thunderstorms and melting snows have worn it to the
hard gray surface on which I now struggle. The path is approximately two and one-half miles long, meandering in a roughly circular route around Mirror Lake. For an instant I can glimpse
through the trees and see the cedar shake roof of my small cabin,
and as always the sight strengthens my determination to reach that
point of triumph.

Around and above me the woods are green and shadowed, and
occasionally I hear birds twitter in alarm at my approach, or a
squirrel or rabbit bolt unseen for cover. I negotiate a slight rise, one
of the most grueling stretches of my morning runs, and my thighs
suddenly ache under the uphill strain, my breath rasping in louder,
quicker rhythm.

Then the high path levels out, sweeps in a sloping crescent to the
south. A steep drop on my left, steep rising bare mountain face on
my right. At my feet Mirror Lake suddenly glitters blue-green, a
jewel nestled deep in a rough green setting.

I draw breath and resolution as I turn onto the final leg of my
run, a series of small rises, then a long gentle grade to my cabin.
That final downgrade is the best of the run, the very sweetest. Lovely
gravity.

Half an hour later I've showered, and I sit now on the wooden porch of my cabin, my feet propped up on the porch rail, a cold can of low-calorie beer on the wicker table beside me. Totally relaxed, I wait for darkness.

I've been jogging for six weeks, since my divorce became final. When Marsha left me I took stock of myself, decided I needed to lose ten to fifteen pounds, strengthen my heart and lungs for the coming lonely battle with encroaching age. I was 43 in March.

Of course age and weight weren't my only reasons for taking up jogging. Tension. Jogging is one of the greatest tension relievers there is, and I was under more tension during the divorce, the unexpected bitterness, than I would ever have guessed I could bear.

And perhaps I couldn't have borne it without the escape and spiritual experience of running, and the isolation of this tiny cabin near Mirror Lake. I've been here two weeks now, and each day I'm gladder I came. Oh, the tension remains, but now I easily hold it at bay.

Seclusion heals. And there is only one other occupied house on the lake, a large flat-roofed modern structure that juts from the side of the east hill like the imbedded prow of a ship. The Mulhaneys are staying there, Dan and Iris. Dan looks to be a few years older than my 43, a beefy, graying man with a sad-pug, brutal face. Iris I've seen once, as she stood staring into the lake, a lithe, long-waisted woman with long brown hair and a graceful neck. One of those women who somehow by their silent presence will be able to exercise an attraction for men even into old age, a woman not just alive but aflame—coldly aflame.

I've not yet spoken to either of the Mulhaneys; it was from the talkative shopkeeper at the one-pump gas station-grocery store near Daleville that I learned their identities. Though Dan Mulhaney I see almost every day. He's a morning jogger. Always a few minutes either side of nine o'clock he pads wearily past my kitchen window as I'm drinking my coffee. We wave to each other. He's never stopped; he can't break stride.

But one morning he does stop.

Mulhaney simply ceases exerting effort and his bulky white-clad form decelerates to a walk with machine-like inevitability. I stand up from the table and take half a dozen steps out onto the porch.

"Morning," Mulhaney says. "Thought I oughta introduce myself." He holds out a perspiring hand. "Dan Mulhaney."

"Earl Crydon." I shake the hand.

"Wife and I are staying in the house up on the hill. Here to get away from things."

"That's why I'm here myself."

"Vacation?"

"No, I'm a free-lance writer, so my office can pretty well travel with me."

Mulhaney rubs large hairy hands on his shapeless T-shirt, stands silently, expectantly.

"Been jogging long?" I ask.

"About three months. I'm up to six miles. How about you?"

"I can do a bit over five, which is quite an improvement over my first outing. I run in the evenings, after things have cooled."

Mulhaney suddenly seems ill at ease. I offer him coffee.

"Better not, but thanks." He begins jogging easily in place to keep up his circulation. "I better get moving before I get stiff." He fades backward, graceful for a big man, waves, then turns and strikes a practised, moderate pace. He jogs in the opposite direction from myself—clockwise. There is about him an air of mild confusion.

Next morning, as I sit sipping coffee in my crude pine-paneled kitchen, I hear Mulhaney's approach at exactly two minutes to nine. When he comes into view I raise my hand to wave, but he doesn't look in my direction. His pace is faster than usual, and on his perspiring flushed face is an expression of perplexity, of muted fright. Almost as if he is running *from* something.

"Morning!" I call through the window.

His head jerks in my direction and he smiles mechanically, gives a tentative wave. The rhythmic beat of his footsteps recedes.

That evening, as I jog through long shadows past the precariously balanced Mulhaney house, I can hear shouting coming from inside, a man and a woman, abrupt, heated words that are only desperate, indecipherable sounds when they reach my ears. I jog on.

The next several mornings I watch Mulhaney jog past my cabin window and each time his beefy face wears that same quizzical, fearful expression. Then, on Friday morning, I hear the broken, slowing rhythm of his footsteps, and even before he comes into view I know that he's stopping to talk. I finish my coffee and rise to walk onto the porch to greet him.

Mulhaney invites me to join him and his wife that evening for cocktails and some outdoor-grilled steaks—after I've returned from jogging, of course. I accept, some side of me faintly resenting this intrusion on my self-imposed isolation, and tell him I'll run earlier this evening so I can be there at dinner time. We decide on eight o'clock.

I get to the Mulhaney house at five minutes to eight, feeling fresh and relaxed after my early run and cool shower. Dan Mulhaney is waiting for me by a redwood gate at the top of a long winding flight of mossy stone steps that leads to the side of the jutting, angled house. We shake hands as he works a pitted metal latch and opens the gate. "My wife Iris," he says, pride of possession in his voice.

Iris is standing near a white steel table on a brick veranda bordered by thick twisted ivy. She's wearing white shorts and a violet-colored blouse that brings out the violet of her eyes. She smiles. "A drink, Mr. Crydon? Scotch, martini, beer?"

"Beer. And it's Earl, Mrs. Mulhaney."

"Then it's Iris." As she walks toward an open door she says, "I understand you're a compulsive exerciser like my husband."

"I like to run."

I walk with Mulhaney to a no-frills barbecue pit and examine three still-raw steaks.

"Extra-lean," he assures me, as Iris returns with my beer in a glass and with her own martini glass replenished. We drift to the center of the veranda and sit at the white metal table. There is a hole in the center of the table for an umbrella, and round plastic coasters for our glasses.

"Beautiful place," I say, looking around me at glass and squared redwood. A red Porsche convertible squats in the gravel drive.

Iris shrugs. "I hate it."

I raise my glass and look at her, noticing the sheen of her eyes and the faint flush on her cheeks. The results of more than one or two martinis. "But you're staying here," I say.

"Daniel's idea." Her fingertips brush a faded purplish splotch on the side of her neck.

"Both of us had the idea, actually," Mulhaney says quickly. He swivels in his chair to check the wink of flame above the rim of the barbecue pit. "Hey, I better keep an eye on those steaks." He stands and moves away.

"The salad's tossed," Iris says after him. She fixes a violet stare on me. "Daniel sort of twisted my arm to get me to come up here, Earl." A sip of martini. "Marital difficulties. Private matter."

I shift in my hard white chair, slightly embarrassed. "No need to tell me about it, Iris. I'm not qualified to give advice." I wonder how "sort of" was the arm twisting.

"You're not married?"

"Divorced."

Even her smile is violet. There is an unmistakable intensity there.

"I've had enough woman trouble to hold me for a while," I say, and truthfully.

"Well done?" Dan Mulhaney calls to me, probing the largest steak with a long-tined fork.

"Sure," I tell him, "go ahead and burn it."

Iris smiles at me and rises to get the salad.

Again that expression on Mulhaney's face, as if someone—or something—is chasing him.

I sit by my kitchen window, sipping coffee, and glance at my watch. He's early this morning.

The next morning he stops to talk.

"Hot for morning," he says, wiping his glistening face with his T-shirt.

I lean on a cedar porch post. "It is if you're jogging." I can see that Mulhaney is bothered by something more than the heat.

"Any large wild animals around here?" he asks. "I mean, have you ever seen any foxes, bobcats or—anything?"

"Never anything bigger than a rabbit. There used to be bears and cougars in this area, but not for years."

He nods, his broad red face grotesque with a frown in the harsh morning light. "Have you ever been around hunting dogs, Crydon?"

"Not often."

"You can walk where there are a dozen of them lying in the sun, watching you and not watching you. Nothing happens. But if you run they'll sometimes chase you as if you were game."

"Instinct."

Mulhaney seems hesitant to speak further, but he does. "In the evenings, when you're running, do you ever get the feeling that something's—well, behind you?"

"I never have."

"There's an old Gaelic saying to the effect that if you run fast enough long enough, something is bound to give chase."

"Like the hunting dogs. And you think something's chasing you?"

"I don't think it—it's a feeling. Imagination, I guess. But I'm not the imaginative sort." He snorts an embarrassed laugh. "If I were you I'd think Dan Mulhaney was due for a psychiatric checkup."

"Have you ever considered turning around?" I ask him. "Running back toward whatever you think is behind you?"

I'm surprised by the fear in his eyes. "No, no, I couldn't do that."

As he stands talking to me, helpless in all his aging bulk, I feel a wash of deep pity for Mulhaney, of comradeship. I tell him to wait and I go into the cabin. When I return I hand him my revolver. Perhaps this seems extreme, but it is only a small-caliber target pistol. And what if Mulhaney is right? What if something is running behind him, stalking him? This is still reasonably wild country.

"Carry this tucked in your belt if you'd like," I say. "If nothing else, it should make you feel more secure."

He holds the small pistol before him in gratitude and surprise. "You don't have to do this."

"Why shouldn't I? I haven't fired that gun in over a year, so I won't miss it."

"I'll pay you for it."

"Give it back to me when you leave here, or when you feel you haven't any more use for it."

Mulhaney grins, tucks the pistol into the waistband of his shorts beneath his baggy T-shirt. He really is grateful. We shake hands and he jogs up the path, his footsteps somehow more confident on the hard earth.

I go inside, pour another cup of coffee, and wonder if I've made a mistake.

But the pistol has nothing to do with Thursday's tragedy.

At ten o'clock in the morning a horn honks outside my cabin, a series of abrupt, frantic blasts. I walk to the door and see Iris sitting behind the wheel of the red Porsche. Her hair is tangled, wild. Her eyes are wild.

"I need your help, Earl! Something's happened to Dan!"

I shut the cabin door and trot to the car. "Where is he?"

"On the path. He went jogging this morning as he always does, but he didn't return. I went looking for him, found him lying on the ground. He—he doesn't seem to be breathing."

I move around and get in on the passenger side of the car. Iris rotates the wheel expertly, turns around in the front yard of my cabin, and the Porsche roars back up the path.

Dan Mulhaney is on the highest part of the path, where the hill drops abruptly toward the lake on one side and to the smooth rock that rises steeply to a wooded crest on the other. He is lying on his stomach, his body curiously hunched, his head twisted as if he's straining to get air. We get out of the Porsche almost before it stops rocking, and I know immediately Daniel Mulhaney is dead.

As I'm feeling automatically and hopelessly for vital signs, my hand touches the cool steel of my revolver still tucked in Mulhaney's waistband. He is lying on the gun, concealing it.

"Does your cabin have a phone?" I ask Iris.

She nods, staring at her husband. "He's so still, so wax-like. He's dead . . ."

"We can't be sure. Go to your cabin and call a doctor, Iris. I'll stay here."

She nods once, gets into the Porsche, and backs some distance to a wide space at the base of the rise, where she can turn the car around. When she is out of sight I reach beneath Mulhaney's body and remove the gun. It hasn't been fired. I tuck it inside my belt, beneath my shirt. I didn't count on this happening; I don't even have a permit for the gun.

"It looks like a heart attack," the doctor says, 45 minutes later, as Iris and I look on. The doctor sighs and slowly stands. He's a middle-aged but somehow older-appearing man from nearby Daleville, a general practitioner. "You say he jogged regularly?"

"Faithfully," Iris says. She seems to be in mild shock.

The doctor shakes his graying head. "It's a pattern. Overweight, middle-aged, probably high blood pressure. Trying to run like a man of twenty-five and his heart gave out, would be my guess. Thousands of them die like this across the country every year. It's a pattern."

"He was so . . . so healthy," Iris says.

"Maybe he just thought he was," the doctor answers softly. "An ambulance is on the way. We'll take him to Mathers' Funeral Home in Daleville if that's agreeable with you, Mrs. Mulhaney."

Iris nods.

"Why don't you take Mrs. Mulhaney home, give her this with a glass of water." He hands me a small white pill and glances at Iris. "A sedative. Nothing strong."

I get into the car beside Iris and she backs down the road, turns the car, and drives slowly toward her jutting redwood cabin. There is little I can say to her that will help, so I stare straight ahead in silence.

At the cabin she thanks me, assures me that she'll be all right, and with the small white pill clenched in her hand goes inside.

Half an hour later, from my cabin window, I see the ambulance carrying Dan Mulhaney's body carefully negotiating the narrow path. No need for speed, flashing lights, or siren. For the first time since the divorce I take a strong drink, sour mash bourbon on the rocks. I feel a sadness out of proportion to my mere familiarity with Dan Mulhaney.

It's impossible for me to work the rest of the afternoon. Clouds have moved into the area, casting even more gloom, and each hour brings a stronger threat of rain.

At five o'clock, much earlier than usual, I decide that I should run to beat the rain. It takes me only a few minutes to get into my jogging shoes, gray shorts, and faded red T-shirt. The gun I lent Mulhaney is still loaded, and rather than take time to unload it, or leave it in the cabin while I'm gone, I transfer it to the waistband of my shorts. Jogging is what I need to shake off my depression, to obscure the impressions of this morning.

I'm breathing hard by the time I reach the scene of Mulhaney's death. For an instant I feel a shuddering dread, then reassure myself by remembering that Mulhaney was older than my 43 years, as well as overweight. I jog past the death site, instinctively avoiding the exact spot where the body was found. I find myself running between the tire tracks of the Porsche, tracks that must have been left when Iris drove along the path and discovered the body, and when she drove us back to try to help Mulhaney.

And I wonder, why would she come back this way, the long way, instead of continuing past my cabin, the way the car was pointed? That way we could have reached Mulhaney in less than a minute. As my feet pound along the path, I see in the gray dust this morning's footprints from Mulhaney's shoes, exactly like my own footprints only reversed. But his footprints don't describe a straight line; rather they move from one side of the path to the other, with varying spaces between them. He must have staggered in considerable pain before falling.

As I continue to run I keep staring down at the footprints pointing in the opposite direction from the way I'm jogging. Mulhaney staggered an incredible distance, almost all the way up the steepening hill. Why would a man in that much pain continue to run, to push himself? I know what that takes, even without the agonizing spasms of a heart attack.

I stop running.

Still breathing hard, I walk slowly back the way I came.

Now I can see the more subtle veerings of one set of tire tracks, hardly noticeable unless under close scrutiny. The zigzag, irregular patterns of Mulhaney's footprints are paralleled and bounded by the snaking set of tire tracks.

I stop walking where Mulhaney's body was found and backhand the sweat from my forehead.

It's a cold sweat.

She killed him. Dogged him up the hill with the car, at a point where he was already exhausted from over an hour of jogging. On one side of the path the bare face of the mountain rising steep and smooth, and on the other side the long drop to the lake. He had to keep running until he collapsed. If Mulhaney hadn't been dead on the path, Iris probably would have pushed his body over the edge to fall toward the lake. An accident, it would seem. Iris knew her husband was dead when she came to me for help.

Thunder suddenly crashes, echoing about me, but still it doesn't rain. I jog on toward my cabin, through air charged by the imminent storm.

A tingling of alarm through my body, and I hear the car's strangely atavistic roar.

The Porsche rounds the curve near my cabin and speeds toward me. I know it will reach the base of the hill before I can. *I will be in the same position Mulhaney was in!*

Iris works it artfully, varying her speed, always a split second from running me down, keeping me gasping, struggling to gain precious inches of life-sustaining ground.

As I glance back, I see her behind the wheel, her hair flowing beautifully, a fixed dreamy expression on her face. I know why Mulhaney didn't use the gun, know how much, in his possessive, brutish fashion, he must have loved her. I've no such compunctions, only chilling fear.

Unlike Mulhaney, I've had my brief respite while examining the tire tracks and footprints, enough to regain some of my stamina. I put on a burst of speed, draw the gun from my waistband, and twist my body to fire as accurately as possible. The gun kicks in my hand and I see astonishment on Iris' face.

It takes three shots to stop her. The Porsche stalls and nestles against the rocky side of the hill, one rear wheel off the ground. The windshield is starred and Iris is slumped sobbing over the steering wheel. I walk back and see no blood. She isn't hit.

"I was afraid you'd jog early," she says from the cradle of her arms on the steering wheel. "Was watching your cabin, hoping you wouldn't leave." Her head flies back and she stares madly at the sky. "It was supposed to rain!" She begins pounding the steering wheel with her fist. "It was supposed to rain early this afternoon and wash away the tracks!"

I help her out of the car and we walk toward her cabin to phone the county sheriff. Iris sobs, cursing almost with every step. Right now I'm sure she hates the weather forecaster even more than she hated her husband.

I live year-round in the city now. And I still jog. As my feet pound the hard earth I sometimes wonder about Daniel Mulhaney, if he really thought he was being pursued, stalked, or if he had some sort of premonition of his death, sensed some manifestation of his wife's hate.

An uneasiness comes over me at times as I run through lengthening evening shadows, and I remember what the prematurely aged doctor at Mirror Lake said. *It's a pattern* . . . And I remember what Dan Mulhaney said about how if you run fast enough long enough, something is bound to give chase.

And now and then I glance behind me.

Donald E. Westlake

This Is Death

A short story by Donald E. Westlake—but not at all what you might expect. No humor or hilarity this time, and no tough hard-boiled detective. Instead—a ghost story. "No matter how much they may joke about it, people are still afraid of the supernatural" . . . a memorable reading experience . . .

I t's hard not to believe in ghosts when you are one. I hanged myself in a fit of truculence—stronger than pique, but not so dignified as despair—and regretted it before the thing was well begun. The instant I kicked the chair away I wanted it back, but gravity was turning my former wish to its present command; the chair would not right itself from where it lay on the floor, and my 193 pounds would not cease to urge downward from the rope thick around my neck.

There was pain, of course, quite horrible pain centered in my throat, but the most astounding thing was the way my cheeks seemed to swell. I could barely see over their round red hills, my eyes staring in agony at the door, *willing* someone to come in and rescue me, though I knew there was no one in the house, and in any event the door was carefully locked. My kicking legs caused me to twist and turn, so that sometimes I faced the door and sometimes the window, and my shivering hands struggled with the rope so deep in my flesh I could barely find it and most certainly could not pull it loose.

I was frantic and terrified, yet at the same time my brain possessed a cold corner of aloof observation. I seemed now to be everywhere in the room at once, within my writhing body but also without, seeing my frenzied spasms, the thick rope, the heavy beam, the mismatched pair of lit bedside lamps throwing my convulsive double shadow on the walls, the closed locked door, the white-curtained window with its shade drawn all the way down. *This is death*, I thought, and I no longer wanted it, now that the choice was gone forever.

My name is—was—Edward Thornburn, and my dates are 1938-1977. I killed myself just a month before my fortieth birthday, though I don't believe the well-known pangs of that milestone had much if anything to do with my action. I blame it all (as I blamed most of the errors and failures of my life) on my sterility. Had I been able to father children my marriage would have remained strong, Emily would not have been unfaithful to me, and I would not have taken my own life in a final fit of truculence.

The setting was the guestroom in our house in Barnstaple, Connecticut, and the time was just after seven p.m.; deep twilight, at this time of year. I had come home from the office—I was a realtor, a fairly lucrative occupation in Connecticut, though my income had been falling off recently—shortly before six, to find the note on the kitchen table: "Antiquing with Greg. Afraid you'll have to make your own dinner. Sorry. Love, Emily."

Greg was the one; Emily's lover. He owned an antique shop out on the main road toward New York, and Emily filled a part of her days as his ill-paid assistant. I knew what they did together in the back of the shop on those long midweek afternoons when there were no tourists, no antique collectors to disturb them. I knew, and I'd known for more than three years, but I had never decided how to deal with my knowledge. The fact was, I blamed myself, and therefore I had no way to *behave* if the ugly subject were ever to come into the open.

So I remained silent, but not content. I was discontent, unhappy, angry, resentful—truculent.

I'd tried to kill myself before. At first with the car, by steering it into an oncoming truck (I swerved at the last second, amid howling horns) and by driving it off a cliff into the Connecticut River (I slammed on the brakes at the very brink, and sat covered in perspiration for half an hour before backing away) and finally by stopping athwart one of the few level crossings left in this neighborhood. But no train came for 20 minutes, and my truculence wore off, and I drove home.

Later I tried to slit my wrists, but found it impossible to push sharp metal into my own skin. Impossible. The vision of my naked wrist and that shining steel so close together washed my truculence completely out of my mind. Until the next time.

With the rope; and then I succeeded. Oh, totally, oh, fully I succeeded. My legs kicked at air, my fingernails clawed at my throat, my bulging eyes stared out over my swollen purple cheeks, my tongue thickened and grew bulbous in my mouth, my body jigged and jangled like a toy at the end of a string, and the pain was excruciating, horrible, not to be endured. I can't endure it, I thought, it can't be endured. Much worse than knife slashings was the knotted strangled pain in my throat, and my head ballooned with pain, pressure outward, my face turning black, my eyes no longer human, the pressure in my head building and building as though I would explode. Endless horrible pain, not to be endured, but going on and on.

My legs kicked more feebly. My arms sagged, my hands dropped to my sides, my fingers twitched uselessly against my sopping trouser legs, my head hung at an angle from the rope, I turned more slowly in the air, like a broken windchime on a breezeless day. The pains lessened, in my throat and head, but never entirely stopped.

And now I saw that my distended eyes had become lusterless, gray. The moisture had dried on the eyeballs, they were as dead as stones. And yet I could see them, my own eyes, and when I widened my vision I could see my entire body, turning, hanging, no longer twitching, and with horror I realized I was dead.

But *present*. Dead, but still present, with the scraping ache still in my throat and the bulging pressure still in my head. Present, but no longer in that used-up clay, that hanging meat; I was suffused through the room, like indirect lighting, everywhere present but without a source. What happens now? I wondered, dulled by fear and strangeness and the continuing pains, and I waited, like a hovering mist, for whatever would happen next.

But nothing happened. I waited; the body became utterly still; the double shadow on the wall showed no vibration; the bedside lamps continued to burn; the door remained shut and the window shade drawn; and nothing happened.

What *now*? I craved to scream the question aloud, but I could not. My throat ached, but I had no throat. My mouth burned, but I had no mouth. Every final strain and struggle of my body remained imprinted in my mind, but I had no body and no brain and no *self*, no substance. No power to speak, no power to move myself, no power to *re*move myself from this room and this suspended corpse. I could only wait here, and wonder, and go on waiting.

There was a digital clock on the dresser opposite the bed, and when it first occurred to me to look at it the numbers were 7:21—perhaps twenty minutes after I'd kicked the chair away, perhaps fifteen minutes since I'd died. Shouldn't something happen, shouldn't some *change* take place?

The clock read 9:11 when I heard Emily's Volkswagen drive

around to the back of the house. I had left no note, having nothing
I wanted to say to anyone and in any event believing my own dead
body would be eloquent enough, but I hadn't thought I would be
present when Emily found me. I was justified in my action, however
much I now regretted having taken it, I was justified, I knew I was
justified, but I didn't want to see her face when she came through
that door. She had wronged me, she was the cause of it, she would
have to know that as well as I, but I didn't want to see her face.

The pains increased, in what had been my throat, in what had
been my head. I heard the back door slam, far away downstairs, and
I stirred like air currents in the room, but I didn't leave. I couldn't
leave.

"Ed? Ed? It's me, hon!"

I know it's you. I must go away now, I can't stay here, I must go
away. Is there a God? Is this my soul, this hovering presence? *Hell*
would be better than this, take me away to Hell or wherever I'm to
go, don't leave me here!

She came up the stairs, calling again, walking past the closed
guestroom door. I heard her go into our bedroom, heard her call my
name, heard the beginnings of apprehension in her voice. She went
by again, out there in the hall, went downstairs, became quiet.

What was she doing? Searching for a note perhaps, some message
from me. Looking out the window, seeing again my Chevrolet, knowing I must be home. Moving through the rooms of this old house,
the original structure a barn nearly 200 years old, converted by
some previous owner just after the Second World War, bought by
me twelve years ago, furnished by Emily—and Greg—from their
interminable, damnable, awful antiques. Shaker furniture, Colonial
furniture, hooked rugs and quilts, the old yellow pine tables, the
faint sense always of being in some slightly shabby minor museum,
this house that I had bought but never loved. I'd bought it for Emily,
I did everything for Emily, because I knew I could never do the one
thing for Emily that mattered. I could never give her a child.

She was good about it, of course. Emily *is* good, I never blamed
her, never completely blamed *her* instead of myself. In the early
days of our marriage she made a few wistful references, but I suppose
she saw the effect they had on me, and for a long time she has said
nothing. But I have known.

The beam from which I had hanged myself was a part of the
original building, a thick hand-hewed length of aged timber eleven
inches square, chevroned with the marks of the hatchet that had

shaped it. A strong beam, it would support my weight forever. It would support my weight until I was found and cut down. Until I was found.

The clock read 9:23 and Emily had been in the house twelve minutes when she came upstairs again, her steps quick and light on the old wood, approaching, pausing, stopping. "Ed?"

The doorknob turned.

The door was locked, of course, with the key on the inside. She'd have to break it down, have to call someone else to break it down, perhaps she wouldn't be the one to find me after all. Hope rose in me, and the pains receded.

"Ed? Are you in there?" She knocked at the door, rattled the knob, called my name several times more, then abruptly turned and ran away downstairs again, and after a moment I heard her voice, murmuring and unclear. She had called someone, on the phone.

Greg, I thought, and the throat-rasp filled me, and I wanted this to be the end. I wanted to be taken away, dead body and living soul, taken away. I wanted everything to be finished.

She stayed downstairs, waiting for him, and I stayed upstairs, waiting for them both. Perhaps she already knew what she'd find up here, and that's why she waited below.

I didn't mind about Greg, about being present when he came in. I didn't mind about *him*. It was Emily I minded.

The clock read 9:44 when I heard tires on the gravel at the side of the house. He entered, I heard them talking down there, the deeper male voice slow and reassuring, the lighter female voice quick and frightened, and then they came up together, neither speaking. The doorknob turned, jiggled, rattled, and Greg's voice called, "Ed?"

After a little silence Emily said, "He wouldn't—he wouldn't *do* anything, would he?"

"Do anything?" Greg sounded almost annoyed at the question. "What do you mean, do anything?"

"He's been so depressed, he's—Ed!" And forcibly the door was rattled, the door was shaken in its frame.

"Emily, don't. Take it easy."

"I shouldn't have called you," she said. "Ed, *please!*"

"Why not? For heaven's sake, Emily—"

"Ed, *please* come out, don't scare me like this!"

"Why *shouldn't* you call me, Emily?"

"Ed isn't stupid, Greg. He's—"

There was then a brief silence, pregnant with the hint of murmuring. They thought me still alive in here, they didn't want me to hear Emily say, "He *knows*, Greg, he knows about us."

The murmurings sifted and shifted, and then Greg spoke loudly, "That's ridiculous. Ed? Come out, Ed, let's talk this over." And the doorknob rattled and clattered, and he sounded annoyed when he said, "We must get in, that's all. Is there another key?"

"I think all the locks up here are the same. Just a minute."

They were. A simple skeleton key would open any interior door in the house. I waited, listening, knowing Emily had gone off to find another key, knowing they would soon come in together, and I felt such terror and revulsion for Emily's entrance that I could feel myself shimmer in the room, like a reflection in a warped mirror. Oh, can I at least stop seeing? In life I had eyes, but also eyelids, I could shut out the intolerable, but now I was only a presence, a total presence, I *could not* stop my awareness.

The rasp of key in lock was like rough metal edges in my throat; my memory of a throat. The pain flared in me, and through it I heard Emily asking what was wrong, and Greg answering, "The key's in it, on the other side."

"Oh, dear God! Oh, Greg, what has he done?"

"We'll have to take the door off its hinges," he told her. "Call Tony. Tell him to bring the toolbox."

"Can't you push the key through?"

Of course he could, but he said, quite determinedly, "Go *on*, Emily," and I realized then he had no intention of taking the door down. He simply wanted her away when the door was first opened. Oh, very good, *very* good!

"All right," she said doubtfully, and I heard her go away to phone Tony. A beetle-browed young man with great masses of black hair and an olive complexion, Tony lived in Greg's house and was a kind of handyman. He did work around the house and was also (according to Emily) very good at restoration of antique furniture; stripping paint, re-assembling broken parts, that sort of thing.

There was now a renewed scraping and rasping at the lock, as Greg struggled to get the door open before Emily's return. I found myself feeling unexpected warmth and liking toward Greg. He wasn't a bad person; an opportunist with my wife, but not in general a bad person. Would he marry her now? They could live in this house, he'd had more to do with its furnishing than I. Or would this room hold too grim a memory, would Emily have to sell the house, live elsewhere? She might have to sell at a low price; as a realtor, I knew the difficulty in selling a house where a suicide has taken place. No matter how much they may joke about it, people are still afraid of the supernatural. Many of them would believe this room was haunted.

It was then I finally realized the room *was* haunted. With me! *I'm a ghost*, I thought, thinking the word for the first time, in utter blank astonishment. I'm a ghost.

Oh, how dismal! To hover here, to be a boneless fleshless aching *presence* here, to be a kind of ectoplasmic mildew seeping through the days and nights, alone, unending, a stupid pain-racked misery-filled observer of the comings and goings of strangers—she *would* sell the house, she'd have to, I was sure of that. Was this my punishment? The punishment of the suicide, the solitary hell of him who takes his own life. To remain forever a sentient nothing, bound by a force greater than gravity itself to the place of one's finish.

I was distracted from this misery by a sudden agitation in the key on this side of the lock. I saw it quiver and jiggle like something alive, and then it popped out—it seemed to *leap* out, itself a suicide leaping from a cliff—and clattered to the floor, and an instant later the door was pushed open and Greg's ashen face stared at my own purple face, and after the astonishment and horror, his expression shifted to revulsion—and contempt?—and he backed out, slamming the door. Once more the key turned in the lock, and I heard him hurry away downstairs.

The clock read 9:58. *Now* he was telling her. *Now* he was giving her a drink to calm her. *Now* he was phoning the police. *Now* he was talking to her about whether or not to admit their affair to the police; what would they decide?

"Noooooooooo!"

The clock read 10:07. What had taken so long? Hadn't he even called the police yet?

She was coming up the stairs, stumbling and rushing, she was pounding on the door, screaming my name. I shrank into the corners of the room, I *felt* the thuds of her fists against the door, I cowered from her. She can't come in, dear God don't let her in! I don't care what she's done, I don't care about anything, just don't let her see me! *Don't let me see her!*

Greg joined her. She screamed at him, he persuaded her, she raved, he argued, she demanded, he denied. "Give me the key! Give me the key!"

Surely he'll hold out, surely he'll take her away, surely he's stronger, more forceful.

He gave her the key.

No. *This* cannot be endured. *This* is the horror beyond all else. She came in, she walked into the room, and the sound she made will always live inside me. That cry wasn't human; it was the howl of every creature that has ever despaired. *Now* I know what despair is, and why I called my own state mere truculence.

Now that it was too late, Greg tried to restrain her, tried to hold her shoulders and draw her from the room, but she pulled away and crossed the room toward . . . not toward *me.* I was everywhere in the room, driven by pain and remorse, and Emily walked toward the carcass. She looked at it almost tenderly, she even reached up and touched its swollen cheek.

"Oh, Ed," she murmured.

The pains were as violent now as in the moments before my death. The slashing torment in my throat, the awful distension in my head, they made me squirm in agony all over again; but I *could not* feel her hand on my cheek.

Greg followed her, touched her shoulder again, spoke her name, and immediately her face dissolved, she cried out once more and wrapped her arms around the corpse's legs and clung to it, weeping and gasping and uttering words too quick and broken to understand. Thank *God* they were too quick and broken to understand!

Greg, that fool, did finally force her away, though he had great trouble breaking her clasp on the body. But he succeeded, and pulled her out of the room, and slammed the door, and for a little while the body swayed and turned, until it became still once more.

That was the worst. Nothing could be worse than that. The long days and nights here—how long must a stupid creature like myself *haunt* his death-place before release?—would be horrible, I knew that, but not so bad as this. Emily would survive, would sell the house, would slowly forget. (Even I would slowly forget.) She and Greg could marry. She was only 36, she could still be a mother.

For the rest of the night I heard her wailing, elsewhere in the house. The police did come at last, and a pair of grim silent white-coated men from the morgue entered the room to cut me—it—down. They bundled it like a broken toy into a large oval wicker basket with long wooden handles, and they carried it away.

I had thought I might be forced to stay with the body, I had feared the possibility of being buried with it, of spending eternity as a thinking nothingness in the black dark of a casket, but the body left the room and I remained behind.

A doctor was called. When the body was carried away the room door was left open, and now I could plainly hear the voices from downstairs. Tony was among them now, his characteristic surly monosyllable occasionally rumbling, but the main thing for a while was the doctor. He was trying to give Emily a sedative, but she kept wailing, she kept speaking high hurried frantic sentences as though she had too little time to say it all. "I did it!" she cried, over and over. "I did it! I'm to blame!"

Yes. That was the reaction I'd wanted, and expected, and here it was, and it was horrible. Everything I had desired in the last moments of my life had been granted to me, and they were all ghastly beyond belief. I *didn't* want to die! I *didn't* want to give Emily such misery! And more than all the rest I didn't want to be here, seeing and hearing it all.

They did quiet her at last, and then a policeman in a rumpled blue suit came into the room with Greg, and listened while Greg described everything that had happened. While Greg talked, the policeman rather grumpily stared at the remaining length of rope still knotted around the beam, and when Greg had finished the policeman said, "You're a close friend of his?"

"More of his wife. She works for me. I own The Bibelot, an antique shop out on the New York road."

"Mm. Why on earth did you let her in here?"

Greg smiled; a sheepish embarrassed expression. "She's stronger than I am," he said. "A more forceful personality. That's always been true."

It was with some surprise I realized it *was* true. Greg was something of a weakling, and Emily was very strong. (*I* had been something of a weakling, hadn't I? Emily was the strongest of us all.)

The policeman was saying, "Any idea why he'd do it?"

"I think he suspected his wife was having an affair with me." Clearly Greg had rehearsed this sentence, he'd much earlier come to the decision to say it and had braced himself for the moment. He blinked all the way through the statement, as though standing in a harsh glare.

The policeman gave him a quick shrewd look. "Were you?"

"Yes."

"She was getting a divorce?"

"No. She doesn't love me, she loved her husband."

"Then why sleep around?"

"Emily wasn't sleeping *around*," Greg said, showing offense only with the emphasized word. "From time to time, and not very often, she was sleeping with me."

"Why?"

"For comfort." Greg too looked at the rope around the beam, as though it had become me and he was awkward speaking in its presence. "Ed wasn't an easy man to get along with," he said carefully. "He was moody. It was getting worse."

"Cheerful people don't kill themselves," the policeman said.

"Exactly. Ed was depressed most of the time, obscurely angry now and then. It was affecting his business, costing him clients. He made Emily miserable but she wouldn't leave him, she loved him. I don't know what she'll do now."

"You two won't marry?"

"Oh, no." Greg smiled, a bit sadly. "Do you think we murdered him, made it look like suicide so we could marry?"

"Not at all," the policeman said. "But what's the problem? You already married?"

"I am homosexual."

The policeman was no more astonished than I. He said, "I don't get it."

"I live with my friend; that young man downstairs. I am—capable—of a wider range, but my preferences are set. I am very fond of Emily, I felt sorry for her, the life she had with Ed. I told you our physical relationship was infrequent. And often not very successful."

Oh, Emily. Oh, poor Emily.

The policeman said, "Did Thornburn know you were, uh, that way?"

"I have no idea. I don't make a public point of it."

"All right." The policeman gave one more half-angry look around the room, then said, "Let's go."

They left. The door remained open, and I heard them continue to talk as they went downstairs, first the policeman asking, "Is there somebody to stay the night? Mrs. Thornburn shouldn't be alone."

"She has relatives in Great Barrington. I phoned them earlier. Somebody should be arriving within the hour."

"You'll stay until then? The doctor says she'll probably sleep, but just in case—"

"Of course."

That was all I heard. Male voices murmured a while longer from below, and then stopped. I heard cars drive away.

How complicated men and women are. How stupid are simple actions. I had never understood anyone, least of all myself.

The room was visited once more that night, by Greg, shortly after the police left. He entered, looking as offended and repelled as though the body were still here, stood the chair up on its legs, climbed on it, and with some difficulty untied the remnant of rope. This he stuffed partway into his pocket as he stepped down again to the floor, then returned the chair to its usual spot in the corner of the room, picked the key off the floor and put it in the lock, switched off both bedside lamps and left the room, shutting the door behind him.

Now I was in darkness, except for the faint line of light under the door, and the illuminated numerals of the clock. How long one minute is! That clock was my enemy, it dragged out every minute, it paused and waited and paused and waited till I could stand it no more, and then it waited longer, and *then* the next number dropped into place. Sixty times an hour, hour after hour, all night long. I couldn't stand one night of this, how could I stand eternity?

And how could I stand the torment and torture inside my brain? That was much worse now than the physical pain, which never entirely left me. I had been right about Emily and Greg, but at the same time I had been hopelessly brainlessly wrong. I had been right about my life, but wrong; right about my death, but wrong. How *much* I wanted to make amends, and how impossible it was to do anything any more, anything at all. My actions had all tended to this, and ended with this: black remorse, the most dreadful pain of all.

I had all night to think, and to feel the pains, and to wait without knowing what I was waiting for or when—or if—my waiting would ever end. Faintly I heard the arrival of Emily's sister and brother-in-law, the murmured conversation, then the departure of Tony and Greg. Not long afterward the guestroom door opened, but almost immediately closed again, no one having entered, and a bit after that the hall light went out, and now only the illuminated clock broke the darkness.

When next would I see Emily? Would she ever enter this room again? It wouldn't be as horrible as the first time, but it would surely be horror enough.

Dawn grayed the window shade, and gradually the room appeared out of the darkness, dim and silent and morose. Apparently it was a sunless day, which never got very bright. The day went on and on, featureless, each protracted minute marked by the clock. At times I dreaded someone's entering this room, at other times I prayed for something, anything—even the presence of Emily herself—to break this unending boring *absence*. But the day went on with no event, no sound, no activity anywhere—they must be keeping Emily sedated through this first day—and it wasn't until twilight, with the digital clock reading 6:52, that the door again opened and a person entered.

At first I didn't recognize him. An angry-looking man, blunt and determined, he came in with quick ragged steps, switched on both bedside lamps, then shut the door with rather more force than necessary, and turned the key in the lock. Truculent, his manner was, and when he turned from the door I saw with incredulity that he was *me*. Me! I wasn't dead, I was alive! But how could that be?

And what was that he was carrying? He picked up the chair from the corner, carried it to the middle of the room, stood on it—

No! No!

He tied the rope around the beam. The noose was already in the other end, which he slipped over his head and tightened around his neck.

Good God, *don't!*

He kicked the chair away.

The instant I kicked the chair away I wanted it back, but gravity was turning my former wish to its present command; the chair would not right itself from where it lay on the floor, and my 193 pounds would not cease to urge downward from the rope thick around my neck.

There was pain, of course, quite horrible pain centered in my throat, but the most astounding thing was the way my cheeks seemed to swell. I could barely see over their round red hills, my eyes staring in agony at the door, *willing* someone to come in and rescue me, though I knew there was no one in the house, and in any event the door was carefully locked. My kicking legs caused me to twist and turn, so that sometimes I faced the door and sometimes the window, and my shivering hands struggled with the rope so deep in my flesh I could barely find it and most certainly could not pull it loose.

I was frantic and terrified, yet at the same time my brain possessed a cold corner of aloof observation. I seemed now to be everywhere in the room at once, within my writhing body but also without, seeing my frenzied spasms, the thick rope, the heavy beam, the mismatched pair of lit bedside lamps throwing my convulsive double shadow on the walls, the closed locked door, the white-curtained window with its shade drawn all the way down. *This is death*

EDITORIAL POSTSCRIPT

The story you have just read was nominated by MWA (Mystery Writers of America) as one of the five best new mystery short stories published in American magazines and books during 1978.

David Ely

Going Backward

You will get nothing usual from David Ely—you know that by now. And his stories—strange, provocative, disturbing—always have deeper levels of meaning. In this one the acute observations and perceptive details form a nightmare mosaic which reveals a curious kind of "civilized" crime that has terrifying implications for all of us . . .

The old farmhouse in Herkimer County hadn't been lived in for many years. When the young people moved in, they found field mice in the parlor, and bird droppings in the kitchen; there were cobwebs everywhere, and dust, and mold. They set to work at once cleaning and making repairs. Walter patched the roof while Charles replaced weakened floorboards. Lewis and Jane began clearing out the barn, and Victor chopped away with a rusty sickle at the tangle of weeds and vines in the yard. Susan, sweeping upstairs, was disturbed by the discovery of a fox skeleton. She was superstitious, and considered this a bad omen. "We won't be happy here," she predicted to the others.

It was Lydia who found the trunk in the attic, full of old clothes and hats. She shook them out and aired them, and inspected them with interest. Some went back all the way to the 1890s, she knew. That evening she and Jane tried on a couple of the dresses, and after redoing their hair into severe Victorian buns, they made a surprise appearance at supper. Lewis and Charles, seized by the same amiable spirit, rushed off to the closet where Lydia had hung the clothes, and returned as a pair of lean and long-legged Gay Nineties sparks in checked suits, complete with handlebar mustaches drawn in chimney soot. "Remember the Maine!" cried Charles, striking a warlike pose before the hearth.

Victor got out his violin and played reels while the others danced by the candlelight, their laughter leaping and fading in the sweet summer darkness that enveloped the house. Walter and Susan, hearing the music, came over from the cottage across the lane to join the dancing. "Costumes first!" cried Lydia, so the newcomers had to rummage about in the closet to find something to put on.

Susan chose a beribboned bonnet, and Walter found a derby. When Victor's arm tired, Lydia and Jane sang duets, and then Charles performed what he remembered of a monologue from "The Drunkard," and after that they sat on the porch listening to the owl in the woods and the tinkling of the windchimes Jane had hung in the pear tree.

The night air was soft and warm; they could count the stars. "Oh, I wish—" Lydia began. Susan tried to stop her: "Don't wish! It's bad luck!" Lydia wouldn't mind her. "I wish it really were 1890," she said, "and I wish we could stay in it forever." Susan sucked in her breath. "There's something moving in the woods!" she said. The others laughed—Susan was always seeing things that moved in the dark—but she went inside and made Walter come in, too, to keep her company.

The seven young people, being artisans of modest means, had found in the farm property exactly what they had to have—ample living and working space for virtually no rent. Naturally, there were reasons for this bargain. The house was just barely habitable, and the cottage had only one room whose floorboards weren't rotted. There were no amenities—no electricity, no telephone, no running water. The artisans used kerosene lamps and candles for light. Water they drew from an old well; so far nobody had fallen ill. A fire took the chill off the occasional cool summer evening—but how they would manage to keep from freezing in the storms and snows of an upstate New York winter, the young people had no idea. At least there was plenty of wood around. They used it for cooking, having found a woodstove that drew nicely.

A further reason for the token rent was the fact that the place was isolated. The lane had once gone all the way east to the village, but had been cut off when a change in the water regime of the zone created a swamp, submerging the low-lying land in muck and weeds. The north and west sides of the property were blocked by thick, vine-choked woods. The only way out was to the south, through an old pasture that hadn't been used for years. This led to an apple orchard, likewise abandoned and growing wild. Beyond that a cow path meandered down to the Henneman farm, where there was a dirt road which eventually reached the village.

A jeep could have bounced across the pasture, but the young people had no motor vehicle of any kind. They walked to the village—nearly three miles away. When they had heavy things to transport they pushed along a wooden cart they'd found in the barn.

Charles, light-spirited, began wearing his Nineties suit into the village when it was his turn to go in for food and supplies. The fabric had a yellow check pattern, and he could be seen for quite some distance across the pasture, strolling along like a dandy in his high collar and derby hat. Lydia reproved him, for he'd ripped the back of the coat. "If you like that style, I'll make you a suit," she told him. "I'm copying a dress for myself." Lewis wanted a suit, too. So did Victor, but he was shy about being overweight, and didn't want Lydia to take his measurements, so she did it by guess, and the suit fit him quite well.

By the end of summer, she and Jane had created a period wardrobe, fashioning new clothes and altering old ones. It amused them to dress up. Lewis and Charles were cultivating real handlebar mustaches. Victor had found a pince-nez in an old desk. He parted his hair in the middle, practised fierce expressions, and gave imitations of Teddy Roosevelt, whom he somewhat resembled. In the evenings they would sing or dance or sit around playing Nineties' games—holding spirit séances, and acting out charades. With mock solemnity Charles would initiate discussions of "current" issues—would there be war with Spain? Would McKinley defeat Bryan for the Presidency?

It wasn't just a joke, though. In this forgotten rural corner of Herkimer County the young people were in fact living much the way their great-grandfathers had lived. It was as if they had taken a backward step through time. They didn't miss the Twentieth Century. Their air was pure and sweet; their water had a wholesome tang. The woods were alive with squirrels and birds; a family of pheasants lived at the edge of the pasture.

"Just think," said Victor. "We've discovered what it means to live a cleaner, simpler, healthier life. We don't have any waste or pollution, and we're away from the consumer mentality. Buy, buy, buy—that's all people know how to do nowadays. If only they could see the way we live. If only we could show them!"

As far as possible, the young people lived off the land. Jane established a vegetable patch behind the house. Everybody helped with the weeding. There were blackberries in the woods, and mushrooms down by the swamp. Susan traded earthenware pots for a pair of pullets from the Henneman farm, so there were fresh eggs. Life wasn't easy, but morale was high. Even the prospect of winter wasn't daunting.

They took turns minding the shop in the village where their craftwork was displayed for sale, and thus they became well-known to the local people, who regarded them with a tolerant eye. Villagers would drop by to admire Lewis' fieldstone sculpture and Jane's lacework. Occasionally they would barter—a crate of apples for one of Victor's straw baskets, or a sack of sweet corn for a pair of Charles's wooden serving spoons.

The villagers would listen with apparent attention to Victor's expositions of what he came to call his 1890 philosophy of life, and they derived much enjoyment from the occasional spectacle of the wooden farm cart creaking and clattering along the street. For the most part, however, the locals left the artisans alone. No one went calling at the old farm, except for a few children, who wandered out to watch Lydia at her loom or Walter and Susan at their potter's wheels. When school began, not even the children came.

Fall brought brisk days and frosty nights. The woods burst out in gold and scarlet leaves, and a dozen pumpkins ripened in the vegetable patch. The tourist season was over, so the young people closed the shop in the village. They were busy laying in food and supplies for the winter. To save on fires, Walter and Susan left the cottage, and moved in with the others.

Charles built storm windows for the north side of the house. Lewis and Walter split logs and chopped kindling. Jane caulked the floorboards. Susan discovered a sled and some snowshoes in the barn, and just as well, for it snowed early and heavily that year. They spent Christmas snowbound, all except Jane, who had gone home to Buffalo for her younger sister's wedding, and couldn't get back until after New Year's Day.

Charles lined the lane with life-sized snowmen, and Lewis sculptured the heads into likenesses of such Nineties notables as Queen Victoria and Bismarck and John L. Sullivan. Lydia so cultivated the birds with crumbs and crusts that the kitchen windows were wingdark at feeding time. There were snowball fights, and moonlit tramps through the icy woods, and skating on the Henneman stock pond.

The cold, however, made working difficult. Fingers got stiff; materials, too, became contrary. In February, when a two-day blizzard struck, the young people gave up entirely and spent all their time trying to keep warm. The two-day blizzard was followed by a three-day blizzard, and the following morning Susan peered out through the shutters, and shrieked, for the snow had drifted so high in the lane that Charles's figures were buried to the neck, and the lifelike heads, with the severe and dignified expressions Lewis had given them, were staring at her with rigid curiosity out of their white unwinking eyes.

During the winter the young men managed to make the trek into the village at least once a week to buy a sled-load of provisions, and to let people know that all was well out at the farm. It was harder going in March, when the thaw made the pasture spongy, and muddied the cow path. The arrival of spring set them all working again, invigorated by the freshness and warmth of the season, and proud that they had got through the winter so well, with no worse casualties than Victor's violin, whose soundboard had warped from the damp and cold.

In April a reporter from the county weekly newspaper came out, having heard that the group might be worth a little story. "They tell me 1890 is your bag," the reporter said, which displeased Victor, who had taken a dislike to modern slang; but as the reporter was a pleasant young man, and seemed sincerely interested in what he saw there, Victor soon warmed up and explained everything at great length. The weekly reporter wrote an article which in turn stirred the daily newspaper in Albany to send one of its feature writers, accompanied by a photographer. They did a Sunday picture story—"Craft Commune Turns Back Clock"—with photographs of Jane and Susan with their leg-of-mutton sleeves, churning butter, and of Lydia with her topknot, laboring at her loom, and of the men working, too, and then one of the entire group in full costume, posed formally in front of the barn, and looking very authentic.

On April 22 the young people had their first sightseers, a husband and wife from Troy, who explained that they happened to be driving through the village when they remembered the feature story in the Albany paper, and so had stopped to ask how to get out to the farm.

Victor welcomed them and showed them the workshops and living quarters. The man from Troy was fascinated by Lydia's loom, and his wife was so charmed by Lewis' stone pieces that she kept crying out in amazement, "You did that? You really made that yourself?" Before they left, the visitors asked if they might buy something. They chose a lace handkerchief, and a small rug, and a stone owl, and then in a burst of enthusiasm decided on a pair of ladderback chairs.

Charles and Walter helped them carry their purchases across the pasture and through the abandoned apple orchard and down to the cow path behind the Henneman farm, where the car was parked.

"I really admire what you kids are doing," the Troy man said, shaking hands, "and I know you'll have a real big success."

The next day a family from Schenectady came by in the morning, admired everything, and bought a stack of Victor's baskets. That afternoon two girls from Herkimer came bouncing across the pasture on their motorcycles, making a terrible racket, but they were so merry that the artisans forgave them, and invited them for supper. The girls said they'd better call home first. Lydia explained there was no telephone. The girls stared at her. "No phone?" one of them said. "Honest? Well, God, I mean, that's quaint."

The weather turned warmer and the woods greened. There were frogs in the swamp, and rabbits raiding the vegetable patch. A family of raccoons, it was discovered, had wintered in the cottage. Visitors would occasionally appear, having hiked across the pasture. They were friendly and agreeable, and always apologized for disturbing the young people. Their number increased in June. By the middle of the month hardly a day would go by without a few of them, frequently several at a time.

On Saturdays and Sundays there was a constant flow of people. They peered at the workshops in the barn, took snapshots of the house, and listened with reflective expressions to Victor's explanations. Susan didn't care for the sightseers. They were polite and quiet, but all those clicking cameras made her nervous, and there were cigarette butts and peanut shells strewn about the yard. Victor urged her to be tolerant.

"These people are really interested in the way we live," he said. "Our example is going to make them question their own standards." Over the winter he and Jane had stitched samplers bearing such mottoes as "Waste Not, Want Not" and "Make Do With Less." The visitors had bought them all, which Victor considered a sign of their receptivity to a simpler way of life. "I still wish they wouldn't come," Susan said.

But the tourists kept coming. Even rainy days didn't keep them away. They came, looked, and bought. There was no need to reopen the shop in the village. Everything was snapped up on the spot. The young people couldn't make enough for the demand. Rather than depart empty-handed, visitors would ask for something as a souvenir—a handful of nails, or a mug which had cracked in a firing. They even wanted to pay, although naturally the artisans couldn't accept money for such things.

"You fellows ought to build a decent driveway in here," said one man, as he watched Charles and Lewis labor across the pasture with the cart. "That's the first rule of business—easy access for your clients." Lewis explained that they didn't have the money to build a drive, and besides it wasn't their property. "Well, at least you ought to do something about where folks park their cars," the man said, and it was true that the cow path was a mess. Scores of automobiles backing and turning had churned up the earth and broken down the sides of the banks. When it rained, mud sucked at the hubcaps. On busy days the racket of honks and grinding engines could be heard all the way across the pasture.

Susan put up a note on the barn asking people not to walk in during working hours, but the idea that they were out there reading her note distracted her, and she thought she heard them whispering. Besides, the taller men peeped in at the window right behind her, so in a way it was worse than having them inside. She finally compromised, opening the studio from eleven to twelve every weekday morning. Visitors fingered the wet clay and sniffed the glazes, even though she kept telling them not to.

"They just don't pay attention," she lamented to the others. "They drift around like sheep, and how can you communicate with sheep?" Victor maintained a more positive attitude. "They're not sheep," he said. "Many of them are sincerely interested in fighting against the insane waste of the consumer society. Why, I've even gotten some invitations to speak before their local civic organizations."

Victor had problems, too. A little boy got sick all over some new baskets, and somebody's dog ran off with his deerstalker cap and ate it. The most annoying thing was the discovery that a novelty firm in Utica had copied the "Waste Not, Want Not" sampler and was producing it in plastic by the hundreds, machine-made.

By late July the litter in the yard had increased to the point where Victor felt obliged to put out one of his large baskets as a trash receptacle. A few days later a tourist tossed a smoldering cigarette butt into it; the basket and its contents caught fire and burned, leaving a large withered patch in the grass. Lewis went into the village to buy a metal trash can. On his return he helped some people push their car free of the mud at the cow path, and he noticed how the gouging and tearing of the cars had not only widened the track but extended it several yards into the old orchard. When he reported this, Susan gave a little shiver. "The cars are coming," she said. "The cars are making their own road."

The first guided tour appeared August 3—twenty men, women,

and children preceded by a man wearing an armband and holding a little megaphone. They were vacationers at a nearby Adirondack resort, making a day trip, and they insisted on getting autographs. "I think what you're doing is wonderful," one man told Jane. A woman admired Lydia's dress, and wanted to buy it. Lydia said no as politely as she could. The woman had crowded up beside the loom and was fingering the dress as Lydia tried to work. Susan shut the barn door, but people kept opening it and peering in.

"Please go away," she told them. The visitors seemed abashed and confused. "But we've got tickets," one of them said plaintively. Susan finally went off into the woods to be alone. A family was having a picnic there. The wife offered her a chicken leg. "Say, you must be one of the actresses," she said. "I don't mind saying it's a swell show."

Susan began weeping at sunset. She cried late into the night. The next day she put on her bluejeans and sweater, and left. Walter went with her, arguing. The others could hear their voices in the pasture. Later Walter came back. "She can't stand any more," was all he would say. He tramped around the barn cramming tools into his knapsack, and then he left, too.

Victor started after him, but a woman visitor stopped him, taking his sleeve. "Hi, there," she said, and she told him her name and where she was from, and she asked if she could take her little boy into the kitchen and make him a sandwich. She offered Victor a dollar. "I don't know how much it is," she said. "Do you have a price list?"

The departure of Susan and Walter discouraged the others, and they told Victor something would have to be done about the sightseers. "If there were just a few, it would be all right," said Lewis, "but we can't work with all these people crowding in." Victor agreed, and said he would go into the village to talk the situation over with the chief of police, Mr. Grimes.

As Victor crossed the pasture and orchard, he saw that there were brightly painted arrow-shaped signs pointing the way to the farm. He tried to wrest one from the earth, but it was securely implanted. All he managed to do was get a splinter in his hand. The signs were fixed along the cow path, too, and even at the Henneman place. Mr. Henneman stood by his gate, smiling, in his Sunday clothes. He was charging a quarter for every car he let through.

At the police station Victor told Mr. Grimes that the tourist situation had got out of hand and requested the assistance of the law.

Mr. Grimes said that the police could prevent trespassing on private property, but he pointed out that the loss of new business would hurt the town, and cited the example of his brother's gas station, which had tripled its sales. "And by the way," he added, "you kids have been selling merchandise out there without a license, which could mean a heavy fine, so if I were you I wouldn't push on the trespassing thing. Anyway, I've only got two men, and one of 'em's sick."

By mid-August there was a snack stand in the pasture where a woman sold plastic-wrapped sandwiches and cold drinks. In the lane itself a college boy strolled back and forth hawking slides and postcards showing the artisans at work, all in photographs of unnatural clarity and eye-shattering color. In one photo Victor's hazel eyes were an electric blue; in another, Jane's maroon shawl was as bright as blood.

"Who said you could sell these things here?" Victor asked. The college boy said it was his father, who had a little printing business at Lake George, and he added that he had persuaded his father not to charge the young people anything, even though the slides and postcards were valuable publicity. "I told him you were into ecology and stuff," he explained.

Lewis came back from the village one afternoon to say he'd been told at the post office that the county authorities planned to drain the marsh and rebuild the lane. A tourist overheard him, and expressed concern. "Don't let 'em do it, boys," he said. "It'll ruin this place if you get cars in here. Fight that road—fight it." Victor said the opening of the lane probably wouldn't matter much. Motor cyclists and beach buggies came roaring across the pasture as it was, and an enterprising villager had established a jeep service, ferrying visitors from the cow-path parking lot at a dollar a head.

The first tourists of the day were arriving early, shortly after breakfast, and the last ones were still wandering about after sunset. Sitting on the porch in the evening, the young people had been startled more than once by an apologetic voice from the darkness, asking for the loan of a flashlight—and of course Victor or Charles or Lewis would have to guide these tardy sightseers back to their cars.

The number of tourists increased and it was this that led to Charles's accident. People were anxious not to miss a thing, particularly when the artisans were exercising their skills. Charles's woodworking had a dramatic flair to it, the chips flying as the forms took shape under the strokes of his chisel, so he always had quite a crowd pressing eagerly around. One afternoon someone was bumped from behind and jostled Charles's elbow, causing him to run his chisel deep into his hand.

Jane medicated the cut, and bandaged it, to stop the bleeding, but Charles was awake half of the night with pain. The next day he decided to go to the doctor, and was about to set off when the woods burst into flame, having been ignited by some visitor's carelessness with matches, and he had to stay and help fight the blaze.

The fire burned with a great snapping and crackling of branches. Charles and the others snatched up the available tools—two spades, a rake, and a snow shovel—hoping to block the flames by digging a fire trench. They worked furiously, half blinded by smoke. The tourists gathered to watch. "You'd better send somebody to tell the fire department," one man suggested to Victor.

Many visitors had cameras and were busily filming the dramatic scene. A dead tree flared like a torch. It fell, hurling glowing brands. Lydia hurried around with a bucket of water, extinguishing them. "There are some over there," a woman told her, pointing to some blazing tufts of grass. The edge of Jane's long dress began smoldering. She had to rip off that part. Charles's cut was bleeding through the bandage. He felt faint and sick, and had to totter back from the heat.

"Hold it," a man said to him, and snapped his picture in a close-up. The snack-stand woman was doing a brisk business, for the fire had stimulated appetites, particularly among the children.

When the breeze shifted, the fire stopped advancing, and slowly burned itself out. Victor asked some men to help carry buckets from the well to douse the embers, but by then it was quite late in the day and the guides were summoning everyone. "You kids deserve a big round of applause," one man said, and he would have shaken Victor's hand, if it hadn't been so grimy.

Lewis and Jane took Charles to the village to see the doctor. Late that night Lewis returned alone, explaining that Charles had been driven to the hospital in Utica for tests, and Jane had gone, too, to be with him. They wanted their things sent to Jane's family in Buffalo, for they had decided not to return to the farm.

"Not even if the tourists stop coming?" Victor asked.

"The tourists aren't going to stop coming," Lewis answered.

The next morning Victor noticed visitors picking up twigs and handfuls of grass and putting them in their pockets. "Why are you doing that?" he asked. A man answered that since there were no craft artifacts left to buy, he and his wife wanted something to take home as souvenirs. A young woman came up to Victor. "Let me pay you for these," she said, showing him some pebbles. He gazed at her, bemused. "No charge for pebbles," he said finally. The young woman looked distressed. "Oh, I wouldn't feel right, not paying," she said, but she kept the pebbles anyway.

Later Victor saw that people were taking pieces of rotted floor boarding from the cottage. He went over to stop them. "You need to get the bad part out," a man told him. "That way the air can get in and dry out the rest."

Lydia was dismantling her loom, and Lewis was packing his tools. "Stay a little longer," Victor urged them, but when they asked him why, he had no answer. From the east came the howl and rumble of the earthmovers and the trucks. Work on the swamp had begun. "We'll stay the night, anyway," said Lewis. "We'll leave tomorrow."

That afternoon Victor helped Lewis and Lydia load the cart, and push it into the village, as they wanted to put their possessions and those of Charles and Jane into the shop for safekeeping. On the main street they noticed two women wearing dresses like Lydia's—long skirts, large sleeves, and high collars. One woman was shielding her smiling face from the sun with a parasol. They asked about these costumes at the post office, and the postmistress, Mrs. Chadwick, said it was a new fashion from New York, quite the rage, despite the discomfort in summer. "They'll never get me in an outfit like that," said Mrs. Chadwick, but Lydia saw she now wore her hair, Nineties-style, in a chignon.

The young people brought back bottled water. The well was thick with refuse, and they were afraid to drink from it. They found people in the house. Victor asked them to leave. One man requested his autograph. "I'll never forget this wonderful place," the man said. He and the other visitors went across the lane to the cottage, and sat on the steps there, gazing back at the house.

Twilight came in through the ruined woods, turning everything a melancholy brown, like a faded photograph. Some tourists had gone; others remained. They were still there at dark. When Lewis brought the food out to the table on the porch, he could see dim figures standing in the lane, like the snowmen he and Charles had made in winter.

"Maybe we ought to eat inside," he said to Lydia, but she told him there were people in back, too, looking in that way. "What do they want?" she asked. "Why don't they go away?" Victor came out on the porch; he wouldn't eat. The distant earthmovers had fallen silent for the night, but from time to time the young people could hear a cracking sound from the cottage across the lane.

"There's a big hole in the floor now," Lewis said. "I went over an hour ago to look. They're breaking it up." Victor was walking restlessly about the porch. He stopped, and said, "They're not breaking it up. They're consuming it."

Visitors' cigarettes glowed like fireflies in the yard. The moonlight was reflected by white things; shirts swam in the darkness, and tennis shoes took steps. A chain of pale faces drifted in the lane, shifting and bobbing in a soft flow of talk. "Oh, why don't they go away?" Lydia said again. "What do they want?"

The young people remained on the porch all night, huddled together. The first light of day showed that the yard and lane were empty, and yet voices came from the pasture. New people were arriving. "They've never come this early," Victor said. From the east the earthmovers began pounding at the swamp. Dust clouds rolled up crimson in the sunrise.

"Let's go," Lewis said. Tourists were gathering in front of the house, smiling and pointing their cameras. Lewis took Lydia's arm; together they went down the steps and along the lane, trying not to notice the people around them. "Hi, there," a woman said. "I'm Myra Morton from Aurora. Is the museum open, or is it too early?"

Lewis kept going, guiding Lydia by the elbow. Someone asked for his autograph. Someone else snapped their photograph. "You got a swell place here," a man said enthusiastically. Near the barn Lewis turned to look for Victor and saw him well behind them, walking slowly, and glancing this way and that, as if unsure which way he ought to go. Lewis shouted back at him to hurry. Victor waved, but didn't quicken his pace. Halfway across the pasture, Lewis looked back again. There were many tourists walking across the trampled weeds, and he couldn't see past them. "We'll wait for Victor in the village," he told Lydia.

Victor's eyes smarted, and his head ached. A bitter odor still breathed out of the burnt woods, where charred trees were dying. He thought of returning to the house to take something with him—perhaps his violin, ruined though it was—but there were people touring the rooms, and he didn't want to have to push his way among them.

He was discouraged when he approached the pasture. There

weren't just people there, but cars as well. Several were parked just beyond the barn. Others were bumping across the rough ground, following the jeep tracks. In the distance, just visible among the apple trees, was a tour bus, rocking and bucking along. Victor decided not to leave that way, and turned back along the lane.

As he passed the house, he saw a woman come out of the front doorway onto the porch. She was putting a plate into her purse. She saw him, and smiled vivaciously. "Hi there," she said. Farther on was the vegetable patch. A tourist had pulled up a carrot. He, too, noticed Victor, and grinned, and waved the carrot. "Where do I pay?" he asked. "In the house?"

Victor hurried along the lane. It was padded with the dead leaves of many years. Broken branches had fallen there, too. He had to pick his way carefully in places. The going became more difficult the farther he went. Only when he paused to disentangle his feet from some vines did he realize that there was a group of tourists behind him.

"Please don't follow me," he said, and his voice was uneven, for the exertion of his walk had brought his breath up quick. The tourists regarded him in a friendly way. "Hi there," one of the men said. "I'm Charley Farson from Binghamton, and this is my wife, Nella." His wife wiggled her fingers at Victor.

Victor swung around and continued to push his way through the undergrowth. He could tell by the voices that the tourists were still following him, but he didn't want to look at them again. The lane was completely overgrown. Brambles tore at his clothes and slashed at his hands. He heard the tourists exclaiming as they helped free each other from the thorns. A trickle of blood ran down his forehead; his palms were crisscrossed with little cuts.

The closer he got to the swamp, the louder grew the thunder of the earthmovers. The ground was no longer firm, but spongy. His feet sank in more with every step. He saw glints of water through the trees to his right, so he circled off the other way. The trees were dead there. They had been dead for years. It was a forest of dead trees and stumps and fallen logs that lay half submerged in the swamp.

The effort of pulling his feet from the clinging mire wearied Victor. He was sweating heavily, and gasping, and was half blinded by the perspiration mixed with blood that coursed down his forehead. The tourists were close behind him, conversing. He glanced back one last time. "Please don't follow me," he repeated. Some of them waved at him. One man had his camera out. "Watch the birdie," he said, and snapped Victor's picture.

Victor lumbered on in the mud. His feet thrust ankle-deep sometimes. Once he went to his knees, and had to crawl out. He was smeared with muck. He began running—a heavy, staggering run. His breath burst from him in sobs. He couldn't tell how far ahead of the tourists he was. His eyes smarted from the perspiration; he strained to see his way. The swamp-light was pale and greenish, shadowed by the dim slanting streaks of the dead trees. They were branchless, like torsos without arms.

Victor lurched against these naked trunks; they were light as cardboard, and went toppling slowly down with a soft sighing sound. Ahead he saw a light patch and thought it might be a path, and so, confused and exhausted, he went floundering into a softness that sucked at him and sank with him until he was waist-deep, while the people came up behind, remaining at a safe distance and watching with great interest as he struggled there, losing strength and sinking still. The man with the camera had just enough time to finish the exposures on the roll of film.

EDITORIAL POSTSCRIPT

The story you have just read was nominated by MWA (Mystery Writers of America) as one of the five best new mystery short stories published in American magazines and books during 1978.

Bill Pronzini

Caught   in   the   Act

Loomis caught the stranger in the act. But what act? Loomis was
certain the stranger had stolen something. But what? . . .

When I drove around the bend in my driveway at four that
Friday afternoon, past the screen of cypress trees, a fat little
man in a gray suit was just closing the front door of my house.
Surprise made me blink: he was a complete stranger.

He saw the car in that same moment, stiffened, and glanced
around in a furtive way, as if looking for an avenue of escape. But
there wasn't anywhere for him to go; the house is a split-level, built
on the edge of a bluff and flanked by limestone outcroppings and
thick vegetation. So he just stood there as I braked to a stop in front
of the porch, squared his shoulders, and put on a smile that looked
artificial even from a distance of 30 feet.

I got out and ran around to where he was. His smile faded, no
doubt because my surprise had given way to anger and because I'm
a pretty big man, three inches over six feet, weight 230; I played
football for four years in college and I move like the linebacker I
was. As for him, he wasn't such-a-much—just a fat little man, soft-
looking, with round pink cheeks and shrewd eyes that had nervous
apprehension in them now.

"Who are you?" I demanded. "What the hell were you doing in
my house?"

"Your house? Ah, then you're James Loomis."

"How did you know that?"

"Your name is on your mailbox, Mr. Loomis."

"What were you doing in my house?"

He looked bewildered. "But I *wasn't* in your house."

"Don't give me that. I saw you closing the door."

"No, sir, you're mistaken. I was just coming *away* from the door.
I rang the bell and there was no answer—"

"Listen, you," I said, "don't tell me what I saw or didn't see. My
eyesight's just fine. Now I want an explanation."

"There's really nothing to explain," he said. "I represent the Easy-
Way Vacuum Cleaner Company and I stopped by to ask if you—"

"Let's see some identification."

He rummaged around in a pocket of his suit coat, came out with a small white business card, and handed it to me. It said he was Morris Tweed, a salesman for the Easy-Way Vacuum Cleaner Company.

"I want to see your driver's license," I said.

"My, ah, driver's license?"

"You heard me. Get it out."

He grew even more nervous. "This is very embarrassing, Mr. Loomis," he said. "You see I, ah, lost my wallet this morning. A very unfortunate—"

I caught onto the front of his coat and bunched the material in my fingers; he made a funny little squeaking sound. I marched him over to the door, reached out with my free hand, and tried the knob. Locked. But that didn't mean anything one way or another; the door has a button you can turn on the inside so you don't have to use a key on your way out.

I looked over at the burglar-alarm panel, and of course the red light was off. Tweed, or whatever his name was, wouldn't have been able to walk out quietly through the front door if the system was operational. And except for my housekeeper, whom I've known for years and who is as trustworthy as they come, I was the only one who had an alarm key.

The fat little man struggled weakly to loosen my grip on his coat. "See here, Mr. Loomis," he said in a half-frightened, half-indignant voice, "you have no right to be rough with me. I haven't done anything wrong."

"We'll see about that."

I walked him back to the car, got my keys out of the ignition, returned him to the door, and keyed the alarm to the On position. The red light came on, which meant that the system was still functional. I frowned. If it was functional, how had the fat little man got in? Well, there were probably ways for a clever burglar to bypass an alarm system without damaging it; maybe that was the answer.

I shut it off again, unlocked the door, and took him inside. The house had a faint musty smell, the way houses do after they've been shut up for a time; I had been gone eight days, on a planned ten-day business trip to New York, and my housekeeper only comes in once a week. I took him into the living room, sat him down in a chair, and then went over and opened the French doors that led out to the balcony.

On the way back I glanced around the room. Everything was

where it should be: the console TV set, the stereo equipment, my small collection of Oriental *objets d'art* on their divider shelves. But my main concern was what was in my study—particularly the confidential records and ledgers locked inside the wall safe.

"All right, you," I said, "take off your coat."

He blinked at me. "My coat? Really, Mr. Loomis, I don't—"

"Take off your coat."

He looked at my face, at the fist I held up in front of his nose, and took off his coat. I went through all the pockets. Sixty-five dollars in a silver money clip, a handkerchief, and a handful of business cards. But that was all; there wasn't anything of mine there, except possibly the money. I shuffled through the business cards. All of them bore the names of different companies and different people, and none of them was a duplicate of the one he had handed me outside.

"Morris Tweed, huh?" I said.

"Those cards were given to me by customers," he said. "*My* cards are in my wallet, all except the one I gave you. And I've already told you that I lost my wallet this morning."

"Sure you did. Empty out your pants pockets."

He sighed, stood up, and transferred three quarters, a dime, a penny, and a keycase to the coffee table. Then he pulled all the pockets inside out. Nothing.

"Turn around," I told him.

When he did that I patted him down the way you see cops do in the movies. Nothing.

"This is all a misunderstanding, Mr. Loomis," he said. "I'm not a thief; I'm a vacuum-cleaner salesman. You've searched me quite thoroughly, you know I don't have anything that belongs to you."

Maybe not—but I had a feeling that said otherwise. There were just too many things about him that didn't add up, and there was the plain fact that I had *seen* him coming *out* of the house. Call it intuition or whatever: I sensed this fat little man had stolen something from me. Not just come here to steal, because he had obviously been leaving when I arrived. He had something of mine, all right.

But what? And where was it?

I gave him back his coat and watched him put it on. There was a look of impending relief on his face as he scooped up his keys and change; he thought I was going to let him go. Instead I caught hold of his arm. Alarm replaced the relief and he made another of those squeaking noises as I hustled him across the room and down the hall to the smallest of the guest bathrooms, the one with a ventilator in place of a window.

When I pushed him inside he stumbled, caught his balance, and pivoted around to me. "Mr. Loomis, this is outrageous. What do you intend to do with me?"

"That depends. Turn you over to the police, maybe."

"The police? But you can't . . ."

I took the key out of the inside lock, shut the door on him, and locked it from the outside.

Immediately I went downstairs to my study. The Matisse print was in place and the safe door behind it was closed and locked; I worked the combination, swung the door open. And let out the breath I had been holding: the records and ledgers were there, exactly as I had left them. If those items had fallen into the wrong hands, I would be seriously embarrassed at the least and open to blackmail or possible criminal charges at the worst. Not that I was engaged in anything precisely illegal; it was just that some of the people for whom I set up accounting procedures were involved in certain extra-legal activities.

I looked through the other things in the safe—$2000 in cash, some jewelry and private papers—and they were all there, untouched. Nothing, it developed, was missing from my desk either. Or from anywhere else in the study.

Frowning, I searched the rest of the house. In the kitchen I found what might have been jimmy marks on the side door. I also found—surprisingly—electrician's tape on the burglar-alarm wires outside, tape which had not been there before I left on my trip and which might have been used to repair a crosscircuiting of the system.

What I did *not* find was anything missing. Absolutely nothing. Every item of value, every item of no value, was in its proper place.

I began to have doubts. Maybe I was wrong after all; maybe this was just a large misunderstanding. And yet, damn it, the fat little man had been in here and had lied about it, he had no identification, he was nervous and furtive, and the burglar alarm and the side door seemed to have been tampered with.

A series of improbable explanations occurred to me. He hadn't actually stolen anything because he hadn't had time; he had broken in here, cased the place, and had been on his way out with the intention of returning later in a car or van. But burglars don't operate that way; they don't make two trips to a house when they can just as easily make one, and they don't walk out the front door in broad daylight without taking *something* with them. Nor for that matter, do they take the time to repair alarm systems they've crosscircuited.

He wasn't a thief but a tramp whose sole reason for breaking in here was to spend a few days at my expense. Only tramps don't wear neat gray suits and they don't have expertise with burglar alarms. And they don't leave your larder full or clean up after themselves.

He wasn't a thief but a private detective, or an edge-of-the-law hireling, or maybe even an assassin; he hadn't come here to steal anything, he had come here to *leave* something—evidence of my extra-legal activities, a bomb or some other sort of death trap. But if there was nothing missing, there was also nothing here that shouldn't be here; I would have found it one way or another if there was, as carefully as I had searched. Besides which, there was already incriminating evidence in my safe, I was very good at my job and got along well with my clients, and I had no personal enemies who could possibly want me dead.

Nothing made sense. The one explanation I kept clinging to didn't make sense. Why would a burglar repair an alarm system before he leaves? How could a thief have stolen something if there wasn't anything missing?

Frustrated and angry, I went back to the guest bathroom and unlocked the door. The fat little man was standing by the sink, drying perspiration from his face with one of my towels. He looked less nervous and apprehensive now; there was a kind of resolve in his expression.

"All right," I said, "come out of there."

He came out, watching me warily with his shrewd eyes. "Are you finally satisfied that I'm not a thief, Mr. Loomis?"

No, I was not satisfied. I considered ordering him to take off his clothes, but that seemed pointless; I had already searched him and there just wasn't anything to look for.

"What were you doing in here?" I said.

"I was *not* in here before you arrived." The indignation was back in his voice. "Now I suggest you let me go on my way. You have no right or reason to hold me here against my will."

I made another fist and rocked it in front of his nose. "Do I have to cuff you around to get the truth?"

He flinched, but only briefly; he had had plenty of time to shore up his courage. "That wouldn't be wise, Mr. Loomis," he said. "I already have grounds for a counter-complaint against you."

"Counter-complaint?"

"For harassment and very probably for kidnaping. Physical violence would only compound a felony charge. I fully intend to make that counter-complaint if you call the police or if you lay a hand on me."

The anger drained out of me; I felt deflated. Advantage to the fat little man. He had grounds for a counter-complaint, okay—better grounds than I had against him. After all, I *had* forcibly brought him in here and locked him in the bathroom. And a felony charge against me would mean unfavorable publicity, not to mention police attention. In my business I definitely could not afford either of those things.

He had me then, and he knew it. He said stiffly, "May I leave or not, Mr. Loomis?"

There was nothing I could do. I let him go.

He went at a quick pace through the house, moving the way somebody does in familiar surroundings. I followed him out onto the porch and watched him hurry off down the driveway without once looking back. He was almost running by the time he disappeared behind the screen of cypress trees.

I went back inside and poured myself a double bourbon. I had never felt more frustrated in my life. The fat little man had got away with something of mine; irrationally or not, I felt it with even more conviction than before.

But what could he possibly have taken of any value?

And how could he have taken it?

I found out the next morning.

The doorbell rang at 10:45, while I was working on one of my accounts in the study. When I went out there and answered it I discovered a well-dressed elderly couple, both of whom were beaming and neither of whom I had ever seen before.

"Well," the man said cheerfully, "you must be Mr. Loomis. We're the Parmenters."

"Yes?"

"We just dropped by for another look around," he said. "When we saw your car out front we were hoping it belonged to you. We've been wanting to meet you in person."

I looked at him blankly.

"This is such a delightful place," his wife said. "We can't tell you how happy we are with it."

"Yes, sir," Parmenter agreed, "we knew it was the place for us as soon as your agent showed it to us. And such a reasonable price. Why, we could hardly believe it was only $100,000."

There was a good deal of confusion after that, followed on my part by disbelief, anger, and despair. When I finally got it all sorted out it amounted to this: the Parmenters were supposed to meet here with my "agent" yesterday afternoon, to present him with a $100,000 cashier's check, but couldn't make it at that time; so they had given him the check last night at their current residence, and he in turn had handed them copies of a notarized sales agreement carrying my signatures. The signatures were expert forgeries, of course—but would I be able to prove that in a court of law? Would I be able to prove I had not conspired with this bogus real estate agent to defraud the Parmenters of a six-figure sum of money?

Oh, I found out about the fat little man, all right. I found out exactly how clever and audacious he was. And I found out just how wrong I had been—and just how right.

He hadn't stolen anything *from* my house.

He had stolen the whole damned *house*.

Stanley Ellin

Reasons Unknown

Right under the wire, at the very last moment, just in the nick to be published—we had despaired, almost given up hope. But trust Stanley Ellin to keep his word and write his annual story for EQMM . . . It's a strong, hard-in-the-gut, contemporary story, with marvelous dialogue, that will hand many a breadwinner a stiff jolt where it hurts. You want to know the facts of life in today's job market? Okay, read . . .

This is what happened, starting that Saturday in October.

That morning Morrison's wife needed the station wagon for the kids, so Morrison took the interstate bus into downtown Manhattan. At the terminal there, hating to travel by subway, he got into a cab. When the cabbie turned around and asked, "Where to, Mister?" Morrison did a double take. "Slade?" he said. "Bill Slade?"

"You better believe it," said the cabbie. "So it's Larry Morrison. Well, what do you know."

Now, what Morrison knew was that up to two or three years ago, Slade had been—as he himself still was—one of the several thousand comfortably fixed bees hiving in the glass-and-aluminum Majestico complex in Greenbush, New Jersey. There were 80,000 Majestico employees around the world, but the Greenbush complex was the flagship of the works, the executive division. And Slade had been there a long, long time, moving up to an assistant managership on the departmental level.

Then the department was wiped out in a reorganizational crunch, and Slade, along with some others in it, had been handed his severance money and his hat. No word had come back from him after he finally sold his house and pulled out of town with his wife and kid to line up, as he put it, something good elsewhere. It was a shock to Morrison to find that the something good elsewhere meant tooling a cab around Manhattan.

He said in distress, "Jeez, I didn't know, Bill—none of the Hillcrest Road bunch had any idea—"

"That's what I was hoping for," said Slade. "It's all right, man. I always had a feeling I'd sooner or later meet up with one of the old bunch. Now that it happened, I'm just as glad it's you." A horn sounding behind the cab prompted Slade to get it moving. "Where to, Larry?"

"Columbus Circle. The Coliseum."

"Don't tell me, let me guess. The Majestico Trade Exposition. It's that time of the year, right?"

"Right," said Morrison.

"And it's good politics to show up, right? Maybe one of the brass'll take notice."

"You know how it is, Bill."

"I sure do." Slade pulled up at a red light and looked around at Morrison. "Say, you're not in any tearing hurry, are you? You could have time for a cup of coffee?"

There was a day-old stubble on Slade's face. The cap perched on the back of his graying hair was grimy and sweatstained. Morrison felt unsettled by the sight. Besides, Slade hadn't been any real friend, just a casual acquaintance living a few blocks farther up Hillcrest Road. One of the crowd on those occasional weekend hunting trips of the Hillcrest Maybe Gun and Rod Club. The "Maybe" had been inserted in jest to cover those bad hunting and fishing weekends when it temporarily became a poker club.

"Well," Morrison said, "this happens to be one of those heavy Saturdays when—"

"Look, I'll treat you to the best Danish in town. Believe me, Larry, there's some things I'd like to get off my chest."

"Oh, in that case," said Morrison.

There was a line of driverless cabs in front of a cafeteria on Eighth Avenue. Slade pulled up behind them and led the way into the cafeteria which was obviously a cabbies' hangout. They had a little wrestling match about the check at the counter, a match Slade won, and, carrying the tray with the coffee and Danish, he picked out a corner table for them.

The coffee was pretty bad, the Danish, as advertised, pretty good. Slade said through a mouthful of it, "And how is Amy?" Amy was Morrison's wife.

"Fine, fine," Morrison said heartily. "And how is Gertrude?"

"Gretchen."

"That's right. Gretchen. Stupid of me. But it's been so long, Bill—"

"It has. Almost three years. Anyhow, last I heard of her Gretchen's doing all right."

"Last you heard of her?"

"We separated a few months ago. She just couldn't hack it any more." Slade shrugged. "My fault mostly. Getting turned down for one worthwhile job after another didn't sweeten the disposition. And jockeying a cab ten, twelve hours a day doesn't add sugar to it. So she and the kid have their own little flat out in Queens, and she got herself some kind of cockamamie receptionist job with a doctor there. Helps eke out what I can give her. How's your pair, by the way? Scott and Morgan, isn't it? Big fellows now, I'll bet."

"Thirteen and ten," Morrison said. "They're fine. Fine."

"Glad to hear it. And the old neighborhood? Any changes?"

"Not really. Well, we did lose a couple of the old-timers. Mike Costanzo and Gordie McKechnie. Remember them?"

"Who could forget Mike, the world's worst poker player? But McKechnie?"

"That split-level, corner of Hillcrest and Maple. He's the one got himself so smashed that time in the duck blind that he went overboard."

"Now I remember. And that fancy shotgun of his, six feet underwater in the mud. Man, that sobered him up fast. What happened to him and Costanzo?"

"Well," Morrison said uncomfortably, "they were both in Regional Customer Services. Then somebody on the top floor got the idea that Regional and National should be tied together, and some people in both offices had to be let go. I think Mike's in Frisco now, he's got a lot of family there. Nobody's heard from Gordie. I mean—" Morrison cut it short in embarrassment.

"I know what you mean. No reason to get red in the face about it, Larry." Slade eyed Morrison steadily over his coffee cup. "Wondering what happened to me?"

"Well, to be frank—"

"Nothing like being frank. I put in two years making the rounds, lining up employment agencies, sending out enough résumés to make a ten-foot pile of paper. No dice. Ran out of unemployment insurance, cash, and credit. There it is, short and sweet."

"But why? With the record you piled up at Majestico—"

"Middle level. Not top echelon. Not decision-making stuff. Middle level, now and forever. Just like everybody else on Hillcrest Road. That's why we're on Hillcrest Road. Notice how the ones who make it to the top echelon always wind up on Greenbush Heights? And always after only three or four years? But after you're middle level fifteen years the way I was—"

Up to now Morrison had been content with his twelve years in Sales Analysis. Admittedly no ball of fire, he had put in some rough years after graduation from college—mostly as salesman on commission for some product or other—until he had landed the job at Majestico. Now he felt disoriented by what Slade was saying. And he wondered irritably why Slade had to wear that cap while he was eating. Trying to prove he was just another one of these cabbies here? He wasn't. He was a college man, had owned one of the handsomest small properties on Hillcrest Road, had been a respected member of the Majestico executive team.

Morrison said, "I still don't understand. Are you telling me there's no company around needs highly qualified people outside decision-making level? Ninety percent of what goes on anyplace is our kind of job, Bill. You know that."

"I do. But I'm forty-five years old, Larry. And you want to know what I found out? By corporation standards I died five years ago on my fortieth birthday. Died, and didn't even know it. Believe me, it wasn't easy to realize that at first. It got a lot easier after a couple of years' useless job-hunting."

Morrison was 46 and was liking this less and less. "But the spot you're in is only temporary, Bill. There's still—"

"No, no. Don't do that, Larry. None of that somewhere-over-the-rainbow line. I finally looked my situation square in the eye, I accepted it, I made the adjustment. With luck, what's in the cards for me is maybe some day owning my own cab. I buy lottery tickets, too, because after all somebody's got to win that million, right? And the odds there are just as good as my chances of ever getting behind a desk again at the kind of money Majestico was paying me." Again he was looking steadily at Morrison over his coffee cup. "That was the catch, Larry. That money they were paying me."

"They pay well, Bill. Say, is that what happened? You didn't think you were getting your price and made a fuss about it? So when the department went under you were one of the—"

"Hell, no," Slade cut in sharply. "You've got it backwards, man. They do pay well. But did it ever strike you that maybe they pay too well?"

"Too well?"

"For the kind of nine-to-five paperwork I was doing? The donkey work?"

"You were an assistant head of department, Bill."

"One of the smarter donkeys, that's all. Look, what I was delivering to the company had to be worth just so much to them. But when every year—every first week in January—there's an automatic cost-of-living increase handed me I am slowly and steadily becoming a luxury item. Consider that after fourteen-fifteen years of these jumps every year, I am making more than some of those young hotshot executives in the International Division. I am a very expensive proposition for Majestico, Larry. And replaceable by somebody fifteen years younger who'll start for a hell of a lot less."

"Now hold it. Just hold it. With the inflation the way it is, you can't really object to those cost-of-living raises."

Slade smiled thinly. "Not while I was getting them, pal. It would have meant a real scramble without them. But suppose I wanted to turn them down just to protect my job? You know that can't be done. Those raises are right there in the computer for every outfit like Majestico. But nobody in management has to like living with it. And what came to me after I was canned was that they were actually doing something about it."

"Ah, look," Morrison said heatedly. "You weren't terminated because you weren't earning your keep. There was a departmental reorganization. You were just a victim of it."

"I was. The way those Incas or Aztecs or whatever used to lay out the living sacrifice and stick the knife into him. Don't keep shaking your head, Larry. I have thought this out long and hard. There's always a reorganization going on in one of the divisions. Stick a couple of departments together, change their names, dump a few personnel who don't fit into the new table of organization.

"But the funny thing, Larry, is that the ones who usually seem to get dumped are the middle-aged, middle-level characters with a lot of seniority. The ones whose take-home pay put them right up there in the high-income brackets. Like me. My secretary lost out in that reorganization too, after eighteen years on the job. No complaints about her work. But she ran into what I did when I told them I'd be glad to take a transfer to any other department. No dice. After all, they could hire two fresh young secretaries for what they were now paying her."

"And you think this is company policy?" Morrison demanded.

"I think so. I mean, what the hell are they going to do? Come to me and say, 'Well, Slade, after fifteen years on the job you've priced yourself right out of the market, so goodbye, baby?' But these reorganizations? Beautiful. 'Too bad, Slade, but under the new structure we're going to have to lose some good men.' That's the way it was told to me, Larry. And that's what I believed until I woke up to the facts of life."

The piece of Danish in Morrison's mouth was suddenly dry and tasteless. He managed to get it down with an effort. "Bill, I don't want to say it—I hate to say it—but that whole line sounds paranoid."

"Does it? Then think it over, Larry. You still in Sales Analysis?"

"Yes."

"I figured. Now just close your eyes and make a head count of your department. Then tell me how many guys forty-five or over are in it."

Morrison did some unpalatable calculation. "Well, there's six of us. Including me."

"Out of how many?"

"Twenty-four."

"Uh-huh. Funny how the grass manages to stay so green, isn't it?"

It was funny, come to think of it. No, funny wasn't the word. Morrison said weakly, "Well, a couple of the guys wanted to move out to the Coast, and you know there's departmental transfers in and out—"

"Sure there are. But the real weeding comes when there's one of those little reorganizations. You've seen it yourself in your own department more than once. Juggle around some of those room dividers. Move some desks here and there. Change a few descriptions in the company directory. The smokescreen. But behind that smoke there's some high-priced old faithfuls getting called upstairs to be told that, well, somebody's got to go, Jack, now that things are all different, and guess whose turn it is."

Slade's voice had got loud enough to be an embarrassment. Morrison pleaded: "Can't we keep it down, Bill? Anyhow, to make villains out of everybody on the top floor—"

Slade lowered his voice, but the intensity was still there. "Who said they were villains? Hell, in their place I'd be doing the same thing. For that matter, if I was head of personnel for any big outfit, I wouldn't take anybody my age on the payroll either. Not if I wanted to keep my cushy job in personnel, I wouldn't." The wind suddenly seemed to go out of him. "Sorry, Larry. I thought I had everything under control, but when I saw you—when I saw it was one of the old Hillcrest bunch—it was too much to keep corked up. But one thing—"

"Yes?"

"I don't want anybody else back there in on this. Know what I mean?"

"Oh, sure."

"Don't just toss off the oh, sure like that. This is the biggest favor you could do me—not to let anybody else in the old crowd hear about me, not even Amy. No post-mortems up and down Hillcrest for good old Bill Slade. One reason I let myself cut loose right now was because you always were a guy who liked to keep his mouth tight shut. I'm counting on you to do that for me, Larry. I want your solemn word on it."

"You've got it, Bill. You know that."

"I do. And what the hell"—Slade reached across the table and punched Morrison on the upper arm—"any time they call you in to tell you there's a reorganization of Sales Analysis coming, it could turn out you're the guy elected to be department head of the new layout. Right?"

Morrison tried to smile. "No chance of that, Bill."

"Well, always look on the bright side, Larry. As long as there is one."

Outside the Coliseum there was another of those little wrestling matches about paying the tab—Slade refusing to take anything at all for the ride, Morrison wondering, as he eyed the meter, whether sensitivity here called for a standard tip, a huge tip, or none at all—and again Slade won.

Morrison was relieved to get away from him, but, as he soon found, the relief was only temporary. It was a fine Indian summer day, but somehow the weather now seemed bleak and threatening. And doing the Majestico show, looking over the displays, passing the time of day with recognizable co-workers turned out to be a strain. It struck him that it hadn't been that atrocious cap on Slade's head that had thrown him, it had been the gray hair showing under the cap. And there was very little gray hair to be seen on those recognizable ones here at the Majestico show.

Morrison took a long time at the full-length mirror in the men's room, trying to get an objective view of himself against the background of the others thronging the place. The view he got was depressing. As far as he could see, in this company he looked every minute of his 46 years.

Back home he stuck to his word and told Amy nothing about his encounter with Slade. Any temptation to was readily suppressed by his feeling that once he told her that much he'd also find himself exposing his morbid reaction to Slade's line of thinking. And that would only lead to her being terribly understanding and sympathetic while, at the same time, she'd be moved to some heavy humor about his being such a born worrier. He was a born worrier, he was the first to acknowledge it, but he always chafed under that combination of sympathy and teasing she offered him when he confided his worries to her. They really made quite a list, renewable each morning on rising. The family's health, the condition of the house, the car, the lawn, the bank balance—the list started there and seemed to extend to infinity.

Yet, as he was also the first to acknowledge, this was largely a quirk of personality—he was, as his father had been, somewhat sobersided and humorless—and, quirks aside, life was a generally all-right proposition. As it should be when a man can lay claim to a pretty and affectionate wife, and a couple of healthy young sons, and a sound home in a well-tended neighborhood. And a good steady job to provide the wherewithal.

At least, up to now.

Morrison took a long time falling asleep that night, and at three in the morning came bolt awake with a sense of foreboding. The more he lay there trying to get back to sleep, the more oppressive grew the foreboding. At four o'clock he padded into his den and sat down at his desk to work out a precise statement of the family's balance sheet.

No surprises there, just confirmation of the foreboding. For a long time now, he and Amy had been living about one month ahead of income which, he suspected, was true of most families along Hillcrest Road. The few it wasn't true of were most likely at least a year ahead of income and sweating out the kind of indebtedness he had always carefully avoided.

But considering that his assets consisted of a home with ten years of mortgage payments yet due on it and a car with two years of payments still due, everything depended on income. The family savings account was, of course, a joke. And the other two savings accounts—one in trust for each boy to cover the necessary college educations—had become a joke as college tuition skyrocketed. And, unfortunately, neither boy showed any signs of being scholarship material.

In a nutshell, everything depended on income. This month's income. Going by Slade's experience in the job market—and Slade had been the kind of competent, hardworking nine-to-five man any company should have been glad to take on—this meant that everything depended on the job with Majestico. Everything. Morrison had always felt that landing the job in the first place was the best break of his life. Whatever vague ambitions he had in his youth were dissolved very soon after he finished college and learned that out here in the real world he rated just about average in all departments, and that his self-effacing, dogged application to his daily work was not going to have him climbing any ladders to glory.

Sitting there with those pages of arithmetic scattered around the desk, Morrison, his stomach churning, struggled with the idea that the job with Majestico was suddenly no longer a comfortable, predictable way of life but for someone his age, and with his makeup and qualifications, a dire necessity. At five o'clock, exhausted but more wide-awake than ever, he went down to the kitchen for a bottle of beer. Pills were not for him. He had always refused to take even an aspirin tablet except under extreme duress, but beer did make him sleepy, and a bottle of it on an empty stomach, he estimated, was the prescription called for in this case. It turned out that he was right about it.

In the days and weeks that followed, this became a ritual: the abrupt waking in the darkest hours of the morning, the time at his desk auditing his accounts and coming up with the same dismal results, and the bottle of beer which, more often than not, allowed for another couple of hours of troubled sleep before the alarm clock went off.

Amy, the soundest of sleepers, took no notice of this, so that was all right. And by exercising a rigid self-control he managed to keep her unaware of those ragged nerves through the daylight hours as well, although it was sometimes unbearably hard not to confide in her. Out of a strange sense of pity, he found himself more sensitive and affectionate to her than ever. High-spirited, a little scatter-brained, leading a full life of her own what with the boys, the Parent-Teachers Club, and half a dozen community activities, she took this as no less than her due.

Along the way, as an added problem, Morrison developed some physical tics which would show up when least expected. A sudden tremor of the hands, a fluttering of one eyelid which he had to learn to quickly cover up. The most grotesque tic of all, however—it really unnerved him the few times he experienced it—was a violent, uncontrollable chattering of the teeth when he had sunk to a certain point of absolute depression. This only struck him when he was at his desk during the sleepless times considering the future. At such times he had a feeling that those teeth were diabolically possessed by a will of their own, chattering away furiously as if he had just been plunged into icy water.

In the office he took refuge in the lowest of low profiles. Here the temptation was to check on what had become of various colleagues who had over the years departed from the company, but this, Morrison knew, might raise the question of why he had, out of a clear sky, brought up the subject. The subject was not a usual part of the day's conversational currency in the department. The trouble was that Greenbush was, of course, a company town, although in the most modern and pleasant way. Majestico had moved there from New York 20 years before; the town had grown around the company complex. And isolated as it was in the green heartland of New Jersey, it had only Majestico to offer. Anyone leaving the company would therefore have to sell his home, like it or not, and relocate far away. Too far, at least, to maintain old ties. It might have been a comfort, Morrison thought, to drop in on someone in his category who had been terminated by Majestico and who could give him a line on what had followed. Someone other than Slade. But there was no one like this in his book.

The one time he came near bringing his desperation to the surface was at the Thanksgiving entertainment given by the student body of the school his sons attended. The entertainment was a well-deserved success, and after it, at the buffet in the school gym, Morrison was driven to corner Frank Lassman, assistant principal of the school and master of ceremonies at the entertainment, and to come out with a thought that had been encouragingly flickering through his mind during the last few insomniac sessions.

"Great show," he told Lassman. "Fine school altogether. It showed tonight. It must be gratifying doing your kind of work."

"At times like this it is," Lassman said cheerfully. "But there are times—"

"Even so. You know, I once had ideas about going into teaching."

"Financially," said Lassman, "I suspect you did better by not going into it. It has its rewards, but the big money isn't one of them."

"Well," Morrison said very carefully, "suppose I was prepared to settle for the rewards it did offer? A man my age, say. Would there be any possibilities of getting into the school system?"

"What's your particular line? Your subject?"

"Oh, numbers. Call it arithmetic and math."

Lassman shook his head in mock reproach. "And where were you when we really needed you? Four or five years ago we were sending out search parties for anyone who could get math across to these kids. The last couple of years, what with the falling school population, we're firing, not hiring. It's the same everywhere, not that I ever thought I'd live to see the day. Empty school buildings all over the country."

"I see," said Morrison.

So the insomnia, tensions, and tics continued to worsen until suddenly one day—as if having hit bottom, there was no place for him to go but up—Morrison realized that he was coming back to normal. He began to sleep through the night, was increasingly at ease during the day, found himself cautiously looking on the bright side. He still had his job and all that went with it, that was the objective fact. He could only marvel that he had been thrown so far off balance by that chance meeting with Slade.

He had been giving himself his own bad time, letting his imagination take over as it had. The one thing he could be proud of was that where someone else might have broken down under the strain, he had battled it out all by himself and had won. He was not a man to hand himself trophies, but in this case he felt he had certainly earned one.

A few minutes before five on the first Monday in December, just when he was getting ready to pack it in for the day, Pettengill, departmental head of Sales Analysis, stopped at his desk. Pettengill, a transfer from the Cleveland office a couple of years before, was rated as a comer, slated sooner or later for the top floor. A pleasant-mannered, somewhat humorless man, he and Morrison had always got along well.

"Just had a session with the brass upstairs," he confided. "A round table with Cobb presiding." Cobb was the executive vice president in charge of Planning and Structure for the Greenbush complex. "Looks like our department faces a little reorganization. We tie in with Service Analysis and that'll make it Sales and Service Evaluation. What's the matter? Don't you feel well?"

"No, I'm all right," said Morrison.

"Looks like you could stand some fresh air. Anyhow, probably because you're senior man here, Cobb wants to see you in his office first thing tomorrow morning. Nine sharp. You know how he is about punctuality, Larry. Make sure you're on time."

"Yes," said Morrison.

He didn't sleep at all that night. The next morning, a few minutes before nine, still wearing his overcoat and with dark glasses concealing his reddened and swollen eyes, he took the elevator directly to the top floor. There, out of sight on the landing of the emergency staircase, he drew the barrel and stock of his shotgun from beneath the overcoat and assembled the gun. His pockets bulged with 12-gauge shells. He loaded one into each of the gun's twin barrels. Then concealing the assembled gun beneath the coat as well as he could, he walked across the hall into Cobb's office.

Miss Bernstein, Cobb's private secretary, acted out of sheer blind, unthinking instinct when she caught sight of the gun. She half rose from her desk as if to bar the way to the inner office. She took the first charge square in the chest. Cobb, at his desk, caught the next in the face. Reloading, Morrison exited through the door to the executive suite where Cobb's assistants, getting ready for the morning's work, were now in a panic at the sound of the shots.

Morrison fired both barrels one after another, hitting one man in the throat and jaw, grazing another. Reloading again, he moved like an automaton out into the corridor where a couple of security men, pistols at the ready, were coming from the staircase on the run. Morrison cut down the first one, but the other, firing wildly, managed to plant one bullet in his forehead. Morrison must have been dead, the medical examiner later reported, before he even hit the floor.

The police, faced with five dead and one wounded, put in two months on the case and could come up with absolutely no answers, no explanations at all. The best they could do in their final report was record that "the perpetrator, for reasons unknown, etc., etc."

Management, however, could and did take action. They learned that the Personnel Department psychologist who had put Morrison through the battery of personality-evaluation tests given every applicant for a job was still there with the company. Since he had transparently failed in those tests to sound out the potentially aberrant behavior of the subject, he was, despite sixteen years of otherwise acceptable service, terminated immediately.

Two weeks later, his place in Personnel was filled by a young fellow named McIntyre who, although the starting pay was a bit low, liked the looks of Greenbush and, with his wife in complete agreement, saw it as just the kind of quiet, pleasant community in which to settle down permanently.